DECEPTION

LORETTA ENRIGHT

DECEPTION

Copyright © 2024 by Loretta Enright
All Rights Reserved.

No portion of this book may be reproduced in any form without permission of the publisher or author, except as permitted by U.S. copyright law.

LorettaEnright@hotmail.com

ENRIGHT PUBLISHING

ISBN: 979-8-9893997-0-3

Cover photo by Elizabeth

Printed in the United States of America

To my mother,
who always believed
I could write a book,
and to B, the survivor.

*What truth there is in this story
is stranger than fiction.*

CHAPTER 1

"You'll be okay, Nicky," Callista said, holding him close, or as close as she could get to the gurney that was strapped into the air ambulance. "In a few days Mom and Sienna and Max will be back home with you. Be good. I love you."

The blond-haired wraith of a child didn't move. If you didn't watch closely, you'd miss that he was even breathing, she thought. He's groggy, they sedated him so he'd sleep for most of the plane ride. She straightened slowly, wiped a stray tear from her cheek, and turned to her husband. Just looking at him burst the dam.

"Mark, I can't do this," she whispered. "I won't see him for a week, I won't know how he's doing, it's like tearing off an arm!"

Mark's arms held her. "It's okay, you can do it. You know this is the only way we can get him out of California and back home. We can't drive the RV like we planned, in case there's an emergency. We have to get him back to his hospital, his doctors at Holcome. There's no other way." He rubbed her back and sighed. What a nightmare, a 15-hour open heart surgery and then – kidney failure. Why, he thought angrily, why? Why didn't anyone even suggest this was a possibility?

The Beechcraft shuddered. Callista looked up, fear rippling through her stomach. What if this was the last time she would see Nick? And she began to shake.

"Mrs. Hampton – Callista, it's time for you to go, Mark has to strap in and we have to run some quick routine checks on Nick." The flight nurse smiled gently. "We'll take good care of them." Callista shuffled down the ramp, watching as the nurse took out a stethoscope and Mark crammed himself into a small seat behind the gurney. And then the doors were closed.

Mark strapped in and watched the nurses. After years of visits to Holcome International Medical Center for Nick's heart care, he'd met pretty much everyone in the Cardiac Unit, including Peggy and Dar who'd volunteered for this air duty. Both were trained as flight paramedics as well as cardiac nurses. They knew Nick quite well, he was a favorite in Holcome's CICU, with his collection of car pictures and wild sense of humor.

"He's stable," Peggy said to Mark. She took off her flight nurse beret and let her platinum hair fall loose. "We'll be off in a few minutes."

"This setup is pretty amazing," Mark said., "I know you have all kinds of equipment in here, but it's well-placed, out of sight."

"And that's why only you could ride with us and have that premium cramped seat," Peggy laughed. "If we had to, we're equipped for emergency surgery, racks and racks of instruments, IV equipment, oxygen, the works. I could even do a trach on you if necessary."

"No thanks," Mark said, wondering what kind of huge explosion there would be if the plane crashed with the oxygen and tanks of other gases on board. "When do we arrive?" The plane shuddered again and started moving backwards out of the boarding area.

"About four hours. Jeff has to fly around some storm that's brewing over the Rockies. We should be at the airport about seven o'clock in the morning, then a quick ambulance ride and we're there, but you know your way around the hospital, so you know exactly where you'll be. Try to rest." She turned and moved quickly up front to her seat next to Dar.

And Happy Thanksgiving, Mark thought. It was barely Thursday, or was it still Wednesday? The air ambulance had arrived Monday in California, but the weather grounded the flight home and the crew was forced to stay in San Jose. They'd gotten the green light only a few hours ago and rushed to get everything prepared before the next weather system moved in.

He felt the pressure as the little plane accelerated along the runway and suddenly they were up, the dots of San Jose slowly diminishing. My God, Mark thought, a year ago who would have thought we'd be spending a month in a RV park in California and commuting to the Stanford Medical Center from Redwood City. Just another *segue* in Nick's young life, or rather saving Nick's young life, with severe congenital heart defects that went undetected for the first nine active months of his life! Misconnected arteries, a left lung with minimum blood flow from the heart – it was one wild ride after another, surgeries, interventions, three years ago the mother of all surgeries, 21 hours, followed by two more the same week. And now this visit halfway across the country to Stanford, to live or die at the hands of Dr. James Hendrix, pioneer in childhood special ops, so to speak. Things had deteriorated in Nick's chest over the last year and this was the only way for him to survive. Mark sighed. And now kidney failure. Why? Were they failing when they got here? Too many hours on heart-lung bypass over the years? Did something happen at Stanford? Or was it destiny? Destiny...his last thought before sleep overwhelmed him.

***

"We're leaving for home tomorrow?" Max asked Callista as they drove back to their RV at one in the morning. "What about the laundry? I don't have clean underwear." At 14, chores were the last thing on his mind until he discovered his drawer was empty.

"And you smell like it," Sienna said with a toss of her blond ponytail. Just turned 16, she claimed the front passenger seat, banishing Max to the cramped back row. Max slipped his foot under her seat and kicked.

"Mom-meeee! Max kicked me!"

"Guys, please, I have a headache. Stop it or you can walk the rest of the way." It was a false threat, the creepy turn-off and side road to the RV park was the last place Callista wanted to drive, let alone drop off the kids to walk. It was so dark sans street lights, you could just imagine the near occasion of crime and it was the same among the trailers crammed in the large bay front trailer village. There was only a small retaining wall between the back of the grounds and a finger of San Francisco Bay that stretched south. None of the area was lit.

"We've got to get going. It will take four days to get back home and Dad will need someone to give him a break at the hospital. Hopefully it won't be too long down there at Holcome and we can get home."

"Won't be too long, like being stuck here four weeks got to be too long?" Max yawned.

"It wasn't supposed to be this way, we were counting on Nicky coming through like he always does after heart surgery, ready to escape in a week. Having his kidneys go out was an unexpected complication."

"Is it permanent?" Sienna asked. She hated to see her little brother sidelined.

"Who knows. Dr. Chen said it could be a couple of weeks, a couple of months, a year, or forever. Real encouragement. We just have to go with it and make the best of it. I'll feel better when he's back home and at Holcome Medical Center."

They arrived at the RV and Callista surveyed the rooms. There's no way I can drive this rig home, we have to leave it here, she thought. What can we take, what do we leave? And that car, what a joke! How to condense a trailer full of our lives into a small Jeep SUV with hardly any backside room? It's too late to start now, she sighed.

"Bed," she called after her teens as they went into the bunk area at the back. "We'll just have to get on this in the morning, okay?" She didn't wait for an answer but went up the two steps to the master bedroom. Worry for Nick was eating her up. She shook her head. My God, I'm so tired I can't stand it. Just for a minute, I've got to lie down, she thought, as she burrowed in among the pillows strewn on the blue bedspread. Just for a minute.

It seemed like such a short time later when the buzz of the vibration woke her. Groggy, she looked around. Mark.... She blinked as the vibrations continued. The phone! She sat up quickly and then saw it on the bed stand. "Hello, hello?"

"Callista, it's me!"

"Mark! Are you okay? What's wrong?"

"Wrong? I'm just calling you to let you know we touched down okay and are on the way to the hospital. Everything is fine. Nick is coming out of sedation and looks like he's enjoying himself. Flirting with the nurses. Well, as much as he can with that damned tube in his nose."

"Thank God, thank God. What time is it?" It was still dark outside.

"Probably 5am or so by you. I'll call later when we have a room. Love you!"

Callista put the phone down and sighed deeply. One step on the massive checklist of life finished. She got off a quick text to her mother, *Landed. All okay.* She knew Ellie wouldn't mind the early morning message. Then, dizzily, Callista lay back on the bed, desperately needing more than three hours of sleep to face the day.

❋❋❋

Just like on *Emergency* reruns, Nick thought, as the gurney went through the double doors of the emergency room from the ambulance bay. He looked around at the ivory wall tiles with red geometric designs, that tile was everywhere in the whole hospital, he'd seen enough of it in his nine years. Up ahead it looked like a convention, a couple dudes decked out in suits and ties and a small army of nurses in blue scrubs. He sighed, still a little groggy.

"Looks like a welcome committee," Mark said.

Katelyn waved them over. Mark remembered her, the nurse manager from the Cardiac Intensive Care Unit upstairs. "Mark, glad you made it and in good time. You and Nick will be going upstairs shortly." She turned toward the older of the two men, tall, lanky, with a close-cropped beard and dark hair with gray showing here and there. "Nick, these are your doctors. This is Dr. Baudette, chief of Cardiac Surgery." She nodded to the shorter man, about Mark's size and age, bald, with tufts of hair poking up around his ears. Intense eyes. "This is Dr. Loomis, chief of Pediatric Services. He's also a nephrologist and will be in charge of your care."

Dr. Baudette extended his hand to Mark and then quickly bent down to Nick. "I hear you know everything there is to know about this place, Nick. I'm the new chief of cardiac surgery and if you need any intervention at all, I'll be doing it. Dr. Arthur and I work closely together and we've consulted with Dr. Hendrix, who is quite pleased with his repair job."

"He drives a Porsche," Nick offered, struggling to speak around the tube at the back of his throat, "but wants a Ferrari."

Baudette laughed. "I heard you're a car whiz." He turned to Loomis, "What do you drive, Chuck?"

A look of distaste briefly crossed Loomis' narrow face. He seemed as if he wanted to be anywhere but greeting a new patient. "An Alpha Romeo Spider, nothing that matches your Corvette, Richard."

"A 'vette?" Nick seemed to light up. "Bring me a picture. The Spider, too."

Dr. Baudette clapped him on the shoulder and nodded to the nurses. "Upstairs with this one, blood work, and hook up his machinery. Welcome back, Nick."

CHAPTER 2

"They told us at Stanford the beeping was a machine error," Mark told the technician. As soon as Nick was hooked up, the machinery in his room started the incessant beeping.

"Machinery error?" The tech laughed. "The machines respond to the heart signals. Either his magnesium or potassium levels or both are abnormal. He's got tachycardia, you know, an arrhythmia. The numbers have to be just right or the heart goes wacky. That's why the machines beep." She was hooking up an IV. "This will take care of it."

"How's my favorite little man?" Katelyn asked from the doorway. "You should feel pretty good to be here, Nick, our CICU is like a second home."

Nick nodded. He was in this very room four years ago for two and a half weeks. In fact, he'd had a five-hour surgery in this room for chest closure, attaching clamps to hold his sternum in place. All the CICU rooms were equipped so they could be turned into surgical suites – there were banks of electronic monitors plus cabinets and drawers of hidden equipment. The bed was center stage next to a pole on which hung IV bags. The window was curtained, but overlooked a courtyard five floors below. A bed for a caretaker was beneath the window. Nick could see the other rooms in the circle, all the same, with the nurse station in the middle. Second home.

"He's still vomiting," Mark said. "It started two weeks ago. He has gastroparesis, an empty stomach does him no good, but he hasn't eaten real food for the longest time. He was even throwing up blood. Now he coughs, even around that nasoduodenal tube. God, that must be uncomfortable with a tube from your nose down to your gut. He needs a major repair job."

Katelyn nodded as she looked over his chart notes. "I see an Ear Nose and Throat consult tomorrow for the cough. Dr. Arthur will be in next week and I'm sure Gastroenterology will be called today. We'll get him fixed up." She patted Nick's arm and smiled. "Can't wait to see some more car pictures. There must have been some good ones out in California."

"Porsche," Nick tried to say, but the effort made him gag around the tube. "We were by a Porsche dealer," it came out garbled. He just shook his head and a tear slid down his cheek.

"Oh, honey, just hang on a little longer," Katelyn said. She blew him a kiss and left.

***

Chuck Loomis lounged back in his leather chair. He'd just finished reading through the highlights of Nick Hampton's medical history. Hard to believe the kid lived this long, he must live a charmed life, he thought, or it was good medical care. He laughed at that. All the care was here at Holcome International, mostly under the guidance of the chief cardiologist, Arlene Arthur, competent and completely incorruptible. She ran her department and surgeons very tightly, no one stepped out of line. Pity that.

He gazed around his office, with built-in bookcases filled with medical books on stuff he never heard of, but they looked good; his bragging wall behind him with the twenty diplomas, certificates, awards for outstanding service, and a couple publication covers featuring his articles. Pediatric Services was his domain at this place, he was in charge and excellent in his job – the letter on his desk proved that point, a thank you from parents for his outstanding work in saving the life of their precious little child.

The huge windows just to the left looked out over city, plenty of trees to break up the monotony of offices and other buildings. Stanton did a good job of changing with the times, making the downtown area visually pleasant, while funneling the view of visitors toward the center of the city and the red brick bastion that was Holcome International Medical Center. Blocks of buildings surrounded the huge medical complex, with long hallways interconnecting its specialty services. Almost the entire first floor of this building was taken up by a vast atrium with banks of elevators and admissions offices and desks, but it was beneath his view. He didn't care. Double doors on the side wall to the left led to a spacious conference room, not that any patients or families ever got close to entry; he controlled the access for meeting with other doctors on his turf.

Loomis turned back to Nick's file. Neil Hawthorne, the hospital administrator, demanded he meet the little bugger at 7:30 this morning. Why? It was Thanksgiving, senior staff didn't work holidays. Yet there was that suck-up Baudette waiting to greet the kid. So what if Nick was an icon at the hospital for the last nine years. His sordid thoughts were interrupted by a muted buzz inside the bottom drawer. He yanked it open and grabbed the blue Tracfone that was blinking. His "number phone," only numbers and texts, no names. "*Good price,*" he read with a smile. One of his little side enterprises was going well. "*Anytime,*" he texted back. Then he noted a red flag on the message icon of the red phone, a twin to the blue.

"*Your new patient might be a fit.*" Damn it, no wonder he forced me to meet the kid this morning. Hawthorne knew everything and controlled everything, as hospital administrator he was over the top. Who was he to tell me what to do with patients in my department, Loomis thought angrily. He threw both phones back into the bottom of the drawer, his mind going back to the early September meeting with Hawthorne and Anton Gregory from Houston, who was the mastermind behind the so-called plan this Nick Hampton kid might fit into. He remembered the conversation well:

"You dumbass, you played that too close, way too close! And you lost!" Gregory's deep voice boomed.

"How was I supposed to know the kid would move into trouble so fast? His numbers weren't *that* bad!" Loomis retorted.

"It's your *job* to think about these things in advance. Now I'm doing damage control because you had the mother thrown out of here for causing a disturbance." Neil Hawthorne's quiet voice seemed more threatening than Gregory's outburst.

"She was fricking yelling in the hallway! What was I supposed to do, wait till she barged in on me or unloaded all her complaints on that fat ass assistant here?"

"Her kid died," Gregory said evenly. "We had everything ready to launch our plan and now this. We have to start over. Fix it."

And then, the stupid administrative assistant, Miranda something or other, Loomis thought angrily. She must have heard them in the conference room but pretended she didn't know what I was talking about when I confronted her. She acted so innocent. Then she lost the papers I left on her desk, they just disappeared. I hope to God she never read them, I'm glad I got her out of the office before she could figure anything out.

Enough of this, he thought. The hell with this place. I'm going home. It's a holiday. Nick Hampton is obviously a survivor, he can survive over the weekend and then some without a nephrology consult.

❊❊❊

An ear-splitting bang made Callista jump up from the bed. What the hell? Another flash of lightning and another boom of thunder. It was pouring outside. Geez, I thought it didn't rain here in sunny California. The clock said eleven in the morning. So much for leaving at noon. She grabbed her phone and saw a message from her mother.

Better you don't leave today, bad weather. Try tomorrow. Glad Nick and Mark got back okay. Love ya all. See you soon.

"Kids! We got lots of work to do, get up!" With groans, they stumbled out of the back bedroom like the walking dead.

"Food, I need food," Sienna said, reaching the pantry. "The Pop Tarts are calling me."

Max was in the bathroom. Callista banged on the door. "Quit admiring your physique and get out here." He came out in his pajama bottoms. At 14, he was fast getting a manly look about him, including a little darkness over the top lip. He looked a lot like his mom, with dark brown hair and big brown eyes that melted the hearts of the girls in his class.

"How did she know what I was doing?" he asked his sister. Sienna was almost as tall as Callista, but Max was starting to catch up, only half a head shorter. She pushed him. "Cuz she knows how proud you are to look like a Marvel superhero. Not."

"Okay, here's the plan," Callista announced. "Laundry. Sienna, pile the baskets in the Jeep and you and Maxie go to the laundry shed. You can drive that far without hitting anything, can't you? Then we pack. Take shorts for the ride, but we're going back home, where it's cold – it's almost December. Pack only what you need. School stuff, jeans, sweatshirts. There isn't going to be any room in that puny little rental. We leave the rest here. Dad will have to fly out with Grandpa Hampton and drive the RV back. We take our snacks, drinks, nothing we have to cook, we'll eat fast food."

"What about the pillows, we brought our pillows from home," Sienna whined.

"If they fit. Look guys, we pack what we can today and we're outta here tomorrow morning. I'd like to get out of California as soon as we can."

"What about the food? I mean you have all kinds of good stuff here, Mom. Are we leaving it behind?"

Callista nodded. "Roberta next door will take care of it. And Max, be sure to get all the computer stuff packed, it's worth a bundle of money, it doesn't get left behind."

They drove off at ten o'clock the next morning, Sienna in the front, Max crammed into a quarter of the backseat. Sienna had moved her front seat back to accommodate her legs; Max's limbs were doubled over tightly. Suitcases and boxes were stacked next to him, the cooler by his elbow. Under his feet were his computer games and sketching materials, but there was no way he could reach any of it. It was going to be a long four days.

CHAPTER 3

"Honest to God, it's been a merry-go-round around here," Mark told Callista over the phone. The reception was good this time, no dropped signals wherever it was that she was *en route*. "It's like the State Fair, constant parades of people all with their jobs to do sticking and poking Nick."

"Is he okay?" Callista asked frantically, smashing the phone to her ear. "Is he okay? I was such a wreck when he left I didn't think I would ever see him again."

She could hear Mark, "Hey, Nicky, yell hi to Mom."

"Mmmmoooommm!"

"I can hear him, I can understand him! What's going on?"

Mark settled on the bed under the window. Nick was sitting up and watching a DVD – *Cars* again – in bed. His color was back and he actually laughed aloud at the movie.

"Well, first he had a blood transfusion, his hemoglobin was down. Then ENT came in, suspected the tube in his nose and down his throat was causing the cough. I mean it's hard to swallow spit with that sucker in place anyway and a dry throat makes for a cough."

"Dialysis?"

"No, that guy hasn't shown up. He must be getting lab numbers though, to know if it's needed. I don't have a clue."

"Who is he?"

"Some guy named Charles Loomis, the head of Pediatric Services and also a nephrologist, I guess. We met him fresh off the plane Thursday morning when we met Baudette. Looked real inconvenienced to be there. I don't know what to think of him, hardly said a word."

Callista sighed, yet another personality to deal with in a hospital already loaded with overly inflated egos. At least Nick was in CICU, where the staff was superb.

"Then last night, they pulled the nose tube. Nick woke up today and it's been great."

"Oh, wow, I'm so relieved." Callista wanted to sit down and cry, but she was in a little Super 8 motel room, Max and Sienna finishing up McDonald's chicken nuggets and some fries. It was never good for a mom to cry in front of the kids.

"You're kind of behind on the driving schedule," Mark went on.

"Yeah, well, we didn't leave until noon yesterday, it was raining on Friday pretty bad so we stayed. Then it took longer to pack, everything here takes longer. That rental sucks, it's so small we have to pry Max out of the back seat every time we stop."

Mark started laughing.

"Seriously. Then we got to Tehachapi in the mountains. It was so dark and actually getting cold and I didn't feel like plunging off a mountainside, so we found a little motel and stayed over. It snowed overnight, can you believe it? And all we had to wear was shorts and tee shirts! We went to church this morning looking like bums and then took off and if we'd continued ten more minutes last night, we'd have been down the damn mountain! Mark! Cut it out!" The laughing was loud enough the nurses at the central station looked up.

"We only made it to the edge of Arizona and New Mexico. There was a winter storm warning ahead. No way I wanted to drive in that!"

Mark's Notebook, Monday night –

December 2 already! Better day, Nick was up and walking around. He wanted to get dressed in his shorts and tee shirt. It's good to see him acting normal, even if only for a half hour at a time. I am feeling good about this. That Loomis guy checked in about 8am, said labs were ordered and they would do dialysis to even Nick out. Can't figure that guy, didn't explain what they were looking for, only that there were certain levels to be maintained. Even I know that. He didn't even ask Nick how he was feeling. Callista made it almost across New Mexico. Tomorrow through Okie panhandle. Hoping to be here Thursday. She said her mom and dad would stop by tomorrow. Nicky will like company. We are leaving CICU tomorrow. Not happy about that. It sounds like they are planning discharge, going to Step Out, a pediatric section with less medical staff hanging around, we will be more on our own to get used to life without a hospital leash. The blue bowl stays handy, but there's a lot less vomiting, thank God.

***

It was Tuesday afternoon when company arrived.

"Nicky, what are you doing here by the elevators?" Ellie asked when the gray doors swooshed open.

"Grandma! Grandpa!" He threw his arms around both of them. "Group hug!"

"We're a little too large for the hug with your little arms," Paul observed. "How are you, kid?"

"Yeah, we expected you to be bedridden and all hooked up like you usually are at this place," Ellie said with a laugh.

Nick practically skipped along. "Nah, they've been working on me, giving me real food, pulled out that stupid tube that was choking me. How do they expect a person to get better with a tube down their nose?" His blue eyes twinkled.

"Where are we?" Paul asked as he looked around. "I've never been in this area before."

"You only came to the heart rooms after surgery. This isn't as cool."

Cool to an almost-ten-year-old had many meanings, Ellie thought. He looked good, though, sparkly almost; he'd even brushed his teeth.

It was a bit of a walk, turning this way and that and across an indoor bridge-like path and finally past the nurse station and off to the right. The room wasn't as high-tech, not all the hidden medical instruments, just a TV, a tray for eating while in the bed, a couple of chairs and a small sofa-like thing against the wall.

"Hey! Glad you could make it," Mark called across the room. He had his laptop on a small table, his iPhone next to it. "Just finishing up some work." The odd couple had arrived, he thought, Paul about a foot taller than Ellie, his dark hair lightly streaked with gray. It was longer on the top, Mark noticed, and had a wave to it. He held his weight well on his frame, she was a little pudgy. Both were retired, sort of. Paul did his accounting work from home, very busy during tax season. Ellie, a former news reporter, did some freelance book editing for various and sundry authors. Her white hair made her look like a sweet little old lady. Not. Little old ladies don't go jetting off to California to help them while Nick had surgery. He remembered her telling him, "You can't leave two teenagers alone in a RV park, duh." Whenever she was called, "Mom, can you come and help," Ellie was on the way. She took flight behind the wheel of her car and had the speeding tickets to prove it.

Ellie gave him a hug. "Glad *you* made it. No end in sight?"

Mark looked tired, circles under his blue eyes, a well-started scruffy beard on his cheeks. "We're in this part of pediatrics, it's called Step Out, so I'm thinking we could be home by Christmas. This is where they put people on the way out."

Paul spotted some car pictures on the room's windows. "Business as usual, I see." He peered closely, "You got these at a Porsche dealer in California? I'm surprised they let you breathe close to those machines. Is that a 911 Sport Classic?"

With a yelp, Nick did a little dance. "You're darn right! I love it. I'm going to have one some day!"

There was a buzz, and Mark picked up the phone. "Okay...okay, I can do that. I'll be right over." He hung up. "I scored a room at Ronald McDonald House a couple blocks from here. When Callie gets here, we can split the hospital stuff and one of us can stay there with the kids overnight. I have to go sign the papers. Is it okay for you to stay an hour or so?"

"Of course," Paul said. "Take your time. Everything else okay? How is work? This whole thing must have been tough with you starting a new job in September and then taking off in mid-October." He sat his six-foot-plus frame on the edge of the bed, then reached into a jacket pocket. When Nick saw the green and red Altoid tin, he started clapping his hands.

Mark yawned a bit. "Sorry. Not the greatest bed in here. Yeah, work is okay. The thing about working at a cyber-based firm is you can work from almost anywhere. Once you have the key to the clients' networks, you can do what you want off-site. If the boss is happy and keeps sending me stuff to do, I'm happy. Look guys, is it okay if I grab a shower and shave while I'm gone? When my dad visited, he brought me a change of clothes,..."

"No problem," Paul interrupted and Mark was out the door in a minute.

Digging in her black purse, Ellie pulled out a rectangular little gift bag and held it high. "What am I bid for this?" Nick made a grab for it.

"No, little boy, you need to bid."

He thought and then said, "A dollar."

"You have money in this place?"

"No, I'll get it from Grandpa! What is it?" He reached up and grabbed it before she moved it away. "A movie!"

"Thought you could recite *Cars* by now," Ellie said. She handed the DVD to Paul and asked him to load it into the player.

"*Hellfighters?*" he asked. "Are you kidding? He's a little kid, this isn't for him. The language...."

"Was that an explosion in the background on the cover? Oh boy, this looks good. Who's John Wayne?"

Both grandparents stared at him. "You don't know?" Ellie shook her head. "This is from Uncle Rusty. He liked it when he was a kid."

"He sent this all the way from South Carolina? Oh cool!" He settled onto the bed, the blue bowl handy. "This is going to be fun!"

CHAPTER 4

"Hey, cuz, wait up!"

Miranda turned to see Tera Storm striding rapidly toward her. Tera wore the navy blue uniform of the Elite Corps well, she could wear a garbage bag and still look exceptional, her dark hair flowing over her shoulders like a veil framing her flawless oval face.

They hugged and then entered the hospital cafeteria. "How's the new assignment working out," Tera asked, raising her voice above the noisy background.

"It's gone," Miranda answered as she grabbed a tray for the food service line. "Today's my last day." She picked up a frosted breakfast roll, an orange, and juice.

"What?" Tera eyed the food offerings speculatively. Nothing looked appealing; she'd only returned from London the day before and her inner clock was still out of sync, not a single pang of hunger to be felt. They moved toward a table in the middle of the seating area, surrounded by nurses in scrubs, medical technicians, maintenance – an early-morning sampling of the thousands of staff at the hospital.

"Yesterday I was told to get out, I'm a security risk for a suspected data breach. Yeah, right. I don't even have upper level access for patient records. I'm pretty sure Dr. Loomis is behind me getting canned." She sighed as they sat down. "He went off kilter after that black lady came by a couple of months ago. She was asking to see her kid's doctor. She wanted to know why her kid died, but the atrium in our circle is confusing, unless you know who you're looking for, you can just stand there, lost. Loomis was looking at her through a slit in the blinds and then he told me to call security on her."

"Security?"

"She was causing a disturbance," Miranda said sarcastically. "Disturbing the peace because her kid died. Shame on her." She bit into the roll and made a face. "Gah, I won't miss the day-old crap they serve here." She looked at her cousin, taking in the light blue, almost transparent eyes. "Things really went downhill when I came in early one day afterwards to catch up on data and heard an argument in Loomis' conference room. Loomis and Hawthorne, the administrator, and some guy with a really deep voice. He was actually yelling at Loomis, called him an f-ing dumbass and said something about a plan.

"Loomis came out of the office afterwards and asked why I was there and what I heard and told me if I ever repeated anything said in that office I'd get fired. He was totally crazy-looking, those black bug eyes of his like deep pits. That really scared me. Then he came at me two days later about some papers he lost. He said he'd left them on my desk and what did I do with them? I'd found a mess on my desk and tossed the stuff in a folder and put it in my drawer. But he had me so rattled I couldn't find them. He started checking my messages on the portal, asking who I was talking to on the phone. Suddenly I got dropped down to part-time and transferred to Geriatrics and now out the door."

"That sucks. Do you have any job prospects?" Tera's fingers drummed on the table. "You know I can get you something up in the Cities, with...."

"Oh God, there he is," Miranda interrupted. "Tera, get away, go somewhere else or he'll get after you, too."

Tera stared, dumbfounded at Miranda's words and her obvious terror. She carefully glanced around and saw Dr. Loomis in the doorway, surveying the people in the room. He was such a jerk, standing there like a feudal lord or something. The little tufts of hair around his ears stuck out in such a way that he resembled a Roman athlete with a laurel wreath on his head, except he was bald and beady-eyed and the tufts were the only bits of hair he had. Keeping her back to him so he couldn't identify her, Tera got up from her chair and whispered, "Keep me posted." Then she sidestepped away.

Miranda watched Tera move over to a group of other employees raucously talking about the upcoming Vikings football game. When she looked back, she could see Loomis' eyes boring into her. Tera Storm would have glared right back at him, she was that kind of person, but Miranda was so uncomfortable she looked down.

Wonder what they were talking about, Loomis thought, his eyes following the dark-haired gal across the room. Nice enough looking, sexy long hair, but in with the Elites, the specialized administrative assistants who could go anywhere and do anything, fit into any office in the vast hospital campus. Not to his liking, the whole group was off limits in his mind, far too competent. But he'd never seen that young woman around the hospital before. His wedding ring started to feel itchy as he moved out of the room.

※※※

"Nickeeeeeee!" Sienna danced on her tiptoes across the room that Thursday evening and swooped her little brother into her arms. A solid nine-year-old in the arms of a willowy sixteen-year-old made both of them stumble backwards. Callista braced them up quickly. They'd made good time, it was only a week after Thanksgiving.

"Yew, you need a shower. Why are you so grubby?" Nick rubbed his head on her shoulder. "But I love you anyway."

Max vaulted onto the bed and lay flat on the top of the white bedspread. "This feels so good, you have no idea how hard it is to be folded up like a slinky in a corner of the back seat of a little car. Boxes to the left of me, boxes behind me, boxes under me, boxes falling on top of me, no room to even fart." He saw his parents kissing. "Hey! Get a room!" He looked down, "What's this blue bowl for?"

"Puke," Nick said and watched his brother screech and toss it away. "You forget to wash your face or something? There's something dark on it."

"He needs to shave," Sienna said, squeezing him. "He's growing up and has to learn to use a razor without cutting his throat. I wish."

CHAPTER 5

<u>Mark's Notebook –</u>
It's like a shooting gallery. You get off a shot, the duck goes down, but then pops back up and you have to shoot at something else, just keep shooting. First relaxants like Mirtazapine, an anti-depressant, and Cyproheptadine. IV Tylenol for stomach pains that suddenly materialized. GI consult, keep Mirtazapine, hold Cyproheptadine, stop B2, switch to Pepcid, start Carafate because now they think there's an unhealed ulcer from California. Zofran usually works fine but it affects the heart. Don't want to do that, Nick is just a month past major heart surgery. Then the next day, stop Mirtazapine, keep Carafate, restart Cyproheptadine, restart PPI, whatever that is, keep Pepcid. Vomiting. Nausea. Pee. This is like Groundhog Day, replaying everything over and over and over.

Loomis stood outside the room studying Nick's chart. They were sure pumping a lot of garbage meds into the kid; it appeared no one had a clue what was wrong with him with the vomiting. Whatever.

Suddenly the door jerked open. A woman with huge doe-like brown eyes and long brown hair was staring at him. "Who are you?" she demanded. The stance was bold, defensive. Must be the mom, he thought. Tee shirt and jeans and fluffy slippers, must have spent the night. Even without make-up, she looked damned good for nine in the morning.

"Dr. Loomis, Pediatric Services," he said, waving his hand, indicating he wanted entry to the room.

She backed up. "I'm Callista Hampton. Where have you been? It's been over a week since Nick was flown here. I thought you guys made rounds every day."

Loomis gritted his teeth. "I see numbers from the blood work, I come when I need to."

"I've got some questions," Callista stated, looking him up and down. He was a few inches taller than her five-foot-seven, a blue shirt and striped tie under his white coat. No pot belly from sitting around too much, bald except for some hairs that forgot to fall out around his ears. He turned. Oh gosh, black beady eyes like a bug.

He stared back, waiting. Damned if I'm going to ask what she wants, he thought.

"The numbers," she said, making a quick recovery. "Aren't the blood pressure numbers too high at 150 over 100? Usually after...."

"They're elevated, but not high enough to cause any symptoms or distress," he recited. What did she know, he hated these doctor wanna be's who got their medical information from Google.

"The blood pressure isn't allowed to get this high after heart surgery. And he looks puffy. There hasn't been dialysis for five days, don't you think he needs it?"

"As I said, I see the numbers from the blood work. Everything looks good to me. We're trying to stimulate his kidneys by giving them something to do, to work on."

Stepping back, Callista gave that concept some thought, but she kept coming back to the same thing, Nick's blood pressure was closely regulated after heart surgery, this was no different in her mind. Both medical problems needed to be juggled, kept even, not one side up and the other down like a see-saw. No, she thought, he's wrong.

Now he turned away, looked Nick over, the kid looked sleepy, worn down. Yes, maybe a little puffy, it showed in the jowls which drooped like those of an old man. Loomis wrote quickly in the chart, then went out the door. He stopped. "We'll remove a liter of fluid and see how he feels." And then he was gone.

"Nice meeting you," Callista said to the door. She turned to Nick. "Is he always that way?"

Yawning, Nick said, "I don't hardly see him. Mom, help me up, I gotta go to the bathroom."

The next day brought a transfusion, the blood was low again, plus a very small amount of blood pressure medication and a diuretic. The smart alecky Nick was down in the dumps, not eating or drinking. He started picking fights with Callista when he wasn't ignoring her. Several times she called Mark to come over to relieve her, but he kept saying he was busy.

***

"Mom, I've had it," Callista told Ellie on the phone. She was nearly in tears. "I drove all that way like a maniac and the kid could care less. I don't exist. They're all being stupid. Now that I'm here Mark stays away at Ronald McDonald House and works on his computer. And the other kids are out of control. That dumb Sienna didn't pack her school books, she left them in California!"

"On purpose?" Ellie asked, knowing the answer.

"She claims she forgot. And Max, we found out he isn't getting credit for his school work. He's going to fail the quarter. He didn't read through all the directions on the orientation page for his online school and clicked off before the end. At the end, he had to list his classes for credit. He didn't do it. What did I do to deserve this?" She finally broke down.

"Where is everybody now?" Ellie asked.

"They're all at the hospital. They left me this hole of a room to clean up. I could scream!"

Ellie had heard about the room earlier. Long-term situations warranted a generous suite with large bedrooms and a microwave, mini-fridge, kind of like a motel. Short-term stays at this location were assigned a room with a queen bed, and a twin with a trundle beneath. With the trundle out, there was no room for the chairs that came with the table. The bathroom was tiny, and the sink outside in the main room.

"What are you going to do?" Ellie asked. "I can come and get the kids and take them home."

"They're going home, all right. I have them re-enrolled at school, they start Monday and I'm leaving this place, the hell with it. It's been almost two months since we left, I can't stand this shit. Mark can sit here and rot, I'm not coming back."

"And Nick?"

"All he does is puke. Says he's dizzy sometimes. I don't know what's going on, no one tells me anything."

Ellie paused a minute, considering an idea that popped into her head. "Okay, what's his blood pressure?"

"Why? Well, the lowest it's been is 130 over 100. It keeps spiking to 150 and more! I can't make anyone believe it needs to be lower. Dr.

Arthur isn't around until later this week."

"When I was pregnant with you I felt that way. Nauseous, head congested. I didn't know it, but my blood pressure was way up. Pre-eclampsia. I ended up on IVs after delivery because it was so high. Maybe that's what's wrong with Nick, high blood pressure."

Silence.

"Callie?"

"You know, I brought that up to the doctor but he said they were keeping it high to make his kidneys work. Maybe you're on to something, Mom. He's had lower oxygen overnight too, and I wondered if it was fluid overload. He's really puffy. It doesn't make sense. He's tired, it's almost like he's going backwards."

Mark took the overnight duty that night. Nick's oxygen levels overnight were low again when he was checked, but there was no concern. The kid was tired and slept hard. Mark felt the same way and got a long stretch of sound sleep considering that cramped little bed.

The bustle of the morning brought them both awake: food carts bumped down the hallway, a couple of nurses were making rounds to get morning notations done – it was a constant background buzz.

Nick's blue eyes were open, and Mark called over, "Hey, bud, how'd you sleep?"

"Okay, I guess. I'm still tired." He was taking big breaths and Mark came over.

"You want to try breakfast?"

Nick opened his mouth to answer, and suddenly his eyes rolled back and he went still. Buzzers you could hear all over the floor suddenly went off. Mark looked at the machinery and saw Nick's oxygen level was next to nothing. "Nick!" He shook him. No response. Then louder, "Nick!"

He ran to the door. "Somebody help! I think my kid is dying."

CHAPTER 6

Mark was pushed out of the way as staff rushed in with a crash cart. Numbers crisscrossed the room as various nurses and doctors reeled off blood pressure, oxygen levels and heart rate multiple times. Nick didn't wake up. Words like "seizure" and "stroke" and "CT stat" came through the intense action around the bed. Mark grabbed his phone.

"Now what," Callista answered with an edge to her voice.

"You have to get over here. Leave the kids. Something happened to Nick, they can't wake him up."

"Oh my God, what happened?"

"He woke up, seemed okay, but sleepy, then just passed out. Oxygen tanked. They just intubated him now. Heart seems okay but," he paused, "he isn't waking up."

Callista tripped over the bed and the trundle trying to get to the bathroom. Max groaned as he turned over when she kicked him. Sienna didn't move. "Max, I gotta run to the hospital, something happened to Nick."

"What did you say? Where are you going?"

"To the hospital. Stay here!" Max was already back down on the mattress.

Throwing on clothes and grabbing a sweatshirt, Callista ran outside. She was surprised it was raining, it was cold enough to snow. The Jeep was slow turning over. "Come on!" Damn California vehicle! Then she tore out of the parking lot and into the main street of downtown Stanton, the hospital campus looming a mere two blocks away. Into the ramp and through the underground tunnels, it was taking forever. She didn't want to run, she would look like a crazy woman, but, in fact, she was totally panic-stricken. What happened?

Hurling herself through the double doors, she saw Mark by the elevator. "They're just taking him to CT – this way," he said. Through another hallway and they could see the gurney ahead.

"Nicky, Nick," Callista reached out for his shoulder as they caught up. Suddenly she was staring into his blue eyes. He was awake, wondering where the tubes came from. "It's okay, honey, you're just going to have a CT. They're going to peek in your head. You've had a lot of them. No big deal." He nodded as he was whisked into the scan area.

She sat in the waiting area, as Mark paced the small space. "I don't have any idea what happened," he said. "One minute he was fine and the next out and hardly breathing. I heard them say seizure and I think that's what they're looking for, but I don't know why."

"When is this going to stop?" Callista moaned softly as the tears began to fall.

***

"That must have been very frightening for you," Dr. Kindly told Mark and Callista as he made himself at home in Nick's Cardiac Intensive Care room the next morning. He was plump with white hair and a beard, and could have passed for Santa. After a round of anti-seizure medication, blood pressure medication and sedation, Nick awakened that morning feeling great. He was extubated, but his oxygen was still low and he had a blow-by of oxygen near his face. He ate and kept the food down. He went to the bathroom. The day before was like a bad dream.

"Nick has what is called PRES, Posterior Reversible Encephalopathy Syndrome," Dr. Kindly said. "Edema in the brain caused the seizure. The good news is in that word *reversible*, the difficulty should be resolved in a week or ten days."

"How on earth does that happen?" Callista asked, stunned. Edema – fluid in the brain – did not sound good. And happening here at the hospital with so many people watching his progress, how could that be?

"Acute hypertension. His blood pressure was not controlled, not when the systolic was up as far as 190. That's what the chart showed. There may have been other symptoms, abdominal pain, nausea or vomiting. It's sometimes hard to see this coming because the symptoms could be other things. But mainly, it was the hypertension.

We gave him blood pressure medication. By tightly monitoring blood pressure and keeping it no more than the 130/80 range, this can be avoided."

Callista and Mark looked at each other. Hadn't they asked the nephrologist about this?

"What are long-term effects?" Mark asked.

"For most people, there are none," Dr. Kindly said. "Sometimes you see an occasional person whose short-term memory is damaged. It isn't significant damage, you understand, but things seem to take a tiny bit more time to be acted on, to answer a question, to understand to do something. That will take about 6 months to resolve. If he has it or not, he will need another scan at that time."

Mark shifted in his chair, reluctant to even consider that medical stupidity caused this problem. "Could this have been fatal?"

Dr. Kindly hesitated, then said, "Yes, if not treated fast enough, the edema puts pressure on the brain and causes a cerebral hemorrhage. But staff here reacted in plenty of time. No danger to young Nick now."

"Can it happen again?" Callista asked, her voice barely above a whisper.

"Perhaps. Blood pressure is the key. Keep it down and there'll be no problem. It's a tad more difficult with kidney patients, what with dialysis and all, but it can be done." He turned to Nick and smiled. "We're going to do some neurological tests in a short while to see how you're doing. Is that okay?"

Nick nodded. "Sure. Better than a tube down my throat again." He made a gagging noise.

Dr. Kindly laughed. "You're one tough kid. You're going to be all right."

Before noon, orders came from nephrology to move Nick from the Cardiac Intensive Care Unit down to Pediatric Intensive Care. Loomis made a brief call to Mark explaining that blood pressure could be monitored better in the Pediatric ICU. An arterial line was to be inserted for future use.

"He couldn't come here and tell us that?" Callista said after the move was completed. "I'm going to get the kids, they're probably not doing homework anyway." She surveyed the area, similar to the cardiac unit, but rooms not as large, not set up for surgery. The nurse station was right out the door. Five women were standing around talking, not one of them came to the room to check on them after the move. What's going on here, Callista thought. Where's the outstanding care this place brags about?

Today she'd walked the two blocks in the morning chill, needing to clear her head. Now, on her way back to Ronald McDonald House, she wondered what to do. It was Thursday, the kids had to show up at school on Monday. She or Mark needed to bring them home, but did they both need to be here with Nick? Could Mark stay home?

What she didn't need at that moment was chaos, but chaos was the only word to describe what greeted her when she opened the door to the small apartment at Ronald McDonald House: pillows strewn every which way – pillow fight? – both kids still in pajamas at almost two in the afternoon. There were candy wrappers on the floor, and as expected, neither computer was logged in for school work.

"What the hell are you doing?" she yelled.

"Mom, be quiet," Sienna hushed her. "You'll disturb someone."

"*I* am disturbed. What have you done all morning? Why does this room look like it was ransacked? Didn't I tell you there's a laundry room downstairs and to wash clothes? Bedding?"

Max shrugged. "Forgot." He lay back with his hands behind his head. "Some really good stuff on cable. Reruns."

"Get up! Do you hear me? Get up! I'm done with this. You can't be left alone more than two minutes. Get dressed. You're coming to the hospital."

"There's nothing to do there," Sienna whined. She tossed her hair. She hadn't washed it in a day or two, it looked greasy. "I'd rather stay...."

"Get dressed. I can't trust you here alone. And I am taking you back home over the weekend. I can't stand this anymore. You're going to school Monday. You can be someone else's worry. Grandma Ellie will be there to babysit."

"I'd rather have Aunt Tera," Max yawned. "She's cool."

"Tera has a job."

"Doing what?" Max asked. "She doesn't look like she does anything except get her nails done."

Max had a point, Callista thought. Her younger sister was precisely done up every time they got together. Tera had flitted in and out of the country for years and now lived nearby in the town of Orion. She worked, for sure, but Callista didn't know what this job was, only that she worked longer hours somewhere here in Stanton, or was it up in the Cities?

"Do we have to have Grandma?" Sienna asked. "She's no fun. She brings that heavy suitcase with her dinosaur of a laptop and works on that."

"She puts vegetables in the food, I spend half the meal digging them out," Max complained. "And she expects us to eat at certain times like six at night. I like to eat when I'm hungry."

"And she says stuff and doesn't care. Remember that time outside the thrift store?"

Max snickered. "Yeah, a woman came out, her butt looked like two basketballs. And Grandma said, 'Oh my, that's unfortunate' loud enough the woman heard it and gave her a dirty look."

"You can't stay home yourselves. You have to get up, go to school, do your homework. You need a haircut, Max. I'll leave all the instructions for Grandma." Callista realized she hadn't alerted her mom about this arrangement as yet, but was sure there would be no problem. Have car, will travel, Ellie told her.

CHAPTER 7

Back home in Trent, Callista spent hours on the computer Saturday and Sunday getting caught up on meaningless school messages – who cares about what kind of water bottle was allowed at school when one of your kids has kidney failure? She didn't get to the grocery store to pick up necessities, didn't realize so much stuff had been left in California. Ellie would have to do the shopping. The house seemed so unfamiliar as she walked around it. And then there was a puddle on the floor in the basement where the water softener leaked. All the water in the toilets was brown. The company was called, and it would be dealt with – next week. She left later on Sunday, hating to drive 100 miles alone in the dark, but stuff needed to be done. Her mom said not to worry.

It was eight o'clock when she left the room at Ronald McDonald on Monday morning. She'd spent well over an hour cleaning it up. She should have felt badly that Mark was stuck at the hospital with no relief over the whole weekend, but she didn't care. You had to get away from a problem to really see it. Walking into Nick's room, she could definitely see it. He looked puffy, almost to the point of being bloated. His left hand was swollen as was his left eye.

"Hey," she pushed on Mark's shoulder under the thin blanket. "What's going on?"

His blue eyes opened slowly and he stared at her blankly, wondering who this woman in a Minnesota Vikings tee shirt was. Then he shook his head as if to clear it. The dark brown hair was longer, down past her shoulders, framing an oval face that looked concerned.

"Wake up. What's been going on? I left Friday and come back and the kid looks like a stuffed sausage he's so puffed up."

Mark dragged himself upwards and sat with his feet over the edge of sofa bed. "Yeah, I saw that, but it was a weekend, you know. Who does anything on a weekend?"

"Has he had dialysis?"

"No, they're still counting on his urine output to increase." Mark shook his head. "It hasn't. I don't know what's going on."

"That doctor show up?"

"Not that I've seen, although most of the doctors check in with the nurse station. You might check with them. I mean he hasn't been to the room here, but maybe he checked in with them and I didn't see him. Maybe you can ask that he come."

Callista nodded and left the room. The same five women were standing around, two with nursing pins, the others must have been assistants. "Excuse me," she said. Ten eyes looked at her. "Has Dr. Loomis made rounds yet today?"

"Rounds?" a very pregnant 30-ish woman asked. "He doesn't do rounds every day. I'm in charge here."

"Can you explain to me what meds Nick Hampton has had, why he hasn't had dialysis? We were told he was sent here to PICU because you would watch his blood pressure better but he's all puffy like he needs an intervention of some sort."

The nurse looked around Callista as though trying to see Nick across the hall. Obviously she couldn't see him through the room windows from the nurse station. It was all for show. She didn't make an attempt to go to the room. "I don't know anything about meds or dialysis. Dr. Loomis is his doctor and we follow his orders."

"Is he going to do rounds today?"

The nurse looked at her blankly.

"Okay, how about you send him a message requesting he check Nick Hampton."

"The doctor on the floor can look at...."

"I said Dr. Loomis," Callista interrupted. "This is a nephrology case, you just said you won't make a move without Loomis' okay."

The nurse shrugged. "I'll check on it."

Callista went back to the room where Mark was packing his small bag. "Don't leave me here all day," she said. "I have a bad feeling."

Mark cocked his head at her. "Oh, oh. What's up?"

"No one has seen Loomis. This is one of his patients. What kind of doctor doesn't check on a nine-year-old patient?"

It was late afternoon when Loomis flipped through the pages of Nick's records at the nurse station. Urine output wasn't increasing. Oxygen dropping at night. Hmm, maybe fluid retention. He sighed. Time to go into the room.

Opening the door, he glanced around. Nick was sitting up in bed playing a handheld game, not in a hospital gown, but wind pants and an orange shirt with some kind of car on it. Mister was sitting in front of his computer, and Missus looking at her phone. He cleared his throat.

They all looked up.

"You wanted to see me?"

"Have you been checking on Nick?" Callista asked. It was almost five o'clock and it had been nine in the morning when she asked for the consultation.

"I get the daily information. The numbers are good."

"Good? Did you look at him? He's all puffed up! He's retaining fluid."

Loomis shook his head slightly. "That's to be expected, he hasn't been very mobile." He waited. Let them drive this car, he thought, offering no other ideas on the matter.

It was the careless attitude that made Callista see red. "Is that what you thought last week when you ignored his blood pressure until it got so high he had that seizure? We asked you more than once whether it was too high, whether his symptoms meant trouble."

"I'm the doctor here," Loomis said, his voice harsh. "I make these decisions."

"And you decided *wrong*," Callista retorted. "He has PRES. Dr. Kindly said there are some memory problems. You decided wrong. What kind of incompetent doctor are you?"

"I am not going to stand here and let you...."

"You should." Mark interrupted. "Dr. Kindly said PRES is caused by acute hypertension. Nick is a cardiac kid, you know what that means? He had massive open heart surgery just a little over a month ago. His lungs were involved. We don't even know if they can handle this amount of fluid. His life depends on a delicate balance in his body and blood pressure plays a very important part in regulating his heart rhythm. It can *not* be played with. The Kidney Foundation has some guidelines...."

"Don't give me that," Loomis interrupted angrily. "I've been in practice for years. And my experience is worth more than some article on Google."

"You could have killed our son. How do you think we feel about that, *Doctor*? We don't think you know what you're doing." Callista felt the eyes at the nurse station boring into her back. Were they shouting? Damn right they were, this was like talking to a post.

Loomis glared at them and then left the room. He stopped at the nurse station and motioned for the pregnant woman to come over. Artesia Cole was the name on her badge. He scribbled some instructions, as well as orders for Lasix as a diuretic to take down the fluid. "Do this exactly as I have it written, do you understand? Do not deviate one iota!" Then he was gone, his white coat flowing behind him.

***

The next morning Loomis found a white piece of paper on his desk. Who the hell was in here, he thought. I'm only here because I couldn't sleep, what am I going to do if the Hamptons claim medical negligence? He picked up the paper – printed instructions to check a HealingWay account, log in: ArtGlo, password Medic123. Games. I refuse to play games, Loomis thought as he crumpled it up. What do I care about some damn whiny blog, everyone and their uncle puts stuff on that site about their broken arm or bad hospital stay, not enough attention to their every little whim. He picked up his gold and silver pen and dropped it. He could feel his heart rate increasing. What if it's the Hampton account? Who is ArtGlo, some of our people, nurses, who get to read it? They let anyone read it? Damned if I will buy into this. He picked up the pen again and dropped it on the desk. Picked it up again and dropped it. Damn it! He threw the pen across the room and it hit the side of the filing cabinet with a loud clunk. He turned to his computer. Stupid games, he thought as he carefully logged in.

And there it was. What the hell, that Hampton woman is vomiting her brains out on the site, describing Nick's condition in wild detail and nailing me, a Holcome doctor, to the wall.

Posted 12/16/19, 11pm – Callista Hampton

Nick continues to retain fluid everyday. So much so that his face is puffy, one eye is swelling, his ankles, feet and legs are swelling. His clothes are getting tight. So far the "wait and see" approach and dosing lasix is all that has been done. While yes, the lasix is now working, he woke three times last night to pee, but his body isn't catching up and taking over. Nephrology guy really doesn't want to do dialysis anymore because he feels it will set the kidneys back but this morning I told him I personally had a major lack of trust for his decision-making since the last time he pushed the limit and waited to see what would happen, Nick coded. He would also like to get him off his IV BP meds. Nick doesn't need much, but every time it's shut off, they have to turn it back on. If they remove fluid he might do a better job keeping the BP controlled with oral meds, don't you think?

So that is where we sit, nothing is getting Nicky ahead. With newly repaired lungs that haven't known how to fully work before, I don't know that it is completely smart to be loading them down with fluid. Since it was the nephrology guy who knew the risks and pushed the issue with his blood pressure, it's his fault Nick got PRES and had the seizure. How could we place 100% trust in him when we can SEE that Nick isn't flushing all the fluid he could be/needs to be? How can I get that head guy to act like a real doctor?

How many people have read this post, he thought. Damn it to hell, how can I shut them up? I can't have stuff like this out in public. I've got to stop them, maybe keep them so off balance they can't think!

❈ ❈ ❈

"Hi Nick, how're you doing?" Tall and soft-spoken, Dr. Arlene Arthur found her way down to the Pediatric Intensive Care Unit from the heights of the cardiac unit. She'd guided Nick's care for all of his nine years.

"Dr. Arthur!" Nick grinned. "I really miss seeing you. Have you been flying around the country?"

"Out of the country, Nick," she said, smoothing her skirt as she sat down. "Hi there, Callista, Mark. Where are the other kids?"

"Grandma is teen-sitting," Mark said. "I hope she's not a wreck when she's done." He appraised Dr. Arthur, her hair a little more gray, a few more wrinkles around the eyes, the reading glasses hung on a red strap that matched her sweater.

"You've been out with Doctors Without Borders?"

Nodding, Dr. Arthur looked over Nick's chart. "Well, this is interesting. You've had some adventures, Nick. How are you feeling now?" She reached out and held his hand, actually checking his pulse. "I saw HealingWay and thought I'd better check what happened while I was gone."

"I'm tired. They gave me some medicine that makes me pee all day and especially at night. I get to bed, get to sleep, have to get up again. Mom yelled at them yesterday and said not at night so I don't get a migraine. You know that will happen if I don't get enough sleep, don't you?"

She smiled knowingly. "When do you plan to enter medical school, Nick? You've got the routine down pretty well. I'll give you a recommendation."

"And cut people open? Are you kidding?"

They laughed. And then the door opened without so much as a knock. Dr. Loomis was standing there, green shirt and dotted tie showing through his buttoned white coat. Nothing could take the glare from his intense eyes as he saw Dr. Arthur.

"Dr. Arthur, I'm surprised to see you here." There was a slight edge to his voice that Callista thought very unprofessional.

"Just checking up on one of my patients. Like you are, Loomis?" It was plainly a question, and an incredulous one at that. She didn't dignify him by standing, just kept sitting with Nick's hand in hers. "It seems like Nick has had some high blood pressure issues." She paused. "Why is that, Doctor?"

"Standard with kidney failure, push the kidneys to get them back on track."

"You *do* know Nick is a cardiac patient, don't you? You can't do the standard when it could cause cardiac involvement and in his case, lung problems, too. You know that, don't you?"

Instant replay, Mark thought. That's what the discussion was two days ago. Go for it, Arlene.

"This is a nephrology issue, nothing for you," Loomis began. But she interrupted him, "I beg to differ, *Doctor*, it is incumbent upon each of us to know how everything connects in a patient. If you'd have picked up your phone and called me I could have enlightened you."

Arlene was on her feet now, staring eye-to-eye at Loomis. "Nick's blood pressure must be maintained below 130 or he could have heart complications. Surely you don't want to deal with that, do you?"

The silence was so thick it was suffocating. Mark held his breath.

He'd never seen Arlene – usually so easy-going – so acid. And Loomis, the jerk, wasn't backing down. She had years of seniority over the man, who did he think he could push around?

Loomis gritted his teeth. There was no way to win this with her, especially here, now, he thought. This is my patient and damned if I'm going to tolerate any interference. But not now.

"I beg your pardon," he bit out, then turned and left the room.

It felt like a huge weight had been lifted when the door closed. Callista felt close to passing out. What just happened?

CHAPTER 8

"It's like a flipping tag team," Loomis was rapidly pacing in his office, his voice elevated. "What she doesn't come up with, he does. She tells me I'm incompetent and caused PRES, and he starts rattling off statistics to buttress their opinion. I can't stand it. I can't stand them!" He stood before the windows, looking out over the darkened streets in Stanton. "Then that damned Arlene Arthur comes in today. I hate that woman, all superior and insulting. I hate her."

"You won't get far picking on that one," came a quiet voice behind him. "She's an icon here. Thanks to her, Holcome is a major cardiac player in this country. Better to bow down as you leave the room." Neil Hawthorne sipped his gin. He'd helped himself to a bottle in the hidden refrigerator in the lower left cabinet of the bookcase. It was not even noticeable, but filled with top shelf liquor and an icemaker. "Here, have one, Chuck. You're way too agitated to think clearly. This Barr Hill gin is exquisite. You want one?" he nodded to the other guest.

"What are you, her cheerleader?" Loomis turned to face his guests. I don't even know who told Neil to come, he thought. I only texted one person on the red phone, and he was in the stuffed chair to the side, saying nothing, his fingertips touching as he held his hands – almost prayerlike, but not this guy – in front of his face. Then, the deep voice, "Were you attempting the same *treatment* as you did with that black kid last August?" The word *treatment* was dripping in sarcasm. "I warned you about that." Anton Gregory was getting irritated and that wasn't a good thing.

"Don't you fucking *know* anything?" Loomis snapped. "Sometimes you have to push the kidneys to wake up. I don't know what's wrong with this Hampton kid, if the kidneys suffered harm as a result of the heart surgery or they were failing in the first place. The point is, kidneys can recover from harm, from injury. It takes time."

"But forcing high blood pressure on a kid you don't know, a kid with cardiac issues, who could possibly become unstable and die is a huge mistake," Gregory said. "You almost destroyed the time element altogether when that black kid died on you last August." The veneer of civility dissolved as he went on. "There is a critical time element to this plan of ours and you damn near destroyed it again. We don't suffer losses well."

Hawthorne put his glass down; he didn't like the direction this was going. He was only here because he was hospital administrator and had to know how the plan that Gregory launched over summer was working out. Branching out to dialysis seemed like a good move, people didn't know that much about it in the first place – and for kids? Parents, terrified at the thought of their child dying of kidney failure, made easy prey. No questions asked and extra dialysis sessions went unnoticed. But destroying confidence of the patient and family wasn't good, it might even make them go to another hospital. Sometimes Loomis was such a jackass, he thought.

"Take control of the situation," Anton Gregory ordered. He got up, smoothed his impeccable black wool suit with minute gray stripes, and started toward the back door. "I have a plane to catch." He glared at Loomis again. "Fix this," he ordered. He didn't bother to say good-bye and his swarthy face appeared to be in a slow simmer of anger. Hawthorne took this as his cue to leave as well, and drained his glass. "Thanks for the refreshment," he told Loomis. "Like he said, take control. I'll back you up." And then they were out the door.

Loomis began to pace again. Control, they think dealing with these people is easy? They're smarter than the average parents who are usually scared out of their wits and say "Yes, Doctor, No, Doctor." These people survived multiple medical interventions and learned all they could in order to help their kid survive. They were right about the PRES. I played it too close again. They could ruin my career, my whole life just by the mere mention of medical negligence. How to get around them? Better yet, get rid of them. He picked up his phone. There was someone in PICU who could help with that.

❊❊❊

Nick was losing ground again. He was tired, cranky, the blood pressure was edging up. He was in PICU, the pediatric intensive care unit, for better blood pressure control and medication access and he wasn't getting anything. There was some nausea, a headache. More than once Callista talked with the nurses at the station and all they said was talk to the nurse manager. And all she said was that she was following written orders, the doctor knew what he was doing.

The kids were already off for Christmas break, they'd only been back to school for a week. Mark made the trip, stayed the weekend to catch up with work at their house, sorted the mountain of mail, and finally returned the Jeep. He leased a Ford Escape; they needed another vehicle since his truck was still tethered to the RV in California. Then he brought the kids down on Monday. And after bumping into each other a hundred times in the cramped room in the space of an hour, he had a long conference with the manager of the Ronald McDonald House and put in an application for a suite, usually reserved for long-term tenants. In Nick's case, who knew what was going on. The hope to be home by Christmas had vanished.

On the way down to Stanton, Mark stopped at Ellie and Paul's in French Lake, east of the Cities. Picked up stuff, dropped off stuff. This year was so crazy, Ellie was debating whether or not to even put up a tree. Besides presents for a Holcome Christmas, Ellie handed him a big green bag of "special stuff," she called it. "Callista will know what to do with it." He had strict orders to take it to the hospital that evening.

Nick was the first one to dive into the green bag. "Decorations!" he yelled. It was crazy, all three kids pulling stuff out of the bag and tossing red and green streamers around and incessantly pressing the buttons on singing ornaments. They found tape at the bottom of the bag and got to work covering every possible inch of the room. Callista sat back on the little visitor bed and held Mark's hand. "I don't know when this will end," she said. "No one tells me anything except 'the doctor knows what he is doing.' Yeah, right."

"Any chance of discharge?"

"Maybe, but I have no idea when. And it's a holiday so we don't have the usual staff." She sighed. "This sucks so bad." Yet seeing the kids having fun and pushing each other around and laughing, well, at least they were together.

Three days later, another surprise. Loomis showed up, white-coated, bald pate shining, beady eyes on his charts. Mark was at the room, Callista and the kids were moving to a very spacious suite at Ronald McDonald House. Loomis looked up. "We're going to do dialysis today or tomorrow prior to discharge."

"Discharge? You mean home?"

"No," he said with an amused snort. "Of course not. You can't go home yet, we don't know if you can handle this on your own. So you have a room at RMH?"

Mark nodded.

"Outpatient then. You can stay there and bring him in for labs every other day and we go from there. We'll leave the internal jugular line in, just in case he needs dialysis, but it's been ten days. Maybe he won't need it." IJ was the set-up with two capped lines hanging out of a main line in Nick's neck for intravenous and dialysis service. The kid made Frankenstein look good.

"You mean he's doing better?" Mark couldn't figure where this was coming from, there hadn't been much communication for over a week, after the encounter with Arlene Arthur. "What about meds?"

With a shake of the head, Loomis was out the door. The next day, dialysis. And then, Sunday, a medical technician arrived and said she was told to remove the IJ connection. Why was that? She told them the doctor said if Nick needed dialysis, they could put a tunneled catheter through his chest into the jugular vein later.

And so, for the first time in several weeks, Nick left the sterile halls of a hospital and rode in the family SUV to Ronald McDonald House. There he found streamers, his family, and the smell of spaghetti and meatballs. And he cried.

CHAPTER 9

New Year's Eve and Callista was alone with Nick in the three-bedroom apartment on the third floor of Ronald McDonald House. They'd just gone to the outpatient department for blood draws. They spoke with the doctor in charge for the day, who gave them no instructions, so the rest of the day was their own. Mark cleared out early with the older kids. He wasn't feeling well, a bad headache coming on and a little dizzy, face feeling like it would burst. It didn't take a genius to figure a sinus infection was coming on. He didn't want to expose Nick to any germs. Besides the older kids had homework to do, they had a nasty habit of forgetting their school books at home.

It was two days of bliss, nothing required of them. Nick's improved strength allowed him to walk farther each day, even to McDonald's a couple of blocks away. There was church on New Year's and Grandma and Grandpa Hampton made the trip from South Dakota to stop by. Callista treated herself to a couple of glasses of wine. Nick began to work on a car model. It was just like things were normal.

They barely got in the door on Thursday, the day after the holiday when the phone rang. "Who's calling now?" Nick asked. It was barely ten in the morning. They'd walked to the hospital for his labs and just returned. It was fun in the cool air and seeing the newly fallen snow. He was so happy he was getting better and he felt stronger each day. He watched his mom talk.

"I don't understand," she was saying. "Things were fine. No, I wasn't told to monitor his blood pressure. I had no instructions. And what was I supposed to monitor it with, no one said to get a cuff." She looked puzzled. "Are you sure? Now? Okay."

She put the phone down. "C'mon Nick, get your jacket. We have to go back to the hospital. They want us in the ER. Your numbers are out of whack."

"What if I need dialysis?" he asked. "I don't got any hook-up."

The nightmare began within fifteen minutes of walking in the door at Holcome. All Nick's numbers were out of the normal range, potassium was high enough to cause heartbeat irregularities or even a heart attack and the blood pressure was edging up.

"Why didn't you take his blood pressure twice a day like you were told?" Dr. Storelee demanded. He was wearing blue scrubs with the Holcome logo, a few reddish blond hairs sticking out from his surgical cap. The pockets of his lab coat bulged with an iPad, pager, and a stethoscope.

"Because I wasn't told to do that," Callista replied, bewildered. "No one, I mean, *no one* told me to get a cuff somewhere, to monitor blood pressure. We left here on Sunday and it's now Thursday and only when we were here for blood work on Tuesday did anyone check his BP."

"Impossible," Storelee snapped. He looked at the chart. "Where are your discharge papers?" Callista pulled the single sheet she signed out of her purse.

"Where's the rest of it?"

"What rest of it? This is it."

"No, you must have lost the paperwork. No one, I mean, no one leaves this place without going over pages of discharge instructions thoroughly with staff."

"Yeah, you should have a copy and signatures of that stuff then," Callista retorted. "It's not there because it never happened. Who was supposed to see that was ordered and done?"

Storelee was flipping through the chart again. "Your doctor should have...."

"Mom, I don't feel so good. I'm getting a headache."

"Look, we can argue until next year about who did what, the point is, what are you going to do *now*? Nick needs help. Didn't you hear him just now?"

"Dialysis would work, but there's no catheter port." He was puzzled. "It says it was removed Sunday before you left. Did you ask for that?" Seeing her face, he looked for initials beside the order. A blob of scribble. An *L* stood out. Oh God, one of Dr. Loomis' patients. "Uh, we have some things we can try," he said quickly. He was in charge of the ER, and for sure, this required emergency treatment.

"Can't you put in a catheter?"

"No, too specialized. They want a tunneled catheter from the chest to the neck, the team for that isn't here because of the holiday. The nephrologist has to call them in, it won't be before tomorrow for sure. We've got to improvise."

Callista's Journal, Thursday night –

It's night now. We are in PICU again. Improvise, he said. Albuterol nebs to start, then Insulin, Dextrose, Lasix, each poured into the IV, one at a time, wait to see if it would work. The potassium would go down, then up again – move on to the next thing. Nicky needs dialysis and that ass Loomis said maybe he wouldn't need it anymore, so he had the access removed. Right. Then that Storelee guy insisted on giving Nick Kayexalate, something to bind to the potassium and take the level down. I didn't want to. Before God I didn't want to, the crap looked like diarrhea in a cup, all brown. You could have taken it straight from the toilet. It was like a last ditch thing to try. So Nick took it. Then the vomiting started. All day and even into tonight. The blood pressure is going up. I am trying not to cry in front of Nick, but it's so hard seeing him falling apart before my very eyes. These damned people here refuse to start IV blood pressure meds. Mark, where are you, I need you so badly.

❈❈❈

"It hurts, it hurts," Nick cried, writhing in the bed. He was holding his stomach, but the pain went around to his back. He'd try to sit up to throw up, and it would hurt worse. His chest incision seemed fine after the catheter insertion, but then a kidney biopsy was ordered while he was under sedation and that left him in excruciating pain for two days. Tylenol couldn't touch it. If he tried to put weight on the leg to go the several steps to the bathroom, he would nearly scream.

"What the hell is going on here," Callista demanded at the nurse station. Surely they could see and hear Nick's suffering the last two days. It was now Sunday evening. They'd been in the hospital since Thursday morning, in PICU since Friday. "I've asked for a consultation for three days about the vomiting since we've been here. I've asked you to pay attention to blood pressure. His heart rate is elevated and you sit here like queens on your thrones! Why is he in pain? Is anyone looking into that?"

"We'll have someone check on that shortly." That was from Artesia Cole, the pregnant nurse manager.

"I've heard that for three days. We'll check, we'll do this, we'll do that. And you do nothing! You don't even go in his room!" Callista was almost shouting. "He's throwing up blood. Have you even checked on that? His stomach lining is being ripped apart!"

"You don't talk to us that way, you're not being respectful."

"And you are not respecting my child. Get the fucking doctor in here!"

"You can't talk to me or my staff that way! I'm going to report you!"

"Go ahead." Callista walked away, tears streaming down her cheeks. I hate you, I hate this place, you stupid bitch. She turned and saw the manager yapping on the phone. Bet it's not for a consult.

"What is this, a third world country?" Ellie asked on the phone awhile later. "Did you get transferred to Bangladesh or something?" It was very early Monday morning. "This can't be the great and wonderful Holcome International Medical Center. Do you need anything? Can I help?"

"Not unless you have a medical degree. They sent in the resident about four hours later and he okayed morphine for Nick. Then that stupid nurse manager came in all huffy about my needing to use the proper words when asking for assistance. You don't say 'I need a consult' you have to be specific about which doctor or which consultation service. Like I know what he needs for pain or puking, or who to specifically ask for. Except for blood pressure, I know who to bitch at for that. And how dare I speak so disrespectfully to them. Good God, my kid is throwing up blood, I should bow down to them to get their attention?"

"Everyone is right but you, all that politically correct crap," Ellie muttered. "How is Nick?"

"The pain in his back and side and stomach is so bad he can't put pressure on the leg on that side. What the hell did they do to him? They didn't need to do that biopsy for another month. Why did they do it? Who ordered it? And everyone is staring at us, phones in their ears, like reporting to Big Brother or something."

"What about Mark? Where is he in all of this?"

Callista ran a hand through her long hair, now a mess after four days confined to an ICU room and no relief. "He's sick. It's a bad sinus infection. He wasn't feeling well when he left last week and couldn't get in to the doctor until Friday because of the New Year's holiday. By then he had a 102 fever. He's down in bed."

"Do you want me to run up there and help out?"

"Kids are back in school tomorrow, he can rest during the day. I'll call him and let him know what's going on, what went on last night. Just hang in there, Mom, I'm sure you can put on your rescue cape and help out sooner than later."

※※※

By noon, things changed. Staff from the Cardiac Intensive Care Unit showed up and transferred Nick upstairs, much to the anger of the PICU staff. It made them look bad. But Nick wasn't two months past open heart surgery and the pain and stress of the weekend threw his heart rhythm way off. It didn't help that the bag of magnesium ordered for an IV on Friday to help correct his arrhythmia fell on the floor as they were leaving; it had not been administered.

All Mark did was call Katelyn, the cardiac unit nurse manager, and she got Nick out of the clutches of pediatric care within a half hour. CICU was all business. A specialist was sent for and an abdominal ultrasound revealed two large hematomas, one of them at the kidney biopsy site, no wonder he couldn't walk. Whoever stuck the needle in him was an amateur, in Callista's opinion. Nothing could be done for any of it, but there was an expectation the hematomas would dissolve on their own with rest. The gastroenterologist began checking the medications and ended up putting a hold on oral medications to give Nick's stomach a rest. The next day, dialysis.

"What are you doing up here?" Dr. Loomis asked two days later. He was holding Nick's chart in hand and another doctor was with him, a tall, thin, younger fellow with black hair swished upward.

"Nick had cardiac distress after all the vomiting and pain."

"I told you I thought Pediatric ICU was better able to handle his care."

"No, they weren't," Callista said evenly. "There was no blood pressure medication given, no one from gastroenterology came to check on the vomiting, he was throwing up blood, for God's sake. He needed a transfusion when he got here."

Loomis snorted. Doing the Google doctor thing again. "That wasn't from the vomiting, the kid isn't getting the nutrition he needs. We may have to start gastric feeding."

"Oh no, you're not."

"Who are you to...."

"I'm the parent and he can barely tolerate water. He's worn out from the weekend. We've got to get him back together."

"Yeah, yeah." He turned to the other doctor. "This is Dr. Dorian Place, who will be assisting with your case. He's new to Holcome." Loomis gave her a hard look, she did look worn out–hair messy and no make-up. Where was her hotshot husband? Should be easier to control the situation with only one of them to deal with, he thought.

"Nick is going back to PICU tomorrow," he said and then was out the door.

Dr. Place paused, looking after him, then at Callista. He shrugged and started after his boss, then hesitated at the door. He turned back, "Nice meeting you. I'm sorry for all this. I'll try my best to do better for you." Then he was gone. When he caught up, he saw Loomis on a red cell phone. Dr. Place couldn't hear the conversation except for some "yes" answers. Then Loomis looked behind and saw Place quietly observing.

"Out of here," he said. "Back to the office."

CHAPTER 10

"Mom, I need help."

"Callista? Why are you whispering into the phone?"

"I don't want them to hear me. There's something going on and I'm scared."

Ellie froze. Eighty miles away and trouble, not so good. "What's up," she said calmly.

"They're after us, they say I threatened the nurses and screamed and they have to have a legal document, some behavior plan we have to sign or they won't care for Nick. You know, about last week. The hospital administrator is involved, some guy named Neil Hawthorne. He sent me a formal notice, there's going to be a meeting. Mark can't come down here, work is overwhelming him and he's tied up in meetings for two more days. I don't want to do this without him, but they don't care. They're demanding to see me. Today. Then the nurses keep coming in here to snoop, look around. They pretend to be checking on Nick but not one of them has taken his blood pressure or temperature. They have someone watching this room constantly." Callista had her back to the nurse station so they couldn't see she was on the phone.

"What do you need?"

"Can you come down here and stay with Nick? I have to get out of here." Her voice broke. "I've been stuck here for almost a week alone, haven't been able to shower or get more than a snack from a vending machine. I'm so tired."

"Sure," Ellie said. "I'm out of here in five minutes. Do you have that thing they want you to sign? I'll take a look. Where are you and how do I get to your room, that place is like a maze." She hung up after a jotting down a few notes. "Hey, Paul, gotta go down to Stanton to sit with Nick for awhile. Something's going on." She gave him the highlights.

Yet another rescue run, he thought, but that's what we're good at, back-up. "Haven't they been through enough at that stupid hospital?" Paul asked, disgusted. "Here," he grabbed a couple of Altoid tins. "And why don't you bring that new Monopoly game with you, Christmasopoly or something like that. Maybe Nick will want to play it, get his mind off his prison." He bent down and gave her a kiss. "Drive carefully."

❊❊❊

Ellie entered the PICU with purpose. According to the directions, just get to the nurse station and hang a left. Yes, there they were, all sizes and shapes, butts draped on chairs and chatting. There was a white coat with a bald head off to the side, silent observer, obviously didn't care there was a light on over there on the right. A tall Somali woman in her robes was pacing inside another room. A baby was crying. The place was noisy and annoying, all those half walls with windows the rest of the way up, damned near no privacy at all.

"Nicky, Grandma is here."

He looked appalling. Circles under his blue eyes, thin arms over the white blanket, a blue barf bowl at his side. A bunch of machines were shoved to the right side of the room in no particular order, cords all over the floor. There was an IV tree and a screen with Nick's heart and blood pressure and oxygen rates zigzagging along. The bathroom was way over in the corner.

"Hey kid, what are you doing here? Last time I saw you, you were walking all over the place and now you're loafing in bed."

A weak smile. "Got anything for me?" She held up the Altoids.

"Yes!" Then, disappointed, he added, "But if I eat them, I might puke." He thought about it a minute. "Oh well, I'll puke anyway. Can you help me open it?"

Ellie caught a movement out of the corner of her eye. Some young fellow in blue scrubs was sitting near the corner. "Hi, I'm Dr. Mom, from the school of hard knocks. Who are you, the guard?" she demanded.

He laughed. "That's a good one."

"This is Robert," Callista said hurriedly. "They decided to have a nurse with us at different times of the day to check on Nick." She lowered her voice. "He's okay."

"Nice to meet you," Ellie said. "Not many guys go into nursing. How's it going?"

Robert grinned. "Not bad. PICU is good duty, the kids don't talk back much, not like on general pediatrics. And then there's Nick. He never follows the rules."

Nick was nodding as he sucked on the candy. "Mmmm, peppermint."

"Anti-puke, too," Ellie said. She turned to Callista who was getting into her jacket. "Where's the paperwork?" Callista handed her a folded up sheet of paper. "You can sit on the bed," she nodded to the side. "Don't let them see you."

"Not my first rodeo, honey." Ellie opened it.

Name: Nicholas Hampton
Pediatric Intensive Care Unit – HIMC
January 8, 2020

The health care team will collaborate to provide the best care for Nicholas to promote positive outcomes. The health care team (physicians, nurses, social work, respiratory therapy, family) will speak using respectful words and tone, listen to each other and ask questions for clarification. Following are Holcome International Medical Center expectations:

- Nursing will evaluate Nicholas according to unit routines and patient needs.

- Consult services and other services will be present and arrive as available and appropriate for patient's needs.

- Level of care is dependent on patient care needs and deemed by the physician and multidisciplinary care team in collaboration with the patient and the family.

- If the family has a concern, they shall bring the concern to the nurse who will communicate it to the provider. If necessary, the provider will discuss the issue with the fellow and then the consultant. If the family is not satisfied with the plan of action as presented by the nurse and chief resident, they may ask to speak to the fellow and/or consultant and they will oblige when the needs of the unit allow.

- All health care providers are knowledgeable and competent to provide Nicholas's care.

- Physical and verbal threats as well as profanity will not be tolerated and security will be contacted.

- If these expectations are not met, the behavioral emergency response team will be activated to de-escalate behaviors.

There it was, on a plain piece of paper, no letterhead to be seen. "This can't be official; there's no indication where it came from. There is no name, no authority listed who's making these demands. And the grammar is so poor, did a third-grader write it? Why does it dump on you and not spell out the responsibilities of staff except saying they will provide care? What if they don't?" Ellie shook her head. "Rank amateurs. Has Mark seen this?"

"He's got a copy and called Patient Liaison to complain and demand changes. This is allegedly a draft, but the way it was presented, this is it, period: Agree or we're out of here."

"Who's responsible for this?"

"That Neil Hawthorne guy, he's the hospital administrator. Look, I'm going to drop if I don't get out of here. I've gotta go, maybe I can nap. Thanks, Mom. And if someone comes by, you don't know anything, right?"

"About what?"

It was nearly an hour later. "Your turn, Grandma," Nick was collecting all the reindeer cards. He'd passed the North Pole three times and only thrown up once. "Oh, oh, here comes some tall guy in a suit."

Ellie sighed. Here it comes. She glanced at Robert who was standing up respectfully. Oh geez, it must be someone in administration. And there he was, very tall, likely six-three, in a dark green suit. He had brown hair, a close-to-the-face beard like that Green Bay Packer quarterback, and gray eyes. He reeked of authority from his perfectly trimmed hair to his wingtip shoes. Behind him stood two nurse types, like acolytes behind the priest. The short one looked about to drop her overdue baby right there on the floor. The other was looking over toward Robert, trying to catch his eye. Flirting? Give me a break, Ellie thought.

"I'm looking for Callista Hampton," the tall guy said, staring at her. "I'm Neil Hawthorne, hospital administrator."

"And I'm Ellie Blakely, Nick's grandmother." She was very pointedly not holding out a hand for an introductory shake. Neither was he. She adjusted her seat on the edge of Nick's bed.

Hawthorne ignored her as he looked around. "Where is Callista Hampton?"

"She isn't here. She went back to Ronald McDonald House to shower and eat something."

"When will she be back?" Very brusque.

Ellie shrugged. "I don't know how long she will be."

"Will she be here in an hour?"

"I don't know how long it takes for Callie to shower, if that's what you mean," Ellie replied, eyeing the nurse station beyond. It appears we have an audience for this matinee, she thought. The bald guy is still back there and watching every move we make.

"How long has she been gone?"

"Half an hour? I didn't look at my wristwatch."

Hawthorne looked at Robert, including him in the inquisition. "When did she leave?"

"Half an hour?"

"What's the problem?" Ellie asked carefully, readjusting her seat on the end of the bed. "Isn't she allowed to leave the floor, go make herself dinner, take a rest?" The implication was clear.

"She was told I wanted to meet with her. Why did she leave?"

Silence.

"Did she tell you anything about why I'm here?"

"Some vague thing about maybe there would be a meeting." Ellie's eyes met his. "She said her husband was busy at home calling Patient Liaison about something. I'm just here for Nick."

She heard some retching behind her. "If you will excuse me, I have to take care of my grandson."

There was a nod from the big man and Robert was at Nick's side. Then Nick moaned, "I have to go. I need the urinal."

Ellie faced the high priest. "Perhaps a little privacy would help for this."

Hawthorne stared at her. "We're medical people, it's no big deal."

"To you, sir, but he's a kid and it's a different point of view." Robert was hastily drawing the thin curtain around that side of the bed.

"When is Callista coming back?"

"I don't know," Ellie said, again, drawing out each word. And truthfully, she didn't. It didn't matter, she wouldn't tell this arrogant jerk the time of day.

"Can you call her?"

"Do you take your cell phone in the shower?" Ellie asked simply.

Impasse.

At the nurse station, Loomis stood behind the nurses who were watching the scenario.

"Who's the old lady," he asked, surveying the white-haired woman in the nice fleece shirt and leggings. Well, not so old, maybe. He picked up some strange vibes from the look and what was going on in front of him.

"Never saw her before, just walked in like she owned the place and went into the room. Then Hampton left. A relative or something?"

Odd, on the intake papers, no relative was listed who could step in and take care of Nick if needed. So who was this old bird? It appeared they were now in an eye-to-eye staring contest, My Way or No Way Neil was not making any headway with that one. Loomis chuckled, he wouldn't have missed this for anything.

"When she gets back, you have her call me, do you understand," Hawthorne demanded a tad sharply. "I'll be in my office. I want to speak with her!"

Ellie shrugged, thinking, the hell I will. She settled further on her perch. If he was waiting for her to get up and bow down as he left, he would have a long wait. He apparently figured that out, because he suddenly turned and the nurses processed out in front of him.

"Nicely done," Robert whispered.

Ellie turned slightly. "It makes me really angry when people barge in and treat you like crap and they know nothing about you. I could be a doctor, I could be a lawyer. No, let's just push people around because they're in charge." She saw the tall guy head for the elevator. The short fellow was still in the nurse station, then he started for the elevator. When the door opened they left together. "And I could be their worst nightmare," Ellie said. "I'm a journalist."

CHAPTER 11

<u>Callista's Journal, Friday, January 17</u> –
I've got to get out of Holcome before I go crazy. There are things going on at home, Sienna has girlie issues, Max is Max, playing with his Legos instead of doing homework. Mark and his dad have to fly to California the 29th because we got notice the RV has to be moved out of the camp as soon as possible. They'll drive it home. Nick is so depressed, he needs to be in his own space, not this prison with people coming in at all hours, looking at him like some kind of bug or zoo animal. Speaking of bugs, got to general pediatrics, there was this bug crawling on the fresh (haha!) sheets on the spare bed. Damned if it wasn't a bedbug. I'm not supposed to say anything to anybody or I'll get kicked out of here, but a bedbug in a hospital? Finally I played dumb and asked someone. And they got all upset and moved us out immediately, saying something about they get the bugs in the hospital laundry in the dirty sheets. Ugh. They rolled in a sterilizing ultraviolet machine after we left. The whole room glowed purple. I don't even want to sit on anything here. I've got my purse in my lap. Mark was here yesterday. Loomis spoke with him, said I didn't need to know what the conversation was about. They argued about that. Nick had to see his doctor and dad arguing? And what didn't Loomis want me to know? He said the biopsy showed a lot of scarring and tissue death, but perhaps a small chance – 25% – chance of recovery. Based on that information, we said we'd go for it and continue dialysis. Things could turn around.

<u>Tuesday, January 21</u> –
Dr. Place is pretty decent. Has a couple kids. He doesn't look old enough to be a doctor. Too bad Loomis has to come with him. Every time the guy makes a suggestion – and a pretty logical one – Loomis slaps him down like a little kid who doesn't know anything. How can Dr. Place stand working with the guy? He kind of snuck down today, said we are going to be discharged

tomorrow to Ronald McDonald as outpatient on his recommendation. He came here from Ridley Children's in the Cities. Said he heard we asked to get transferred there (you think? 80 miles closer?) and he thought that would work out, they have a good program.

"You did what?" Loomis barked at Dr. Place. "On whose authority? What kind of idiot are you? I'm in charge here."

"You said I was in charge of Hampton," Place answered. "And in his best interest, I thought discharge to Ronald McDonald would help him. The kid's mental health is important."

Loomis was standing behind his desk, teeth so tightly clenched his lips looked like a deadly grimace. Dr. Place was before him, all squeaky clean in his fresh white coat, hair slicked up like some teenager. Was that anger flickering in his eyes?

"I also put forward their request for transfer to Ridley for continuing dialysis for three months or so. If there's no kidney improvement, I'm sure they'll be back for transplant. Their cardiac doctors are here."

"You're gonna be damn lucky if *you're* still here in three months. You don't go off making these decisions without the approval of the head of the department and I'm the head of *all* Pediatric Services. Me, not you, hotshot. You want to keep working here? Then you better do as I say, if I say jump, you say how high, do you understand? Or you're out of here!"

Dr. Place backed away slightly and then turned. He knew he did the right thing by Nick and his family and he certainly did not understand Charles Loomis and his rant. What was it to him if the kid received treatment closer to home? He acted like Nick was his possession. What was in it for him?

Loomis stared as the door closed. That one needed to be watched. He could wreck everything they were working for with his stupid principles. I have to whip him into line.

Callista's Journal, Saturday, January 25 –

We're going home today! We had a lab appointment yesterday and Dr. Place showed up — Wow, without Loomis! He said we were accepted for dialysis and kidney care at Ridley Children's. Dr. Jolene Richardson is the head of pediatric neph and we have an appointment on Tuesday with her to determine our needs. He said it is possible the kidneys are plateauing with the care Nick is getting and remaining at a continuous level. Nick may not need dialysis very often, it will be determined by labs, at least that's the way it was run when he was at Ridley. He said he has a note in the medical record:

Per Parents, Nicholas requires a magnesium level >2.
Arrhythmias will occur if he goes below this.
He is also sensitive to hyperkalemia.

Thank God, someone who understands the precarious balance in Nick's life!

CHAPTER 12

"Throw me a cig, Nick!"

Nick rattled the box of candy cigarettes and then threw them to Tera. Her hand flashed out and grabbed them. "Mmmm," she grinned, and soon the white candy was dangling from the side of her mouth.

Sienna shrieked in laughter, her blond pony tail falling apart across her shoulders as she held her sides. Mark and Callista looked at each other. You never knew what Tera would come up with next. Younger than Callista by eight years, Tera was a wild card, enough so that Ellie and Paul sent her to Aquinas Academy for high school, in hopes the Dominican nuns would reshape her undisciplined attitude toward life. There was no telling if they were successful. Mark reached over to refill her iced glass with spiked Ginger Pop. It was a new concoction from Loon Liquor, the craft liquor store in Orion where she lived. The soda was good by itself, but he wondered what kind of affect the vodka she'd added would have. Liquor was quite a part of her past life...or was it? In her case, he couldn't tell fact from fiction.

"So Maxie, what else did you get today for your birthday? I felt like a dork giving you those plastic ribbons for the 3D printer, but you should get what you ask for."

She glanced at Nick. "Like a Ferrari watch."

Nick squealed. His own birthday was in a month at the end of March.

Max looked like he'd grown a couple more inches. He wore his tweed Irish messenger cap on his brown hair, hoping Tera wouldn't notice he skipped washing it. Out of sight, out of mind, right? "Well, the 3D printer was the big thing from mom and dad, but Grandma and Grandpa got shirts I like, the one with the railroad track on it – One Track Mind – was great. And the model of the clock. Mom says it's my brain. When Sienna gets a job, she's going to get me a gift card."

"Says who, smarty!" Sienna punched him.

"What can you make with that printer? Maybe you can make a kidney for Nick."

"Out of plastic?" Nick was horrified. "Like a garbage bag?" He coughed a bit.

"What's that? Are you sick?"

Callista shook her head, "Picked that up two weeks ago, I think at Ridley. He can't seem to shake it."

Meanwhile, Max fumbled in his Minnesota Wild sweatshirt pocket. "I made this."

"Holy crap, is that a gun?"

For sure, Max held out a thin silver pistol with black on the handle. "I downloaded some plans and made this based on a Walther, but smaller than the one James Bond uses," he laughed. "I made a miscalculation with my math for the size so the magazine won't fit, but the rest of it is for real."

"They have plans for guns on the internet?"

"Oh, Tera," Callista said, "they have *everything* on the internet, even plans for bombs. Don't you use a computer?"

"Of course I do, but not for building stuff. Some toy."

"It's not a toy," Mark put in. "Had he done it correctly, it would be the real deal. With just a little adjustment and some metal parts, the next one will shoot." He knew this from his own gun collection.

"Are you shitting me? Oops, sorry Nicky."

"I've heard it before," Nick said. "You should hear mom sometimes."

"You want it?" Max asked. "Keep it."

Tera sat back on the chair, her light blue eyes wide. Several uses came to mind, particularly for a woman driving alone at night.

Sienna laughed at her brother. "Of course, you can't do eighth grade math, you don't listen to anyone about anything, but you taught yourself trigonometry and physics to play that stupid computer game about cars."

"Cars are everything," Nick cut in. "You can do a lot with cars, more than with math."

Tera was sighting down the short barrel, then she held it up, hand steady. Mark's eyebrows rose, she looked very proficient. Interesting. Everything about Tera Storm was interesting. She kept saying image was everything and that included her name, suited more to a pole dancer than a nun. Mark remembered the elbow he'd gotten in the ribs from Callista when he said he'd enjoy church more if Tera was a nun.

"We want cake! We want cake!" The kids were already lighting the 15 candles. Where has the time gone, Mark thought. Max is 15, I wonder when he'll start acting like 15; then, as he remembered his own teen years, I should be careful what I wish for. They divvied up the cake and ice cream and then the kids ran from the kitchen to the living room to watch TV, some movie about car races.

"So how are the kidney wars going?" Tera asked, elbows on the table and chin in her hands. "How's Ridley working out for you?"

Mark and Callista looked at each other. "It's not Holcome," Mark said, carefully. "Haven't quite decided."

Tera could see they were holding back. "Spit it out."

With a sigh, Callista started, "Dr. Richardson met with us on the 28th, the day before Mark and his dad flew out to get the RV in California. That was three weeks ago. We went over the importance of labs being done right away when we come in Mondays and Thursdays, and then deciding if he needs dialysis. They don't do things that way at Ridley. You just come in and get plugged in. Then she said Nick had to be there by eight in the morning. Period. That's his timeslot at Ridley. No way, I said, he gets migraines if he gets less than ten hours of sleep. She seemed to think that over and said if we got there anytime between eight and noon, it would be all right. Usually we get there about 11.

"She's kind of weird. As tall as Mark, really thin, longish brown hair that she wears down. The woman needs a makeover."

"Most of the time she doesn't come in to see Nick," Mark said. "We get a phone call after labs to discuss the numbers. I don't know if she's working at another hospital, but she always sounds like she's talking in a wastebasket, you know, on speakerphone, maybe in the car." He drank some of his beer. "When I'm there I go over the settings while I'm looking over the shoulder of the dialysis nurse to see if she's doing things correctly."

"Then on the third, a Monday, the potassium was high," Callista said. "I was there. Blood pressure was going up, high 140s. Like I want to go through PRES again. I tried to get them to give rescue meds.

There are three different meds we can use that can bring things down fast, but the one we usually use was out of stock. Are you kidding me, this is a major hospital and they're out of a common medication? They admitted him and gave him IV blood pressure meds but not until after he started puking during the dialysis run and kept doing it the whole time. Got a gastro doc to look at the Holcome records and agree to use their strategy. It worked. We were there two nights. Then, before we got discharged, someone decided that he needed dialysis again. Richardson wasn't there. A Dr. Rafaela Yuki was supposed to direct the dialysis."

"Yeah, when Callista called me about that," Mark said, "I wanted to make sure Yuki knew about the lab values, magnesium and potassium. I know it's in the record that was transferred, but who reads anything anymore? Nick was running higher potassium since Monday. So I called her; I said, since the potassium was so high, didn't she think an EKG was needed to make sure there was no arrhythmia. And she said everything was fine. I asked if she had seen Nick that day. 'I know all about what he needs.' And she said she gave the dialysis center the settings to run. So I called Callista and got this panicked call back, everything was wrong. So I called Yuki back. It took her forever to pick up. Honest to God, it sounded like she was at a casino or some party, not at the hospital at all. And she insisted she was working off the numbers, she knew all about Nick, he was fine when she saw him, he didn't need an EKG, blah, blah, blah."

"Only she was never there," Callista said. "I didn't see her, Nick didn't see her, no one saw her, so how could he be fine when she saw him? I guess I shouldn't have yelled at the dialysis nurse to stop the run, she looked like I scared her to death. But I was scared too, the magnesium level was already too low! We got on the phone with Dr. Place at Holcome. He gave us medication suggestions for at home. He didn't know who Yuki was. And when I told him Richardson was suggesting scheduled dialysis, same time, same days every week, he said not to do it.

"So here we are, two weeks later. A couple trips a week for blood work, everything seems fine. Hasn't had dialysis at all. The rest of the time we're just keeping the kids going at school and the tutor working with Nick and Mark can actually do some work."

Again, a cough from Nick from the other room. It sounded really heavy, congested.

"He needs to be looked at," Tera said.

"When did you go to medical school?" Callista demanded with an edge, although she was starting to agree, the cough was lingering too long with no improvement.

Tera ignored her. "He's got heart and kidney issues, and nothing should be allowed to impede forward progress. Could be pneumonia, like Rusty had when he was little."

"Speaking of Rusty, what's up with him?"

"Speak of the devil." Their younger brother's distinctive hockey "Charge" ringtone blasted though the kitchen. He was put on speaker as he talked to the birthday boy and regaled the joys of the South in the winter.

"Did I hear someone ask, 'What's *her* name'?" Mark asked. "A girlfriend?"

Callista shrugged. She knew Rusty got a transfer with his FedEx job to South Carolina because he met a girl online, but Callista was sworn to secrecy. A shy southern belle and her little brother? Well, not so little, he was a good six feet tall.

After the phone call ended, Tera grabbed her jacket and headed for home in Orion, a bit of a drive, about 90 miles. The kids watched from the front bay window as she twirled the midnight blue Mustang in the driveway and went toward the road with a roar.

"That is the coolest car," Nick said. "1999, V-8, with a stick. I love it. That's my second choice if I can't have a Porsche."

"So whose car is it?" Max asked, plopping down at the kitchen table after putting popcorn in the microwave. "Her husband's?"

Mark cleared his throat. "Uh, Aunt Tera's husband isn't around," he said.

"What?" Callista asked, shocked.

"Then why does she have that license plate, Storm 1?" Nick asked. "If he's not around, then she isn't married, so whose name is that?"

"That was her name after she got married," Callista said. She was going to press Mark for more information about her sister's marital issues but the kids began interrupting.

"But if she isn't married, why does she still have that name? How come she isn't still married?" Nick was puzzled.

"What happened to her husband? We were at the wedding,

weren't we?" Sienna asked. She had a faraway look. "Or was that just a reception at Grandma Ellie's? Did they get married somewhere else? I just can't remember what the guy looked like." All she remembered from age 11 was someone tall with dark hair, an old guy of 30.

Embarrassed, Mark broke in, "Well, judging from what I heard when we picked up the Christmas gifts at Ellie's, I forgot to tell you," he nodded to Callista, "well, we could hear an argument in another room. Tera was screaming a lot of words at what's-his-name that I don't think your mom and dad use. And some of it wasn't even in English."

"Must be from when she ran away to Europe."

"Aunt Tera was in Europe?" Sienna choked on her ice cream.

"After high school, after about a year, Tera just up and left. I don't know what she did, maybe she went to school over there. Anyway, she spent a lot of time in Britain. Still does, the guy is from over there." Callista eyed Mark. "What exactly did you hear?"

"He sounded like he wanted out, said he had other interests. He was leaving Christmas Day."

Max dropped his popcorn on the floor. "Then why did he marry her if he wasn't going to hang around? They only got married a few years ago!"

"Get the broom! And I don't have those answers," Callista said. A silence surrounded the table. She gazed over the oak cabinets, listened to the hum of the dishwasher and watched the scented candles flicker on the counter. *Why am I not surprised*, she thought. *How could Tera be so stupid to get into something like this?*

"Is she going to get married again?" Sienna was really worried. "I mean, who wouldn't like Tera? I'm glad Trevor isn't a jerk like that."

"Trevor?"

"Her friend," Max supplied. "They taste each others' lips a lot."

He ended up on the floor as a red-faced Sienna pulled him from the chair, yelling, "We do *not*!"

CHAPTER 13

The desk phone began to ring. Jolene Richardson glanced at it. Oh God, not him again. She refused to look at it, to touch it. Soon the rings stopped, only to resume again. She sat back in her office chair, her thin legs stretched out, her black print skirt covering them like a shroud. The phone kept ringing. She put her hands to her head and wanted to pull her hair. Leave me alone! It stopped again. She knew the number. She knew it was Dr. Charles Loomis at Holcome.

How on earth did I get into this, she groaned. They were colleagues, both working in pediatric nephrology at their respective hospitals. She'd entertained the idea of a transfer to Holcome, the prestige of that place was worldwide, it would've boosted her career tremendously. It was a mistake to covet a job there: he saw it and pounced. She looked around her plain utilitarian office, bookshelves, a gray steel desk, eight stuffed file cabinets, and folders with recent patient files on her desk and on the gray carpet at her feet. No opulent office for her, no cabinet *cum* bar with expensive liquor and wine. Ridley was a hospital that served poor and rich alike, but Holcome served the world – if a person could afford it, or had excellent insurance.

In the end, he lured away Dorian Place, her most promising nephrologist. She wondered what the plan was, and poor Dorian, so naïve to think after only five years in the field he merited a move to Holcome.

The phone rang again, persistently. I want out, she thought, taking a sip of her bottle of flavored sparkling water. She eyed the windows of her office overlooking the mighty river that divided the Cities. Maybe I should leave, go back to Arizona. Or try Colorado, they have a children's hospital. Somewhere too far for him to get any benefit from knowing me.

Her hand inched toward the handset. "Hello."

"Loomis here, what are you up to, Jolie?"

God, how she hated that name! She hurriedly scrolled through the calendar on her iPhone. There it was, the reason for the call, another article due. The University demanded that medical department heads publish regularly in their field, like colleges required professors to do a book a year. But professors taught only a few classes a day, they didn't work between two hospitals like Ridley and the University, they didn't see patients from all over the entire state, from all walks of life. There were only two pediatric hospitals in the state equipped to handle specialized cases and most of the patients did not go to Holcome. Loomis had little to do with his time to earn his fantastic pay.

At first it was simple. He wrote, or had someone write, the articles for her. She got the credit, her administrator got off her back, her job was safe. "What is it?" she asked hoarsely.

"You know what it is. *The Journal of Pediatric Nephrology*. The article is due in two weeks. 'A Timeline For Development of Diabetes Mellitus in Pediatric Transplant Patients'."

"Are you crazy? I know it's a factor in transplant screening for donors, but I know nothing about that post-transplant! I don't think anyone *knows* anything about if or when diabetes will appear with any certainty. What if someone asks what kind of studies I've done on this?"

"Just say it's continuing. Tell them to read the article. BS a bit."

Jolene was leaning over her desk, her heart was pounding. How about an article on heart distress from extortion, she thought.

"What do you want this time?" Her voice was hardly a whisper.

"What? You're fading out." He laughed. "You have a patient of mine, Hampton. He's there for dialysis because it's closer to home. I want him back. They were told it's supposed to be temporary at Ridley, only until something shows itself in his kidneys, whether they will resurrect or die on him. They're already dead," he laughed. "And I've got the lab work to prove it. The parents just don't know it, *you* don't know it because that little test result never made it into the files you received. I want him back and begging for a transplant."

She almost gasped. Nick Hampton had gone three weeks without dialysis, pretty amazing. Yet, according to what Loomis just said, the child's kidneys must be so damaged, he really needed a kidney transplant: End Stage Renal Disease.

"Are you telling me to...."

"I'm *telling* you nothing. I want him in our transplant program. Do whatever you need to, but I want them running back here for their care sooner than later. The article will be in your inbox by the end of the week." He hung up.

Richardson stared at the top of her desk. What kind of game is he playing, she wondered. If the kid was End Stage Renal Disease, he should have been listed for transplant immediately. But he hasn't been as yet. We could do testing, we could do the transplant. How could she betray her hospital and send the child back to Holcome? One word from her and Loomis would...take her out. He'd deny it all, he'd let slip *her* scholarly articles were someone else's work. She'd be disciplined, perhaps even fired.

Her phone rang, and she was startled. The caller ID was a number unfamiliar to her. She hit the speaker button.

"Hello, this is Sabrina McAvoy from Trent Family Clinic. Is this Dr. Richardson?"

"Who are you? How did you get this number?"

"I'm the Physician's Assistant at the Trent Family Clinic. Nick Hampton is here for a cough and I want to check on a medication I want to prescribe. Mrs. Hampton gave me your number."

"I'm not a pharmacist, honey. I'm a doctor. Figure it out yourself."

"No, no, I just want to be sure what I prescribe is okay for Nick, with all his issues, you know. You *do* know, don't you?"

Get me out of here, God, I can't take this anymore. "Yes, yes, I know, what do you want?"

"Well, I was going to give him Cefdinir, it's kind of a broad spectrum...."

"I know what it is." Richardson closed her eyes. Why did it have to be so soon, I haven't even figured out how to act on Loomis's request, if I want to even do what he wants and then get a question like this. I don't want to be involved in this. I don't want to do this.

"Go ahead." And she ended the call.

❊❊❊

"Hey, Herb, how's it going?" Mark finally made it to the pharmacy counter at Walgreen's in town. It was always busy after work.

Herb waved. "It'll be ready in a minute." He turned back to the computer. Mark had a few items to check out along with the refill on Nick's prescription. The cough had dramatically improved. That was one good thing so far. Work was busy, he was now in charge of document review, and people just didn't get it about security online and even contracts. Too trusting. Too busy to care or just brain dead, he didn't know, but it kept him employed.

"Here you go," Herb came over with a small bag. "You know the drill, if you have any questions, ask the pharmacist." He laughed. "How's the kidney kid doing?"

"Fine, just fine. That's who this is for," Mark jiggled the bag. "Nick's had a cough for almost a month and it's finally sounding better after a week on this Cefdinir stuff."

"Good God, Nick is the kidney kid? He's been on this?"

Mark stepped back, suddenly afraid. "Yes. That's what was prescribed. The PA even called Ridley to check...

"I don't care if she called the President of the United States, I'm so sorry, I didn't know."

"What are you talking about?"

"You have to be careful with this stuff. Cefdinir is thought to be nephrotoxic. It shouldn't be used with patients with chronic kidney disease. It may cause irreparable damage."

CHAPTER 14

It was early, the kids were already off to school, Callista and Nick still asleep, no check-in for labs at Ridley for two more days. Mark sighed, it was almost time to hit the road for work in downtown. Life in the big city, traffic jams, people on bikes everywhere, especially in your way and what made anyone think a bike was safe in the winter in this state? Mark constantly feared those thin wheels would slide on the icy pavement and the rider end up under his tires. His fault, of course, because he was *driving* to work and not saving the planet. He clicked the remote and popped bread in the toaster, then picked up his notebook.

<u>Mark's Notebook –</u>

Dr. Richardson gave up on Nick's kidneys two days ago, this after he went a solid 3 weeks with no dialysis even with a cough and that medication that is supposed to be toxic. She denied that, said it was only a theory. She's acting weird, according to Callista, I've seen it myself. She isn't making sense, evasive actually. Refuses to instruct BP med usage, left that up to us, even after he's had dangerously low BP. She refuses to listen to us, our comments, ideas, won't answer questions, says "That's what we always do." Yeah, well, that doesn't work with Nick. Yesterday, I was there. His labs came back at a very good level and she said he needed dialysis twice a week. I asked her why if his numbers were good and he didn't need dialysis for three weeks and she said "His kidneys are in a different place right now." Then some stuff about invisible toxins. If you ask me, she is in a different place.

The undulating sound of a siren in Europe broke into his thoughts. The news reporter was saying something about a vast amount of illness in France, Italy and Britain. Mark could hardly hear the report with all the background noise. Then the story shifted, many people getting very ill with a new virus in Washington state, California, and a lot of people sick on a cruise ship. All the same symptoms. Nothing locally at least, except yearly influenza. This new disease sounded ugly. The governor of New York was on the air every day, constantly ranting about a tremendous increase of infections and people jamming the hospitals. Mark glanced at the clock, then grabbed the toast and his briefcase and ran out the door. It wouldn't be a good thing if he was late for morning meetings with the boss.

❊❊❊

Ping-ping...ping-ping...ping-ping...ping-ping....

Callista opened her eyes. Oh gosh, did she oversleep? Did the kids get to school? She stumbled out of bed, almost slipped on the waxed floor, and grabbed the nightstand for support. The bed with its thick, plush mattress, was so high on the platform it made her feel like she was on a plane. Where was Mark? 9 o'clock, well, at work, then. She could see no lights down the hall, and half slid, half ran to check on Max and Sienna. Not there. Must have gotten off then. Nick was asleep, maybe she could shower in peace.

Ping-ping...ping-ping...ping-ping...ping-ping....

Phone! That was the ring for Holcome. She grabbed her cell. "Hello, hello?"

"Am I speaking with Mrs. Hampton? This is the pediatric nephrology department at Holcome."

"I'm Mrs. Hampton."

"This is just to let you know that based on the lab reports, his numbers qualify Nicholas Hampton to be in the transplant program because of End Stage Renal Disease."

That was it. He qualifies, was it just a numbers game? Callista went down to her computer in the office and quickly sent a message to Dr. Place via the message portal at Holcome. Did he know this? What does this mean? Does he need scheduled dialysis now? The real question she wanted to ask was how do we get the hell out of Ridley.

He answered within 15 minutes, as if expecting the message. Yes, he knew of the calculations to qualify for the transplant and yes, based on those, Nick qualified. No to scheduled dialysis for kids unless absolutely necessary and please continue to ask before cutting any blood pressure medications on your own.

※※※

"Ms. Storm, is that a cigarette you're holding?" The acid tone of Mrs. Harris's voice carried throughout the room. Fifty pairs of eyes turned and stared at Tera in the back row of seats in the large meeting room.

"Geez, I haven't heard that since the nuns in school," Tera said, sitting back in her chair.

"Nuns! Were you in a convent? You don't look like a nun with all that hair." As usual Tera had her dark hair somewhat clipped back, yet flowing over her shoulders.

A couple of the guys laughed, a dirty kind of laugh. That would be Dave and his pal Kenny. Roger Allen cheered. Hard to tell if it was that she didn't look like a nun or the smart remark.

"Reform school would be more like it," another woman jabbed. "Do they still have those?"

"Ms. Storm!"

Tera took the white box with the red circle and shook it. The box rattled loudly. "Candy. I need my sugar fix. I stole this from my nephew."

More chatter.

"Ladies and gentlemen, your attention please." Mrs. Harris had no sense of humor. She glared at them over her half-spectacles. "This is a special emergency team meeting and we have a lot to cover." She was wearing her black power suit, her gray-streaked brown hair pulled back tightly. It was serious business.

They settled down; fifty-plus members of the Elite Corps, all garbed in their navy blue slacks and polo shirts with the Holcome International Medical Center logo, all seated with iPads ready for their assignments. These Elite staff members were highly trained in computer skills, analysis, and medical knowledge to fit into any area of the vast hospital complex long term or short.

"Ladies and gentlemen, the novel coronavirus – SARS-CoV-2, referred to as Covid 19 – is spreading rapidly throughout Europe. I am sure you have seen this on news reports. Fatalities are occurring at alarming rates, people actually dying in ambulances on their way to the hospitals. As of today, March 13th, the World Health Organization has designated it a global pandemic. I understand the United States is going to curtail overseas flights. What started in Wuhan, China, has escaped into the countries of world, mainly through travel and then by interpersonal contact. Strict health measures are being enacted from Italy to Britain, and it is expected some degree of lockdown will be occurring there soon."

Tera shifted in her seat. Europe? Lockdown? Not good.

"It is the best guess of the Center for Disease Control here in our country that we can expect it to sweep across the United States very soon. This virus is a killer, causing acute respiratory distress, bodily fatigue, and a myriad of other symptoms. It appears half the hospitalized cases are headed to intensive care units and from there, ventilators. The vents are the last effort to save them. Most do not come home from that situation. Toward that end, Holcome has lent its infectious disease experts toward research."

"Are we ahead of the game?" Tera asked. There was no call for questions and interrupting a presentation by the director was unheard of.

Mrs. Harris glared. "It's no game, Storm. People who get this are dying. It's nothing to laugh at."

"And I'm not making any jokes," Tera shot back. "What's the rate of infection, the transmissibility? What's the fatality rate per numbers of infection, per 100,000 people? Is there a particular European situation that exacerbates the infection rate such as high rise apartments? Is there an epicenter, perhaps in Bergamo? Is it expected to occur at these same rates here in this country?"

Silence followed the questions. Mrs. Harris grunted. "Storm, I appreciate the fact you've learned your trade in Europe, you don't have to show off. At present, we are 'ahead of the game' as you say, but not for long, not with the mobility of the people in this country. In fact, there are many cases of severe pneumonia in this country. It could be this virus. Doctors here in this state are dealing with this already. Samples have been sent to the state health department for analysis. Holcome, of course, has far more personnel dedicated to this work than the state, we will lend assistance as needed. We have to reassign several of you to laboratories and data tracking. Volunteers?"

A rustle of cloth as people shifted in their seats and hands went up. No one had actually said there was a case at Holcome, but it appeared to be only a matter of time before it arrived.

Harris went on to outline anti-contagion measures, hand washing, use of sanitizer, and face masks, and a six-foot distance from others was to be maintained at all times. Masks would be issued, but due to a shortage in the state, the N95 masks were reserved only for those dealing directly with the disease.

"The hospital administrator is working with Infectious Disease to structure medical containment areas and procedures for cases brought here, but I am assured Elite members will have no direct patient contact. This Corps fulfills many administrative needs at Holcome and if staff falls ill or people avoid coming to work for some reason, you are expected to be here to keep this place running." Silence reigned.

Harris looked across the room. "There is talk that the governor will invoke emergency powers to handle this health problem. There could be a total lockdown but it will not affect our medical facility. Those of you who have not been reassigned, please continue in your current departments. And that includes you, Ms. Storm, Transitional Care wants you back." Her tone implied she thought the decision to be a mistake.

"Is that a surprise?" Tera asked, with a toss of her hair. "I'm just that good."

Laughter broke the tension that overshadowed the meeting room.

A low buzz of conversation surrounded her as she made her way out of the room. Before she knew it, Dave and Kenny were on either side of her.

"You're that good, huh. Just at work?" That was from Dave.

Tera restrained herself from slapping him. He and his dirty mouth plagued her the last two months. They were like dogs after a bitch in heat.

"Europe, huh? What'd you do there, test the guys in Italy and Spain for STDs?" This time her foot did the dirty work, as she kicked Kenny in the shin. A little higher and his kneecap would have cracked. He reeled to the wall. "Shhhit, you stupid bitch."

But she was gone, hurrying ahead through the group. She felt for her phone in her pants pocket. She had to make a call. Now. Where in this stupid place could she get a clear signal? Outside! She had to get out and made her way through the crowd heading toward elevators. There, the courtyard. She slid quickly through the doors and sat on one of the polished marble benches. Only the fountain, denied of its gently falling water during the winter months, kept her company. Once settled, her fingers flew over the keypad. Again. Again. Knees together and bent over as though in pain, she kept working the keys.

"You got a problem?"

Tera jumped and turned. Roger Allen was standing behind her. She hadn't seen him through her curtain of hair. "You okay, Teresa? Do you have an important call to make?"

"Yes, to my h...." She caught herself. "To Hilary, my aunt. She's a medical missionary in Europe."

Roger hooted in laughter. "Medical Missionary in Europe? Give me a break!"

"Everyone deserves a chance to be saved," Tera retorted.

"Maybe you *were* in the convent," Roger said thoughtfully, leaning forward. He seemed to be eyeing her phone. She turned it over.

"Yeah, I got expelled for stealing altar wine." Go away, she thought. Don't come any closer to me.

"What order?"

"Bénédictine," she said hurriedly, and then realized she'd used the French accent as he burst into wild laughter.

"Liqueur, right? That's a good one."

Bénédictine, nice memories from the villa on the Riviera on our honeymoon, she thought for a moment. She shook her head to clear it as he said, "C'mon, I'll walk you back in."

Something seemed off in this conversation. Did he follow her out here? He had his own assignment and they were only given an hour for meetings in the main lecture hall of the administration building. Why didn't he run off to IT? Was he listening for something? Spying?

"No, thank you, I'll be along in a minute. One more try."

He stood there, waiting.

"Alone. That means move along, I can press buttons myself without your help."

"You sure can." He shook his head and moved back toward the door.

Head games, she thought. Her fingers flew again. Come on, answer, damn it! Answer!

Nothing. It was all the same, in ten different languages, five of which she spoke fluently, the call could not be completed.

CHAPTER 15

"Mom, just a warning. Meeting at the hospital today, word of a possible lockdown in the state coming because of that coronavirus. Stay at home orders, soon, I think. Better get what you need at the store while you can. Let Callie know."

Ellie shook her head at the voicemail. The squat governor of the state was a former teacher and a pompous ass, always talking as though people were mentally deficient and he was the only one with a brain. "Hey Paul, you see anything on the news about the state going into lockdown?"

"What the hell are you talking about. The Governor wouldn't dare." Paul came out of his office with his coffee cup, and glasses pushed up on his head. "Where'd you get this?"

"Tera left a voicemail, meeting at the hospital warning hospital staff of the apocalypse. Said something about stay at home orders and getting what we need."

"He can't do that. No one would stand for that." He paused. "There's a month left to tax season, I have clients to meet. Every accountant will have his head. He won't do that!"

The orders came later that day.

There he was in a suit and tie, holding forth in front of the U.S. and State flags. George Wald, Governor. The diminutive Lieutenant Governor and elderly Department of Health director stood next to him. His staccato words were chilling:

"By the authority vested in me by the State Constitution and applicable statutes, I issue the following Executive Order:

"The U.S. Department of Health and Human Services Secretary has declared a public health emergency for the United States to aid the nation's healthcare community in responding to COVID-19. The World Health Organization has recently assessed that this outbreak can be characterized as a pandemic.

"In coordination with other state agencies, local governments, and partners in the private sector, the State Department of Health has been preparing for the COVID-19 pandemic here. For these reasons, I declare a peacetime emergency in this state and order as follows:

"I encourage all individuals to help protect each other by continuing their individual prevention efforts by staying home when feeling sick, frequently washing hands, and monitoring information about COVID-19.

"In order to protect our state's most valuable resource, our children, I am ordering that all schools will go to distance learning beginning on Wednesday, March 18. I further order that schools will be closed starting on Monday, March 16, so that teachers can safely report to their buildings and begin planning their learning strategies."

"As circumstances require, and pursuant to relevant law, I will issue orders and rules to protect public health and safety. All state agencies are directed to submit proposals for such orders and rules to my office.

"This Executive Order and declaration of peacetime emergency is effective immediately."

Given this day of March 13, 2020

- Governor George Wald

"Power grab," Paul muttered, shaking his head. He and Ellie watched the entire press conference in silence, without the usual sarcastic comments the governor's statements elicited from them. "It's only the beginning."

And it was. Four days later, it was announced beginning the next Monday, bars and restaurants and other places of public gathering would be closed. A few days later, there the governor was again before a room packed with reporters for yet another pronouncement, this one that "all non-essential or elective surgeries and procedures, including non-emergent or elective dental care, that utilize PPE or ventilators must be postponed indefinitely."

At that moment, Callista, Mark, Ellie, Paul, and Tera shared the same thought: Where does this leave Nick's kidney transplant?

※※※

The new Holcome CEO, Dr. Terrance Rexalt, was in meetings with the governor weekly. A lot of it seemed to be in press conferences, in some ways one-upmanship, the state health department versus Holcome International. While the state health department complained about lack of testing supplies and that staff could only process a few hundred of the newly developed diagnostic tests daily, Rexalt bragged that Holcome's labs could do at least ten times as many and would be up to 100,000 by the end of the month.

In addition, the state set up a cumbersome website with every detail and percentage examined every which way, an obsessive-compulsive person's dream of nitpicking. The site was impossible to navigate. The only fact clear enough was that people were getting this virus and dying from it from lack of oxygen as lungs became inflamed and then infected. From this came the next statement by the governor.

After recounting his authority and previous executive actions, including one that limited gatherings to less than ten people, Governor Wald went on to demand:

> "All persons currently living within the boundaries of our state are ordered to stay at home or in their place of residence except to engage in the particular activities and critical sector work...All workers who can work from home must do so...."

The list of Critical sector exemptions was very long, covering everything from first responders to those who repaired tractors, from union leaders and election officials to laundry services, all in reference to a national list. There followed, in minutia, a variety of definitions of workers and activities affected or not affected by the order, but who was he kidding? Everyone was affected by it. The only bright spot in the month came on March 26, when the Hamptons received a letter about transferring care back to Holcome's nephrology department and requesting a video meeting on April 6 to schedule hemodialysis for Nick.

CHAPTER 16

"Is this your car? A classic, isn't it?"

Roger Allen came up to the driver door as Tera turned the key in the lock. He was almost going to stroke it in awe when she put her hand out, stopping him. "You'll get fingerprints on it."

He laughed. "1999 Mustang, V-8, you know how to use a stick?"

"No, I pushed it here. You ought to see my other car, it's a Porsche."

Roger stepped back. "Are you a kept woman?" He was serious.

"God almighty, can you ask anything more personal?" Tera asked as they walked through the parking ramp and toward the tunnel which led to the hospital. Why was he here? Was he waiting for her?

"And keep your distance. Get your mask on before anyone sees you and puts you in jail."

Roger laughed again. "It's just that you're interesting. A lot more interesting than the other people in the EE-LEET Corps." There was an edge of mockery in his voice. "That cigarette thing, that was good. I've been working at this place for eight years and everybody does their job, you know. Don't ask questions, just march lock step to your station and go to work. Don't fraternize, just do your fricking job. And no one talks back to Harris. You crossed the line, girl. I like that." He looked appreciatively at her, long, dark hair, eerie light blue eyes, striking figure, very attractive, about the same age. And single.

"Roger, I have been here three years now. I do the lock step too." She glanced at him, tall, with a genial face and close-cropped hair. The short blue sleeves couldn't conceal his nice biceps. "Eight years, huh? You're ready for a bonus." She hoped to change the subject, he was way too intuitive.

He sniffed. "Ten years and not before. Don't you know that? You gotta be careful around this place, you know. The doctors are gods. Cross one and you're out. I probably got here under a quota for blacks, but I'm good at what I do. Maybe without this race stuff I wouldn't have had a shot at the great Holcome International or even staying here. It's almost like you have to know someone." He paused. "So who do you know?"

Tera stared straight into his dark eyes. "No one."

He punched the handicap panel and the first set of double doors opened. "Like I believe that." He brushed his dark navy blue pants and straightened his polo with the HI logo.

"I don't care what you believe. I applied, I was vetted, I got the job, got promoted into Elite. I'm just that good."

He looked at her strangely. No one from the outside got hired that easily and no one from the outside ever, ever made it to Elite. Today she was wearing the uniform, fitted pants and polo shirt like he was, but she didn't always. There was a touch of flamboyance, sometimes, or was it defiance? Like the car, not something a woman ordinarily would drive. There was just something different about her.

"So tell me about these gods," Tera asked, trying to distract him. They were pacing quickly on the tiled floor, the hall brightly lit, a few staff coming by. They were nearing the cut-off, Roger would go up to IT and she would head through the south tunnel to the shuttle.

He sighed. "There's talk, you know. Every place has talk. There's just some people you don't cross. Neil Hawthorne, the hospital administrator, for one. He's a real son of a bitch. You'd think he was putting down an uprising the way he pushes people around. I heard he even gets in the face of parents, I mean you don't dare question one of his doctors. One mom yelled at the PICU nurse to get help for her kid, she didn't say please or thank you or kiss ass and she got in a whole lot of trouble. The mom, not the nurse. That was Artesia Cole, she struts around like she owns the place. Hawthorne was on it in a minute, defending his precious staff. You're wrong, not them. You're always wrong. There was one, I forget which department, the supervisor came on to one of the clerical staff, his admin, like sexual assault. He's still here, she got transferred out."

"Out where? Why didn't she have him arrested or a court order or something?"

"Here? You can't get anything here in Stanton against Holcome staff. They own the town. They sent her to Reno, an affiliate of HI there. A promotion. Like who wouldn't keep their mouth shut for something like that. I heard a couple guys in our group got into trouble like that too, they got after a girl in the Corps. She's gone, they're not. And then Miranda, you heard about her."

Tera shook her head. "No. Transitional Care is pretty much out of the loop, you know."

"She got canned. One of the docs got her demoted, then she got accused of accessing patient files and she was out by the end of the week. I don't believe it for one minute. She was good at her job, but accessing files? She was no computer whiz, I doubt she could access her own files."

That sounds like Miranda, Tera thought. Poor cousin Miranda, working in some chiropractor office now. "Which god was that?" she asked.

"Loomis, supposed to be in charge of Pediatric Services. He's a bear. The gossip is he killed a kid during treatment, but he's still here walking the halls." He looked at his watch. "Whoa, I gotta run. Let's get together for coffee one of these days. Maybe we can sip it through a sanitary straw under the mask. I'll see if I can dig up some more dirt!"

Tera nodded as she turned right and waved. Her hallway was just as lit and just as shiny with the ivory tile and embossed red geometric designs on the walls, but her mood just hit bottom. Loomis was Nick's doctor.

Transitional Care units were attached, but not attached to Holcome. The shuttle carried staff to off-site locations with names like Greenwood Acres and Springwood Fields so no one would think they belonged to Holcome, but just about everything in town belonged to Holcome. There, on the exit door, was a sign announcing that shuttle service would cease over the weekend to prevent the spread of disease.

Fifteen minutes later, Tera pulled her navy mask over her face and entered Springwood Fields, a two-story brick building much like all the rest of the Holcome properties. She was sure if the hospital had housing for the employees, it would be the same red brick with boring double hung windows. The large atrium featured a few overstuffed chairs, and accent tables and the same ivory-colored walls found on every property. Her domain to the right now looked like a bank teller's spot with the Plexiglas between thee and she. There was a small table right off the entry with a sign demanding that masks be worn because the residents were in varying stages of recovery from surgery or in need of short-term physical therapy. A hand sanitizer dispenser was on the table as well as cheap blue masks. All of it was unused now that the state was on lockdown.

She flipped on the computer. Since the news about the coronavirus, people were calling about the patients. Why can't I visit my Dad? When can my Mom be discharged? Who can we talk with to expedite discharge? How contagious is this virus? Is there any cure yet? What is Springwood Fields doing to protect people? Tera made up a list of questions and answers so what she said would be consistent, and basically bullshitted her way through the day, except when she took her breaks and visited her gentlemen.

The unit had two floors, the upper for the women needing short-term care, and the lower for the men. There was a section on each floor for those recovering from cardiac involvement where the residents attended classes on nutrition and did daily workouts to help recovery. The rest of the residents included orthopedic cases who needed to learn about walking with their new knees or hips, recover from surgeries on ligaments and ugly ankle breaks. Holcome referred to transitional care a lot and for lengthier stays than the industry standard, Tera thought, based on some of the questions she fielded. She noted each call and searched out the background information. After all, that's why she was there. This wasn't her real job, but this assignment was to watch for trends in prolonged and unnecessary care for patients. Holcome was on the radar of a very large insurance provider and several complaints had made the company take notice.

Twenty-two large rooms, she went up the eleven on one side during the morning, and down the other side in the afternoon, joshing the guys and making them comfortable with water, a soda, setting up a phone call, or just chatting. Mr. Angelou, so old you didn't call him anything but Mr. Angelou out of respect, just wanted to hold her hand for awhile, calling her Deidre. He was so pleased his wife came each day to see him, in his dementia no longer remembering that she died years before. The nursing home found him on the floor with a broken hip and took him to Holcome for surgery. He'd been there ever since, out of sight, out of mind.

Bob Dodge was placed there to recover from his knee surgery. A month stay was way too long for what he needed and he was antsy to get out. Montez and Diego roomed next to each other down the hall and argued playfully over card games, sometimes demanding Tera referee their poker hands. She kept reminding them that yelling at each other was not proper cardiac rehabilitation. And so it went, day after day. When she wasn't visiting or answering phones, there were pages of insurance documents to fill out, data entry of daily records, and other computer work to keep her busy. It was just that, busy work, mostly, but that was where the data was and that was what she was expected to track.

"Hey Storm!" It was Bob Dodge calling from his room.

"Yeah, Dodgeball?"

"See, I'm doing my knee exercises."

"Correctly? You gotta do them correctly or the hospital will happily charge you another 80K to fix your knee again." She came into his room and plopped down in the chair next to the bed. There was a dresser to the side, a bed, and table/tray, almost like a motel set-up with a nice spacious bathroom. A metal track adorned the ceiling from back when the spacious room was a two-sleeper.

"Do you have to wear that silly mask?" Bob asked, as he eased back in bed. "And when can I walk on my own? Any cases of this bug at the hospital?"

"Not that I know, but I'm not first on the e-mail list, you know."

"How long am I supposed to stay here? When I came here, the doctor kept hedging on the date. Now he doesn't come at all. I want out! And did you hear bars and restaurants are closed?"

She didn't tell Bob his doctor had made his case open-ended, with no date for escape.

"You'd look funny in a bar with a walker," she told him. "Yeah, they closed on Monday and business tanked the next day. The hell of it is that no one knows how this thing is passed, so the health department is stomping on everyone and everything."

"Hey, the governor is on TV at two o'clock again. Want to watch?"

"No way, I have to look like I've been busy." They laughed as she got up and went to the door, carefully looking both ways to make sure all was clear and the mask police wouldn't see her. Bob had some good questions. Exactly what *was* going on with the virus at Holcome? Glancing down at her computer, she saw two messages, one from

Springwood's director and the other from Mrs. Harris of the Elite Corps.

Jan Michelob had been in charge of the Springwood for a year now, not exactly keeping it well-staffed, but then the patients were not in desperate need of care. The news of the moment indicated that only one nurse would be present for the whole building for each shift. Others were being moved to the hospital directly. Nursing assistants would take up the slack. Mrs. Harris's missive reminded the Corps there were layoffs coming for hospital staff. No one from the Corps would be laid off, no one from the Corps could take time off. There could be two or even three assignments for each member, but under no circumstances were they to perform nursing duties. None of them was certified in that field. Tera left her station and went upstairs. No sign of the head nurse and Jan was gone already, no surprise. Tera quickly sat down, flipped a flash drive out of her pocket and proceeded to download files to add to her collection. In an hour, she'd be done and gone for the day, with no trace of her little side trip.

***

The trip on the shuttle bus was like being in a football game, the bus going in and out of traffic like a receiver sidestepping tacklers while zoning in on the goal line. She was barely out of the bus when it pulled away. The last time in the parking ramp, Tera thought as she came up to her car. As she turned the key in the lock, she saw something shiny on the ground by her front tire. Was someone messing around with it? She bent to pick it up.

And suddenly a hand was on her side, traveling up and down in a gross way and then through her hair. It made her skin crawl. She sniffed, cheap after shave. Dave and his faithful sidekick, Kenny. She'd vowed after the rape that no man would ever touch her like that again. She exploded up and back. There was a yelp and scraping feet.

There they were, Dave holding on to the car next to hers like he'd been socked and Kenny dumbfounded. Grabbing her phone from her pocket, she called, "Smile boys, let's get a nice picture for the police report!" The flash caught them by surprise. Just enough time for her to get into the car and start the engine. They looked like they were going to block her in. Dave was actually making a move toward the door.

She slammed the car into gear, starting forward, and not slowly. Dave jumped on the hood of the next car. Kenny ran a few cars down.

Roger saw the flash, he wasn't parked all that far away, he never parked that far since he'd noticed Dave and Kenny sort of stalking Tera around campus. He strolled over.

"She means it boys. I wouldn't mess with her."

"What are you doing here," Dave said sliding off the car. "You got some interest in this? She want some chocolate in her life?"

"Listen, white boy, she's former military. You're lucky she didn't hand you your balls on a platter."

It was a good lie, Roger thought, listening to the Mustang's engine in the distance. A female commando might scare them. It also might scare them to know their little games had not gone unseen. And now he was sure, Teresa Storm had not been at Holcome three years, maybe not even two. Otherwise she'd have known no one messed with David Hawthorne, son of the hospital administrator, the member of the Elite who got away with sexual assault as easily as some people crossed the street; the one whose father could make any and all police or employment complaints melt away.

CHAPTER 17

"Do you get to wear one of those space suits?" Nick asked Dr. Place, who was wearing a facemask that matched his gray gabardine suit. He was also wearing gloves, but since he was sitting at a table and it was a video meeting, they seemed unnecessary.

"When I come into a room, as for dialysis or after surgery, I would be required to wear the protective gown and hood and face shield," Dorian answered. "But this is a video meeting, so I think I'm safe without it. We aren't sitting next to each other." He smiled a little, his own kids asked the same question.

They were on a call on the private Holcome International video system. It gave the sense they all were seated around a conference room table, Mark, Callista, Nick, Dr. Place and then the door was flung wide as Dr. Loomis walked in like Caesar before his subjects. Callista felt they should stand and say "Good morning, Dr. Loomis" like a bunch of school kids from *Little House on the Prairie*. Over my dead body, she thought.

"Mr. and Mrs. Hampton," he nodded. Nick was not mentioned nor was Dr. Place. No "Thank you for attending the meeting" left his lips. "As we resume hemodialysis for Nick here at Holcome, there are a few things you need to know. While Nick is scheduled for dialysis on Monday and Thursday, Ridley did such a poor job with his care and cleaning his kidneys, we have to have you here three times at the start, Wednesday the 8th, Friday the 10th, and Monday the 13th to begin his regular run. Your scheduled time is 8:30am. Call ahead if you're going to miss it, but we're pretty full, so that had better be a rarity."

"No labs scheduled?" Mark asked. "How do you know if he was cleaned out if you don't do prior labs? You haven't done those yet. How do you know the settings for dialysis without prior labs?"

Loomis turned his head and glared at Mark, but before he could retort, Mark added, "Defined nephrology values are lower than levels acceptable for his cardiac levels. Potassium needs to be at 4. Nephrology is okay at 3. You have to be careful. You know that, don't you? You have to watch out for that each time. How can you do that without labs being a standing order?"

"I'll put that in there," Dr. Place said hurriedly. "Actually, I'm assigned as his doctor and that's my job."

"Then why aren't you conducting this meeting?" Mark asked, looking from one to the other.

"Because as head of Pediatric Services, I am in charge of Nick's care. I am in charge of the transplant Nick needs, you go through me," Loomis snapped. Damn him, he's too quick-witted. He took in the not-too-casual polo shirt and slacks, the subtle look of a professional. Something in computers, he remembered. "He does what I say. He tells you what I tell him to say. Right now this is just introductory. Nick qualifies for consideration for transplant because we're looking at a diagnosis of End Stage Renal Disease, but we believe his kidneys could get back their function, even with CKD. Do you know what that is?" Out of the corner of his eye he saw Dr. Place shift in his seat.

Callista was confused, "I thought he was suffering more from AKI, you know, Acute Kidney Injury, not Chronic Kidney Disease or End Stage Renal Disease." She had a hard time even saying those words. "I mean I was confused when I got that call from your assistant that his numbers qualified for ESRD. At Stanford they said...."

"Stanford didn't know what they were talking about," Loomis interrupted. Damn! Hadn't anticipated they would know one alphabet letter from another. Gotta bullshit this.

"Nick is not a textbook case. It could go either way with him. Even though he hasn't had dialysis except for every couple of weeks, we want to do it more often, twice a week, to give his kidneys a break and hopefully kick-start them," Loomis said.

"Do you have any questions?" Dr. Place added. He had no idea what it was Loomis was talking about, it was all nonsense, but the guy was in charge – of them and him.

"Yes," Callista said. "Nick gets migraines if he has less than ten-twelve hours of sleep. I would have to be on the road at six-thirty in the morning to get here by eight-thirty. It can't be done without him getting sick."

"Makes sense," Dr. Place replied. "I'll see if I can get that changed, but it may not be until the 20th. Anything else?"

Mark and Callista looked at each other. It was so overwhelming and Loomis made it downright depressing; his actually saying the words *End Stage Renal Disease* made it scarier than hell.

❋❋❋

What do you want?

The text came out of nowhere. Not even how are you, Tera snorted. Totally rude. She responded:

R U O K?

He was *so* annoying sometimes, and dense. Why else would I be calling except to check on him? It took a whole minute for his response. *Will call if time.*

She sighed, half angry, half relieved that she'd finally gotten through. The news around the world was so grim, so much death. Not that it was going to escape her. There had been construction workers for two solid weeks in her location. Suddenly the pleasant private rooms in Springwood became double rooms, with mere curtains between the residents. Staff had to be gloved and masked and wear a gown of sorts, not the contamination suit, though. The first half of each floor was designated for the short-term care patients, and the other half of each floor was dedicated to those coming from the hospital for care after a case of coronavirus. Those attending these new residents wore full sterile gowns, hoods and face shields. When the new residents arrived, they were on gurneys, some with portable oxygen apparatus. Some looked very ill, still coughing. Contagious?

The first hearse showed up on Monday. Doors were closed as the body was rolled out. It was one of the new ones. Was it an omen of coming days?

❋❋❋

"Indiana Jones" was racing through her head. What? Groggily, Tera realized it was the ringtone on her phone. Three in the morning! Who the hell,...but she knew, that distinctive ring belonged to only one person and with a six-hour time difference, why not three in the morning?

"Yeah."

"Can't talk long. What do you want?"

"To know if you're still alive. Can't get back?"

"I'm stuck here. Europe is locked down, no planes. I wish there was more information out there, we're making it up as we go along."

"Craig, you're not involved in this, are you?"

"You recall I have my license to practice medicine here in Britain. I wouldn't be a decent human being if I neglected to pitch in."

"But you have a job *here*! You live *here*! *We* live here! It's damned dangerous over there now!"

"And I cannot get out of here now. Tera, calm yourself. Most of the time they have me crunching numbers, projecting the path of this insane situation."

"And the rest of the time?" she held her breath, wanted to cover her ears, didn't want to know exactly how involved he was. She knew Craig Storm-Livesey only too well.

"Some hospital work." He hesitated, then the façade cracked slightly. "It's bad. It's so bad. Those news photos cannot begin to capture the agony of it all." He tried to change the subject, "How's your family? How's Nick? Everyone staying clear of this thing?"

"Everyone's healthy, so far. As for Nick, he's back at Holcome, with hemodialysis twice a week to *rest* his kidneys. Doesn't make sense."

He didn't answer, there were voices in the background. Then, "You need to be more targeted in your information search. I've looked over the data, nothing significant yet. Keep at it." It wasn't a request, it was a command. A loud voice in the background. "I'm needed. Good-bye." And he was gone.

Tera looked at the phone. You bastard, I hate you so much, running off to Europe like a VIP and now up to your hips in coronavirus. I hate you.

CHAPTER 18

Ellie's fingers flew over the keyboard, no dainty hand was hers. A couple more paragraphs and it would be done, an op-ed piece on the idiocy of government in an emergency, the power grab of the governor included. She hesitated, a scratching noise by the door catching her ear. Pulling her robe close around her she went to the door and opened it.

Tera practically fell into the entryway, her arms weighted down with plastic Wal-Mart bags. "Geez, Mom, you trying to kill me?" She dropped the bags and slid out of her leather jacket. No matter if the calendar said it was April and Easter was tomorrow, it was cold outside.

As she turned, she blinked. "What are you wearing? It's eleven in the morning!"

"I work at home, I can wear what I want," Ellie replied, peering into the bags. Paul, his hair awry, came down the steps in his plaid sleep pants and an unzipped sweatshirt.

"Did I interrupt something?"

Her parents looked at her, aghast at her words.

"You know Callie is coming over in a few minutes, probably bringing the kids. Are you ready?"

"Doesn't anyone call ahead of time," Paul grumbled as he turned around to go back upstairs.

"She texted!"

"I don't text!"

Ellie laughed at the comment. Too true. "What's in the bags?"

"Callie needed some stuff, you remember that?" Tera said carrying over bags with bread, rice, and other staples toward the kitchen. "This chicken needs to be refrigerated."

"I'm not two. There's my pile over there. You know where the fridge is. I'm going to get my make-up on. And some clothes too, I suppose."

Callista had texted a few days earlier begging them to look for items she could not get at her local stores. When news of the stay-at-home order came, people panicked and cleaned out the shelves. Most stores looked as if they'd been looted, shelves empty, open bottles with contents dripping to the floors, not a paper towel or pack of toilet paper to be found. Meat was scarce unless it was something odd like buffalo. Nick's diet was low potassium, low phosphorus, which meant only certain items met the standard: Minute Rice, an odd light Italian bread, fresh chicken only, no chicken nuggets, frozen chicken breasts, or popcorn chicken. And, of course, chicken was not to be found. But Tera scrounged some up, Ellie suspected from one of restaurants forced to close by the governor. The small towns, like Orion, had ignored the shut-down order as long as they could, but in the end, they were forced to comply. Many restaurants around the capital city had been caught by the closure with refrigerated food that had to be used or thrown away. They bagged stuff up and opened their doors and people forced out of work by the stay-home-order lined up for miles for these needed items.

Coming down the steps a few minutes later, Ellie got a good look at her middle child who was looking out the bay window toward the open areas around the cul-de-sac. We let our kids choose their own paths, she thought, even Rusty taking off to South Carolina. They say when they move out you don't have to worry about them, but I worry more, especially about Tera. Stanford, even Harvard, begged her to finish her advanced degree work with them. She could be teaching absolutely anywhere in the country. But no, Ellie thought, she went to London, she's teaching in London. And this World Health Organization stuff, off to the farthest corners of Africa. She's a mathematician, why is she chasing epidemics?

Oh, hell, Ellie thought with a burst of anger, I know where it came from, Craig must get his thrills doctoring in danger and he's been dragging her along. Was he forcing her to go with him? Paul let him have it on that before they were married. Sweet, quiet Paul got into it with the guy, demanding to know what hold Craig had over her.

"*Me?*" Craig had shot back. "I don't control her. No one controls her, you of all people should know that. She guilted me into working with WHO, she said I was a waste of a human being if I didn't get out of the classroom and *do* something to help people. Then, she got this crazy idea to do her dissertation on statistical prediction and disease outcomes. Paul, I love her, I won't let anything happen to her."

Ellie sighed. Even now, when Tera was officially back home the last three years, she really wasn't, she was gone at least six months each year. It's so hard to build a sense of family with the family missing in action.

"You're looking like you lost weight," she said. "Pregnant?"

Tera whirled. "Mo*ther*! Are you accusing me of whoring around? Thanks a lot!"

"Not necessarily. It hasn't even been four months since Christmas when he left...."

"Don't even go there!"

"Well, I meant to say my sister Maggie didn't know she was expecting until Miranda was a month from birth. It happens. You look too thin, like you've been sick. Are you eating?"

"A lot of extra time at work. Not hungry and I'm not making a four-course meal for just me. And now that the bars are closed, I can't go pick up guys anymore." Tera grabbed a small briefcase with papers in it. After checking them, she handed them to her mother. "Here's your stuff."

Thanks to the electronic age, Tera still oversaw her primary job in analytics at a major insurance company. Ellie had stepped in to cover the actual in-person aspect of the job when Tera began working in Transitional Care at Holcome. The second job was a special assignment from the insurance company's review department.

Ellie didn't bother looking at the briefcase, she'd heard the loud slam of a car door. "Brace yourself."

And the whirlwind appeared through the door, Sienna, Max, and Nick yelling, "Aunt Tera! Grandma!" They nearly took Tera down as they hugged her. Callista came in behind, red-cheeked and wearing a heavy Carhartt jacket. "It's cold out there. What the heck's going on?"

Ellie laughed at her, "What's a little spring snow shower? C'mon, sit down while I get cocoa and some goodies."

"You know we're breaking the law," Paul said, making his appearance in jeans and a Coors Light shirt. "$1000 penalty for being out and about now that King Wald extended the shut down. Mark my words, two weeks to a month to two months and not a second shorter. And we're all going to hell for not wearing a mask at the store." He picked up his cup from the microwave.

"I've got an 'essential' letter," Tera said. "I'll make copies for you all."

"What makes you so special to get a letter," Callista asked. More one-upmanship from her little sister? "Mmmm, this is good, even without liquor."

"You're driving," Ellie said, "but I'm not. Mmm, good. So what's going on out there?"

"It's crazy, it's like doomsday," Callista said. "You go into a store and what's on the shelves is nothing you'd want. Target has arrows on the floor for traffic flow, up one, down another. If you accidentally get into the wrong row you're given terrible dirty looks by other customers." She sighed. "This one old lady was standing in a row, looking at different kinds of noodles. Her cart was going the wrong way, and this jerk came up to her and started yelling, 'Don't you know which way to go? If you can't read, get out of here.' Target is the first to have curbside pick-up for shopping, but it takes hours to get your order."

"And here it is Easter and the churches are closed. I can't believe the bishop allowed this, any religious leader allowed this," Tera said. "I mean when we were little, we'd be getting things together for the Food Blessing later in the afternoon."

"For your information, we still do that, at least last year," Callista sniped. "Or haven't you seen a church lately?"

"What I do is none of your business," Tera retorted, with an edge of anger. I wasn't around for Easter a year ago or the year before that, she thought. It was the middle of spring term at Imperial College, four thousand miles away.

"Uh, uh, uh, ladies," Paul said. "No personal attacks." He reached over toward the counter and picked up a purple gadget, the size of pack of cigarettes. He flicked a switch.

Everyone yelped as his gadget emitted a loud sound like an electrical charge exploding out of a transformer.

"What's that, Grandpa? Can I see?"

"Do it again!" He did. "Yes!"

"His new toy, a taser of some sort."

"How'd you get that? This isn't something you get at Ace Hardware."

"Rusty got it and sent it, I don't know, it may be illegal to ship out of state. I don't care," Paul said. "I think as these shortages happen, it's going to get ugly out there. A guy got jumped and beaten at a gas station the other day."

"You wouldn't dare use that thing," Tera said. Her father hardly ever raised his voice, Mom was the one to crack the whip on the kids.

"Don't be so sure. I take it when I go out at night."

"Even to take the garbage out," Ellie laughed.

"You laugh," Paul said. "I thought I'd need it at Walgreen's last night. There was a bunch of teenage girls about Max's age. They were standing on the street corner screeching amongst themselves in the most terrible language. Then, they were yelling at the cars going by."

"Nothing to do with themselves now that school doesn't exist," Ellie said. "They're like feral cats, roaming around."

"Then they came into the store and roamed the aisles yelling and picking stuff up and tossing it around. There was a female manager on duty and they just ragged on her when she told them to get out. I was ready in case they came after me."

Callista and Tera looked at each other. What on earth was happening in the world?

"So how was the dialysis meeting?" Ellie asked.

Callista shifted in her seat. She felt her eyes tearing up. "Pretty daunting. I mean the last thing a parent wants to hear is your kid is being diagnosed with End Stage Renal Disease...end stage. He's only ten!" Nick was absorbed on his Game Boy and gave no indication of hearing his mom's words.

"Ten!" Tera jumped up. "Nicky, come with me, I have your birthday present!" She ran to the bags by the entry and began searching through them like dog sniffing for a bone. Nick was at her side in an instant. "Will I like it?"

"Of course you will." She pulled up a package and watched as he tore into it. "A Ferrari watch! Just what I wanted. Thank you." He hugged her tightly. "You're the best." He ran off to the living room area where Sienna and Max were playing with the TV, trying to get into Netflix.

"You were saying...," Ellie prompted Callista when Tera sat down again.

"Well, the nephrologist said Ridley didn't do a good job and they are going to need to clean Nick out so he has to have dialysis three times in the next week at 8:30 in the morning. In the morning! That's a two-hour drive! How can I do that? Then Mark reminds him no labs are scheduled, how can he do dialysis without lab values. If looks could kill, I'd be a widow." She shook her head, brown hair falling to each side of her face. "Anyway, he said even if Nick is diagnosed as ESRD, they think his kidneys can still recover, so they want to do dialysis twice a week from now on. It will give his kidneys a rest and help them recover."

"Recover?" Tera asked, settling down in her seat. She'd snuck a bit of rum into her cocoa. "He has dialysis only every two weeks. Why does he suddenly need it twice a week? This was decided without diagnostic labs? They want to force the issue to give them a rest? That makes no sense. Was he just shooting off his mouth? Like the governor saying 72,000 of us will die from coronavirus in the state by August. Statistically impossible, they'd have to be dropping dead in the streets and they aren't." She paused a second. "What are the numbers? Do people recover from ESRD? How many has he worked with who have recovered? In fact, why is Nick on hemodialysis when peritoneal dialysis is preferred to give kids a better quality of life?"

"What do you know about statistics and percentages, you're the one who flunked math at Aquinas," Callista said unkindly.

Tera snorted. "Did you ever see that tutor? He was *hot*! There was a race to see who could flunk the fastest to get an appointment with him. He was a senior exchange student. I won," she laughed a bit, "the grand prize."

"You wasted how much money on tuition?" Callista asked her mom.

Paul cleared his throat. "Not that it's your business, but Tera had a free ride." No need to add that it had been either Aquinas Academy or juvenile detention. Getting expelled from public school in the first month of freshman year was a stunning accomplishment of the worst sort.

"Including room and board? That's crazy, and even then you still darn near flunked everything that quarter," Callista hammered on. "You worried mom and dad to no end."

"I still graduated at the top of the class, or don't you remember I was valedictorian?" Tera snapped angrily.

"Stop it!" Ellie ordered. "Quit your bitching or both of you get out, do you hear me!" Some things never change, she thought angrily.

It was quiet, except Nick whispered loudly, "Did you hear that? Grandma said a bad word."

"You've heard it before," Sienna said, not so quietly. "Big deal."

"You've *said* it before," Max added, then realized the adults were looking in their direction. "I think."

With a sigh, Callista said, "Sorry." She didn't sound like she meant it. In fact, she was looking down, studying the wood table carefully.

"Me too," Tera said, not meaning it at all. "But back to kidneys, didn't you say Ridley wanted scheduled dialysis and that young doctor said you never do scheduled dialysis for kids?"

Callista blinked. Tera was right. There was so much going on, she forgot. What *was* going on, what was right?

"Snow! It's snowing!" The kids were screeching and dancing in the living room, TV forgotten. And it was, large flakes not gently falling, but dropping heavily from the sky.

"Merry Christmas, Mom and Dad," both sisters said together, then laughed. "Jinx!"

"Kids," Callista yelled. "Get your stuff, we're out of here! Thanks, you guys, for the rice and chicken and stuff. I hope these shortages don't last long. And I hope this snow doesn't last, I need spring!"

As they left the house, Sienna pushed Max and he rolled down the slight embankment. Nick hastily rolled a snowball and threw it at her, but Max was running rapidly toward his sister, tackled her and rubbed her face in the whitened grass. Tera hopped past them, then turned and scooped a pile of snow on them all. She ran toward her car and when they realized she was going to escape, they started pelting her with snowballs.

"Kids!" Callista yelled. "Come on! We still have to get to Wal-Mart and I hate driving in snow!"

And then they were all gone.

"It's your fault," Ellie said, turning to Paul. "You couldn't wait, you had to put the snow shovels away early and now this."

CHAPTER 19

Dr. Dorian Place carded himself into Holcome's dialysis center. A dad and yawning child were just leaving after their early morning session and two teens were in Bays 3 and 4. He looked over his shoulder carefully before stepping into the first short hallway, then knocked at the sliding door of Bay 6.

Nick was receiving treatment, machinery humming as his blood was filtered under a nurse's watchful eye; as always he wore jeans and a car shirt, today a Formula One racer kicking up dust across the front of his black shirt. No doubt, he'd be able to recite all the engine specs on it, Dorian thought. Callista was clicking away on her laptop in the corner. She looked up.

"Oh, hi. I've got to thank you for changing the dialysis time to ten. It's a big help, believe me, because I can make sure the other kids are up and online for their classes before we leave." She still thought he looked too young to be a doctor. She noticed his dark hair was sticking out in a few places, barbers were a big casualty of the governor's state shut down because almost everyone was affected by *that* closure, well, except for Loomis, she thought.

"I'll try to get you into an afternoon session as soon as I can," Dorian said. Then he caught himself looking over his shoulder again. "I'm...uh...here today because I thought you might have some questions about transplant and how it works. We didn't go into it at the meeting with Dr. Loomis."

"Where is he?" Callista asked, relieved to have one-on-one with the younger doctor, who was far more user-friendly than his egotistical boss.

"Attending a conference at the University." He turned to Nick. "You don't say much, Nick, but I'll bet you have a lot of questions about what this transplant stuff is about."

Nick squirmed a bit. "Yeah, I don't think I like the idea of getting sliced open like a cantaloupe, you know what I mean? Pretty soon I won't have any nice skin, it will all be a bunch of scars."

"Good point," Dorian agreed. "So you'd rather keep coming here for dialysis instead, for a few years? It's got to be one or the other, Nick. With a transplant you can get back to school and some sports and your pals. Without it you're going to be stuck with some form of medical treatment and dialysis several times a week."

Shaking his head, Nick mumbled, "Yeah, I know. What do we have to do?"

Dorian eased down on the bed. "Some extra tests, not a big deal. The tests will show what it will take to get a kidney match for you. You don't just get one because your mom or dad or grandma offers one of theirs. It has to be a perfect fit for *your* body. A perfect fit is like this," he held both hands toward each other, fingers apart, then moved them into place so they fit together. "It's not just to match your blood type, but there are other factors in your body, stuff we doctors call markers that we have to look at to match. It depends on vaccinations you've had, on your antibodies from illness, on the blood transfusions you've had and the quality of the blood. There are six markers; most people don't have to match all six."

"How do you find someone to match?" Nick asked. "You don't put an ad in the paper or on TV, do you?"

Callista laughed. "That would be too easy, Nick. Once the medical center has the information, you're put on a list that's published around the country. All the information is there. If a kidney becomes available, and it matches you, that's how you get it. But maybe we could try Facebook, maybe at car shows we can pass out flyers that ask people to be donors. These things don't grow on trees, you know. Just pick one and stick it in. People have to be brave enough to want to give one of theirs to you. It's an operation in a hospital."

Picking one from a tree. Dorian sighed. If only it was that easy. If it was, there wouldn't be 90,000 people waiting for a kidney. "Let's say you pass out a flyer at a car show, and some guy named Jesse James wants to give you a kidney. He signs up at the hospital, they have a questionnaire about his health, does he smoke, do drugs, eat healthy. If he passes that, he will get a bunch of tests. If everything matches up, there would be surgery to remove his kidney and surgery for you to receive it. If he doesn't live close by, the kidney could be flown to you for surgery." Dorian was enjoying the extended interaction, this was what he went into medicine for, he thought, the patients, helping them. Here at Holcome there's precious little time to see faces instead of words on a sheet of paper. "Guess where we put the new kidney."

Nick wrinkled up his face. "My butt? I don't even know where these things are, and where would you put the extra one so it won't stick out?"

Callista and Dorian laughed. Dorian reached over and traced a line on Nick's stomach, a vertical line parallel to his navel. "Right there, right up front. We connect the blood vessels and you're off and running."

"Uh, is that the only way you can get a kidney, from someone else?" Nick asked, overwhelmed. "I don't know anybody who would want to get slashed up to do a good deed. I would, like, be waiting forever for that to happen, you know?" His lip quivered a little.

Callista intervened. The next part was a little hard to explain. "That's the way it's done with a live person, Nick. Like dad or me. But some people are in accidents and are dying. Their family is asked if their organs can be donated. Like Alyssa got that heart transplant while you were here a few years ago. Remember that? A guy got hurt in a motorcycle accident and his family donated his heart to her and saved her life. I'm sure someone else got the kidneys and the liver."

Nodding, Nick said, "I remember that. You ever see that, Dr. Place? You do kidneys, but this was a heart!" He sighed. "I was more interested in that heart-lung machine she was on, that was so cool."

"We get to observe all kinds of surgeries and treatments, Nick. I *have* seen that, pretty dramatic stuff." He eased back, more relaxed. Loomis wouldn't be caught dead meeting with a patient and explaining things like this, but Dorian felt the connection was vital. It eased patients' minds if they knew what to expect. It built trust. He'd just read a book, *The Physician's Healing Touch,* by some British doctor from Imperial College, Craig something or other. It urged doctors to stop being distant and to be as human as their patients; he contended sometimes just holding a hand was as important as a surgery.

"Any more questions?"

"How about after? How long do I stay in the hospital? When can I go to school?"

"Each week will be better. You'll have some meds to take so your body doesn't see the new kidney as an invader, like on your Nintendo game, and you'll have to have tests and drink a lot to keep your plumbing working, but I think you'll make it, you'll be in school before Christmas if the surgery is done this summer."

"Yes!" Nick smiled, as he lay back against the pillows.

Dorian got up to leave and nodded at Callista. He looked at his watch, Loomis really wasn't at a conference, he was in some meeting or other and could pop up at any time and ream him to hell for making nice with a family. It made no sense, but Loomis was the boss – his way or no way.

CHAPTER 20

Elsewhere at that moment, Dr. Loomis was standing in his office hallway facing the main door and the administrative desk. Maya was at the keyboard, totally unaware of her surroundings. She wasn't the fastest at her job, but decent. She tried hard to please.

"Oh, hello, Doctor, I'm sorry I didn't see you there. Is there anything I can do to assist you?" She stood respectfully. A rather shapeless, immature figure, pleasant face with a pixie haircut for her black hair. Just too nice, almost groveling.

The idea came to him in an instant. "I have some spreadsheets for you. Please put them in order. I'll email them." He disappeared down the hall. She's so dense, she'll never figure out what they are, he thought, and I hate number crunching. He flung his suit jacket over his office chair and sat at his computer, quickly locating his "Anytime" file and sent the spreadsheets: accounts and dates, amounts paid for services rendered. As he clicked send, a hand touched his shoulder. He whirled.

"Jesus! What the shit are you doing here?" he hissed at Neil Hawthorne. "Can't you come in the main door? How long have you been standing there?" He got up a tad too swiftly.

"Easy, easy. I figured we needed to have a talk and didn't want what's-her-name to see me. Just came from the budget meeting." Hawthorne shook his head. "If this damn order for no elective surgeries continues much longer, we're on track to lose at least four billion dollars by the end of the year."

"What the hell? Are you sure?" Loomis sat back. He motioned to Neil to get him a drink.

"Where do you think we get our money? Donations? The ER? It's from elective surgeries and fat insurance checks. And, of course I'm sure that's the number they are going to publicize. T. Rex is going to call a press conference later today. I don't know how close to reality it is, but I do know that 25% of the staff has been laid off, including nursing staff. Your gal out there," he motioned toward the outside office, "is likely to be gone and Dr. Kadajh can go back to India, for all I care. The doctors who work with you will take a hit in their own departments." He took a long drink of the Barr Hill. For sure, one wasn't going to be enough to allay his fears. "We're at only 35% capacity. There's talk of senior staff taking a 10% pay cut."

Loomis's eyebrows went up. "Is T. Rex going to announce that too?" Rexalt had quickly learned how to work the system, cozying up to the press every chance he could, especially if it made Holcome look good at the expense of the state. And the loss of such a huge amount of money to a major medical institution was sure to make people take notice.

"Anton called from Houston. Wants to know if you've made any progress."

That's what happens when you're the new guy on the block, Loomis thought, always being checked on. "Some."

"Look, some isn't good enough. What's the status? Are there any others in line for the same treatment?"

"How many pediatric kidney failure cases do you think are out there? I mean I know Covid affects kidneys but you can't count on a particular number. And if it affects kids, who knows how they will recover from it. Besides, Dorian Place is too good at his job. It was a mistake to hire him. He has people off hemodialysis within two weeks of their crisis and onto peritoneal dialysis at home. He's useless."

"So what's the story about the Hampton kid, the one who came from California?"

Loomis spoke through clenched teeth. "I've got them believing hemodialysis is the way to go. But I can't stand them second guessing me all the time." He downed his drink and got up to get another. "Telling *me* what to do. I can't stand them!"

"So split them up. Make a Covid policy for only one parent."

"This is pediatric, you know that won't work."

"This is dialysis, make it work. You have to keep him at all costs, and keep him on hemo. If this expansion into pediatric neph works, it has the potential to bring in a good chunk of change. We already have transitional rehab, people who might need extra therapy are sent to one of our places and there they stay." He laughed. "It's working well. It should for you. $100,000 a month on the line for hemo."

"That's $900,000 this year alone! How does that help *us* though?"

Hawthorne stroked his closely trimmed beard and eyed Loomis. "Keeps us employed, for one thing. And maybe, just maybe, you understand, there would be a little bonus down the line." Hawthorne laughed slightly. It was nice to have a financial wizard like Anton Gregory around to devise a scheme like this and its potential payback. "Depends on you making this work, pal." He raised his glass in salute and then drank deeply.

An hour later, Loomis had a pretty good buzz going as he shifted the papers around on his desk. He opened his email and saw the spreadsheets were back. They looked all right to him, that's why he ordered people to do these menial things for him. If he lost Maya, he'd have to demand some assistance. If staff was laid off, for sure that would be a problem. Or not, he oversaw several departments.

How to make this Hampton thing work. First, increase dialysis another day. That would keep them on the run and their minds occupied. He glanced at the record. The kid could stand it. They wouldn't know if he needed it or not. End Stage Renal Disease automatically meant dialysis three times a week to insurance carriers. But the parents – good idea, limit one of them, that way they couldn't bounce ideas off each other. He made a note to call the nurse manager, Dominic Dorrance, to place notices of the new Covid policy around the dialysis center. Nicky boy, you're going to be here for a long while.

CHAPTER 21

He looked at himself in the mirror. Charles Loomis, Head of Pediatric Services. The new light gray wool suit fit quite well and was comfortable for an early-May appointment. White shirt and red tie, a power combination every time, especially for meeting with parents in a panic over their child's health. He loved bestowing the words they'd been waiting for and hearing their heartfelt thank you. He held a power next to God's.

He checked over his e-mail. Ah, the results of the tests for Hampton's transplant. Fast work. The tests were just taken at Monday's dialysis run, the parents didn't even know about it.

HIGH RISK TRANSPLANT
Preliminary testing reveals high antibody load (nearly 100% PRA); Match for all six markers required; 92% graft survival rate at 1 year with complications, expected 5+ year wait.

There was a half page of more information, each line worse than the last. Good God, this can't be happening! Getting an organ to transplant with these parameters, and then into a kid with his heart and lung problems, it can't be done, he thought. No way in hell could it be done. Anywhere. Loomis paced the room. What am I going to say? What can I do? This is going to go out across the country when he's listed and we have so much more to look out for than just a transplant from mom or dad. His hand was poised over the bar, then he looked at his watch. An hour should be okay before the call, he thought as he picked up a glass. I need this *now*. Jesus, no way can I let them know this, he thought. I have to stall. If they find out that biopsy in January showed End Stage probability and the kid wasn't listed for transplant, they'll go all the way to Rex, to the Medical Board on this. Why aren't they stupid like everyone else I have to deal with?

***

Eleven in the morning on the dot. The video conference was different from the last one, a month ago, but they were stuck with it because in-person meetings were still banned. They could see each other, talk to each other, but only as talking heads. Nick sat between Mark and Callista. He was more interested in the stuff on the wall behind Dr. Loomis than what they were saying. He couldn't stand the guy's whiny voice.

"We're going back to doing some elective surgeries," Loomis announced, taking command. He wasn't sure about surgeries resuming yet, it was just a rumor but what would these people know about it. "We can plan for Nick's transplant; barring hiccups with further evaluation, the transplant will be done by the end of summer. But first, there are some gaps in Nick's vaccination records. He has to have those before we can go further. I've posted a list of what's needed. Have your own doctor take care of it. Meanwhile, several specialty appointments are needed, get them set up as soon as you can, things will go faster if you do. The transplant committee will decide by June 5 how to proceed. We don't want any delays."

"When can we be tested as possible donors?" Mark asked. "Let's get that done."

"Depends on insurance," Loomis said. It was a safe answer, everything nowadays depended on insurance. They didn't need to know the real answer was never.

"So, surgery this summer. You'll spend a month here at Holcome or its environs post-op, longer if needed. We will keep his blood pressure at a higher threshold after transplant to prevent clotting and create better perfusion. Around 150-160 systolic."

"Wait a minute," Callista interrupted. "You can't do that. That's how he became ill last winter. He gets headaches and then throws up constantly. You're not doing that to him again."

"Not to mention PRES," Mark added. "We're not going that route again."

Loomis sucked in his breath. "PRES doesn't happen twice," he said with a sudden edge to his voice. "I know what I'm doing. Higher blood pressure is better at first. You better get used to that idea. In fact, it might be a lifetime thing."

Mark and Callista stared at him. "You have to control blood pressure so it doesn't affect his heart," Mark argued. "And what about potassium levels?"

"That may not improve after transplant." Loomis was getting tired of the interruptions. "You have to realize life after transplant is going to be different. Two or three meds to suppress his immune system, plus blood pressure medications, anti-virals and anti-bacterial infusions. You have to prevent any and all infections for a year or longer. You have to be within an hour of a major hospital at all times." At this point, he wanted to paint the worst picture possible. "That's even after a year or maybe for years, in case something goes wrong. And high potassium levels and low magnesium are a direct result of anti-rejection drugs. It happens. You have to watch for this at all times. There will be blood work, scans, biopsies. Rejection is a major and ongoing danger."

"I don't understand this," Mark said pointedly. "Nothing I've read has been this onerous."

"Then you've been reading the wrong things!" Loomis couldn't hide his anger.

Timidly, Callista asked, "About the restriction in dialysis to one parent...."

"Nothing you can do about it."

"But he's a high risk patient! We work better together. What does the CDC say or the State Health Department?"

"Ask *them*. We have our rules, you follow them. Period."

Mark and Callista sat back. It was a lot to take in. As Callista told Ellie later, "If what he said is true, I don't know how transplant is going to improve Nicky's life."

❉❉❉

I can't stand him, Loomis thought as he turned off his computer. He thinks he knows it all. Who is he to tell me what to do? He picked up his half-full vodka glass on the desk and threw it across the room. It bounced off the door, spilling over the carpet. I hate these people. Which one, which one has to go? He took a deep breath. Him. How? There was a buzz from his drawer, he jerked it open and grabbed the red phone.

They met at the helicopter pad off the sixth floor at the hospital end of the huge medical complex. Hawthorne had his suit coat over his shoulder and tie loosened. The spring breeze ruffled his brown hair. It was a good time of the year, he thought, gazing over the city and the green banishing the winter's gray. Except this year.

"Why are we meeting up here, so you can tan yourself?" Loomis was striding across the landing area marked with brightly colored circles like Captain America's shield. By the way he was moving, he was highly agitated.

"How'd the meeting go?" Neil didn't want to give up the delightful peace and quiet but duty called.

"As bad as I could make it and they still argued. You'd think that bastard could scrub up and do surgery himself the way he talks back to me about his research into the kid's medical issues." Loomis gripped the railings around the rooftop.

"Must have a pretty important job somewhere. Your ordinary bricklayer doesn't come across that way," Hawthorne laughed.

"I have to get rid of him. I can handle her. She's sharp, but not as quick or incisive with her questions." Her accusations, on the other hand, were damned uncomfortable, but no need to admit that. "But Covid won't work. That guy would go to the governor himself if he had to and that obsequious dolt would cave in if it would make him look good in the press." Loomis slapped the handrail. "At least you don't have to worry about the hemo going on. I got the evaluation. That kid is impossible to match. They ought to get a cemetery plot now."

A sharp intake of breath made Loomis look over at Hawthorne. So what, it was the truth.

"You didn't *say* that, did you?"

"You think I'm stupid? I told them end of summer."

"That *was* stupid," Hawthorne said angrily. "And how are you planning to get out of that when the end of summer comes and you've got nothing?"

"Don't get your water hot. I'll think of something. I've just got to get rid of *him* first."

Rubbing the side of his face with his hand, Hawthorne knew he had an answer. It was used before, a few places elsewhere, not so many that anyone would notice or connect them. Could Loomis put it together without his damned ego ruining it? Hawthorne sighed. He'd already committed this case to a million dollars in a year's time. That meant until next February. At all costs, they had to keep the kid. He leaned over the rail, hands clasped. "Okay, here's an idea."

***

How do I make this work? Hawthorne says it will, but he never gets his hands dirty, Loomis thought as he returned to his office from the heliport. The vodka glass was where it had landed, a wet stain still on the carpet. Faint odor too. Too bad. He sat at the desk There must be someone else with a different way to create the story, he thought. He punched some numbers to the Wisconsin affiliate office where he did consultations.

"Linda O'Brien."

"Linda...."

"Chuck! I'm honored to hear from you."

"Cut it out, you just saw me yesterday. I need a number for someone at Ridley, someone like you in dialysis."

"Sounds urgent. What's in it for me?"

"This isn't funny. I need someone who will do what I ask, when I ask. Has to do with a letter I need."

A pause. "Why not go to your friend Jolene? You have her on a short leash."

"How do you know that? It's none of your business. Now give me a name and number."

"Cynthia Langley. She's the dialysis nurse manager. You'll find her pliable." She laughed as she gave him the number and email and then hung up.

Loomis reached down to his drawer with the matching phones, bringing both up to his desk. After sending a text on the blue one – same message, "Anytime" – he quickly entered information into the red phone and settled down to have a long chat with Cynthia Langley.

CHAPTER 22

"Storm!"

It was Dodgeball, the voice more like a loud hiss, as though he didn't want to be heard.

Tera Storm was with Mr. Angelou, the poor fellow hardly awake anymore. He was slipping away, alone. She stroked the top of his hand, hoping the sensation would stimulate his mind, his memories of a life so long ago, that didn't have to end this way. Then she got up, sanitized and donned gloves to visit the next room.

"Take that stupid mask off."

"Bob, I can't. Rules. Things are getting more dicey around here." They both knew what that meant; Covid-19 was in the building, three women from upstairs, not transfers from the hospital, passed away and from the foreign sound of the two ventilators down the hallway, more were on the way out.

"You gotta get me out of here. Call that bastard doctor! I'm no dummy, I can see what's going on, and we're sitting ducks here!"

While she agreed, Tera had to play the part. "I understand. I haven't seen Dr. Holliday in awhile. I sent him your records to review, but that's it. He's got a few others here. Nothing." Both Mr. Angelou and Ronnie Duvall had Doc Holliday listed as admitting physician. Same problem.

"Get after him, Storm! You look feisty. Nail him. And what the hell happened to therapy?"

With the coming of the lockdown came sporadic services. Not that they weren't considered essential, but, in fact, the lockdown caused staff lay-offs everywhere. Therapists were sitting at home with no jobs because the business closed due to lack of income.

"How's the knee?" she asked, hoping to derail his anger.

"I think I can manage it at home. Please! Can I check myself out?"

"Against doctor's orders?"

"Hell, he isn't my doctor, is he, if he hasn't seen me in a month of Sundays?" He ran his hand through his graying brown hair. His triangular face looked more gaunt and his eyes bright from stress. "I don't want to die here. It's the middle of May, this should've been a two-week stay, not three months!"

He was right on that. And who would notice if Lila just came and got him? Who'd report it? Not me, Tera thought.

"I'll call, Bob. I'll be feisty for you." She winked and went back to her desk. There she doused her hands in sanitizer. Was that a cough down the hall? Brassy, odd. Not another one. Diego and Montez were rooming together now, it was from that direction. The card games had ceased awhile ago, as did most activity, replaced with increasing depression among the residents. She buzzed for the nurse to check on them.

"Why don't *you* do something, Storm," Carla snapped when she answered the call. "Go down and check on them. Take temperatures. Do something to help us."

"Carla, I'm under orders from my supervisor not to be involved in patient care. We aren't trained for that." Well, she actually was, but only Harris knew that.

"I don't *care*. You can flick a button on a handheld thermometer and report to me. We're swamped here." So Tera slipped into a gown, made sure all the straps were secure, and went down the hallway. She didn't need a thermometer to see Montez pink with fever and chest heaving as he tried to get air. Diego looked panicked. "He's got it, doesn't he! *Madre de Dios*, he's going to die and I am too."

"I'll get him moved out of here into isolation, okay? Just relax. You aren't right next to each other, you should be okay," she lied.

She went back down the hall, but paused by a doorway. Ronnie'd had knee surgery. He got an infection and to clean the festering mess the doctor removed the knee cap. For two months Ronnie lay in bed waiting for things to clear up, then he had surgery to replace the knee cap. He wasn't hard to take care of, dementia eliminated any demands he might have made. It was intended that therapy would return mobility. But there was no therapy.

"Who's that?" he called. "Did you feed the dog today, Martha?"

"Sure did. You be good now, and rest. Watch *Jeopardy*. You'll get smart." He fumbled with the controller. *The Edge of Tomorrow* was on the movie channel. He didn't notice.

After peeling off the gown and other paraphernalia in the change room and rubbing on more sanitizer, Tera went to the phone. First the nurse.

"Covid, I'm pretty sure, Savo Montez. You have to move him to isolation."

"You're sure? What's the temperature?"

"Didn't need it, the guy can't get a breath and he's burning up. He needs isolation. And his roommate, Diego, don't be putting anyone in there for two weeks, he's been exposed."

"Don't tell me what to do. We have to move people around, there are more coming in."

"You're breaking public health protocols, Carla. Do your job."

This afternoon is getting too long, Tera thought, after hanging up. Next call.

"Allie?" Allie Hathaway was the director of Ames Therapy, the outside company contracted to do physical therapy for transitional care.

"Tera! How are you? Staying healthy? Like anyone can these days with this virus lurking everywhere. Have you sanitized your plastic bag from Wal-Mart yet? Or your Amazon package?" She laughed at her comments about a CDC recommendation about how long the virus could last on plastic bags, delivery packages, kitchen counters, and everything else.

"I'm at Springwood here in Stanton, remember? No one has shown up here for any therapy sessions. I've got one guy who has been walking and exercising and may only need a review to get out. He wants out before he gets diseased. And I've got another fellow who's never going to walk again if someone doesn't get down here to work on his leg and restore mobility." Tera's anger was obvious. "You have a contract to fulfill."

"Back off, Teresa Storm, no one is going there. Half my people are laid off because we can't afford them and the governor said if you were afraid to go to work because you might get the virus, you don't have to go to work and no one can fire you or hire anyone to do your job. Get it? There's no one here to do the work. I can't help you or anyone else."

Should I go three for three, Tera wondered, as she slammed the phone down. Doc Holliday is next, the dumbass. Out of the corner of her eye she saw a white ghost moving down the hall.

"Tera?"

The voice was very familiar. "Tom? Tom Kressly? What are you doing here?" She never would have recognized him in the space suit. Then she saw the collar. The dark blue eyes were more mature, but there was still a lurking playfulness in them.

"*Father* Tom Kressly?" He really went through with it, she thought, remembering that night he told her it was over, all their plans for marriage thrown aside because he was entering the seminary.

"For real. What have you been up to? You know you're the only one in our entire class who just dropped out of sight after graduation, well except the ones in jail. How long? 12 years? I'm surprised I remembered your name."

"So when did this priest stuff happen?" she asked. He was still tall, husky, a voice in the deep that had made him a solo in the Academy choir.

"Ordained about five years ago. I've been associate in a couple of places, now in Stanton. What about you? Where have you been?"

"Around."

"Different last name on your badge but no rings. What's up?"

Tera looked at her bare hand. "I don't like to wear jewelry at work. The hand sanitizer can wreck a lot of stuff."

He was giving her an odd look. "And?"

"What," she answered with an edge. "I've been here and there. Spent time in Europe. I don't do any of the social media stuff, it's a bore. *You* didn't answer *me*, what are *you* doing here? No visitors."

He motioned toward his neck. "This gets me in. The bishop started a group of priests to anoint those with Covid, give Last Rites to those dying. It's been done in Europe and a few places here. It isn't right that these people have no spiritual sustenance in their last hours. We're notified of impending death and come. You *do* remember what Last Rites are, don't you?"

"Of course I do. Where did that come from?" She quickly changed the subject. "Aren't you afraid of this?"

"Aren't you? You work here every day. You see it all." Don't remind me, she thought. He had a point. She had a job to do, and he did too.

He went on, "I was at first, but at some point you have to let go and let God. These people need me."

Good old Tom, always for the greater good.

"I know you, Tera." There was a hint of the familiar laugh. "Is it still image is everything? I see some hard edges." In fact, he seemed like he was looking right through her. They had been a power couple in school, after the tutor incident. If anything needed a boost, any committee needed a hand, they were there, T and T. They were kidded about wedding bells, but altar bells won out.

"Look the other way, then." She felt herself tightening up. I don't want to talk to him, look at him. Go away.

He reached through his gown to his pocket. Sure, it was breaking protection, but some things were more important. He pulled out a card and placed it on her desk. "Let me know if you want to talk sometime." His pager went off. "I'll change outside, another call. Say a prayer." And he was gone.

Tera flicked the card into the wastebasket and sighed in relief. The end. She got on the phone with Doc Holliday's office. He was "not in the office" the answering service recited. "Leave a message and Dr. Holliday will get back to you."

Maybe he's got Covid, Tera thought. Or he's stuck on that cruise ship in the Pacific that no country will allow to dock at their port. No matter, the day was done. Time to go home to nothing. She glanced down at the card in the wastebasket, then stooped to pick it up, putting it in her purse, maybe for future reference.

CHAPTER 23

"Oh Nicky, is that a new watch?" Lindsey Dahlin, the assigned dialysis nurse, pulled Nick's wrist over for a closer look. "This is so sweet!" she said in her singsong voice as she rubbed his back. "Was it your birthday?" She bent over him, her fake blonde hair bouncing up and down.

Callista shook her head no, don't tell her. Nick pulled his hand back. They were in the dialysis bay, a six foot by ten foot cell. Lounge chair, bed, equipment, maybe three open feet against the glass wall and sliding door if you went around the bed. He climbed up on the bed and raised his shirt.

"Not talkative, honey? Are you feeling okay?" Lindsey asked in a pouty, sad voice.

Get a life, Callista thought. She looked over her shoulder. As they were coming in the dialysis center, Mark was cornered by Neil Hawthorne, the hospital administrator. They were talking in the tiny meeting area outside the center's secured doors.

Lindsey was making the dialysis connections off to the side. Not 15 minutes later, alarms went off.

Dialysis notes, Thursday, May 14: Lindsey Dahlin

Nick in good spirits, no complaints, treatment tolerated well.

Alarms after 15 minutes of treatment.

Both parents arrived for treatment. They stated that following dialysis they have a cardiology appointment and both parents wanted to be present during that appointment. Manager Dorrance and Administrator Hawthorne met with parents and discussed necessity of only one visitor at a time during dialysis. Parents voiced understanding and complied with visiting rules, with parents rotating at bedside.

Four days later, instant replay.

<u>Dialysis notes, Monday, May 18: Lindsey Dahlin</u>
Multiple arterial alarms.

"Do you know how scary it is to hear those alarms on your kid?" Callista asked Dr. Place. Her brown hair was swept into a long pony tail, and she was wearing a shirt with a *Die Hard* quote. It was funny, but inappropriate, he thought. But everything was inappropriate these days.

"I...uh...I guess the lines need changing. Hemodialysis is intended to be temporary, this has been in for months."

"That's all you have to say?" Mark asked, his voice edged with anger. "If it's only supposed to be temporary, why is Nick still on it? I've read about PD. Why hasn't Nick been changed to that form of dialysis? It would be so much easier on him." They were standing with Nick and Dr. Place in the hallway outside the dialysis center.

Dr. Place shifted his weight uncomfortably. He had no answer for them. "That's a call for Dr. Loomis to make," he said carefully. "He thinks hemodialysis will do a better job for Nick."

Mark rolled his eyes. "Whatever. So what's the remedy for this stuff going on now?"

"I'll schedule Interventional Radiology to insert new lines. It will be a simple procedure. General anesthetic."

"No," Mark said. Today there wasn't anything casual about his dress or attitude. He'd done Zoom meetings in the waiting area with some company presidents about their security options. He'd dressed the part of the expert he was.

"I beg your pardon?"

"There's nothing simple about Nick. He has difficulty with sedation and recovery from anesthesia. He needs a cardiac anesthesiologist to watch for heart problems. No matter what your rules say, we both have to be there with him because we need to oversee all of this."

Dr. Place backed off. "If it's okay with IR, we can do it your way," he said, looking around quickly. Loomis wouldn't like this arrangement, but the procedure had to be done and he could see for Nick's sake, the way Mark and Callista wanted it. "The procedure won't even take a full hour. We can do it before dialysis and then during dialysis we'll be able to check how things are working. Okay? See you Thursday."

"I don't want them to do anything to me." Nick was angry.

"Nick, they have to. Your lines aren't working. In order for dialysis to work, the lines have to be replaced."

"They were fine a week ago. How do you know that silly nurse didn't do something to them."

"Nick, she's a nurse! She'd get fired if she did something like that."

"There's good nurses and bad nurses. And she's so silly, I can't stand her. How do you know she's smart enough to do this right?"

"Same way we know you can handle this on Thursday, okay? We just know."

CHAPTER 24

"Patrice, please. Yes, this is Dr. Loomis. I have two pages that need to be inserted in a patient record. Hampton, Nicholas. I'm emailing them down to you."

Next call. "Dorrance? Dr. Loomis. The Hamptons are due, call me or Neil Hawthorne immediately when they arrive…You're not that busy that you'll miss a kid in a wheelchair. They're coming up from Interventional Radiology. And remember, Backstrom does the dialysis today…I don't care if he has to drive 40 miles to get here."

Loomis sat back and nodded at Hawthorne across from him. "Okay, now what?"

"We wait. I'm sure I'll be paged to come to talk with Mark and will go downstairs then. Zora has the security detail ready." He looked around. "You know, it might be handy to bring a social worker up here, a nephrology social worker, so to speak, to handle the non-existent transplant, and all the other work you do." He snorted. "Knowing Hampton, you're going to be swamped with calls and complaints. The calls could come into this office and you'll be able to keep track of what they're up to. You might need *unbiased*," he cleared his throat, "back-up of your plans. I know just the person, Gwen Deeds."

A bit later, his phone rang. He nodded, then handed it to Loomis.

"Loomis. They did. What time is it? 13:45? 1:45? Okay, now at four o'clock, page Dr. Place and tell him to call Mark Hampton to tell him there is information about the procedure he needs to know. Why don't I do it? Because it's Dr. Place's job, it's his floor."

He handed the phone back to Hawthorne. "We're on."

Neil nodded. "I'll be back in a couple of hours. Everything can just stay in a holding pattern. They can call me here then." He left.

Alone in the office once again, Loomis started checking Nick's online schedule. The woman was as efficient as her husband, she'd already made several pre-transplant appointments. And one by one, he cancelled them all.

Callista's Journal Thursday, May 21, 2020 –

Nick had procedure with IR today. Dialysis catheter needed to be switched out because it was causing problems. Mark and I felt we needed to be there for the anesthesia and the procedure. We were anxious to make sure this new line worked and Nick doesn't handle recovery very well. Dr. Aphid from IR gave permission for both of us to be present due to Nick's history of difficulty with sedation. Had to give Ketamine/Versid via catheter, but needed Propofol to knock him out before taking him up to the procedure room. Best sedation experience so far, no IV until he was asleep. One hour procedure, woke well, no nausea, stable throughout. Cath site oozing a bit, was discharged to dialysis. Both of us wheeled Nick from procedure in wheelchair to dialysis center about 1:45.

Immediately we were met with nurses who said one of us had to leave the center. I left. Mark stayed while dialysis was started about 2 o'clock with a new nurse we never saw before. He was a big guy, like a football player. Didn't look too bright. We switched places off and on and then Nick got hungry. Since I take care of his diet more, Mark left. It was a little after 4pm when Mark came back to the room to get his lunch bag and was planning to leave but Dr. Place called, so Mark took the call. Immediately, 2 security guards rushed to Mark, who informed them he was on the phone with his son's physician. Mark went into the hallway to finish the call. They paused for a short amount of time. Mark came into the dialysis room to ask me a question from the doctor, tried closing the doors to the bay so he could hear better.

Security opened doors and entered the dialysis bay and got between Mark and Nick. Mark informed Dr. Place that he'd need to call him back. Security guy gets in Mark's face, says he can use physical force if necessary, pushes, chest bumps Mark. I heard Mark say "Get your hands off me." I was in the lounge chair next to the bed. I was looking at my phone and the next thing I know, the two guards seem to tackle Mark. They slammed into the bedside table and my chair and threw Mark to the ground with both guards on top of him. All three were on the floor in front of me. Mark continued to tell the guards to get off of him, while trying to push them off.

The guy dialysis nurse moved over to get between Nick and the men. There was a lot of movement. The bedside table crashed into the wall. The security guards got off and let Mark up.

Mark called 911, refused to leave the dialysis bay until Stanton police showed up. It turns out the officer from Stanton Police was contracted to work at Holcome. There is no way to get hold of anyone NOT connected to Holcome, it seems. The Stanton police officer escorted Mark from the bay to the hallway.

I couldn't see any more as they left, but I caught a glimpse of Hawthorne, the hospital administrator, who came to talk with them. They escorted Mark outside and ordered him to leave Holcome property. He parked across the street where he could watch for us when we came out.

I received a call as Nick and I went to the car, it was that creep, Loomis. He said that Holcome was not going to move forward on Nick's transplant. This scared me to death, it was like he just sealed Nick's fate into a grave.

***

"I don't even know if that guy was a nurse," Callista said as they drove home after the dialysis session. Mark was driving but was constantly shifting in his seat. "How is the pain?"

"I feel like something got knocked out of place when they decked me. I don't know what the crap happened. I noticed the guards when we walked in, thought it was unusual for guards in dialysis, real hot spot, you know. But man!" he rolled his neck around. "They asked Hawthorne if it was going to be a trespass and he said no. I recorded it. I wish Nick hadn't seen this. I mean how comforting is it to have your father beat up by hospital guards. Geez, this hurts."

"This whole thing was a mess," Callista said. "Something was wrong from the start. I mean the procedure was okay, but the big moron didn't draw labs before the run and used the wrong size tubing. All he said was 'Oh well.' No second nurse came to verify the dialysis machine settings. Afterwards, he just shoved gauze into the dressing for bleeding, didn't change the dressing, it was as if he didn't want to waste time doing his job correctly. And it was still bleeding when we left. What kind of nurse was this? I'll bet none of these things are written in the record. I'll look."

She was quiet as the Ford Escape moved north. Then, suddenly, "Oh, hell!"

Mark jerked the wheel. "What the...."

"All the specialty appointments we made for pre-transplant have been cancelled!"

As they drove, Nick sat quietly in the back, very drowsy. It was such a long way back and forth and today it seemed to take forever. That operation in the morning, then dialysis. And the security guys. They thought he wasn't paying attention, but he saw all of it, the guys throwing his dad on the floor. Just because an extra person was in the room? He yawned and stretched and went to adjust his seat, straighten his shirt and jacket, except his shirt seemed to be sticking to him. He looked down, there was a red spot on his chest. It was where the catheter line went under his skin. He reached over and took a Kleenex to clean it up. Only it didn't clean up, the Kleenex turned red pretty quickly. He dropped the Kleenex on the floor and tried again. And again. Then he ran out of Kleenex.

"Mom, I think I have a problem."

"Huh? What is it Nicky?" She was groggy, the ride blessedly put her to sleep.

"I'm bleeding."

Jerking around, Callista saw his light blue Star Wars shirt half covered in blood. "Oh my God!" She tore off the seatbelt and tried to get herself up and over the console between the front seats. "Stop the car! Stop!" she screamed. "He's bleeding!"

Mark made for the side of the road. One glance had him frantically punching numbers into his phone. "C'mon, answer." It was after six o'clock; maybe no one was in the office.

"Loomis."

"This is Mark Hampton. We have a problem. Nick is bleeding from the insertion site for the catheter. His whole shirt is bloody. What do we do?" He was calculating his options. We're half way to Holcome and half way to Children's in the Cities. Where to go?

"A little bleeding is to be expected, I'm sure," Loomis said casually. He was online, looking at Mark Hampton's medical record of previous visits at Holcome. Interesting. And with one click, he blocked Mark from ever receiving medical services from them again. He'd already checked to see if the extra pages were inserted into Nick's records. So far so good.

"It's not a little. No way. It's a shirt full."

"Basic first aid, then. You know, pressure. Change his position, see what works."

See what works, sure. "Thanks," Mark said tightly, then hung up.

"How is it?" he saw Callista pressing on Nick's chest, Nick was lying down. She shook her head.

"We've got to back," she said. "Maybe there's something wrong with the line, maybe they have to redo the surgery in IR."

Mark waited for a break in traffic and cut across the little path the cops used to get between traffic lanes. "Maybe we should get an ambulance." He called the hospital from the car. No answer. He called again. "One moment, please." And hold. And hold. After 12 minutes, he hung up. "We're going straight to the ER," he said. It was nearing 7 pm. "I just thought about something. I've got to call Hawthorne."

"Yes, good evening." Neil had just come up to Loomis' office. Both were comfortable, shirts open, drinks in hand.

"Why, hello Mark," he said into his cell phone. "How is Nick after his procedure? Bleeding? How badly?"

"Badly enough that I'm bringing him back. The question is, you told me to get the hell off the property. Can I drop him and Callista at the ER."

"No."

"C'mon, man! The kid can't walk, he's bleeding."

"Mark, be reasonable, you just assaulted two security guards and...."

"I assaulted, give me a break. You know it didn't go down that way, not when the first cop chest bumped me and said he had permission to use violence on me! All because of an extra person in a dialysis center for a kid who just had surgery? That doesn't pass the smell test. It won't stand up in court."

"There is a disorderly conduct charge against you, Mark. You can't come on our property. You've made yourself a danger to the Holcome institution."

"What about my kid! Who is he going to hurt while he is bleeding to death?"

"The answer is no." Hawthorne hung up and looked over to Loomis. "How much heparin did Backstrom give the kid? He isn't a bleeder, is he?"

"No, never mind, they're just exaggerating."

As Mark made the right turn toward the ER entrance at Holcome, Callista saw a crowd by the doors. "Oh God, it's half the police force. Mark, they meant it when they said they were blocking you from coming on the premises. Even from the circle at the entrance and the ER parking lot."

"I'll just have to drop you off at the street. I can't take a chance they put me in jail tonight."

"Nicky, Nicky, come on, I'll have to carry you." They parked across the street in front of the apartment buildings. Callista picked Nick up, and Mark helped her across as far as the curb. Someone must have been watching because a resident came rushing out with a wheelchair. And then they were gone.

❖❖❖

"Ellie, can you help us out?" Mark was on his cell phone, still sitting across the street from the ER. Callista had called and said Nick was taken right in and they were working on him. He was lying on an ER bed, the resident holding a little sandbag-like thing on his chest. His favorite Star Wars shirt was a mess and no sign of the blood flow stopping, she told him.

Ellie looked at her watch. Almost nine. Nothing ever happened during daylight hours, it seemed.

"Sure, what's going on?"

"Nick started bleeding on the way home and we had to turn around and are back in Stanton in the Holcome ER. Can you go up…?"

"And take care of the kids. Sure, on my way. How's Nick doing?"

"They've tried pressure, a tamponade like they do in combat, even a sandbag. Nothing worked. They've called the Interventional Radiology department to come back and re-stitch the catheter, they think it pulled loose. Not here yet."

"Never a dull moment," Ellie said. "Hang in there." She hung up the phone. "Hey Paul, I'm outta here! Up to Trent."

"Now what?" he looked up from the early local news, dreading the answer. Late phone calls meant nothing good.

"Nick's little procedure turned out to be not be so little, he started bleeding and they went to the hospital to have them fix it." She hurriedly put on her jacket.

"You've gotta be kidding. Can't anything go right for them? Got enough gas?"

"Yeah. You know, something seems funny about this. She texted earlier and said there was trouble, would fill me in later, and Mark didn't sound like he was with her. Why wouldn't he go in with her?"

"Covid?"

"The day Covid would keep me from being at my kid's side if there was danger!"

It was 2:30 in the morning when Mark, Callista and Nick came in the door. Nick could hardly walk, his eyes were closed. Mark carefully picked him up and carried him up to his bedroom. Callista looked worn down, hair in disarray and deep circles under her eyes. They'd left at seven o'clock that previous morning, over 18 hours ago.

"Well?" Ellie asked, getting up from the sofa in the living room, her book falling to the floor.

Callista dropped into the dark leather love seat. She didn't bother to turn on the lights.

"A couple things went badly for us, Mom," Callista began with a sigh. "A stitch pulled out from Nick's procedure today. IR had to redo it. We sat in that ER for three hours. I don't know where these people were, took them forever to get there. The ER doctor said he could have done it, it wouldn't have been painful, but Nick balked at the idea of a stranger digging around in his chest and neck."

"What caused the bleeding problem?"

"The jerk of a nurse gave him 4000 units of heparin. That may be the usual dosage to keep his cath line open, but do you give that to a kid right after surgery and expect things to go right? He was still bleeding from the procedure when we left the first time and he was never even checked."

"And the other thing?"

"Didn't Mark tell you? He got thrown out of Holcome International because he was in the dialysis center. There were two of us in the room and the rule says only one can be there at a time. It was after the surgery, for God's sake. The security guards came in and tackled Mark and threw him to the floor."

"Over an extra person in dialysis?" Ellie's eyes were wide. "That's insane."

"Not as insane as the fact they wouldn't let him drive us to the door of the ER. They threatened to arrest him if he did." She sighed. "And all our transplant appointments have been cancelled. It's just been a wonderful day."

CHAPTER 25

Saturday, two days later, a letter arrived from Neil Hawthorne with a copy of the Behavior Plan the Hamptons were now required to follow. It was odd that it arrived so quickly, almost as if it was created prior to the May 21 incident. Also, the mail included a large envelope from the Stanton Police Department. The incident had been investigated, reports filed and mailed with surprising speed for government agencies.

Holcome International Medical Center

May 22, 2020

Mr. and Mrs. Hampton,

The recent verbal and physical altercation initiated by Mr. Hampton toward Holcome International Medical Center staff has been disruptive and has negatively impacted the care environment. This behavior is contrary to Holcome patient and visitor behavioral expectations and the Holcome Dialysis Patient Rights and Responsibilities Code of Conduct which states "Holcome International Medical Center Dialysis Center has an expectation of mutual respect for patients, visitors and staff members. Swearing, yelling or rude behavior by patients, visitors, accompanying patients and staff members will not be tolerated." Additionally, the document states: "physical harm or any type of written or verbal threat will not be tolerated."

The physical altercation initiated by Mr. Hampton on Thursday, May 21, resulted in harm to Holcome International Medical Center staff. This cannot and will not be tolerated. In order to preserve a safe and respectful environment that is most conducive to high quality care for our patients and staff, a set of behavior expectations is imperative and will be implemented effective immediately.

In order for the dialysis center or any Holcome provider to continue providing services to Nicolas, there must be an understanding of mutual expectations and acceptable behavior.

Neil Hawthorne
Hospital Administrator
Holcome International Medical Center

"What the hell?" Mark ran a hand through his sandy hair. He was looking at the police reports and the mailed citations they'd just received along with Hawthorne's pompous letter. He eased back carefully in his chair at the kitchen table. The ice packs on his shoulders slipped a tad and he pushed them back in place.

Callista looked over his shoulder. "That's from the Stanton Police Department, not the hospital. For God's sake, this was in dialysis, not a bar! I was right there and this isn't how it happened!"

Stanton Police Department Event Report

Preliminary
On 5/21/2020 at or about 1620 hours, I, Officer George Lewis, went to the dialysis unit for a disorderly person. I was escorted to the dialysis unit by Holcome Security. Once there Mark Hampton stepped out to the hallway to speak with me. He said Holcome was refusing to allow him in the room during treatment of his son even though his wife was in the room with their son. Holcome advised they have a one visitor per room policy. Neil Hawthorne (Holcome Hospital Administrator) came to the area and spoke with Mark. Mark was told by Hawthorne that he needed to leave the hospital. I escorted Mark outside without incident. Mark gave me the following information.

Mark Hampton statement
He went up to the room to retrieve his lunch from the room his son and wife were in. While he was in the room, he received a call from his son's doctor. Holcome security came into the room and told him to leave. He stated he was talking to the doctor. Security Guard Hartford put his hand on him and they ended up on the ground in the room. At some point, another security guard ended up on top of them in the wrestling match. Eventually everyone got up and he called 911. Security did not tell him to leave.

Billy Strait Statement
Security was told to be at the dialysis center as they have had problems with Mark in the past. Mark was told to wait outside of the dialysis unit as only

one person was allowed in the room with their son and the wife was there at the time. He saw a sanitation employee badge their way in to the dialysis unit and Mark followed him in unauthorized. Guards went to the room to tell Mark he had to leave. Mark was on his cellphone when they got to the room. Mark ignored them while he was on the phone. He hung up and Hartford told him to leave. Mark kept refusing and Hartford put his open hand on his shoulder to try and divert him out of the room. Mark put his hands up and stated, "Don't touch me." Mark "bum rushed" Hartford and they fell up against the wall. Security let Mark up and he called 911. When law enforcement showed up, he was escorted by security to his car, a silver Ford Escape in the parking ramp.

Report by Gregory Backstrom, RN, in Nicholas Hampton's medical records
2 hours into treatment, father visited with patient and mother. Moments later, 2 security guards came in the room and "asked him nicely" to wait outside unit, father ignored them, stated he needed to call Nicholas's doctor. Guard raised his arms in a calm manner and tried to point him in direction of the door. In that moment, father yelled at the guard to keep his hands off him and lunged at guard, now both guards were trying to get him under control and second guard hit his face on the table as three of them fell to the floor. 1 hit their head on the wall leaving a 3" dent. Wife was recording on her phone, Nicholas showed no emotions and watched TV.

Vonn Hartford Statement
Officers told Mark he needed to leave the room. Mark refused to leave. He put his hand on his shoulder to try and move him towards the exit. Mark put his hands up by his chest and said "Don't touch me." He took a step towards Vonn and puffed his chest out. Vonn stepped towards Mark and Mark grabbed him around the midsection like he was going to pick him up and they fell to the ground up against the wall. Billy got on top of them in an attempt to get Mark off him.

Senior Security Specialist Joe Wagner Follow-Up 5/22/2020
As an assist to Captain Zora Zane, I, Sam Spenser, reached out to obtain background. Nurse Manager Dominic Dorrance is away from work for a few days. His e-mail advised to contact Nurse Manager Linda O'Brien who would be covering for him during this time. At 9:03 am on 5/22/2020, I made telephone contact with NM O'Brien in Croixpoint, Wisconsin. NM O'Brien was familiar with that incident. NM O'Brien also told me that she knew that there had been problems in the past with this family and was not surprised this incident occurred.

Disposition
Citation issued to Mark J. Hampton for disorderly conduct.

"I'm fighting this in court," Mark said. "There's no way in hell I started this. I was *under* those cops! Even the chiropractor said these are defensive injuries. I had my arms crossed in front of me in a defensive position against any physical assault. I did not take a tactical stance. If anyone with a brain reads this they would pick up all the inconsistencies. First I'm under the guy, then in the next report I'm on top of him and the other cop is trying to get me off his buddy. I tried to pick a guy up? That one cop was bigger around than my reach; I couldn't have picked him up if I wanted to. Open hand on my shoulder? I puffed out my chest?" Mark shook his head. "The cop did that! How dumb would I be to take on two cops? Who wrote this script for them?"

"Who's this Linda O'Brien that they talked to? She was 100 miles away in Wisconsin! Why did they even talk with her, she wasn't even in the dialysis center that day. Did you see her?"

"Dorrance was there, that's all." Mark stared ahead. "You know, when I called about bringing Nick back when he was bleeding, that jerk Hawthorne told me I was being charged with disorderly conduct. How did he know? These reports were investigated *after* he told me that. Something's going on here."

Callista sat at the wooden kitchen table and put her head in her hands. "I can't do this. Oh God, why? *Why?* He's just a little kid, why does he have to be pushed around and forced to be in this situation. Why are *we* the bad guys, we didn't cause this! And canceling the transplant stuff! This is nightmare!"

Later that day, they were notified on the hospital message portal that there would be a mandatory meeting on Monday in the dialysis center conference room. Several involved parties would attend. Mark could participate on Zoom via his phone because he was barred from being there in person.

CHAPTER 26

Dialysis even on Memorial Day, Callista thought, the schedule must be kept. She answered the Covid questions through her *Die Hard* facemask, but as she turned, the administrator of the intake department, who was behind their screener, waved her arm. She looks like a fool, Callista thought, turning toward the elevators. And then her way was blocked by a female security guard with a crew cut and an attitude.

"Hold on, you can't go to the rooms. I need to accompany you." She took off her radio to answer a call.

Nick frantically grabbed Callista's arm. "Mom, what's going on, are they going to arrest you? Are they going to beat you up like they did Dad?"

Nice work, Holcome, Callista thought. "No, Nick." She turned. "Officer, what is this about? We have to get up to dialysis. We have to be on time, we're not waiting for you." She started walking away.

"Stop! I said I need to accompany you."

"Why, because I'm a drug smuggler? Murderer?"

"Hospital administrator's orders. You are not to walk around this building unaccompanied."

"Why?"

Callista was ignored.

The elevator ride was silent up to the second floor and Nick clung desperately to Callista's arm. When the doors opened, Neil Hawthorne was waiting for her.

"Come along, Mrs. Hampton, we have a meeting in the conference room."

"No, Nick has to have dialysis. It's his appointment time and I can't leave him in there alone."

"I said come along, Mrs. Hampton, there will be no dialysis until we complete the meeting."

I knew I never liked him and his oh-so-important title and his expensive suits and perfect beard, Callista thought, especially after that confrontation with Mom last January. You son of a bitch.

"In case you haven't noticed, Mr. Hawthorne, Nick is a minor and shouldn't be left alone in a dialysis bay while I'm at your meeting. I don't care how good you say the staff is, I'm here to watch over him."

"I said come along." His voice had a menacing edge to it now. "Nick will not receive dialysis until we're done, however long it takes. The security guard will remain with Nick in the room."

The meeting began with Hawthorne saying there were a lot of meetings on the 22nd, the day after the incident; he claimed to be exhausted by the effort. Loomis added the conversations included University nephrologists who also provided nephrology services at Ridley. He, too, claimed to be exhausted by all of the work.

Seriously? Callista stared at them. Exhausted? Who are they trying to fool? She was handed the Expectations and Behavior Plan designed for their family's future treatment at Holcome International Medical Center:

Expectations and Behavioral Plan
Patient Name: Nicholas M. Hampton

• Nick's father, Mr. Mark Hampton, is no longer allowed on any Holcome International Medical Center property. In the event that Mr. Hampton does enter Holcome Clinic property, he will be reported to Holcome Clinic Security and the Stanton Police Department for trespassing.

• Nick's mother, Mrs. Callista Hampton, will be allowed to accompany Nick to his dialysis appointments, with the expectation that all interactions with others are respectful and non-threatening.

• Entrance to Holcome International Medical Center at the West Entrance only.

• Security will escort Mrs. Hampton and Nick to appointment(s) and remain nearby.

• Should Mrs. Hampton be unavailable to bring Nick to an appointment for any reason, another responsible adult should be asked to substitute in Mrs. Hampton's absence so that Nick may continue to receive the care that he needs in a timely manner.

• HIMC has an expectation of mutual respect for patients, visitor and staff members. Swearing, yelling or rude behavior by patients, visitors accompanying patients and staff members is not allowed.

• Physical harm and verbal threats of any type, as well as profanity, will not be tolerated and Holcome Security and/or Stanton Police Department will be contacted.

• Any concerns should be addressed to the Holcome International Medical Center care team or alternatively to the Medical Center's Office of Patient Liaison.

Callista held back a groan as she left the room and went to the dialysis bay. Hawthorne had made it clear the Hamptons needed to find a new dialysis center, that Holcome would not transplant Nick. He also made it clear if Nick's health deteriorated, it was a problem for the parents, not Holcome. He stated the Hamptons could not be trusted because of their actions in the PICU last winter and because of some issue with Ridley they didn't even know about.

Every movement will be spied on and controlled, she thought. This sucks so badly. Everything points to them having all this arranged before we walked in the door on May 21. Why? Why are they doing this to us, to Nick? This could kill him. I didn't say anything, I didn't touch anyone, I did nothing but watch those cops tear into my husband, and *I* need a guard?

CHAPTER 27

"This is such bullshit," Ellie said, slamming the pile of papers onto the picnic table. She looked over her shoulder to see if Nick was in hearing range. He was lying back in a recliner a little way from them and absorbed in a Nintendo DS game. "When did you miss dialysis appointments? Were you billed for those? You'd better request your insurance invoices and check against appointments. Insurance doesn't like paying for stuff that never happened. They'll go after them for that. Naughty words are forbidden. If you don't speak respectfully they're going to call security?"

"Believe me, the dialysis nurses say plenty of 'oh shits' and 'what is f-ing wrong with the line?' Should go both ways. But it won't. It's so embarrassing, the cop went with me even when I used the restroom across the hallway. How bizarre is that? They think Mark might jump out of my purse?"

"How's he doing?" Paul asked. He was lining up hamburgers for the grill. He kept an ear to the conversation as he worked, but the more he heard, the angrier he was becoming at the harsh tactics being used. For what?

Having a Memorial Day picnic at Paul and Ellie's in French Lake at least provided some relief on the long drive home for Callista and Nick. Mark had brought Sienna and Max and they were playing volleyball in the spacious yard, while Mark relaxed in the shade. Of course, if the Covid police caught them, there would be trouble, picnics and visitors were forbidden and a telephone number was publicized for people to inform the authorities about their noncompliant neighbors. But the cul-de-sac was a bit back from the main street, shrouded in trees and there were no pesky neighbors to spy on them.

"Really sore. Has to take pain killers. One report said a guard got his head knocked against the wall and made a dent in it, but I was there, the rolling table made the three-inch dent in the wall when it shot across the room as they pushed Mark. Not a one of them told the truth. There were two cops there in the dialysis center right after we got there. Then, at ten to four, when I went to the restroom, one cop, the woman, left and the big guy came, the guy who chest-bumped Mark. It was a set-up."

"Why, that's the question," Ellie said. "Why go to these lengths? Who gains by it?" She thought a minute, wondering who planned the whole scenario – a critical question, but she said nothing on the subject.

"Not Nick. Telling us they won't transplant, that dialysis is a courtesy until we find another place to go and if anything happens, it's on us to fix? Do you have any idea how scary that is?"

"And what are you going to do about it," Paul asked, his voice tinged with anger as he handed a wine cooler to Callista. "Are you getting a lawyer? Are you going after them? This isn't on you, it's their doing!"

"Dad, we can't," Callista said quietly. "Nick needs dialysis. We have to keep the peace. There are only two hospitals that do pediatric hemodialysis in the entire state. We can't cross Holcome, where would we go if they up and said 'get out'?"

"That Ridley place," Paul said. He wasn't one to raise his voice, but he was close at this point with the frustration of it all. He'd read the papers as well, and frowned as though something was bothering him. He looked at the driveway where the brand new Ford Escape was parked, the dark gray, almost black Ford Escape.

"Didn't they say they said escorted Mark to the silver Ford Escape? Your car isn't silver! That police report was written by someone who wasn't there. You'd have to be blind not to see the difference between silver and a dark gray. I'll bet a hundred bucks this was written ahead of time. You could go to the press with that information, that's proof it wasn't written by anyone who was there!"

"We can't do that either, they warned us off from doing that, they said they already had a press release ready to go with the 'whole' story!" Callista exclaimed. "*Their* whole story! We're stuck!"

A sickening silence followed her words, the enormity of the situation was overwhelming.

Suddenly, there was a screech and laughter outside. Paul looked toward the driveway. "Tera. Funny, I didn't hear the car."

"Stealth mode," Ellie interjected and they all laughed at that.

The kids stormed the patio hauling bags with them. Tera was close behind.

"Rice Krispie bars with chocolate chips! Pig out time!"

"You cut your hair," Ellie said, surprised. Tera's dark hair was now short and curly with blondish streaks.

Slinging down her purse, Tera shook her head. "I got tired of it, too long to take care of." She paused, remembering how gentle Craig had been as he brushed her hair each and every day. "And I don't do this stuff," she gestured to her head. "It would wreck my nails."

"Where can you get your hair done, that bastard closed everything up," Callista demanded. "I need a haircut, these split ends are driving me crazy."

Paul looked in the kitchen. "If you notice, his highness had a trim for his latest TV appearance. They had a shot of his wife supposedly cutting his hair on the front lawn of the governor's mansion. We're in this together and all that sh…crap. Anyone ready to eat?"

The kids were the first to demand food and were put to work hustling everything outside to the picnic tables. Ellie gave Callista a hug. "We'll do whatever it takes to help you out."

The meal was a raucous adventure, as usual, and since it was outside, louder than ever. Max reached up and gave Tera's hair a yank. "Is that a wig?"

"Ow, you little shit. It's really my hair."

"Why did you change it?"

"I'm trying to get a promotion at work. Dress for success, you know."

"Image is everything," they all chorused.

"All you need are flames on your black leggings and you'd have an image, all right," Callista said with a mean laugh.

"Like a hooker? Is that what you mean?" More laughter.

The banter continued. Sienna started to fan herself, end of May or not, it was plenty hot outside. "Mom, are we going to set up our big pool?" Their above-ground fifteen-foot pool took the edge off the heat.

Callista looked at Mark. "Uh, probably not. It wouldn't be fair to Nick. He can't go into a pool because his catheter lines will get wet.

He can't even shower, remember."

Sienna glared at her mother, then got up and went inside. Max quickly followed. Sensing trouble, Tera went right after them, in time to hear Sienna, "Nick, Nick, Nick. Can't do this, can't do that because Nick can't. Can't have pizza, no chips in the house because Nick has to watch the potassium. Nick, Nick...he's all that matters."

Tera reached out and swung her around. "Nick what? You know your mother would do the same for you if you had these difficulties."

"Not on your life. Haven't you noticed? I don't have a mother anymore, where is she when I need her? Taking Nick to dialysis," she finished in a snotty voice. "Or if she talks to me, it's 'Get that homework done,' 'Do the dishes,' 'Go get the laundry.' I'm sick of it. I want a life."

"Don't be silly, who hauled you around to gymnastics and softball games. Your mom. Who coached your basketball team? Your dad. They do what they have to for you guys and right now, Nick needs dialysis or he's done for."

"Since when did you become a cheerleader for the Hamptons? Mom says you're only out for yourself and you should have stayed away. What do you care how I feel, about how any of us feel?"

"What a shitty attitude," Tera snapped back. "You're family. You're important to me and if I think something is going on that's disruptive, I'm going to tell you," she glared at Sienna, "to your face. Grow up."

Sienna gave her the finger and turned away. Max looked at Tera and shrugged. He followed his sister to the video cabinet.

After the bustle of clean-up, the group decided to watch *Ford vs. Ferrari*. Nick patted an oversized armchair and motioned Tera to join him. "This movie reminds me of your car."

"I'm going to tell you a secret. It's not my car." She ruffled his sandy hair.

"Huh?"

"It's Uncle Rusty's. He didn't want to take it to South Carolina so he left it here for me to babysit. Then he got down there and found out everyone drives a Mustang. He's waiting for a chance to come up here and get it."

"But it has your license plate, Storm 1!"

"You have to have a license plate, Nick."

"Then what are you going to drive if he takes it?"

"A Smart Car, you know, the ones that look like the toy Crazy Coupe."

He yelped with laughter. "No way!"

"How about a Humvee, then?"

More laughter. "How about a mini-van! Image is everything."

"Will you guys shut up over there," Callista ordered. "Can't hear the movie."

"As if she can hear us, over that car race," Tera whispered.

"I want a ride in the Mustang."

"You'd like it. The road to my house is all twisty and turny and you have to downshift like LeMans. But I get off work too late, you're done with dialysis and home hours before I can leave."

"What do you do, Aunt Tera?"

"Shuffle papers, do reports. Then I come home at night and look at more papers to see how and why things happen."

"Like *CSI*? Florensics?"

Florensics? Tera looked at him, must be some kind of kidspeak, she thought. "You watch that? Yeah, kind of, but lots and lots of math."

"Boring." He snuggled closer to her. "What's really boring is that ride to and from Holcome. Down the highway, up the highway. There're only so many things you can do, like video games, count out-of-state license plates, count how many cows in a field. I check out billboards, but how often do the billboards change? There aren't that many on the road on the way. I saw a new one though: 'When you die, you *will* meet God.' Do you think it's to get people to behave themselves?"

"It would take more than a billboard, I'm afraid."

"But I'm not afraid to meet God. I already have." A chill cut through Tera's very being.

"Really? When was that?" Her voice was somehow calmer than she felt.

He thought back, "Not the last surgery in California but after that. I don't think they told Mom and Dad about what happened. I know something happened because when I heard voices, they were saying 'He's back.' If I was back, I must have been somewhere else and the only place you can be in a hospital is right there alive or dead, gone someplace. I must have been dead. I don't remember much, just quiet and a feeling of things being so good, so peaceful, so happy. I saw a smiling face, a very nice face I could have looked at for hours. It was familiar, but didn't exactly look like Jesus in the pictures or anybody in church. But it was a good feeling and I haven't felt that way since, but I wish I could."

The subject turned abruptly. "Aunt Tera, why does Mom say mean things about you?"

"I'm not a mind reader, you have to ask her, Nick."

"I like you, why doesn't she?"

"Don't waste time thinking about it. We're sisters. Sisters fight. We do things differently. Maybe she thinks I should do things her way. We don't hate each other, we're just different people. The important thing is we're sisters, and, in the end, we'd do anything for each other, walk on fire, hold back a train...."

He started laughing loudly at that thought and got hushed again. He gave Tera a hug.

CHAPTER 28

Monday, June 1. Tera was sitting at her Southwood Acres desk, computer logged in for the monthly Elite Corps meeting; the good thing about video meetings was no one could see all of you. She dipped the brush into a bottle of very bright green nail polish. Her guys loved her crazy nails. Anything to get them distracted.

Harris droned on and on about the stricter rules of quarantine and avoiding cross-contamination. Tera propped her head on her hand and yawned. Her guys were losing ground. Ronnie's leg was past the point of no return. Montez passed away and, in fact, Diego was given a new roommate not even three days after Montez went to the Covid restricted area. Diego should have been out weeks ago, home and safe from contagion. The same with Bob Dodge. But now, it was a race against time and these people were left at the starting gate.

"There are a couple of openings for staff," Mrs. Harris was saying. "Lay-offs were made but some departments still require support staff. We are looking for someone in Pediatric Services."

"I'll take it!" Tera called out, once again interrupting the boss lady.

"You, Storm? What do you know about Pediatrics or nephrology, especially when you would need to report there in a week?"

"I'm a quick study. It's a week, plenty of time to learn more than the doctor."

There was a buzz of laughter. "What's so funny? I'm just that good," she retorted. More laughter.

Her phone buzzed. It was Roger, who'd also logged into the online meeting.

Are you crazy, Teresa Storm? The guy you'll be working for is Charles Loomis, the biggest asshole on earth.

Oh, I know who he is, Tera thought. Nick's nemesis. Time to jump into the fray and get down and dirty.

An hour later, the forms were complete. She didn't care if Jan Michelob approved them or not, Regina Harris would squash Jan like an ant. And speak of the devil, here was the dirty dishwater blonde herself, bearing down on Tera in all her administrative glory.

Jan slapped a thick stack of papers on Tera's desk. "You're behind, Storm. Stop faking you're so busy and get these processed." She looked down. "Ugly nails. Get that shit off of them."

"How can I be behind if these were on *your* desk? I can only work on them if they are on *my* desk." Tera deliberately did an overcoat on one nail.

"And be sure they are marked Covid deaths."

"What if they weren't? Do you get a bonus or something for upping the Covid numbers?" Tera asked innocently. When raw anger crossed Jan's face, Tera added, "It's dishonest. Angelou didn't die from Covid. He wasn't tested, he had no cough, no symptoms. And how do I know about any of these others?" She flipped the papers.

"Just do your job, Storm, or you're out of here!"

"I *am* out of here. Good luck replacing me, Jan." Tera sat back, a wicked smile on her lips. She dumped the papers on the floor. "Do your own damn dirty work."

It wasn't half an hour after Michelob left that there was an urgent call.

"Storm!"

Pulling on her mask, Tera went swiftly across the hall. "What is it, Dodgeball?"

"When do things close down here? When does that bitch of an administrator take a hike? I heard her talking to you. Nice nails, by the way."

"She leaves around five, what's on your mind?"

His voice dropped to a whisper. "One day this week, Lila is coming to get me."

Tera didn't leave until six. How could she fake that she didn't know about his escape? "You sure you want to do this, Bob? There's a nurse on duty around the clock, aides. Someone will see you."

"Listen, Storm, I wait until after you're gone and I go walking. There's nobody down here who knows this. I take the walker, I hold the handrails in the hallways, well, not sanitary, but I soap up afterwards. I can do this. I would rather take a chance and go through my regular doc than this Holliday who never shows his face around here. Ever. Can you help me?"

Jan left early on Fridays. Friday was Tera's last day. Who the hell cared what happened on a Friday night?

"Friday," she whispered with a wink. "I know nothing."

On the way back to her desk, she thought she heard crying. It was one of those days. She headed down the hall toward this side of the Covid partition, as if a partition would keep people safer. In the last room, Diego was on his knees on the hard floor, imploring the Señora de Guadalupe to save him.

"Diego?"

He turned. "I am going to die here. Already Montez is gone. This fellow was just put here two days ago, he does not need rehabilitation. He is sick. I hear the wheeze, I see his skin turn pink, there must be a fever. I need help, Ms. Storm. By our Holy Lady, you have to help me." His shoulders were heaving as he sucked in air. Was he in cardiac distress?

"Me?"

"I need a priest." The tears flowed freely. "I want to confess. This may be my last chance before I meet my holy God. I have to see a priest."

"Someone calls a priest when the Covids are dying. You don't even have it."

"But I may be dying. He has to come. That is what a priest does. He comes to the sick no matter what. Please, Ms. Storm, help me. You are smart, you can do many things. Do this for me and I will pray for you from the other side."

She nodded and turned. Cheery thought, the other side. Did he have a premonition?

As she returned to her desk, Tera thought hard about a way around the rules. In most places only a designated nurse or administrator made the calls to the archdiocese for a priest to come and anoint a dying Covid victim, so there would be some order in what was done. Order? As if there could be order with a virus killing off twelve people daily around the state. And now a lot of hospitals ignored patient calls for chaplains. It wasn't right, she thought, he wants a priest, he should have one. She pulled out the card she'd thrown into her purse a week ago. St. Raphael's was close.

"Father Tom here."

"Tom, I have a patient here who wants to go to confession. He thinks he's going to die."

"Tera? What do you have to do with this? Usually the Covid calls go from a designated nurse to a diocesan line. I'm called from the archdiocese."

"It's not a Covid, Tom. It's a cardiac guy whose roommate was taken away and died from Covid and now his new roomie seems sick. Diego is ill. He feels like his end is coming and he's very stressed. He wants to confess, and your Spanish is impeccable."

"I don't know if I can just come in, visitations are restricted." He hesitated. "And I need administrative permission to enter quarantine."

"Are you a priest or aren't you? The hell with the rules. Someone needs you."

Another pause. "You know, I might just have to rethink the mean thoughts I've had since I saw you last. Okay, I've cleared my calendar, be there in a few. You'll hear the motorcycle."

The Harley, Tera thought with a slight smile at the summer memories. He may wear a collar but some things never change. She wondered if he still was more likely to throw a punch than talk... no, that wouldn't do. Hastily, she scribbled Diego's name and room number on a Post It, stuck it where Tom would see it, then headed upstairs to check on a couple of patients whose families requested updates.

Someone else heard the motorcycle as it arrived. Garbed in his protective gear, the priest stopped only long enough to pick up the Post It stuck on the Plexiglas at the empty main desk. He was en route down the hall from the entrance when Jan Michelob accosted him.

"What are you doing here?"

"Call for a visitation."

"I didn't call you. You can't come in here unless I okay it. I make the calls."

"You didn't call?" Tom asked, seemingly puzzled. "I received a call for spiritual assistance and I'm answering the call. It doesn't have to be a Covid, you know. I'm here for the salvation of all." He edged around her toward Diego's room.

"Where are you going?"

He nodded toward the room.

"He's not dying."

"Do you know that for an absolute fact?" He stared down at her, in an intimidating way. "I don't think you do. Now get out of my way." The tone was threatening, quite unpriestly. And he was gone, not waiting for an answer.

Thirty-six hours later, Diego had a heart attack and passed away.

CHAPTER 29

Dr. Jolene Richardson steeled herself when she saw the number on her phone. "Hello?"

"Jolie, did they contact you?"

Richardson was in the Ridley dialysis center, patients were waiting for her. She saw Cynthia Langley looking her way. No time to waste.

"I have patients waiting, Loomis. Who are you talking about?"

"The Hamptons. They should have contacted you by now about transferring to Ridley for care, transplant."

"Yes, I received a request for consideration."

"You told them no, didn't you, as we discussed in May?"

"I told them I don't make the decision, it goes to a committee. They usually go to the committee. It meets later today."

"What a joke you are. Stop it."

"I can't do that! You told them to go elsewhere, we're elsewhere. You can't change that the application was made and the committee has it. The official committee decision will have more weight than me just kicking them out."

"You should have told them no, you won't take them. They're a risk to your institution. They're violent, they caused trouble at Ridley too."

Richardson hesitated. What was he talking about, trouble at Ridley?

"Look in the updated medical records that were just transferred to you. It's a red flag if I ever saw one."

He heard a sharp intake of breath. "What did you do?" she hissed.

Laughter. "Don't get your water hot. A true and accurate account of their time at Ridley is in the record, that's all. Now cancel that transplant meeting or do I have to talk to the CEO about all those wonderful articles you didn't write?"

Richardson slammed the phone down and started ruffling through paperwork, but not seeing any of it. I've got to get out of here, she thought. I've got to get away from him. She didn't see Cynthia, the dialysis nurse manager, answer a phone call and turn away, speaking quickly and nodding, then jotting down instructions. Looking over her shoulder, Cynthia smirked and hung up.

❋❋❋

A few hours later, Gwen Deeds was on her way to her first official patient meeting, accompanying Dr. Loomis. What a great deal, she thought, to have an office to herself working directly with a specialty department, not on call for whenever the hospital needed an intervention by a social worker. Dr. Loomis was so gracious and really happy to have her there, he was giving her a special assignment already: the Hampton family. He'd had her call the Midwest Kidney Network and inform them about the May 21 police incident and the behavior plan the parents had to follow. On his recommendation, she'd assured them there was no danger whatsoever for Nick to wait for the kidney transplant evaluation. She'd also received a call from the Dialysis Nurse Manager at Ridley, who gave her a heads-up that Nick would not be allowed into Ridley's transplant program.

As Gwen approached the dialysis center conference room, there seemed to be a discussion going on between Mrs. Hampton and Neil Hawthorne in front of the open door. Neil, of course, was totally the man in charge, wearing a lightweight blue suit, white shirt, and subdued tie. Mrs. Hampton looked downright shabby in jeans and a tee shirt with writing on it.

"There will be no dialysis until we conclude this meeting," Hawthorne was saying.

"What do you have to talk about, we have the behavior plan, we got a letter Friday about not being able to make any appointments here. Another meeting makes no sense."

"Please come into the room, now!"

Callista followed him. Her eyes fell on a woman with a mass of freckles and a pile of red curly hair like Annie just entering the room. It must be that Gwen Deeds person, her name was on the plan. Just another hospital flunkie along to witness them flay her.

"For the record, did you receive the letters and the behavior plan?"

Hawthorne began. His hands were folded before him and she could see his nails were buffed and carefully manicured. Callista wanted to throw up just looking at him playing God.

"Yes." She looked around. For the record? There was no stenographer or recording device in sight.

"You're expected to follow the plan to the letter. If there is any disruptive behavior, you will be removed and someone will be assigned to take care of Nick."

"You can't do that, I'm his parent. You can't just yank some hospital staff member out of an office and have them take care of a kid with kidney failure and cardiac problems. What would you do, put him in foster care?"

"That's my job, Mrs. Hampton," the redhead spoke up. "I'm the social worker for Pediatric Services and I would find a suitable guardian."

"Excuse me? Guardian? What gives you the right to take my kid away because I'm late, maybe my car breaks down or I say a *naughty* word if I twist my ankle."

"I'm a social worker, a mandatory reporter. We have the right to protect your child and see that he gets treatment."

"He *is* getting treatment. But not right now because you're holding him hostage without dialysis while you lecture me. We haven't missed a single appointment here."

"But you have elsewhere. You're not to be trusted."

Callista stared from one to the other. This can't be happening, what are they talking about?

Loomis shifted in his chair, a smug look on his face. Neil's idea about filing a child negligence complaint just might work, he thought. It would lay the groundwork for the hospital getting guardianship and keeping the kid here to insure his continued dialysis. It was tried before in a rehab case but without proof against the family situation, the court turned it down. Yes, we'll create some proof. This could get interesting.

His eyes appraised her carefully. Her arguments weren't bad. She looked good today, except for the black tee shirt with bold yellow letters proclaiming: "You tell 'em I'm coming and hell's coming with me," a quote from the movie, *Tombstone*. Not up to it, he thought. She's right where we want her, desperate. He spoke, "We'll consider transplant evaluation in six months. At that time, we'll schedule needed appointments. Until then, we'll continue dialysis until you find another provider."

Hawthorne got up to leave without so much as a "good day." That left Loomis and the social worker sitting across the table. Loomis pushed over a letter. "This a recap of our conversation today."

Callista glanced at it and stared back at him. "So?"

"Let me be clear about one significant point. If and when we decide to accept Nick into the transplant program, your husband will not be evaluated for a possible match because of his actions."

"You can't do that, he may be a perfect match. Without testing him you might be killing our child!"

Loomis shrugged. "Your husband will not be tested." He pushed back his chair and waited for Callista to leave the room.

I am going to go out of my mind, Callista thought as she entered the dialysis bay. I can't take this anymore. I just hope Mark recorded that meeting. Loomis' words kept replaying in her mind, "He won't be tested."

Dialysis was underway. Nick chuckled at the game he was playing on his iPad. He looked up and winked at his mom while the tubes connected to his chest ran his blood out for filtering and back in again. In and out, in and out. Things seemed calm. She stuck her head out of the door of the dialysis room. "I have to go to the restroom."

The guard dragged herself up and accompanied her 20 steps to the restroom across the hallway. Whatever. Why a guard on her with a ten-year-old kid? Why tied to a freaking care plan that could not be violated or the hospital could take him away from his family! Wrong was right and up was down.

Coming out of the restroom she saw a male form in the dialysis room. A bit taller than medium height and not a single hair crowning his head. Damn it! Loomis!

"What are you doing here! You've had your say!" Callista demanded as she slid open the door to the dialysis bay.

He seemed to be at the point of ignoring her, but then turned, slowly, infuriatingly. "I'm a nephrologist, you know, and Dorian is off this week."

"Nick is not your patient," Callista said evenly. "You won't let him into your transplant program so you have nothing to do with him."

The anger was boiling within her.

"But a doctor is supposed to check dialysis progress," Loomis said smoothly as he stared at her. He thought the dark brown hair flowing over her shoulders at this moment rather becoming.

"Yeah, a doctor, but not you." Was that a chuckle she heard as she went toward her purse? Had he gone through it? Nicky's eyes met hers over the iPad. Another wink. She turned.

"And that letter you gave me. What happens if I can't get here, like I get the Covid crap and we can't find anyone who can drop everything and bring Nick here. Can Mark bring Nick down here?"

"Absolutely not. Mark cannot put one foot on this campus or he will be arrested. I'll see to that." Loomis shifted his weight. "Your care plan requires Nick to be here for dialysis at 9:30am on Monday and Thursday. When a third day for dialysis is added, same thing. Period. If you violate this plan, you're out of here. We get someone else to take care of Nick. I don't care what happens, your husband can't come in this building."

Burn in hell, she thought. Don't say anything, don't say anything, her brain told her. Burn. In. Hell.

Her chocolate eyes had turned to blazing lava and she stood before him, intimidating. Anger seemed to radiate around her in an aura. He thought he could hear her voice.

"Are you threatening me?" he demanded, his voice a little too loud. The dialysis nurse turned slightly toward them. Maybe I guessed wrong, he thought, both together were a *force majeure*, but she was quite explosive.

"My lips aren't moving," Callista rasped. "I have said nothing to you." Burn in hell!

Loomis glared at her. The silence drew out, then he turned and left, heading down the corridor to the elevators up to the nephrology offices. A few minutes later, he opened the door, almost in relief. Then he saw someone there, a woman standing by the empty administrative desk.

"Who are you and what do you want?" he demanded.

She turned slowly and flicked her ID badge toward him. "Storm. I'm the new admin for your office from Elite."

He shook his head as if to clear it. She seemed familiar somehow. Above medium height, short curly black hair, well turned out in a maroon suede jacket and nicely fitting pants. Real nicely fitting pants. Around 30.

"You're out of uniform! If you're from Elite, you know better. How long have you worked here?" he demanded.

"Three years."

It annoyed him, and she had these eerie blue eyes that you could see through. Three years, that wasn't long enough to be assigned to this department, he thought. I wonder who she slept with to get promoted....

"No one."

Loomis blinked and took a step back. Did I say that aloud, he wondered.

"I said there was no one else who was qualified to work here. They gave the opening in your office to Elite to see if someone can manage to stay longer than three months. That's why I was sent here."

"You think you know anything?" with just an edge to his voice. This day was getting confrontational on too many levels.

"You'll find out," she said calmly. "Is this mine?" pointing to the mahogany desk guarding the hall to the offices. She didn't wait for an answer, just set down her tiny purse and then, turning toward him, asked, "What do you have for me to do, Doctor?"

A slight note of insolence in her voice?

Loomis went toward his office without answering.

Tera watched him stride away. She'd seen him taking in the goods from top to bottom. That may be a way to get to him, she thought. Anything to force him to make a mistake. Let the games begin.

CHAPTER 30

The letters came about transplant. It was a one-two punch right to the gut.

Holcome International Medical Center

June 9, 2020

Dear Guardian of Nicholas Hampton:

Dr. Loomis identified your child as a potential candidate for kidney transplantation, with a diagnosis of unknown kidney disease (unspecified injury to unspecified kidney).This letter is to inform you that your child's case was discussed at the Multidisciplinary Kidney/Pancreas Transplant Selection Conference on Tuesday, June 9, 2020. The consensus of the Selection Committee was that there is an outstanding issue and because of this your child's case has been deferred from being approved as a candidate for kidney transplant. The outstanding issue is <u>social concerns.</u> At this time your child does not meet listing requirements. Your child's case will be reviewed at a Multidisciplinary Kidney/Pancreas Selection Conference in six months.

We thank you for placing your trust for your child's care with Holcome International Medical Center and we look forward to working with you.

Johnson Biggs, M.D., Holcome Center for Transplantation

Ridley Children's Care

June 10, 2020

RE: Nicholas Hampton

Dear Mr. and Mrs. Hampton,

The Pediatric Kidney Transplant Multidisciplinary Team met on 6/8/20 to review Nick's medical history and your request for kidney transplant evaluation. At this time, we are unable to offer an evaluation for kidney transplant or a return to our dialysis unit for dialysis therapy. The matter will be reconsidered in two months.

Jolene Richardson, M.D.
Director, Pediatric Nephrology

Mark had questions for these big shots dangling Nick's life by a thread. He requested information from Holcome Patient Liaison as to which doctors attended the transplant conference. He wanted to talk with them and find out if they really made this decision or if it was made for them. As for Dr. Richardson, he'd left so many messages, he was sure her inbox was full.

***

Sienna flounced down on a chair on the end of the table. "I am *so* bored. This is going to be such a lousy summer! No driver's ed because of the *virus*, no sports, no Fourth of July fireworks, did you see that in the paper? Everything cancelled! I want to get out of here! Can we go somewhere in the RV? Run away from home?"

"Much as I would like to," Callista said, "we can't. The campgrounds are closed because of Covid. Besides, I don't think your father is up to driving that big RV anywhere, and I can't drive his truck, it's a manual transmission. My truck can't haul trailers. Besides, we've been told Nick now has to report to Holcome three times a week for dialysis or else."

"Or else what?"

"They appoint a guardian to take over his care."

"You mean put him in foster care?" She laughed. "Go for it, maybe the rest of us can have a life then." She got up and headed for the stairs. "Only kidding. Haha"

"Was she?" Mark asked.

Two days later, while Callista was working in the kitchen preparing the evening meal, weighing and measuring everything Nick would consume, Mark announced the requested insurance invoices arrived. He told her they showed all dates for dialysis had been paid in full, not a missing appointment date among them, verifying that the report of missing appointment times was a blatant lie in the Holcome records. The bottom line, however, was chilling. Each month, Holcome International Medical Center received $100,000 in payment just for dialysis services. The doctor consultation fees were extra. Even the time for those nasty meetings with the administration about the "incident" had been paid in full!

"Your mom said there could be fraud," Mark said, "keeping him on this more expensive dialysis so Holcome can make a buck. File a complaint and ask for an investigation."

She'd dropped her measuring cup, spilling flour all over the counter on the kitchen center island. Callista stared at him. $100,000 a month for everyone in there? Was that what she heard those nurses talking about, if they get to 100 patients, do they get a bonus? She'd overheard the conversation going on in the room behind the dialysis manager station, how they were up to 60 patients. One nurse laughed about the bonus and said, "I don't know, we've never gotten that many. The trick is in keeping them so our numbers are steady."

How do you keep a dialysis patient, Callista thought. Didn't they either get better or get a kidney? Or, God forbid, die? If what Mark said was true, that would be millions of dollars if they somehow kept the status quo, keeping the patients on dialysis.

"Oh yeah," she replied. "I'm on it."

CHAPTER 31

Only a week left in June and how many more to go for the summer? Callista didn't want to think about that. It was awful adding another driving day to her schedule, three days of dialysis meant 600 miles of driving each week. Nick was dozing on the bed while dialysis filtered his blood. Callista was in that before sleep restless stage, body saying yes and brain saying no. They were in the first room of the pediatric dialysis section. Two small children were newly assigned to dialysis, in rooms down the next hallway. Was it from Covid? Was it from too many heart surgeries like Nick? Or just born that way? She didn't feel like asking. Things were getting her down without someone else's depressing details. But the nurses would be happy, more patients toward their precious goal.

She watched as Nick's eyes fluttered open. As he glanced over toward the nurse station, she saw his blue eyes suddenly bug out, his jaw drop. The guard in the corner turned her head and was staring as well.

What the heck? Callista got up as though to go to the restroom so she could see whatever was causing the stares.

It was a woman, very tight black pants, a black, sort of lacy top, the jagged sides flowing down past her thighs and just enough cleavage showing up top to make it interesting. Four-inch heels. She handed a paper to the dialysis manager and stared him down as he met her eyes and then began fumbling hurriedly at his desk. An executive, Callista thought, the worst kind, a woman with an attitude, ready to grind down anyone in her way. Power to burn flowed around her in an aura from her heels to her black curly hair with blonde streaks. Callista blinked. She looked quickly at Nick who opened his mouth to speak, and she shook her head. He mouthed, "Tera."

Callista looked back, her little sister? Tight jeans and tee-shirted

Tera? Dressed and acting like an executive woman with total power, who could decide who lived or died? What was she doing in the dialysis center? Only people directly concerned were allowed inside the secured doors. She must be working in this department, then. Is this the mysterious job she has, she wondered. Nephrology. Then it hit her. Oh, God, she's working for the enemy, Dr. Loomis! She ducked back into the room and realized her heart was pounding and she was dizzy. What the hell was Tera doing here, at Holcome? What was she doing working for that son of a bitch?

❅❅❅

Tera moved easily through the ER parking lot toward the ramp and her car. The downside of being in the ramp again was having to watch out for Dumb and Dumber, Dave and Kenny. She shifted the clothing bag to her other arm and searched for her keys. Better to stash the power suit and briefcase with papers during the mid-afternoon break time than in front of other employees leaving for the day. Up ahead she could see a vaguely familiar white truck. As she got closer she saw the broken heart emblem on the back window. Was that Callista's white truck? Both her truck and the Ford Escape sported the broken heart emblem. What was she doing here? Dialysis was Monday and Thursday, not Wednesday.

"Stop right there! What the hell are you doing here?"

Tera turned to confront Callista ten feet behind her, Nicky running to catch up.

"I work here."

"You work for *him*! That ugly bastard who's refused to list Nick for transplant, who almost killed him with that high blood pressure last December. You work for that son of a bitch?"

"I just started two weeks ago."

"And you should have quit as soon as you heard his name. You *know* this! You *know* he's the bastard who's out to get us, who's tied Nick to this crappy dialysis program, who's ruining my family! You know this and you still work for him! That makes you just as bad as he is." Callista was so angry tears were flowing down her face and she was shuddering in anger. "I hate you."

"Mom!" Nick was pulling on her arm. "Stop it! You're being mean!"

"Look at her, Nick, the aunt you love so much! She's working for that guy who damn near killed you."

"I can explain," Tera started. "You've got to believe me, I've had nothing to do with what's happened to you. I...."

"Do you think I would ever believe you? You've always lied to cover your tracks, always up to something behind our backs. You're a liar and cheat, and if your husband left you, that's why. You never should have come back home, no one needs you here, no one wants you here, especially if you're working for Loomis."

Nick was close to tears, "Mom, stop it."

"Look at her, Nick, dressed all nice now, but a regular slut when she came into the dialysis center, dressed just right so the guys could see plenty." She was breathing hard, consumed with overwhelming anger. "You're disgusting, Teresa, and I hate you, I never want to see you ever again. You're *dead* to me." She lunged forward and gave Tera a powerful shove. The briefcase and clothing bag went flying.

"Moooommm!" Nick wailed.

"Get in the truck, Nick. Don't bother to say good-bye. She doesn't exist anymore." Callista opened the doors to let him in the back seat, then swung up behind the wheel. From her vantage point, she gave a last stare at her sister. Sister? No more.

❊❊❊

Tera had no idea how the rest of the afternoon passed. She sat at her desk with her eyes straight ahead. It was Wednesday, late start, which is why she'd gotten away with the trip to the dialysis center to pick up certain records that morning, certain records pertaining to the events for the week of May 18, including the events of May 21. People always complied when confronted with a show of power. How bad was it that Callista and Nick had a different dialysis schedule and saw her. Why didn't anyone tell her it was Monday, Wednesday and Friday now? But then, why would they? Why would they think she cared? She hadn't been a part of their lives for so long, she'd become a nonentity, a nothing.

Loomis was busy in his office or on the phone with Gwennie, his new pet ever at his side. Gwennie fawned over him like he was the very sun that rose in the morning, the stupid suck up, Tera thought. More than once she appeared disheveled leaving his private office. Fun and games and a little booze in your favorite doctor's office. Tera knew about the refrigerated booze hideaway. Loomis was late on Wednesday when he was in Wisconsin, and Monday, when he sort of made rounds. She'd had plenty of time to look the place over, especially to find the back door through the conference room. It was an exit in case of fire, but also served to be a handy entrance for people who didn't want to be seen. She hoped it was only a matter of time before someone would show up.

Tera didn't remember getting back to the Mustang or even hitting the freeway. Callista's voice rang in her ears over and over. I am just trying to help and the best way to do that is from the inside, she thought. I have to trap him, but I can't tell her.

Flashing blue and red lights appeared in the rear view mirror. Oh God, she groaned, looking at the speedometer. She downshifted as she pulled over, thinking 25 miles over the speed limit was not going to go down well.

A pleasant-looking young man arrived at the window.

"Good afternoon, ma'am. Do you know why I wanted you to stop?"

"No officer," she said. A classmate had told everyone to admit nothing if they ever got stopped by a cop; the gang from Aquinas knew every trick to stay ahead of the law.

"Ma'am, you were going a good amount over the posted speed limit. Do you have your license?"

Her purse and briefcase were lying on the floor of the passenger side where she'd thrown them and the purse latch must have broken because the contents were scattered all over.

"Yes, officer. Everything fell, if you don't mind, I'll just reach over." She grasped an ID and handed it over, then realized it was her hospital ID, not license. "Excuse me, that's the wrong...."

"You work at Holcome, Ms. Storm?"

"Yes, if you hang on, I'll...."

"No need. I'm not going to write this up. You people are heroes. You all there are doing tremendous work against this virus and pandemic. You must be headed home. I just urge you to be driving a bit more slowly." He tipped his pointed hat and walked back to the maroon squad car.

Her head on the steering wheel, Tera felt the first tears coming.

Hours later, she was curled up in an oversize lawn chair on the deck, a black frosted tumbler of vodka in hand. It was dark, the moon shone on the lake, the nocturnal insects were playing their merry tunes and water lapped against the rocks on the shore. Three years ago, when we got back here, I had everything I ever wanted, she thought. Everything. Back with family, a loving husband, a good future ahead of us. The large house on the lake was an unexpected bonus, an inheritance of sorts. Now, it was basically empty. She poured more liquor into the glass, the waterfall of liquid knocking the ice cubes noisily into each other.

And now, it's all gone. I've lost everything, she thought as she drank deeply. A big empty house and nothing else. My only sister, her kids, my husband....The honey in the Smirnoff smoothed out the alcohol taste, eased the sense of loss somewhat. Absently, she poured more into the tumbler. Everything's gone. Now what, she asked herself, staring over the lake.

CHAPTER 32

"Indiana Jones" again. Tera felt paralyzed, her eyes fused shut. She couldn't move. Where was she? Still outside? Didn't smell like outside. She forced the eyes open, definitely a mistake, the room whirled around and around and her stomach was very queasy. The noise stopped, then it started again. The ringtone was too loud; she found the phone by her pillow and slid her finger over the answer icon.

"Teresa?"

"Ummm."

A pause. "Is everything all right?"

She didn't answer. She felt like she was hardly breathing, and so cold! She tried to feel for her heart, still in uniform? Shoes still on her feet? Why? God, I must be dying, it's so hard to breathe, I feel so weak.

"Have you been drinking?"

"May...be." The mouth didn't want to work and the stomach was roiling.

"Good God, woman, you can't do that. There's work to do, you have to keep at it."

"Shut up, C...Craig Livesey, I'm not a f...f...fucking m...medical student."

"And I am not in a fucking lecture hall. There is a pandemic raging around us, the Prime Minister nearly died two months ago. This is dead serious here and there. You have a job to do."

Silence.

"Are you there? Do you hear me? You have to keep at it, a drunken binge isn't going to help anything, you stupid woman!"

The phone fell from her hand. What's "it" she thought. Why does he keep calling me, who is Craig Livesey to me anyway? The room was going around again. It was better with her eyes closed.

But sleep wouldn't come. Her memories drifted in and out in her stupor, like a dream sequence, but she knew it was a past reality. Was it eight years ago, the argument at the airport? Research for her dissertation in mathematics. She had a grant to gather data from epidemic locations and met up with a WHO group bound for Uganda but had no idea he was in charge of it; he was the last person she wanted to see, their previous working relationship destroyed by his drunken behavior. Ugly, ugly, ugly, he was hell bent on blocking her from the trip, but couldn't, she wasn't affiliated with the School of Public Health. So many bad things said, and they'd forgotten the students were multi-lingual.

She shook her head, remembering afterwards, a small room in the back of the treatment cottage. Craig looked somewhat comfortable, slouched on the narrow bed, a red leatherbound book braced on one leg, with the other stretched out on the blanket. He was wearing khaki cargo shorts and a blue scrubs shirt. Vivid blue, even now an intense memory:

"What are you doing here," he'd demanded. "These are my private quarters and my private time. Get out."

"It's been a week now, I have a couple of ideas about your data and how to gather it, if you're interested. It would probably make your goals clearer to the students."

"My goals? You have no clue what my goals are, what the purpose of this venture is."

"You gave them a syllabus, posted online. I would be an idiot if I hadn't prepared for this trip." Except she'd missed the name of the doctor taking the group to study a post-epidemic situation.

No acknowledgment whatsoever from him that she'd even spoken. "And I just wanted to apologize for...for the scene at the airport. You make me so angry sometimes." She hesitated a bit. "I did leave London, a year ago. My sister had a baby, a little boy, Nick. Chubby cheeks and blue eyes. Cute. And then at a check-up they found a heart murmur."

She remembered finally having his attention, his dark brown eyes fully focused on her.

"And?"

"He had to have open heart surgery. He'd made it to 10 months without anyone finding out he was missing a pulmonary artery, arterial atresia, a missing valve...it was so scary. No one could figure out how he stayed alive missing so many critical pieces."

Craig sat up and put the book aside. "Surgery where?" He ran a hand through his hair, a nervous gesture she knew well. What's he bothered about, she thought.

"At Holcome International Medical Center."

He nodded, the world knew of Holcome and its cardiology advances. "Good, good. And the outcome?"

"He needed another surgery six months later. I was in the waiting room with them, part way through it, the doctor sent a message that there was bleeding into the lungs and he didn't think they could stop it. I cannot imagine what it's like to be a parent and have to sit hours and hours and wait for a surgeon to give you life or death news." Her voice broke slightly. "But Nick came through it." She looked at Craig directly. "Is that why you teach? So you don't have to tell people bad news?"

"No,...not exactly," but she knew by his hesitation that he was lying as soon as the words were out of his mouth. Dealing with patients and their families would surely involve contact he did not want to make. She was surprised he was involved with the students enough to lead a trip into their field of study. As long as she'd known him, even that crazy year he'd spent at Aquinas, he'd avoided almost all emotional investment. Almost all....

The book fell as he moved next to her. "What are you doing here?" he asked, taking her hands in his. "You should be back in the States, helping out, just being there would be an encouragement to your sister."

"I wanted to, I wanted to be there with my family, but I just didn't fit in. Once I chose this path, the doctorate, teaching, doing it *here*, I guess I cut myself off from them. Life went on without me and I'm on the outside looking in, totally alone. It's a curse to have a gift," she said desperately. "A curse and I hate it. I don't belong anywhere."

She captured his brown eyes and stared at him. "You must know what I'm talking about, Craig Livesey. You must have the same feelings somewhere inside of you where you hide everything. You're on the outside, too. You're only 26, you don't just get to be a doctor, write, and hold down a major teaching position – there's a cost to it and it just sucks your life away."

Vaguely, so very vaguely, she'd seen pain in his eyes. Whatever wall he'd built around his soul seemed to have cracked, the icy professor had disappeared, suddenly revealing a vulnerability that frightened her. He put his arm around her and then slowly pulled her close, his warmth surrounding her. "I know exactly what you're saying." And then, hesitantly, he kissed her gently. "But you needn't feel alone anymore."

Tera felt herself drifting away from the past as her body started slipping toward a numbed sleep. We've been together ever since, she thought. It was like finding the missing piece of a puzzle, we completed each other. And where has that gotten me? She groaned as she tried to turn over in the bed and get some covering to allay the deep cold she felt. Not alone, he'd said. I'm sure as hell alone now. The son of a bitch, I love him and at the same time, I hate him.

CHAPTER 33

Mark stood at his computer in his home office flipping through newly arrived mail. Ah, something good. One thing on the never-ending checklist surrounding their life now could be eliminated. He picked up the letter and brought it to the kitchen.

"Thought you'd like to hear this," he said. "It looks like our complaint has gone on to the Medical Review department at the insurance company to determine if there will be a full investigation of Nick's case. They have six months to decide."

"Yes!" Callista exclaimed as he began to read the short missive granting approval to the review. They were interrupted by Mark's phone.

"Hampton." He listened a minute. "Okay, let me put you on speaker." He warily looked at Callista, his facial expression had turned in an instant.

"This is James Meng. Am I speaking with Mr. and Mrs. Hampton?"

"Yes." Callista and Mark looked at each other. Meng? Who...?

"I am a county social worker tasked with investigation of complaints of child neglect. A significant complaint has been filed against both of you, charging neglect of your son, Nicholas M. Hampton."

"What!"

"A complaint has been filed with the county against you, and because of the nature of the charges and health condition of the child, I must meet with you within five days to assess the situation. When will it be convenient...."

"Who the hell did this?" Mark demanded. He let his breath out noisily. One more obstacle in trying to establish a normal life in their household.

"I am not allowed to tell you that information," the voice on the phone said. "If you could let me know when would be a good time...."

"Are the names of Dr. Charles Loomis or Gwen Deeds on this complaint?" Callista burst in.

"I am not allowed to tell you that information. I have five days to meet with you to assess the situation. Because of Covid protocols, you cannot come to our office. Where is there a suitable place and when is there a suitable time to meet outdoors and masked?"

Callista slipped her hand in Mark's. Where did this come from? How serious was this? What powers did the county have to force them to comply with any action that might be recommended? The meeting was set for the following week, on Tuesday, June 30, in the parking lot of the local public library.

"It's got to be Loomis, damn it!" Mark swore after the conversation finished. "What the hell is he doing?" He looked at Callista. "You don't think your beat-up face after you got smacked with the soccer ball had anything to do with this, do you?"

Callie sighed, the raucous backyard game was coming back to haunt her. "I thought my hair covered the bruise. I wasn't there a half hour before that crazy social worker showed up. She was relentless, kept asking Nick if you hit me often. She probably wrote down that he wouldn't answer her because you intimidated all of us. All they had to do was make up some story and report it."

❋❋❋

The library was located in the middle of a sorry little strip mall. There was a small area with a couple of tables and chairs for outdoor patrons on the sidewalk and that's where they met.

"Hello, I am James Meng. Mr. and Mrs. Hampton? Where's Nick?" He looked around. A pleasant Asian, he held a clipboard and a recorder.

"Nick had open heart and pulmonary repair surgery last November," Mark stated. "It's 95 degrees out here. Extremes of heat aren't good for him. He's in the air-conditioned Escape."

James looked over. "Ah. No mention was made of his medical complications, only some kidney trouble."

"Then what *was* mentioned," Callista asked boldly. It wasn't just too hot for Nick, the whole situation was too hot in her opinion.

James handed them a list of charges brought by unnamed sources.

Social Services
Covering all of Blaine County

It was reported by a person familiar with the case that
– Parents' extreme behavior and threatening manner is preventing Nick from receiving the best care and options for his medical situation;
– This pattern of behavior has existed at three different medical institutions, including Stanford in California, Ridley Children's Care, and Holcome International Medical Center;
– Reporter states Holcome recommends Nick be transferred to Ridley but Ridley declined to take Nick back because of these behaviors;
– This mandated reporter consulted with the hospital ethics committee for approval in submitting this report;
– Second reporter said transplant evaluation should have happened by now but due to the father's behavior, it was put on hold for 6 months. Nick is not in any danger;
– In June, Mark came into unit without escort and security asked him to leave, he stated he was on the phone with a provider, security told him he had 5 minutes then he needed to leave. Mark continually removed his mask and would not follow directions, tried to go into dialysis bay and shut door, security informed Mark the doors had to stay open, Mark didn't cooperate and began being 'physically assaultive towards security guard.' He was trespassed from hospital, not an option for transplant.

"Sir," Mark began, "if we were a problem at Stanford, why didn't we know about it back then? I have the number of the Vice President in charge of Hospital Operations. I can call her right here and now and ask her. You can ask her. We also have no information from Ridley regarding anything like this. Who made these charges?" Callista kicked him under the table. He glanced down. While most of the written report had black lines where names were redacted, she found one that was missed, and it was all too familiar: Dr. Charles Loomis.

"I can't say."

"You don't have to," Callista broke in. "You missed blanking out a name. Dr. Charles Loomis is behind these charges. He is the doctor who was in charge of Nick's care, but conveniently has refused to even list Nick for a transplant until the so-called transplant committee re-evaluates the risk we present. What has any fake risk we present to do with giving a kid a lifesaving transplant? You should be investigating why he filed a false child neglect report."

James sighed. "I have to speak with Nick, can you bring him out?"

Nick approached wearing dark glasses and matching Dukes of Hazzard shirt, shorts, and mask. Tall for his age, you'd never know he'd been operated on so much.

"Hi, Nick, I'm James Meng."

"Howdy," Nick said. "I'd shake your hand but we can't get that close."

James didn't know if Nick was kidding or not. "Do you know who I am?"

"Yeah, some kind of social worker."

"Do you know what that is?"

"Yeah, you ask a lot of questions."

James laughed. "Do you have any concerns? Are there any problems in your life?"

"Besides wasting my life driving down to Holcome for dialysis? No."

"Mom and dad get along okay?"

"Sure. And so do my brother and sister."

James straightened up, turning to Mark and Callista. "There are other kids in the family?"

"You don't know that? Sure, Nick has an older sister and brother."

"I have to speak with them, can we set up a video meeting? Thursday? I just have to see them and make sure they are all right. Then I have to speak with the principals at Holcome, uh sorry, I mean the reporters. From what I can see, I am going to assess this case as unfounded and close it." He sighed. He saw no neglect problems he was required to report. Quite the opposite. That meant more paperwork to close the case.

At home, Callista attacked the computer, located the official Holcome form, Revocation of Authorization For Viewing Protected Health Information, and with a wicked smile on her face, filled it out, officially barring Charles Loomis from any contact with the Hampton family.

"What's the next move?" Mark asked as he moved his back around, trying to abate the stiffness. "There are two pediatric hospitals in this state and they're in collusion in preventing Nick from even being listed for transplant. We have to go elsewhere."

Callista put her head on his shoulder. "We have to call Harbison in Wisconsin and University of Iowa and ask for evaluation," she said. "They're the next closest major hospitals. We're stuck."

CHAPTER 34

Ellie looked up from the computer to see Paul coming down the stairs.

"My, aren't we color-coordinated," she commented, taking in his gray tee shirt and gray plaid flannel sleep pants. "You're the only one I can think of who would wear flannel on July first." Sometimes, though, the air conditioning made her add an extra blanket to the bed.

"Same thing I wore to bed last night." He was a night owl, she was a morning person. That's how they'd gotten along so well for 45 years.

She stretched and removed her computer glasses. "Got a message from Callie. They met with that child protection guy. He said he was going to close the case, gave them an impression it was a wild goose chase."

"Can he do anything about a frivolous complaint?" Paul asked while punching buttons on the coffee machine.

"Of course not, county employee, they only do one job. I don't even know if passing it on to another department for fraud is part of the job description." She looked at her notes. "Did you know a hospital *can* go to court to request a guardian *ad litem* – temporary – to be appointed for a patient if it is believed that the person making decisions on behalf of an incapacitated person isn't acting in the patient's best interest? I read about it on *Quora* from a couple of years ago."

"Oh, that's not a good thought," Paul said. "Not the way Holcome is setting them up with a neglect complaint and all. I hope they can find a lawyer with enough guts to go after Holcome for all this disorderly conduct stuff and help in a guardianship battle, too. I wouldn't put it past Holcome to fight them if they get a chance to go to Iowa or Harbison for transplant evaluation." He sighed. "A dirty business, that's for sure." He added creamer to the coffee, and after tasting it, started spooning in sugar.

Ellie shook her head. "Nothing is going right for them. How about Rusty down south? Anything good going on down there? Have you heard anything about his plans for the Fourth?"

"He said he's going to Myrtle Beach with the girl's family."

"Myrtle Beach? It'll be crawling with people! Is he nuts or something? Covid!"

"Says he loves the smell of the ocean. And what about our daughters, are they coming over?"

"Something's up," Ellie said as she stood at the breakfast table. "I asked Callie if she was coming over the Fourth, even though we aren't supposed to gather, of course. She didn't say yes or no, just asked if Tera was coming. I called Tera, asked if she was coming over and she asked if Callie was coming. There's something going on, they must have had an argument. And Tera hasn't dropped off any finished paperwork for me to take to the Coalition. She's behind on that. She's hasn't even e-mailed me, off the grid for a couple of weeks."

"What are you working on now?" Paul asked, noting her pad of yellow legal paper on the table. The woman had a desk, but she seldom used it. Yellow paper meant she was taking notes for another news commentary piece.

"Just some notes on the current state of the state," she replied. "This whole thing sucks, this virus thing, people are dying who didn't have to, businesses are shut down. I want to make someone pay for this disaster and I promise you someone *is* going to pay for the grief Callie and Mark are going through. Maybe I'll write a book." He knew her pen could drip acid, but felt no pity for her targets. There was a box upstairs with fan mail and hate mail from her years as an investigative reporter. So be it, he thought. 2020 was turning into a year of tragedy.

※※※

Callista's hands worked the muscles hard. Mark lay on the bed while she pushed and prodded his shoulders and upper back and neck and rubbed in Aspercreme.

"I don't know why I go to the chiropractor," he moaned. "I can't even sit upright for two days afterwards."

"You have to get an MRI. It's been six weeks since those clowns threw you to the floor and you still have little mobility, you can't even turn your neck to the side."

"I should sue the cops for medical costs," he said. "Fat chance of that happening. Covid has shut down the courts, there isn't even a way my disorderly conduct case will be heard in court in Stanton until next year!" In a video hearing, his lawyer pled not guilty to the charges and that was it for 2020. The governor held every aspect of government under his command, it would be months, maybe even a year or more, before things could resume in person, such as court cases, license renewals, and other important aspects needed to keep a state running.

"This back problem is ruining my sex life," he sighed.

Callista snapped his gaudy cartoon print boxers on his back. "Who's got time, I'm always on the road. What do you want to do for the weekend? Mom and Dad asked us over, but I don't want to go, Tera might show up, the bitch."

"You can't go through life hating your only sister." He took her hand as she bent to help him up.

"Watch me." She thought a minute. "There's a car show over in Wisconsin on the Fourth, you want to go there?"

Mark slid on his slippers. "I can't even think of trying it, my back hurts so badly sometimes. Take the kids."

❊❊❊

"Storm! Wait up."

Tera turned as she was about to put keys into the Mustang's car door. "Hey, Rog, you being my guardian angel again?" It was good to see him, a normal human being for a change, without an M.D. and a nasty attitude.

"Haven't seen you since you got back to the main campus. Geez, that was a month ago almost." It was a good lie, he'd been keeping an eye on her almost every day since she'd come back to campus, the thought of Dave and Kenny lurking nearby was reason enough for his watchful eyes. Roger leaned on the car next to hers.

"The important thing is I haven't seen Dave and Kenny," Tera replied.

"Oh, they've been around. Up to no good, I'm afraid." He didn't dare tell her how much no good he'd overheard from their mouths.

"So what's up, any plans for the Fourth?"

"Plans?" Family plans now shot to hell, the answer was straightforward. "No. Stay home, sleep in, read."

"Oh come on, don't you have family? We can still gather in tiny groups," he laughed. "Gotta have admission tickets to come over for burgers."

"This Covid stuff has really screwed over everything. Are we six feet apart?" It was a deft subject change on her part.

He made his move, something he'd wanted to do for months. "You want to get a beer? There's a little place not far from here."

"Are you asking me on a date?" She seemed truly puzzled, but not laughing at the thought.

"Having a beer is a date?" He grabbed her hand and was pleased she didn't pull back. "You need to lighten up." He still knew nothing about her. No LinkedIn, no Facebook, no yearbook alumni information from local schools. You needed a password to see anything online about Aquinas Academy, the private school was only fifty miles away but it turned out private school really meant private. He'd Googled her name, not even a passing reference on Whitepages or Spokeo. Teresa Storm did not exist. And since she was irregular in attendance at the monthly meetings, there was no way to know how long she'd really worked at Holcome.

"No beer," Tera said, her stomach recoiling at the thought of alcohol.

"Maybe not beer, maybe there's a pop machine," he said. "C'mon. It's not far, give me a ride over in your flashy wheels. Let's see who you can run over this time."

She laughed. For the first time in months, it was a genuine laugh. She appraised Roger carefully, there was a powerful look to him, he was pleasant, easy to like; and she was desperate to escape the loneliness that was eating away at her life.

"Okay," she agreed. They were soon out of the ramp and headed toward the river. The Hazel Nut Grille was practically deserted. They sat on a bench facing the river after he'd ordered their drinks at an outdoor kiosk.

"So what are you really doing for the Fourth?"

"Nothing."

"You want to come over? My sister is having a family gathering, just her and her guy, me, and the folks."

"Roger, *family* gatherings. In case you haven't noticed, I'm a little pale to be a member of your family."

"So who cares? Small group, you're part of my group. We can hang out, you know?"

She looked over at him, so honest, and his interest in her not hidden. It would be good not to be alone. "Okay, you win." Where would this go, she wondered, as his arm edged around her. Anything would be better than the nothing she had now.

❊❊❊

Music from *The Bastard*, a new hard-edged rock album, blared out from the DJ stage and over the parking lot, or what could be seen of it under the 100 cars which had proudly shown up that morning in the huge parking lot of Evangelize! Church. Lyrics were not exactly church-appropriate, but no one was really listening. An event! Hoods up, people were in groups, bent over engines, masked and not, distant maybe, it didn't matter. It was a chance to be together with other human beings. Every once in awhile, the announcer would call out a raffle prize winner, or a special event. The heat, the smells, the voices, at last!

"Oh my gosh! Oh my gosh!" Nick yelled, bouncing up and down in his seat. "This is great!" Callista had hardly stopped her white truck when he jumped out of the passenger door.

"Stop right there!" Callista yelled. He did, but danced from one foot to another. "Here are the rules." She turned to Max and Sienna and Trevor. "Meet back here in two hours, in time for the burn-outs." Max, messenger cap atop his head, nodded. He had a briefcase with his sketching pads and pencils: Another car show, another chance to make money. He had his phone for orders, he'd take pictures of a car and provide the sketch within a week. Others wanted their picture done on-site. He was glad to oblige. He'd made $350 at the last show in the fall. He moved off. Sienna and Trevor likely didn't heard a word, they were deep into each other's eyes.

"Hello over there! Did you hear me?"

"Yeah, yeah, two hours. We're going to look for the General Lee."

Their friends Nira and Hanley were likely there and hanging out with their dad's refurbished orange spectacle, complete with the

Confederate flag atop the roof. Just then they heard the Dixie horn and were off. She's growing up too fast, Callista thought, seeing Sienna in a tanktop and shorts so short they were worthy of Daisy Duke. I think I'm missing something here, she thought, a tad puzzled.

Nick's arm yank brought her back to reality. "C'mon, Mom!" It was all she could do to restrain him to a walking run toward the Challenger Club group. And that was only the beginning. They were all there, the Mustangs, the Corvette Club, Challenger Hellcats, even a Porsche or two with a much-revered gleaming black 911 off to the side. Nearby, a gray DeLorean, both doors up in the air, was surrounded by people lined up to have their pictures taken inside of it. The owners were decked out like Marty and Doc, with white hair flying, a scene from *Back to the Future*. A little way down the row the Ghostbusters ambulance greeted spectators, with suited characters sporting weed blowers ready to take on ectoplasm.

Bold food trucks adorned one side of the lot: blue, red – lots of red – and a white truck touting homemade ice cream. A lot of the stuff was Hispanic, taquitos, rancheros, tacos and nachos, plus corn on the cob, a Hot Hog truck with pulled pork sandwiches, and soda and chips. She'd brought a lunch for Nick, there was no way to know the phosphorus and potassium content of every little thing offered to eat. He begged and begged, but she was adamant.

But he was distracted from food now. "I love this stuff!" Nick stopped at each car and spoke with the owners. He was a familiar character at shows, and well able to discuss the capabilities of engine power.

"Hey, Nick! Heard your surgery was a success!" "Nick, you look great!"

He was in his element, even with the ends of his dialysis threads clunking like a wooden wind chime as he moved. Occasionally he lifted his shirt and showed off his scars. More than one adult turned away from seeing a ten-year-old so drastically cut up by surgeries. Tears were openly shed in a few cases.

Then he saw it! A pink Lamborghini. He was off.

"Nick!" Callista yelled, taking off after him, the dark hair in its high ponytail flying out behind her. She was wearing a tank top and shorts and sported oversize dark glasses. More than one head turned as she went after him, ignoring the catcalls. Nick was shaking the owner's hand and talking away when she got there. Again the Dixie horn. Closer. She looked around and saw a crowd as usual around the General Lee just a row over. Calista moved over to get a better look.

Oh my God, oh my God! Sienna was draped across the hood wearing a small bikini top and Max was sketching her! Trevor was taking pictures. Hanley and Nira appeared to be taking orders for the photos!

"Sienna Marie!" Callista screamed. "Sienna!" No one heard her. She started to go when Nick began pulling at her arm.

"Mom, he wants to take me for a ride. I'm going to go with him!"

"Who is taking you? You don't ride with strangers, Nick!"

"Mom! I've got to do this! He said he's gonna leave soon." He had her arm and pulled. "Come on! He said you could come."

She looked from her eldest child to her youngest helplessly. I can't do this! As he dragged her along, she tried to figure out where the greatest danger existed.

No one was happy by the time the day ended.

CHAPTER 35

He saw her lounging back in her chair, legs crossed and staring down at her phone. Dark glasses again like a couple of weeks ago and then, for sure, it had been from an alcohol binge. He knew the signs well enough, his wife Jeannette was a drunken bitch. Loomis shook his head. Didn't think Storm would binge again so soon, must be a real drunk, he thought. I'm going to nail her – great way to start the week. He was at her desk in three seconds.

"Storm! You know better than to use office time for personal matters."

There was no startled jump or gasp. She simply turned to face him. "I'm sorry, it won't happen again."

"And what's with the glasses? Eye problem again?" He was very sarcastic. "Or hiding something?"

"Personal questions are inappropriate. But if you must know, I lost my contacts." She swept off the glasses and the eerie transparent blue eyes met his insect eyes in a frigid glare. She knew the color anomaly could creep people out. Who better to annoy? And he could plainly see there was no sign of bloodshot or puffiness this time. No sign of the heavy drinking that could've killed her two weeks before.

"Do you want to see the prescription?" Tera asked. He'd been put off his venomous diatribe last time when she produced a medical letter – forged, of course – about her "eye condition." Would he be stupid enough to ask for more proof? He'd been taken aback by the name of the ophthalmic surgeon she'd allegedly seen, a media darling, braggart, a top man in his field – and also a former Aquinas classmate.

Loomis glared at her. Cold as steel, he thought, "I'm going to write you up. Harris will probably like more strikes against you. I understand you got kicked out of your last assignment. Michelob had nothing good to say about you, especially since a patient disappeared on your watch."

"I'm not responsible for what happens after hours." Dodgeball had sent her flowers to thank her for his escape. She stared at Loomis, not hostile, just a straight-on stare, like a game of chicken. Who would blink first?

He turned and went to his office.

Tera folded up the glasses and put them into her purse. She didn't wear contacts.

✷✷✷

The next day was Wisconsin Wednesday. Loomis was gone for consultation at the small Wisconsin affiliate of Holcome International. Gwennie was out of the office and Dorian was in pediatrics, dealing with the family of yet another child brought in with Multi Inflammatory Syndrome – Covid. Tera sank down into the chair of the mighty Dr. Charles Loomis – huge, and with enough cushion that she felt almost dwarfed. The light from the windows was enough to see what she'd come for in that huge office at the end of the hallway.

The wall of file cabinets, the hum of the refrigerated unit, the brag wall, the very large window opening to an excellent view of the city, all to be expected for a department head, along with the glass and chrome desk. Surprisingly, no personal pictures around, the stuff that lets people know you're a real human being. She opened the center drawer carefully: the usual items, silver engraved pens – Mont Blanc, no less – clips, a folder or two. Taking those out, she peeked inside to see weekly schedules downloaded off the portal. Carefully she looked over each piece and the back, and inside of the folder. His computer password would be handy and it would be written down. With a system that required password changes every few weeks for security, no one could remember random upper and lower case letters, numbers, and special symbols. It would be on his phone, of course, but a back-up would be hidden in the desk. Pictures fell out of the other folder.

The first was of the whole family, wife shorter than the master, smile a little off, a little puffy-looking around the eyes, wearing a slinky black dress accented by an exquisite gold and diamond choker with a matching tennis bracelet. Nice. Loomis was in a navy suit with silver threads, all spiffy, that thing on his face a smile Tera had never seen. Teeth weren't clenched either. And the boys, twins. She looked at the back, ah yes, a picture for the local church directory from a couple of years ago. Church? Seriously? The other picture was of the boys, unfortunately duplicates of Loomis only with full heads of brown neatly trimmed private-school hair. They looked about 16-17. And there, on the back at the very bottom was a weird collection of random upper and lower case letters, numbers, and special symbols. She took a picture with her phone.

Carefully, her gloved hand felt around inside the drawer. There was nothing else.

The two large drawers to the right side must be inconvenient, she thought, he was left-handed. The top had hanging files, papers sitting perfectly inside. She skimmed the titles, opening one or two: blank stationary; hospital policy information; pediatric staff backgrounds, which really should be locked in a file, not available in a desk any prowler could read. Hers contained only hiring information from Holcome and a copy of the contract, the same with Dorian and Dr. Kadajh, with the latter's end-of-service date. There was an empty folder for Gwen Deeds. She was empty, all right, Tera thought. Beyond that, toward the back, she saw a yellow pad of paper, some blank postcards, and envelopes.

She'd just slid open the bottom drawer when she heard the click of a door. It was a rather awkward position to be in, poised over the bottom drawer of the head doctor's desk. Footsteps. A door opened and closed. It was Dr. Place. Loomis usually kept his door closed and without a glimmer of light, there was nothing to attract any attention. She was safe.

The bottom drawer was a mess, papers were strewn all over on the bottom. She took a photograph of the layout and then began removing things carefully, one by one. Interesting, all were labeled Nick Hampton. And beneath the mess were two Tracfone cells, one red, one blue. She didn't touch those, snapped a picture of them and then sat back and began to read.

Ethics Advisory Board Consult Note June 23, 2020
Topics for Consideration

Parents are continuing dialysis and medications, but have formed hostile relationship with medical team at multiple centers, family has severed ties with multiple other centers

Aggressive behavior at Holcome, behavior plan in place since January 2020

Have been turned down for transfer to Ridley because of parent behavior

Previous interactions with social work and child psych share concerns for demonstrated aggressive tones/stances with staff and described as "volatile, angry and verbally aggressive"

Claims moving forward with transplant eval has been interrupted due to behavior by parents which is negatively impacting Nick's care

Claims current "parental behavior" will impact success of transplanted graft; set behavioral plan for 6 months, then resume eval process potentially

No concern about care parents give to Nick outside hospital

"Summary of ethical issues" – It is the obligation of the state to protect vulnerable populations, specifically of children. If the minor child is placed in danger or harmed due to parental decisions, it is the obligation of care providers to act on any concern/suspicion for neglect or maltreatment. "There is concern that Nick is being harmed by not proceeding with transplant evaluation due to aggressive and violent behavior demonstrated by parents"; plan to report to local authorities; "should not be misinterpreted as a lack of concern or support for parents."

There were no signatures on the document. Were these notes for the meeting or from the meeting? Or made up? The page seemed to be presentation notes, except for the summary; no internal consistency: no problems about care, yet plan to report to local authorities. Report for what? Who was making claims which were listed, Tera wondered. Ellie had passed on the child protection complaint, all on alleged parental neglect, and more than once saying Nick was in no danger by a delayed evaluation, but the Ethics Summary in front of her seemed to say he was being harmed by not proceeding. Parental behavior will impact success, the report said, but they had messages and a written report from Dr. Place about their care for Nick being outstanding.

The next page was absolutely chilling, especially the beginning portion on likelihood of transplant:

Preliminary testing reveals high antibody load (nearly 100% PRA) = high risk transplant, 92% graft survival rate at 1 year with complications, 5+ year wait

Callista and Mark absolutely did not know about the five-plus year wait. They were told by the end of summer. What a lie! And then Mark was thrown out and all was delayed. Was that a way out of a fake promise? Five years! Jesus, I would give that kid one of my kidneys today if I could, she thought. But without the evaluation and marker testing for compatibility, no one could even think about helping. Nick was stuck *in situ*. She paused over two pages from Ridley dated the same day, same signature, but different accounts of the same occurrence at the hospital in February. Which was correct?

Tera went through paper after paper, then saw a copy of the recent missive from Callista to Patient Liaison. What was that doing in here, it would've been on the message portal and certainly not addressed to him. Then she saw scribbled notes on the sides of what looked like an official report to county child protection.

Glancing at her watch, Tera realized it was getting late, no more today. She quickly scanned all the papers with her phone and was carefully replacing every page back in the drawer when a Post It drifted out of the stack of paper, a memo saying to contact someone named Patrice in the Medical Information department. She pocketed it. And there, off to the side, the form for revocation of access against Loomis from Callie. Oh God, Callie didn't sign it! Hurriedly Tera copied it and put the original back. She could still get that revocation back to Callie and Mark for a signature in the afternoon mail.

Half an hour later, Loomis was through the outer office at warp speed, not so much as a glance at Tera. He made it to his bookcase and opened a cabinet for a glass. Then the cooler, ice, and the Grey Goose vodka. He hated having these office hours in Wisconsin. Annoying drive and Linda O'Brien was a fawning female, always asking what she could do for him. Looking for another payoff, as if what she got for her report to police on the Hampton incident wasn't enough. He eased into his chair and pulled out the folder with his spreadsheets, all nice and neat and....

An odd odor assailed his nostrils. Not unpleasant but oddly familiar. Was someone in here? He jerked open his drawers, one after another. Everything was in place, even in his bottom drawer, but the odor prevailed. He put his head down and looked across the top of his desk, looking for fingerprints, a hair. He got up and looked at his chair for the same. Nothing.

Then, "Storm!" he yelled.

Tera looked up, then around. Seriously, Loomis was yelling from his office? Heart attack? One should be so lucky. She got up, going over in her mind each move she'd made in that office, any mistake that could have been made.

"Yes, doctor?" She walked calmly into the office.

"You've been in here. I can smell your scent."

She didn't blink, but her mind did. Of course, she forgot she was wearing that.

"How many times have I told you never, I mean NEVER set foot in my office, ever! I'll have you fired for this."

There was movement behind her. Loomis could see Dorian come in behind her. He looked even taller, his dark suit making him look like an avenging angel of some sort.

"What are you doing here?"

"I heard you, just wanted to make sure everything was okay."

"It's not okay, this woman doesn't know her boundaries."

"I *was* in here," Tera came forward. "Refilling the sanitizer, the printer paper. And I always use hand sanitizer – my own – before coming in and afterwards, because I wouldn't want to bring any virus particles in your office, sir. I use White Tea and Sage," she drew a sachet from inside her shirt and tossed it lightly on his desk. "Your wife might like it, sir. Bath and Body Works at the Mall."

What the hell? He stared at her, why did she do that? He fixated on the sachet, as if it were a discarded human organ from a surgery, "Why!" he finally rasped.

"It's in the contract you signed, sir, with the Elite Corps." That wasn't what his "why" meant and she knew it. Game time, Tera thought. "We see to everything in office supply. Ask Dr. Place. Ask Ms. Deeds." She caught herself, hearing that aloud made her want to laugh.

Loomis waved her off. She noticed his hand frantically reaching for the glass.

Place was coughing as he backed away. Ms. Deeds, that was a good one. As he went to his office he saw everything she said was true, but there was not even a hint of White Tea and Sage anywhere.

❋❋❋

I'm getting a headache, Tera thought as she parked herself on the bench near the fountain of the inner courtyard of the medical complex, offices on one side, hospital with patients on the other. The courtyard was the only bit of peace in the whole place.

She rubbed her forehead with her knuckles, as if that would help. Now I know there's something going on behind all of this, I know it and there's so much to figure out. She leaned forward and covered her face with her hands.

"Mind if I have a seat?"

"What are you doing here?" she said rudely. "Keep your six feet away."

"I *am* the chaplain, you know. We're allowed in now, no permission needed." Fr. Tom glanced at her as he sat down at the other end of the bench, placing his black bag of sacramentals on the ground. She was a picture of total stress. "Got a call from Pete a couple weeks ago, asking what's up." He stared at the fountain, then faced her. "He recognized the forgery on that letter. You were the best forger at Aquinas. Wanted to know if you were back and/or in trouble."

"It's difficult to explain. Something I've got to think through and I don't even know where to begin. Go away, I'm getting a headache." It was getting worse, and she was starting to take short breaths.

"Ah!" He reached down into his bag and pulled out a red can of Coke. "Maybe you *should* have gotten an eye check."

She almost laughed at that, but it hurt too much. He pulled the tab and handed her the can. "This will help. Part of my supply if I don't have time to eat between sick calls."

"Pete got a call from the doctor himself, demanding to know if he'd treated you. Pete stalled, I mean he didn't know about the name change, and said the usual doctor/patient stuff and he couldn't tell unless he saw what the hell the guy was talking about. You know Pete. He said the son of a bitch emailed him a copy of the letter about your eye condition right then and there. When he saw it was some scam you were running, Pete went on the attack, asking the guy what the hell was wrong with him doubting anything he, the great Cordileone, wrote." Tom chuckled. "So what's going on?"

I'm trying to bring him down, Tera thought. Leave me alone. "It's complicated." She made a move to gather up her purse. "I have to go."

Again, she felt he was staring right through her. "Why'd you run off after school?"

"You broke my heart," she retorted. "I couldn't stand it." She stared at him evenly. The same high cheekbones, close-cropped reddish hair, maybe a hint of an auburn beard starting, she could see it at the edges of his mask. He hasn't changed much, she thought.

"And you broke mine. Do you know how many times I tried to find you? I sent letters, emails. I needed to talk to you. You totally disappeared. Where were you? For the longest time I wasn't sure I was on the right path being in the seminary."

"You're a dumbass. Everyone knew you were headed for the priesthood, except maybe you." It was a lie, no one had seen it coming, least of all her – a gorgeous hunk of a man, she the envy of their classmates – and the deep pain and depression took a long time to resolve.

"You still could have kept contact."

"And feel like I was going to be damned for stealing a priest from the altar?" She shrugged. "I was in Europe, school. Got busy."

"Are you in some kind of trouble?"

She didn't answer. How could she possibly explain how everything in her life was exploding around her?

Then out of the blue. "Have you been faithful to your Baptism?"

Defiant and with no hesitation, "No," she answered. Angry at God for stealing Tom away, she hadn't entered a church for years after their break-up. Things were still iffy on that score since she was dumped again by someone she loved.

"I can fix that."

"Confession? I can't confess to you, I know you too well." She stared at him, the dark blue eyes were dead serious. Always saving others, she thought. Do I need saving? Is this Diego praying for me from the other side? Chilling. After all those years, in all those godforsaken countries, I'm home and *now* I'm alone? Those damned phone calls stopped, Callie won't talk to me, I've got nothing.

"And I know you, Teresa," Tom was saying quietly. "I know your heart. You're in something over your head and you need a lifeline." He took her hand. "Let me help."

CHAPTER 36

"Max! Run out and get the mail." Callista was sitting in the den next to Nick, ready to help him with the English assignment on his laptop. He wasn't in summer school, but she didn't want him to enter the next grade level behind his classmates. She got up when the door slammed and drifted through the kitchen, the cerise roses Mark brought her still held a heavenly smell. He did that now and then, he said he wanted her to feel special. It helped, it really did in this crazy household, that's why she walked through there when she didn't have to.

She met Max in the entryway while he was kicking off his sandals. He handed her the pile of mail and silently went upstairs. The kids were grounded. Well, Nick wasn't. That Fourth of July adventure was too much for her to handle, they were lucky they weren't confined to their rooms with bread and water for a month, they were just confined to home, and no Trevor.

Bills from Holcome, ads, a local newspaper, where was acknowledgment from Iowa or Harbison that the request for transfer of medical information had been received? When called, Iowa said they didn't have it yet. More garbage mail. Ah, letter from James Meng from Child Protection: his report. She moved into Mark's office so they could read it together. The most important part came in the last two paragraphs.

Summary and Recommendations

This family came to the attention of County Child Protection due to a report of neglect – failure to provide medical care. This worker observed Nick. He appeared to be healthy and happy. He interacted with his parents appropriately. This worker met with Mark and Callista regarding the report. Mark stated the hospital is upset with him because he is invested in his son's care and wants the best care possible for him. The family is working with the hospital and following their direction. This worker spoke with Gwen, the social worker at the hospital. She stated the family has been doing better over the last two weeks regarding following the directions of the hospital staff. She also stated Nick is not currently in any danger. In meeting with this family, this worker, along with the SDM tools, assessed the Child as being SAFE in the care of Parents. The risk assessment places the Child at being LOW risk for future maltreatment.

Ongoing Services
This family is not going to receive case management services and there will be no ongoing services provided through Family Assessment. Since this report was assigned for Family Assessment, there will be no determination of maltreatment made. Letters of notification were sent to the family and mandated reporter 07/29/20. The records pertaining to this report will be kept on file for at least five years.

James Meng, Family Assessment Social Worker 07/29/20

"*We're* doing better the last two weeks?" Mark asked. "I wasn't even there."

"Neither was Gwen. How could she write this, she was on vacation. Did he talk to someone else? Wouldn't that be illegal to say you're Gwen when you're not? How would anyone know anything except the spies in dialysis?" Callista shook her head. As she turned away she saw another letter on the floor. From Holcome. It didn't look like a bill. She slit the envelope and pulled out a paper. It was the revocation of authorization for Dr. Loomis, and a green sticky arrow was pointing to where the signature was missing.

"Oh God, did I mess this up. Look."

"Do it! Sign it and get it right back in the mail!"

***

They were seated in the conference room off of Loomis' office. Three of them, maskless, at the big table, six feet apart. Loomis was going over the patient records, checking Dr. Place's notes as if he were a bungling student.

"Why did you recommend peritoneal dialysis? You know with initial cases of kidney trauma we start with hemodialysis. Gwen, you know this case, the Kelly family? What's up with this?"

"The insurance company doesn't want to pay for the more expensive treatment," Dr. Place cut in. "We have rules to follow."

"Then write an exception. Tell them best medical practice calls for hemo and hospital care for awhile."

"But...."

"I can give you a template, Dr. Place," Gwen broke in, "if you've never done this." She sounded so sweet and kind. Dorian shook his head and went back to doodling on the white paper before him. Most of the conversation on individual cases was run of the mill, with comments rattled off by Loomis but nothing of consequence and no notes were taken. No notes, no record in the file of treatment discussions and all the other items that make up patient care. How does he know what the hell he's doing, Dorian wondered.

"Why don't we have Storm in here to take notes?" he asked. "Other providers have the admin in the room for the monthly patient conferences, the stuff that goes into patient records. Seems to me it would be her job to keep track of meetings."

Gwen laughed. "She's busy enough with her little front office. What does she know about anything *we* do?"

Dorian's lips tightened. Probably more than you do, he thought, making a show of looking at his watch. "Uh, I have a meeting in a few minutes. If you'll excuse me...." He got up and headed to the door. What the hell am I doing here, he wondered as he went into his office. He looked around at its files and his desk. I wanted this job. I wanted to get what this place had to offer, the *crème de la crème*. Good for my career. And now I wouldn't want anyone on this earth to know I'm working for this ass. He picked up his briefcase and left the room.

CHAPTER 37

Monday and a late start again. Ivory linen jacket over a red v-neck clingy sweater, shorter pants this time – ivory to match – but the same spikes. This gets old, Tera thought, playing two parts, two names, two lives. Medical Information today. Let's see why there's a stone wall when it comes to the name Hampton.

The department was cubicle heaven, over one hundred little gray stalls with people and their double screens as one entity, only eyes flitting back and forth. There was no movement in the room, only the slight hum of machinery. No one was in the main office area minding the store, so Tera moved over to a lovely young Hispanic woman who was busy sorting paperwork. It was Patrice, the name on one of Loomis' papers. Tera put on the smoky glasses. She wore a white mask with the Holcome logo over her face, only executives wore the white mask.

"May I help you?" Patrice asked.

"Yes, I am from the Department of Hospital Oversight," Tera said, her tone just a notch short of executive-to-peon condescension. "We're conducting an audit of random files to make sure things are caught up, you know requests and transfers and such. It's a spot check. Do you have anything, for example, about anyone named Hampton?" Tera had seen the name among papers on the desk.

"Oh yes, I have some things here." She held up a few papers.

"And what is the disposition of that paperwork?"

Patrice looked puzzled. "You mean, what am I supposed to do with it? These are special. Some of them require social worker or doctor approval for action, you know?"

"Is that customary to require approval?" Tera reached down and picked up the first sheet, the revocation of authorization for viewing patient information for Dr. Loomis, dated July 22. It was the second one, which she'd mailed back to Callie and Mark. She knew they would've put it in the mail within 24 hours. "Or this paper. I see it was signed weeks ago. Why hasn't it been date-stamped and processed? This would be an example of an infraction of requirements that I am looking for, but I'll do you a favor. You're supposed to send these through immediately. If you do that now, I won't write it up."

She watched as Patrice hurriedly scanned and officially filed the revocation. "And I see record transfer requests on your desk. Look at the dates. Over a month delayed. Please scan and send copies of the transfers for those two hospitals to this email," she handed Patrice a card. "I will personally present them to Dr. Loomis for his signature. And I won't write this up either."

Patrice sighed. "Thank you. Thank you so much for helping me. I wouldn't want to lose this job."

So humble and trusting, just the type Loomis would prey on, Tera thought. She turned and saw the maestro of the silent symphony was just returning to her office, but she stopped to observe a few seconds, then came to confront the mysterious interloper talking to one of her peons. Strike first, Tera thought. She removed the glasses.

"Excuse me," Tera said, approaching and flashing her ID from Hospital Oversight. "We are conducting an audit of random files. I want the access keys for the following records." She handed the list to the woman.

"Who are you," the director demanded. "I don't have to hand anything over to you without authorization."

"*I* am your authorization. I'm the Assistant Director of the Department of Hospital Oversight. Look in your directory. See this form, it's on Holcome letterhead and addressed to your attention, Mrs. Kirkpatrick, and is a verifiable request that you cooperate with the audit. We receive federal funds and the feds demand oversight. We have to go through some files thoroughly. Please stop wasting my time."

Mrs. Kirkpatrick stared at the over-confident female storm trooper. "I never heard of this department." She folded her arms over her chest. "I intend to call for...."

Tera whipped out a Holcome staff directory and opened it to a marked page where her picture and that of her imaginary superior were posted. Ellie looked particularly severe in the photo. Office number and phone extensions, e-mails were listed. "Be my guest."

Kirkpatrick looked at the pictures and then up at Tera. She seemed puzzled as if she'd never heard of this department and most likely she hadn't because it was pure invention. Tera hoped Kirkpatrick couldn't smell the distinctive odor of a fresh print job. Then with a disgusted look, Kirkpatrick sat at her desk and clicked her screen alive. She searched for the files, entering codes to gain access. Over her shoulder she asked, "Should I e-mail these to you?"

"Do you really think that's secure in this day of hack or be hacked?" Tera said with an edge of sarcasm. "On paper please, and I am aware that the passwords are a lengthy combination of letters, symbols and numbers, so be careful. I don't want to come back down to this level to reproach you." Tera's steady glare was compelling and the woman began to write on a piece of yellow legal paper.

"I can't give you Hampton. It's got a block on it."

"Excuse me? A block? By whom?"

"The medical provider. None of their records can be released without his signature. A written signature. Not even to themselves. Especially the Miscellaneous file they want," Kirkpatrick chuckled.

Holy hell, that Loomis controls everything, Tera thought. Maybe even those requests Patrice was sending.

"That's not hospital policy," Tera snapped, snatching the yellow paper.

"Providers can do what they want." The tone was arctic. Tera left. It wasn't a total loss, though, a signature might be easy to duplicate, thanks to the calligraphy classes at Aquinas. She imagined Mrs. Kirkpatrick would now be calling some higher-up executive on her, but they'd never find her, not with the name on the ID.

Back upstairs on the fourth floor, Tera stopped in the restroom long enough to shed the linen and don a navy jacket, an optional uniform accoutrement, over the v-neck. She was getting tired of being sniped at for being out of uniform. She quickly changed her pants and shoes. With a glance at her watch, she entered the Pediatric Services office, looking around to make sure they were currently empty and sat easily at her desk. With an eye toward the elevator, she reached down into her briefcase and pulled out her slim Notebook. Logging in, she downloaded the release permission and filled it out. It would just need a signature and then it could go into the hospital intraoffice mail. She doubted there would be any questions. No one in their right mind questioned anything from the office of Dr. Charles Loomis. If these requests required a doctor's signature, they would have one according to the letter of the law. She hit the print icon.

The sound of the elevator doors made her look up. Good God, Loomis was early. And there was some other guy with him, tall, lightly bearded. He and Loomis looked friendly, was he one of the three voices Miranda mentioned? She glanced down, still sending to the printer, so she shut the screen and dropped the Notebook to the floor. Ah, there it was, two pages hanging out of the printer. She quickly went over and grabbed them, barely having time to get them over to her desk. Then she noticed the yellow paper from Medical Information. It was like a beacon in front of her. She carefully folded her hands over it as the door opened.

Loomis was in a hurry toward his office and shot right past her, but the big guy slowed down, raised his eyebrows.

"Hello," he said. "I'm Neil Hawthorne, hospital administrator." He extended his hand. Oh shit, Hawthorne? Related to that sex fiend Dave from the Elites? For sure, he was eyeing her in a very unprofessional manner. They were two from the same mold.

Tera put out her carefully manicured hand. "Pleased to meet you. Is it Doctor or Mister? I'm always being corrected by Dr. Loomis to use the proper form of address."

"Both." Hawthorne laughed at her surprise. "I'm a doctor of hospital administration but not a medical doctor. So I guess that makes me a Mister too."

"Really?" she smiled and then added smoothly, "And which do you prefer or does it depend on the person you're trying to impress?"

His laugh boomed out. "Where did you get this one, Chuck? She's actually got a sense of humor."

For some reason, Loomis was glaring at her, the dirty goat. Fraternizing with his pals, let's dig the knife in some more, Tera thought. "I'm from the Elite Corps," she said. "They thought it best to send one of us to work with Dr. Loomis since regular staff has a high turnover in this office. He's extremely particular in his work requirements and we're trained to work in extraordinary situations."

"And you're out of uniform again, Ms. Storm." That red sweater was really nice, her out of uniforms were...on the edge; he had to make a power move before Neil got hooked any further by her uncommon looks.

She flicked the jacket with its logo at Loomis. "I'll just button up and you won't know the difference."

They disappeared down the little hallway, Neil laughing at Loomis' discomfiture. Tera realized her hands were shaking. She hoped her conversation was enough that the gaudy yellow paper went unnoticed. And Hawthorne was definitely not the one with the deep voice.

"I hate her," Loomis said while Hawthorne went to the bar drawer for the Barr Hill gin and brought out the bottle and two glasses. "You want this or the Grey Goose? Come on, lighten up, Chuck. She's a looker."

"I hate her, I get the feeling she's toying with me, just short of insulting, you know what I mean? Your wife is like that too. She knows damn well she's out of uniform. Extraordinary situations, bullshit. And you fell for it." He was tapping his fingers nonstop on the chrome and glass desk.

Hawthorne took a long drink and sat in the stuffed chair while Loomis opened the Grey Goose, his anger so obvious that he spilled some of the expensive liquor on his desk.

"Why don't you bed her?" The gin had loosened him up and he laughed loudly. But he stopped when he saw Loomis almost sneer. "What's the matter, not your type? Since when?"

"There's something off about all of this."

"So get rid of her. You have a reputation for switching staff every couple of months. What's the problem?"

"She's just too good at the job. Annoying. I'll have to wait a bit longer, there's not even a little chink in the worker bee that I can use to get her out of here."

"Right," Hawthorne was sarcastic. He knew Loomis and didn't understand the hesitancy. "You're enjoying this and you know it. Maybe you want someone with excitement. I hear from Dave there's a real hellcat in the Elite Corps. One of the women rebuffed his overtures." Hawthorne chuckled. "Knocked him on his ass, in fact. And then threatened to run him over in her car. Drives a Mustang, can you believe it?"

"You'd better tame that kid of yours, Neil. We can't keep bailing him out and bribing his prey to shut up. I thought once was enough."

Hawthorne sniffed. "He's got some issues, to put it mildly. He's good at his job here, hard work might straighten him out. Or that gal will. He was hanging out after work, I suppose waiting for her, and she saw him and pulled a gun on him."

Loomis choked on his drink. "Here? At Holcome?" His beady eyes got wide.

"Yeah, in the parking ramp. I don't know if it was real, maybe a plastic toy so it got through security, but he said she held it like a commando and it was aimed below the belt. He feared for his manhood. Says she's been hanging out with a black guy from Elite, built like a football player. Maybe she likes the dark side. He saw them at one of those outdoor patio bars, holding hands...and more."

Loomis was pensive, eyes narrowed. Gutsy move. He couldn't think of anyone he'd ever worked with at the hospital – filled with passive grunts who only did their jobs – who would be that bold. Except....

Hawthorne cleared his throat. Loomis had gone weird, like he was a million miles away. "So let's get down to business," he said. "You know the Hamptons have tried to revoke your access to Nick's medical files."

"What else is new." Loomis sat behind his desk, and running his hand up and down his glass of vodka. He was sick and tired of the Hamptons. He wished they would go away, but Holcome had promised dialysis – nothing else, no treatments whatsoever, but that was enough to put the wife in his dialysis department three times a week. She was a pain in the ass, she knew too much. He should have gotten rid of her instead of the husband, but it was easier to get a guy out on trespass and disorderly conduct than a mother.

"We can stall it, say we have a medical rotation and you're part of that, although Place is listed as his doctor. The deal is they keep at me about the whole situation. Letter after letter. We need to harass them right back. In fact, we need to escalate it. Do you hear me, escalate it!"

"So what do you want to do? They're not stupid."

"I'm creating an Office of Security Oversight...."

"What the hell is that?"

"An office to oversee security," the words held a sarcastic edge, "at the hospital, supposedly on all the campuses, against the likes of

Mark Hampton. The office won't be anywhere else but here but it'll look good on the letterhead. Then they have to bitch to the person there and she can get back in their faces and enact sanctions. I want them beaten down, do you understand me? Totally dependent on our care, unable to get peritoneal dialysis, unable to have time to go to any other hospital because they are scheduled here three times a week." He drained his glass. "If they don't show up, they lose care for the kid. That will prevent them from leaving. We need to keep them here at all costs. The kid needs dialysis and we need the money."

And just down the hall, while Loomis and Hawthorne were guzzling their alcohol, Tera knocked at Dr. Place's door.

"Dr. Place, I just received these requests for records to be sent for Nick Hampton to the University of Wisconsin in Harbison and the University of Iowa. The request is asking for expedited service for these. Oddly, there is a hold on them, requiring a doctor's signature. Would you please take care of this for them?"

"Sure. Why would these require a signature?" he asked as he bent over them and signed, adding Director of Pediatric Dialysis after his name. "So how do you think things will go now that we'll have extra staff to trip over?" He nodded to the extra office. "I just got an email that they might be moving someone in part time to share Gwen's office next Monday."

"We're trained to handle all types of situations, Doctor, all types of people. You know that."

"Doesn't anything bother you, Storm? Not even Charles Loomis leering at you?"

"Leering, sir? I hadn't noticed." Of course she had seen the bastard!

"Give me a break. You're either blind or playing me," he laughed, then glanced at his watch. "I've got to get going. See you tomorrow."

Tera obediently backed out the door, papers in hand. She glanced at her watch. Just enough time to hand deliver them to Medical Information. Kirkpatrick was gone for the day and the closing receptionist had never seen her before and never would again.

CHAPTER 38

Yelling upstairs. Sienna was screaming at Max about something. It was mid-August and school couldn't start soon enough, Callista thought, except what was school? With Covid 19 still around, schools needed to reinvent themselves. The Trent district planned to go into a hybrid mode, each district could create their own definition of hybrid, however. Some considered staggered starts hybrid. For others, classes every other day. Trent was going to be sort of like that, Monday and Wednesday classes in person for the maroon group, Tuesday and Thursday in person classes for the yellow group. The group not in class would participate online. It would work, right? Fridays were left as preparation days for teachers and homework days. Callista was not hopeful.

And then there was Nick. In-person school was not on the horizon for him for this year because of his dialysis schedule. As the opening day approached it was decided the Hamptons had to have a meeting on Zoom with the new principal and a teacher from the special education department who would create accommodations he would need. Meetings and more meetings. Callista and Mark felt stressed out by having to continually explain Nick's squeezed timeframe, the need to remain at home, the need for online learning through Trent's online Academy. It was a clear case of a medical disability, a so-called "other health condition," but it had to be explained over and over because kidney failure wasn't on the little list the state had created for the Department of Education. And with dialysis three days a week – afternoons now – every minute of her spare time was eaten up when she could be using it to keep her household in order.

***

There was just enough light through the huge office window that the overhead light was unnecessary. It was amazing how quiet things were an hour or so early around the offices, traffic in the hallways a mere trickle and the phones dead silent. Tera sat in the huge chair of His Majesty Charles Loomis, and eyed the blue phone and the red phone from the desk's bottom drawer. Now if she had this right, she could remove the SIM card from one and put it into an identical phone. That phone would copy it and retain the information, even after the SIM card was removed and returned to the original phone. Messages and telephone calls could not be made on the clone without carrier service, but they could be saved for future reference. And future reference was all she wanted. She took the red phone, removed the SIM and put it into an identical red Tracfone, then repeated the process with the blue phone. Her copied phones had a piece of tape on them to distinguish them from the parent phones. Who knew what treasures she'd find from this little venture.

After replacing the phones, Tera looked over the drawer again, the same shuffle of printed paper, but wait! She saw a new one with a Ridley letterhead with some scribbles on it and the name Hampton.

Ridley Children's Care

September 1, 2020

Dear Mr. and Mrs. Hampton,
The Pediatric Kidney Transplant multidisciplinary team met on 8/24/20 to review Nick's medical history and your request for kidney transplant evaluation. At this time, we are unable to offer an evaluation for kidney transplant or a return to our dialysis unit for dialysis therapy.

Trust is fundamental for every successful patient and provider relationship. ~~When there is a lack of trust, it hinders the ability to effectively communicate and the ability to deliver care.~~ Due to a breakdown of the therapeutic relationship between your family and our team, we told you in June that we did not think it would be in Nick's best interest to move toward a kidney transplant at the University and Ridley at that time, nor did we offer him dialysis services. In Nick's best interest you should ~~either~~ continue his care at Holcome International Medical Center. ~~or establish care at another institution where you and your family feel that you can establish a relationship of confidence and trust in his care team.~~

Jolene Richardson, M.D.
Director, Pediatric Nephrology
Medical Director, Pediatric Dialysis

What the hell was he doing scribbling on a note from Ridley? Meeting August 24? That date was a week away! And the letter itself to the Hamptons held the date of September first. A future letter? Tera sat back, sick with the realization that Loomis and Gwennie were creating a letter to deny transplant evaluation to Nick, in the name of Ridley Children's Care. On the back of the page was a Post It with a note telling Gwen to send the final version to Cynthia Langley, the dialysis nurse manager of Ridley's Dialysis Center. Was Holcome running Ridley's transplant department? Running Nick's health care no matter where he was?

She heard the click of the outer office door. Quickly she photographed the letter and left the office. They literally bumped into each other in the hallway, she cringed as she felt Loomis sideswipe her, why is he so early, she thought. But Loomis was more aghast than she was at the full body contact. "What the hell are you doing here?" he spluttered, glaring at her so hard it should have hurt his beady little eyes. In fact, he'd been in such a hurry to get to the office, the little tufts of hair by his ears were uncombed and standing on end.

"Checking the supply of toilet paper in the executive restroom." She continued on her way, her disgust leaving her feeling as if hundreds of ants were crawling all over her.

He was taken aback at the answer, and staring at her departing form, suspicion started in the pit of his stomach. He went into his office, none of her annoying scent, he looked at his black computer, nothing there. But he couldn't shake the feeling she was at his very desk. Sickening.

❉❉❉

Awhile later, Mark looked up as his phone pinged. He was balanced on his chair, eyes darting between screen and papers, trying to make sense out of a poor imitation of a security contract. Did working at home during Covid vacuum brains out of people's heads? Then he saw it was a message from Tera. Seriously? Callie blocked her from calls and texts, but Mark didn't have time for that nonsense. He worked when he could, in between forays with medical distractions. Tera never contacted him anyway. Except now.

T: *Mark, this is important.*

M: *What do you want?*

T: *You need to put a block on Gwen Deeds the social worker, don't allow her to access Nick's records. Do it now.*

M: *Why are you butting in? Not your business.*

T: *Thought we all were trying to help Nick.*

M: *You're a lot of help.*

T: *Don't believe all you hear. Don't go A.D.D. on this, do it now.*

M. *Image is everything, right? And yours sucks.*

T: *Be sure you have the right image.*

CHAPTER 39

"Run this by me again, would you? I'm up here on Mondays, Monday mornings for sure, to keep track of the activity of one family?" It was Zora Zane's job to assess situations and this one was unreal and it wasn't just the liquor. Here was a department head obviously cozy with the social worker who worked with him. Totally an off-limits relationship, yet the hospital administrator was guzzling away in the same room and sanctioning it. They were seated in the comfortable chairs in the office, liquor in hand. Captain Zora Zane of the new Office of Security Oversight had been a little surprised at drinking during work hours, but when in Rome do as the Romans do. Loomis relaxed easily on the wider stuffed chair, a glass of Grey Goose in hand. Next to him in the chair without a sheet of paper's width between was Gwen Deeds, the social worker, her Moscato d'Asti in a long-stemmed glass nearly drained. It was her second and her cheeks were rosy. Loomis had his arm around her. Neil Hawthorne, who initiated the meeting, had his gin, and Zora enjoyed a double Johnnie Walker Blue Label.

Clearing her throat, Zora said, "You don't need me to do this."

"Yes, yes we do," Hawthorne said leaning forward. "I'm pissed, you understand. And getting more pissed every day. Every shitting little thing that annoys them they're on the phone, on the portal, bitching at me. Like I'm responsible for billing errors?" He laughed, because he knew he *was* responsible. It was set up for the first of the month, Gretchen in billing would launch another round of harassment. It was a game of you complain, I restrain. "I want to deflect them over to you. Tell them you have full power in all things non-medical. You'll be their only point of contact, and I don't care what you tell them, how you tell them, what you do to retaliate, just get them off my back."

"Are you okay with this?" Zora asked Loomis. No point in asking

Gwen, she was so sauced she'd do a table dance if asked. "They're your patients. This isn't exactly a proper doctor-patient relationship, is it?"

"You do what you're told," Loomis said evenly. "I'm the doctor. And if I decide I want them put down, they get put down. They have this idea they can whine enough that the husband can get reinstated. Like hell."

Zora had read the paperwork about the altercation. None of it made any sense, but it wasn't her investigation. She was here to do what the big guys at Holcome wanted done.

"Come on," Hawthorne said, getting up. "Let me show you to your office. You'll be sharing with Ms. Deeds." He stopped, that had an odd ring to it. He shook his head. "We have a late start on Mondays. You'll be here Monday mornings. The only one here will be the admin. She won't bother you." They entered the spacious entryway.

Tera looked up as the door opened, there was Hawthorne, a little undone, his tie loosened and top button open. He was escorting, or being escorted, by a husky woman with well-done biceps in the gray uniform of the Holcome Security. Captain's bars. Her blond hair was so short it looked like a crew cut. Tera stood, gathered up the new security notebook and came forward.

"Would you please sign in? It's a security requirement."

"I *am* security, honey," Zora bragged. "See the uniform?" She took in the Elite blue, the dark curly hair and nearly perfect facial features beneath, except for those creepy light blue eyes. They ruined everything. "What are you, eye candy?"

"Mm? What's *your* flavor?" Then Tera dropped one eyelid down in a wink. This will throw the bitch a curve, she thought.

Zora took a step back and blinked. What the hell? She turned quickly and went into the office, but not fast enough, Hawthorne caught the interchange. Damn but that Storm was good. "So here's what we want," he started to explain to Zora, closing the door.

Tera rolled her eyes and went back to transcribing. Maybe a quarter of an hour later, the smell of alcohol made her look up and there was Neil Hawthorne watching her.

"Yes sir," she said pleasantly, taking the ear buds out.

"Do you have a first name? T. Storm, sounds like a rapper. Thunder Storm?"

Oh God, he's got a real buzz, she thought. "Personal information, sir. Not allowed," she answered, thinking if he could read, it was in the directory.

"Sir this, sir that." He was tall enough to lean over the little Plexiglas barrier between her and the outside world. "Why don't you call me Neil." He was smiling at her, although licking his lips was probably what he wanted to do.

"You're the hospital administrator, I don't think that would be appropriate."

"I *am* the hospital administrator and I make the rules. Lighten up." He was clearly trying to make points. "In fact, I think I'm going to steal you for my personal use...uh administrative assistant. How does that sound? Big raise, more time off?"

"You would need to go through Mrs. Harris, who runs Elite. And you would get nowhere. We are assigned three months at a time to a particular department. I was sent here because Dr. Loomis has a reputation for being hard to work with. He's stuck with me, and I with him."

"Your time here is almost up, I'll get you reassigned. Damn, you know your stuff, you're good. Maybe you could get some of it into my son's head. Do you know Dave? He works with Elite. He's never mentioned you. You're definitely not like the streetwalkers he talks about."

Oh yeah, I want to work with you and run into your stupid son who deserves to be locked up as a sex offender, she thought. The son I pulled the gun on.

"I haven't gotten to the monthly team meetings as much as most members. I was working at Springwood. As you know, Mr. Hawthorne, department meetings come first."

"Do you want to meet after you're done today for a drink? We can talk about working for me. It will definitely be better working for me." The voice was oozing friendly way too much. Again, the big cat licking its lips before it pounced.

Tera froze, but her salvation came from an unlikely source.

"What are you doing, Neil, talking with that lazy peon? She can't get work done on time. I gave her stuff to do last Friday and it still isn't done." Loomis was at the doorway, staring angrily at Hawthorne.

"Oh, Doctor, I'm so sorry. I'll have those papers prepared for you to sign in 15 minutes." What was this, a turf war? There were no papers. She watched them leave, feeling like her mind had just been raped. Then her phone pinged. Roger.

R: *You want to go for a beer?*
   Tera sighed. God, yes. One normal person in this asylum.
T: *Absolutely. My treat.*

❖❖❖

It was hard to breathe, the dew point was so high it was like a jungle outdoors that Sunday afternoon. Ellie glanced at her weather app. Nothing today, but for sure a tornado watch for the southern half of the state tomorrow. She shifted uncomfortably, Callie and Nick would be in Stanton tomorrow, right in the middle of the predicted storm zone.

She got up and went into the house. The good news is Nicky will be getting the evaluation at Harbison, in Wisconsin, Ellie thought. Callie said they'd received the appointment times from the transplant coordinator and the visit would be in mid-September, a couple of weeks off. She'd offered to stay with Sienna and Max, but Mark's parents were coming up from South Dakota. Left a free week, so to speak. Not really, no week was free anymore. There was nothing part time about filling in for Tera at the Insurance Coalition. Directing the workers was a pain in the ass.

Ellie jumped when Paul came up behind her and slid his hands around her hips. He kissed the back of her neck. "Deep thoughts?" She turned, she always had to bend her neck back to look up at him. I'm a hobbit, she thought. And he always says he doesn't want to come down to my level.

"Just thinking about stuff, work," Ellie replied. "How things have changed so drastically in the last few months, especially at the Coalition." She surveyed the kitchen. Ugh, who wants to cook on a day like this and nowhere to go out to. Drive-through was a bore.

"So who's the boss at the Coalition while Elgin is in the hospital? Is Craig still doing work for them? Seems like they're pretty busy over there in London."

"He's keeping up. I send the stuff, he has a 24-hour turn around. I don't really know what his schedule is and Tera doesn't say anything, I'm worried they aren't in contact at all anymore."

"Bad situation all around. That argument before he left was vicious."

And afterward was vicious as well, Paul thought. Tera depressed was Tera and alcohol. I don't think I'll ever forgive that guy for getting some of those freshmen at Aquinas into that, getting *her* into that when he was there, Paul thought. Craig was an exchange student, older, and had a fake I.D. He'd fled London one step ahead of some scandal that would've embarrassed the uppity member of Parliament in the family. I sure as hell wish those nuns would have stopped all that drinking stuff – stopped *him* – sooner than later. Too late for regrets now, she's married to him.

"Hey, did you see that piece in the business section?" Ellie asked.

"You read the business section?" Paul was about to laugh but saw she was dead serious.

"Ridley Children's Care is going to be incorporated in a new venture, a merger with the University. And a couple of separate health care partnerships, AlexaHealth for one, are being bought out by this new entity because Alexa couldn't afford to keep going after all the elective surgeries were stopped by the governor. Then the workers got laid off. They're calling it U-Ridley Health Care. It'll eat up most of the clinics in the Cities. Isn't that a monopoly?"

"You'd think so, but that's a problem for the state Department of Commerce. And they'll look the other way if they get some benefit out of it. You know how government works," Paul added sadly. "A lot of the time, not at all for the little guy."

CHAPTER 40

"It's creepy outside," Nick said as they walked from the Holcome main doors toward the Emergency Room parking lot. There were hundreds of parking ramp spots at that campus, but none of the underground ramps could accommodate the height of her truck. Callista preferred driving her truck, at least she could see the road when driving and the headlights were very bright.

The sunlight gave everything a hyper-yellowish glow. Callista opened her weather app and saw a tornado watch, nothing new there, except the risk factor was over 70% and they were right in the middle of it. Why now, why today, she thought, I have 110 miles to drive!

"C'mon, Nick, we've gotta make a run for it." They were surrounded by tall buildings. Leaves were past fluttering, they were actually shaking from the wind on the trees lining the main street of Stanton. It wasn't until they left the safety of the core city and hit highway 72 going north that they could see the black, boiling clouds to the west, not too far to the west, and stretching for miles from south to north. Which way was it going? To the northeast? Leaves were blowing across the road now, at an angle. There went an empty white Wal-Mart bag, inflated and lifting off.

Callista floored the accelerator. Nothing but little towns to the north and wide open spaces, perfect for wind storms and blizzards. The golden light turned dark gray within 20 minutes. Big drops began to squash on the windshield. Eyes ahead, she had a death grip on the wheel. The exit to Orion was just ahead. Make a run for it to Tera's? She lived in the woods somewhere to the east, not a good idea if trees started flying. The highway curved to the left now, she had a more than adequate view of the black sky, with a tinge of green. Hail.

"Mom, what's that over there?" Nick was pointing to the right.

White smoke was whipping around at ground level. "Some fool

burning stuff outside," she said. "That won't last long if it rains." She eyed it carefully. Smoke? So wispy, it had to be, right?

Truck or not, it began to shudder with every blast of wind. The rosary hanging from the rearview mirror started to swing wildly. The road curved to the right but by now she could hardly see the road, it was so dark and a downpour started, it seemed as if she were driving through a waterfall. There was literally nothing but a gray wall in front of her.

"I have to pull over Nick," she called, trying to sound calm. "I can't see." She looked back at him in the rear mirror and saw the gray-black cloud covering the road behind her. Was it coming her way? She couldn't just stay there, could she? A branch banged on the top of the truck. Where had that come from, there were no trees around, but the wind was ferocious.

"Mommy!" Nick screamed. Ten or not, it was the first word that popped into his head. She looked in the mirror. Pure terror was etched on his face as he stared out the window. He looked like he was trying to crawl out of the seat belt, the clouds looked like they were boiling right down on the pavement behind them. She crammed herself through the space between the front and back seats and held him. There was a blanket in the back and she quickly covered them with it, but not before hail was clunking on the top of the vehicle and she could see huge stones bouncing like popcorn in the field next to them. She started to pray.

It was over quickly. The back window of the cab was shattered, glass all over, good thing they'd covered up with the blanket. Several branches had come from nowhere near and now lay askew in the truck bed, as if they were being hauled away. There would be dents on the top from the hail. The road ahead was littered with leaves and stripped arms of bare wood. Wasn't there supposed to be a farm house over there to the left? Carefully, she brushed Nick and herself off and made him bring his bag up front. She started to get the truck moving, the wind had forced it sideways across the road.

Her phone was ringing and ringing. Callista picked it up.

"Are you okay? I couldn't get through on the phone to warn you," Mark said frantically.

"We're alive."

Finally back at home an hour later, Callista was exhausted when they made it up the driveway. It was only lightly raining, nary a twig had fallen onto the road. Supper was take-out, the hell with the diet stuff.

It was while they were at the table munching on Arby's roast beef that Sienna exclaimed, "Holy crap!" She was cruising her phone and showed the picture.

"What's that?" Nick asked.

"Water spout," Max said. He was looking at it closely. "A tornado over water. That's massive," he said in awe.

"Maybe it's on the news!"

They scrambled from the table and got their TV revved up.

The first scene was from a helicopter, Chopper 6 showing a massive fire in a small town. "High winds tore the sign of this Fuel Stop station out of the ground and sent it flying on a collision course with a tank truck filling the underground storage units. The explosion was felt for miles. So far the station is a total loss and firefighters are battling blazes in several nearby buildings. They have also set up a line to prevent the flames from entering the wooded areas around the downtown. We'll have more information for you on the ten o'clock news. This is Dan Cooper for Channel 6 News reporting from the town of Orion."

"Orion," Callista breathed, turning from the screen. She picked up her phone and punched Tera's speed dial number only to hear the constant annoying beep of the circuits busy, over and over and over.

※※※

"Neil, you've got to put a stop to this crap. This is two months in a row, August and now September, that our billing has gotten messed up and each time you're adding interest to amounts that I already paid!" Mark was in a slow burn. As if his wife and kid caught in a tornado wasn't enough stress. No way could the billing "errors" be coincidental. And 30% interest! Not to mention that there was a letter telling him the pre-authorized plane trip from California last November was *not* pre-authorized and was going to a collection agency for $50,000. Never mind that a person could not take one step into one of those air ambulances without a pre-authorization. Only Neil Hawthorne could create such havoc.

Neil was sitting back at his desk on the seventh floor of the management building, the tallest in Stanton, the two floors above his dedicated only for use by the CEO and his private staff. He had seen the roiling clouds the day before and was thankful it was all to the north. And as usual, first thing on the first, here was Mark Hampton. Storm would've taken care of this jerk, he thought. She never would've passed him on to me, she'd have destroyed him on the spot. I've got to figure out how to get her here. And I've got to figure how to get back at the Hamptons for daring to fight with me, with Holcome!

"Well, Mark, I don't run the billing department, now do I?" Hawthorne replied in answer to Mark's accusations. "Have you called them?...They say they have no idea how that happened, eh? Well why don't you believe them?...Mark, you're crazy if you think this is a conspiracy against you. You have some mental issues." He hung up.

The next call wasn't so low key.

"Zane! I told you to handle the Hampton case. He just called me and I don't want to be bothered. What the hell are you waiting for?" He dropped the phone in the cradle. I've got to get them off my back, he thought. Neutralize them somehow. If their complaints ever go public, we'll be in a world of hurt. Everyone roots for the underdog and you can't get any further under than a kid with dead kidneys.

❖❖❖

It was mid-afternoon when Mark came storming into the kitchen. "Ridley's blocked us!" He'd been trying to get an appointment for Nick with Ridley's gastroenterology office because sometimes medications caused a war in the kid's gut. But this time the portal wouldn't let him make the appointment and when he called demanding an answer, he was told Nick was blocked from getting any services at Ridley without permission from someone whose name was not revealed. He'd have to waste time reaching out to a supervisor to untangle the mess.

Not an hour later, the FedEx courier arrived at the Ridley Dialysis Center and stopped at the nurse station. "Delivery for Cynthia Langley," he said through his purple mask. Cynthia looked up.

"That's for me," she came forward. She liked these deliveries, the couriers so nice and professional in their black and purple uniforms, black shoes and FedEx caps. She especially liked what they delivered. No signature was required in this time of Covid. The courier just handed the padded envelope off to her, wrote on his handheld device, and left for the next stop in the hospital.

Looking over her shoulder, Cynthia made sure everything was all right and no one watching, then disappeared into her office down the hall. There she tore open the envelope and out fell six $100 bills. She smiled. Getting these for the next few months was quite a pick-me-up. It was a great way to start September. She'd have to thank Loomis, maybe send him a gift and maybe part with a bill to Linda O'Brien for suggesting her.

She shredded the FedEx envelope, then sat at her desk and put the money into her purse hidden in the back of the bottom drawer. From the other side of the drawer she retrieved 25 letters, all addressed to Jolene Richardson, the Jolene Richardson who no longer worked at Ridley, she'd run away to Phoenix in July. But that didn't stop Richardson from getting mail and writing answers postmarked from Ridley. Cynthia laughed, she loved the digital age, anything could be lifted from one file to another, any name could be used as a signature from one letter to another, so in a way, Jolene was still in charge.

The last letter from Mark Hampton was hilarious. She sat back and unwrapped a Salted Nut Roll. He says he wants to repair the relationship, blah, blah, blah so they can come back for transplant at Ridley, she thought. Yeah, the situation with Yuki, for sure, clearly negligent, the stupid woman hadn't even shown up for work that day. Cynthia took another bite of the candy bar, savoring the sweetness.

You're damned right you didn't find out about a bad relationship until later, because I didn't write it until later, she chuckled. The account flagged? No appointments allowed? You haven't seen anything yet, you poor fools. Loomis wants you blocked and blocked you will be.

Cynthia finished the candy bar and crumpled up the wrapper. She brushed off all the little crumbs that had fallen, symbolic, she thought, of brushing away all the complaints of the Hamptons.

CHAPTER 41

The State Fair was officially cancelled due to the virus, but someone dreamed up a scheme to make money anyway and food vendors and some sideshow acts had lined up at the fairgrounds. For $20 bucks, a car- SUV- van-load of people could drive through the unlively grounds where the Midway rides used to thrill the hearts of so many, and stop at food stands with cotton candy and cookies and footlong hotdogs. You'd think the State Fair was only about weird food, not showing off prize animals, the best pies and breads, and sucking up those tasty milkshakes at the dairy building. This poor substitute for the Great Summer Get-Together offered nothing like that, no alligator on a stick or bacon strips twirled around huge french fries. But people lined up for miles to come anyway and finally feel good about something at the culmination of a hot and stifling summer amid the Covid restrictions.

Roger was sitting on a bench near the closed beer garden. You weren't supposed to get out of the car, but there was a patio dining area offering snacks and clandestine beer out of sight of the police patrol. It was about a block away from the main parade of sad but hungry fair fans. He'd paid his $20 to get in, the hell with the rest of the nonsense. It was good having a three-day weekend, civilian clothes, shorts and a muscle shirt, and the sun felt good on his bare skin. "Hey, sorry I'm late." Tera came up behind him. Cut-off jean shorts and tank top, dark hair uncurled and framing her face, she looked like she was barely 20.

"You go to a tanning spa or something?" Roger asked, giving her a long hug. "You know that's dangerous, skin cancer."

"I run. That's outdoors, in the sun. Surely you've seen it." She looked up at him with a playful little smile.

"Do you run away from something or to something," he asked

easily, the double meaning obvious.

"Depends on the day. Usually away from work and the smell of Holcome." They laughed. The odor of disinfectant around the place was nauseating. "Today, maybe to. Plus I do my own outside chores." Damn, there are a lot of them, too, she thought, still clearing the garbage from the storm a week ago. Roger looked particularly nice, relaxed and handsome.

"Let's slide over to a table and get something to eat." She'd driven the 90 miles from her home on the lake, sans breakfast, for Elgin's memorial service and didn't stay for the luncheon; she didn't want to face the inevitable questions about the Medical Director: When was he returning from London? He was slated to take over the company, wasn't he? But she was here now, and away from all of that. Even if it made for a long day, driving across town to the State non-Fair, it was nice to be with Roger, to talk about anything but work, and feel his arm tightly around her, claiming her as his own, as they walked toward a table.

"This whole shut-down stuff is so stupid," she said. "I'm surprised they're allowing this mini-State Fair. And imagine that, no decontamination tents because someone touched your goodie bag. I'm glad we got to golf a few weeks ago."

"Yeah, golfing was fun. You sure don't know much about it, needing so-called help. Hah! Anything to get my arms around you," Roger said, pulling her in for a kiss. They'd been getting together frequently in front of the Hazel Nut Grille in Stanton after work. The outdoor venue was small, not the greatest, but at least a place to have a semblance of a life. It was nice being together and watching the Hazel River drift by in the evenings.

She sipped her Castle Danger Cream Ale, better to not be tempted to say more. Then she reached for a fry from the pile in the bowl on the table...the same time Roger did. Their hands collided. Before she knew it, he was holding her hand and looking into her eyes. "I love you," he said quietly. He was leaning toward her and their lips lingered together with a promise of more to come.

Her mind drifted a little, looking down at her hand in his. Forever and faithful, she thought. I promised it. But this is here, now, real. He loves me and I surely love him.

Then, suddenly, his grip tightened. "You've got a ring mark on your finger! You're *married*! What the hell is going on?" He was up and out of his chair, staring down at her like a scorpion he wanted to crush. "Are you playing with me? You make me fall in love with you and you're *married*?" His voice was getting louder. "Big thrill with a black guy?" There was no mistaking the raw anger.

Tera stared up at him, her hopes destroyed. "Shut up and sit down," she said hurriedly, "or people will notice." The end. She'd dressed the part for the memorial service that morning, even down to the wedding ring which felt so foreign on her finger after so long an absence. Had to keep up the public image at all costs. And now it was costing her.

Roger's biting words shot through her reverie. "My father fell for a white girl when he was in college, at Macalester, back at the end of the sixties. She was rich and used him. She dated him to get noticed because black and white didn't mix back then. She broke his heart when she dumped him. I'm not letting you do this to me." He was turning, moving off.

"Don't go, please. I need to talk to you about something." There was no going back now; she needed to unleash everything.

"More lies?"

She sighed. Why was life so complicated? "Sit down, I'm not going to talk to you looking up like this. Jesus, you look so threatening." Was she wrong about him? Would he be able to put aside his blistering anger and help? Her heart was breaking, but, in the end, she had a job to do and he was the one who could help with it. Tentatively she asked, "How good are you with computers?"

"What the hell are you talking about? I do IT. What do you think? Or do you mean illegal? You mean dark?" He sat back. This was a direction he didn't want to go in. This whole conversation was jumping around too much. "I don't do illegal, you got that?" I gotta get out of here, he thought, she's scaring me. "I'm leaving."

"Not illegal. You remote into files. At Holcome, you have that access because you've got to fix stuff." She waited and he was slow to answer.

"I don't know what you're asking me to do, I can't lose my job."

"You won't. Look, I can explain, but not here." She thought a minute then added absently, "It really wouldn't be appropriate for you to come to my house or...."

"What the hell," he interrupted. "Are you holding back on me? Suddenly afraid to be alone with me?"

She covered her face with her hands. When can I just be Teresa Storm and be like everyone else? Not sparring with dangerous medical people and pilfering records and information, analyzing data and accounts, and making up stories to cover my ass. Not looking out to see if anyone was watching, not jumping to the tune of someone thousands of miles away. Just normal.

"If we went where we're known, someone might notice us."

"Shit, you pulling that on me? It's me, Roger! I'm black, you're white! You didn't give a damn about being seen with me before this. Or at my sister's. You're disgusting. I'm getting out of here." He got up again, violently slamming the chair.

"Did you know Dave Hawthorne was watching us at the Hazel Nut more than a few times."

Roger stopped, considering that thought. "So what. You're worried about that jerk? Last time he was around you were ready to shoot his dick off."

She rolled her eyes, that incident was unfortunate, but necessary to get that creep to stop stalking her.

"Quit playing games!" Roger's harsh voice cut through her thoughts. "You've been using me for something. I don't know what, but I sure as hell just made a big fool of myself."

"No. Listen, we can talk about this later. You know where French Lake is?"

"That town on the east side? Yeah, I've driven through it."

She pulled out a piece of paper and started scribbling on it. She knew her parents would be home after the barbecue at Callista's. "This is the address. Go there, meet you in an hour and we can discuss… things."

He didn't want the paper, he didn't want to even look at her. "Why should I?" He hurt so badly inside he wanted to shake the hell out of her. Was she deceiving me from the start, he wondered. Every time we got together, every time we kissed, was it all a lie? Oh God, this hurts so much…I love her.

"Please, trust me," she said "It will make sense, honest to God. I just can't explain it here."

He snatched the paper and was turning away. She hesitated, then got up slowly. "I'm sorry Roger. I really do like you, a lot. It wasn't supposed to go that way, believe me." But it was surely headed that way. With regret, she felt her finger, naked without the ring for months now. Forever and faithful, one step above hell, it seemed, especially when married to a ghost.

CHAPTER 42

Still so much to clean up. The two big trees barely missed the house going down and were still lying where they'd fallen, one blocking access to the lake and one blocking the main entrance to the home. Tera was hauling broken branches from the yard and piling them up. That's why they call this Labor Day, right? Manual labor from dawn to dusk. She was so tired she could hardly stand. The meeting with Roger and her parents took hours. Roger wasn't obtuse, he was dumbfounded by the plot going on around him, and he was reluctant to be a part of the solution. It was a chance, a gut feeling that he would cooperate when he knew how high the stakes were, but he gave no assent at the meeting. His anger was so palpable, the glaring eyes like a scourge every time he looked at her. Mom was right again, she thought. She warned me that I was playing with fire by going out with him so much. Playing with fire, and he was burned by the deception, hurt because he thought I could love him. I do and I wanted it to be for real so badly. She wiped tears from her eyes and sat on the trunk of the big tree, wishing with all her heart that she could die and everything would be all over.

The sound of an engine startled her and she quickly looked around. A black truck? The door opened and out popped a sandy-haired little head. "Aunt Tera!" Nick was racing around the branches like a football receiver running a pattern, and he nearly downed her when he ran into her.

"Oh God, am I glad to see you, little guy." She held him at arm's length. "How are you? Have you grown! What are you doing here? And a new truck!"

"Duh. Dialysis. Monday, Wednesday, Friday. The end of the world could come but I have to be there, you know. Mom killed the white truck, the transmission. Too much Holcome. And that tornado wrecked it so bad it wasn't worth fixing."

Callista was walking toward them, jeans and tee shirt, hair down around her face and Tera couldn't read her. Anger? Another emotional outburst about to explode between them? I can't take it, Tera thought. I can't take being battered two days in a row.

"You said you had to go to the bathroom bad, Nick, so in the house with you." A gas station would've been better than driving three miles into the woods, Callista thought, but the Fuel Stop in Orion was no more. The woods themselves would have been better, but the kid insisted he needed a civilized toilet.

"Oh, yeah." He winked at Tera and ran toward the house but stopped, surveying the size of it and the mess.

"Go in through the garage," Tera called.

He ran in the open door and they heard him squeal, "Oh gosh! A black 911!"

"Go to the bathroom!"

Callista surveyed the damage. "You really took a hit, didn't you? Lucky nothing landed on the house. Were you home?"

Tera nodded. "Scary. I left work early and got home just before the explosion in town. Then the power went out." She shifted her weight. "Why don't you come in and cool off? I have to sit down before I fall down."

Callista seemed reluctant. "We just stopped because he said he had to go...and I was kind of worried when I heard Orion got hit." She eyed her sister, bare arms scratched, dirt on her face and leaves stuck all over, jeans torn. Was her face tear-streaked?

"I've got to take a picture of this, Mark won't believe it," she laughed, taking out her phone. "Image is everything."

They sat on high chairs at the island in the kitchen, powdered lemonade mix made a fast drink with ice in the large frosted black tumblers. Callista really hadn't planned to stay, she didn't want to apologize, she wanted to stay mad at Tera, but seeing her kid sister literally swallowed by that huge empty house made her sad. She knew she'd go out of her mind if Mark left her.

"Mark told me you texted him, well, it was like two weeks later. I filled out the form. What's the problem with Gwen Deeds?"

"Aside from the fact she was in on the Child Protection stuff? Isn't that enough? That her office is right there in the same hallway with the great and mighty Charles Loomis and they confer regularly?"

"Well, that's all probably enough reason, but why tell us now? There's been crap going on all summer and you haven't said a damn word," Callista was getting angry again. "You've been no help to us."

No help. Good God, they have no clue Loomis will never, *ever* free Nick from dialysis, Tera thought.

"Look, I can't just run in there and tell people to help my sister. In fact, it's in my best interest and yours to not know you. I can find out more that way."

"You don't make any sense. You're hiding something." No matter what they talked about, they were arguing within five minutes, it had been that way since day one.

Tera got up and went to her computer in the office. She came back with the copy of the letter from Loomis to Deeds about the Ridley decision to continue blocking transplant evaluation. She threw it at Callista. The expressions changed swiftly on Callista's face, from hostility to puzzlement, and then anger.

"Where did this come from?"

"I stole it from a desk, okay? You see those strike outs? Someone is writing this piece of shit and someone else is correcting it. They're doing it together, do you understand? These assholes at Holcome are writing a letter supposedly from Ridley! You have Loomis blocked? Think again. There's more going on than you can imagine. Do you see those dates? This was written *before* the meeting."

Nick came running down the hallway. "Five bedrooms! And Mom, you should see Aunt Tera's. It's the width of the house with a stone fireplace in the bedroom like in some English castle. The windows are huge and the lake looks like a painting! Mom, come and see!" He grabbed her arm.

"Not now, Nick."

"Mom!"

Callista shook her head and got up. "What have you got to do with all of this, Tera? You said you stole this."

"You have to trust me. I have to stay there and get whatever information I can get. You just need to take care of Nick. Keep fighting, you understand? Keep at the bastards."

Callista only got as far as the expansive great room, built out toward the lake, hefty wooden beams aloft and a huge gray stone fireplace on the south wall. "Is this place really yours?" she gasped.

"Craig knew someone who wasn't coming back to the States. We just walked in three years ago, sight unseen. Fully furnished, even the stupid 911." No one needed to know it had belonged to Craig's guardian, the soulless bastard his father appointed to ride herd on their wayward teen who'd been such an embarrassment. The house was an inheritance of sorts, or maybe restitution from the fellow who'd stolen more than just money from his charge. Yes, they'd walked in with a sense of total awe. And then, one week later, walked out again. They'd made the massive sea change of a move to the States to get away from being on call – what with Imperial College and WHO jerking their chains all the time – for a semblance of a stable life. But then, as usual, he got called, another crisis emerged and he couldn't say no, so they were off to join a medical team investigating a suspected Marburg outbreak in Uganda.

"This is better than a five-star hotel!" Callista turned in a circle, noting the built-in bar, leather furniture, the painting on the wall. The hallway to the left seemed to stretch forever. The payments would be thousands of dollars a month. Someone wanted to get *rid* of it?

Tera shrugged. "It was empty, that's all I know. Still is, as far as I'm concerned. Hey, your anniversary is coming up. Twenty, right? You want to spend the weekend here? I can go up to your house."

"What?" Callista turned to look at her. "What are you talking about?"

"You can't go anywhere, you're trapped during the week. If you write down Nick's diet, I'm sure I can figure it out. You need a break. And this is free, after all, and it's better than a hotel."

CHAPTER 43

So stupid. 6:30am. Callista could see them standing there in the pinkish light of dawn at the end of the driveway, be-jeaned and sweatshirted, crammed school bags on their backs, black cases with Sienna's saxophone and Max's trombone ready to be stashed in the bandroom's lockers. Welcome to junior year, welcome to freshman year. The bus pulled up. School didn't start until eight o'clock, but the powers that be decided their bus route started 12 miles from the school and zigzagged its way into town – a solid hour of zigzag.

I give the school district four weeks before school shuts down and it's back to online learning, she thought. For us, online is easier, if those dopey kids just did their work. Max would never be a self-starter unless he was totally interested in a topic and then he couldn't turn it off, that's all he would work on for days. Sienna was okay, down in the dumps because Trevor wasn't in any of her classes. Nick had to log in to the online Trent Academy this morning, but not at eight o'clock. He'd be lucky to be ready by 10:30, and would be missing a couple morning classes; she hoped they could work with the teachers on getting the classes on an archive link. He was so exhausted after dialysis he couldn't wake up early, and God forbid waking up early for school would incite a migraine. What kind of life is that for a ten-year-old, she thought, three days on the road down to Stanton and no time to himself, blood pressure taken, weight taken, twelve pills a day to choke down. His pals from school never called, only Brian who lived next door came over because he liked to play with Nick's Legos. It's a hell of a way to live.

Mark was off to work. Although his boss ordered everyone home and online, there were still some things that needed to be done in person, depending on client requests. So right now, the house was silent. Loads of laundry and weeding the garden were on the day's schedule. Callista trudged up the stairs.

O God, I'm so tired of this. Running here, running there. Blood work, this number is too high, that number could kill him. I don't even know if what they're saying is true. I don't trust them! Any of them! And school. Like a bunch of mosquitoes stinging all the time, pick, pick, pick. They want to schedule a full special education assessment. When will I have time for that with three days of the week shot to hell driving down to Holcome. The kid begs to go to school. I begged for all his homework and the teachers said he should just get well and sent nothing. Now I'm taking up the slack, teaching the missing links of fourth grade, reviewing high school work, and going crazy. When can I have a minute for me?

God, why are you doing this to us? She sat on the floor next to the bed, and was reaching for her shoes when the tears came. "Why?" she sobbed aloud. "Why did any of this happen? Why is Nick having to suffer? Why can't he be normal? Why! I can't do this any more." She couldn't stop crying.

A hand touched her shoulder. She started. Where...what time was it? An hour gone by? Had she fallen asleep? She looked up and saw Nick's blue eyes. He handed her a Kleenex. "I'm sorry Mom if you're feeling like crap today. I'll log on and do my work, okay? Why don't you just take a nap, I'll be fine."

❋❋❋

The week rolled on. Late on Friday afternoon, Tera was working with tweezers to free yet another paper jam in the copier when she heard the office door open. Good God! Roger! He was pushing a cart with some boxes – the new computer. Gwen and Zora had nearly come to blows over sharing the single computer in their office. Rather than referee, Tera had ordered new equipment for them. She got up slowly, but kept her eyes down, she was shaking inside.

"May I help you?"

"You need to sign for this and then let me know where to put it. The orders from Mrs. Blakely in 440 were to be sure all the computers here have certain access capabilities."

Mrs. Blakely? That meant he was in! He was going to do surveillance on the items they discussed. Quickly she reached down and pulled a card out of her purse with the passwords to the office computers. He was looking elsewhere. She pushed the card across the desk.

"Here are the passwords. The biggest office belongs to the head doctor."

It was nearly an hour when he returned and slid the card across the desk.

"You know that Mrs. Blakely is a class act. Too bad her daughter isn't." And he was gone.

Not much later, Tera walked through the parking ramp. Roger's biting words really hurt, enough that come hell or high water she and alcohol would meet again that night. I don't care if I get sick, I don't care if I die from alcohol poisoning, I want oblivion.

She didn't see Roger a couple of rows over, leaning against his vehicle, watching her and then checking out the parking ramp. Now that they weren't a couple at the Hazel Nut, it wouldn't take long for Dave and Kenny to start stalking her through the ramp again. He'd stationed himself in the background, watching every day until he was sure she was safe. No matter what, he wouldn't be much of a man if he ignored the potential danger those two were and the risk they presented to her or any woman for that matter. What the hell is wrong with that jackass of a husband, leaving her here alone to run this game, he thought. I swear if I ever see the guy I'm going to take him out.

CHAPTER 44

"What the hell do you mean, they aren't coming for dialysis the rest of the week?" Loomis' eyes were lit up and his face was definitely bright red with anger. "What did you do, damn you!" He was up and out of his chair and glaring at the young doctor from across the desk.

Dorian Place looked shell-shocked at the verbal attack. All he did was stop by to tell Loomis the Hamptons wouldn't be at the Dialysis Center, they were going for a transplant evaluation at the University in Harbison, Wisconsin.

"They wanted to get a transplant evaluation. You won't authorize it here for whatever reason, so they're going elsewhere. The dialysis will be done at Harbison."

"Damn it! How did they get in at Harbison! There's a hold on their records so they can't be transferred without permission. The records weren't supposed to be sent anywhere." He glared at Dr. Place. "Anywhere, do you understand. You signed off on them, didn't you?"

Dorian remembered Storm bringing the paperwork a few weeks before.

"You're a doctor but I *own* this department," Loomis said. "You do what I say, the patients get treated the way I say and when I say."

"That's hardly the norm, Dr. Loomis. At Mercy...."

"This isn't Mercy, this is Holcome and I run this department. This is going into your record, by God. Someone wants a recommendation for you, they'll get one all right."

"This isn't anything to write up negatively. I followed hospital protocol."

"You didn't ask me, you didn't follow *my* protocol. I do what I want and there's nothing you can do about it. Get out of here."

Loomis sat back down. Just what he needed, they were going to a top flight hospital and staff there would be asking questions about why hemodialysis instead of peritoneal, why wasn't the kid fully evaluated yet, why wasn't he listed for transplant and on and on. The results of the bloodwork – the results the Hamptons didn't know about yet – indicated the search for a kidney needed to begin as soon as possible and that was months ago. Questions would be asked. Harbison was one of the best in the country. Dr. Cora Eveleth, the head of Harbison's pediatric nephrology department, had over 35 years of experience in the field. He'd met her at a conference and hearing her credentials had made his paltry ten years of service look sad. She was as abrasive as he could be, but she knew her stuff and in the experience department, she made him feel like a two-year-old. Damn it to hell, how could he sidetrack this little trip.

"Gwen!"

The yell was heard all over the office.

"Gwen! Where the hell are you?" Loomis walked rapidly out of his office. Gwen was chatting on her cell phone. He stuck his head through her door and yelled again, "Gwen!"

She dropped the phone. "Chuck!...Dr. Loomis I mean. Whatever is wrong." She began fluffing her red curls.

"Stop that. You've got some calls to make." He stopped and turned around. Through the window he could see Tera at her desk, this was something he definitely didn't want anyone to hear, least of all her. Something wasn't right about her being assigned to his office, and today, for sure, something wasn't right. Dark glasses again, only he caught a glimpse of the eyes, red streaked. She was a bit slow, like she was really hung over. Damn, another binge, and for a whole weekend? Who would've thought, a woman so obviously gifted in body, and maybe even her mind, would be a slave to the bottle.

"Chuck? What is it you want me to do?"

"I want you to call," he went and closed the office door and then turned to face her, "the dialysis doctor at Harbison. Sheila something or other. And then the transplant social worker. And send a link to the Hampton records to the social worker. Your cover letter will highlight some information they need."

※※※

"Did you take a look at this list?" Callista asked as Mark drove the Ford Escape along the freeway through the bowels of Wisconsin that Tuesday afternoon. It was a long stretch of nothing but road and trees, no billboards, no farms, just two ribbons of cement; and today, very little traffic. It was surely not a place to have a breakdown. The trees were starting to turn to fall colors so the ride wasn't all ugly.

"This schedule is so crammed I wonder if they allowed time for a bathroom break or overnight sleep! Listen to this, and I don't know any order, just that it will take two full days and dialysis too, tomorrow and Friday!" She read the list: Four consults with various specialties; tissue typing, meetings with nutrition, pharmacy, social work – on and on.

"I'm surprised financial wasn't first," Mark said dryly. "It's always first."

The nephrology consult was at eight o'clock sharp, Dr. Eveleth did her office hours first thing in the morning. Then, as Mark suspected, financial matters. From there to the labs, and dialysis for the afternoon. It would be the same on Friday, dialysis in the afternoon and then they could head for home. As for the rest, it was waiting room after waiting room, a needle poke here and there and talk, talk, talk.

During dialysis they met Dr. Sheila Vanderbeek, and that was the first inkling that all was not well.

"What are the possibilities of switching Nick to peritoneal dialysis?" Mark asked. "Your transplant coordinator was surprised he was still on hemo, she said you switch your kids over within a week of kidney diagnosis."

"Well, I don't know if Nick's a good candidate for that."

Mark and Callista looked at each other. "Why?"

"You have to check in monthly with us. That would be almost 300 miles one way each month. You can't miss any appointments. I don't think you'll be able to meet that schedule."

"You don't even know us. How can you say that?"

"It's so far. It's a problem having monthly appointments, believe me, and you're coming a long way. Winter would be a problem. I don't think it would work."

Where have I heard this before, Mark thought. "Did you receive our records from Holcome?"

"Yes I did."

"There were no missed appointments there."

"There were some occasions noted in which you were scheduled for appointments but turned up hours later, you demanded treatments, you were rude...."

"Wait a minute. That wasn't Holcome stuff. I don't know how it got in their records, but that isn't true."

"And I've been driving three times a week from our home to Holcome," Callista added. "That's like 600 miles a week. My truck died. Doesn't that count for something? We know how important dialysis is, Dr. Vanderbeek." Callista was beside herself. Nick needed peritoneal dialysis. They needed him to have it so he could be at home and half their lives wouldn't be wound up continuously on the road.

"I'm sorry. Besides, I talked with Dr. Place. He said they will offer PD for you. I'd prefer it be done and managed at your home hospital."

"Did Place tell you I can't be there for the procedure? Did he tell you they won't train me for using PD for Nick? Only Callista will be trained in our household that way. We both need to be trained, what if Nick has an emergency and she's not in the house," Mark pleaded. "We both need this training!"

"I'm sorry."

There was a brooding silence in the Ford Escape on the way home on Friday. Shafted again, first at Ridley, now at Harbison. How far did the claws of Holcome reach? They were nearing Prairie City when the phone rang.

"Mark Hampton please."

"Speaking."

"Mr. Hampton, I'm Jane Taylor, the transplant social worker. Do you have a minute to talk?"

"Well, I'm driving home right now. If you can hear me all right, fire away."

And she did. "I received a letter and the records for Nick from Holcome, from their transplant social worker, Gwen Deeds. The letter was rather puzzling. Then she followed up with a phone call and said you were banned from the Holcome property for a vicious fight, you were difficult to work with."

Oh my God, Mark thought. "Ms. Taylor, can I speak frankly?"

"Please. That's why I called. What I read and what I saw when I met you are opposites. Something's not right here, I wanted to hear your side of the story."

And he told it.

After an excruciatingly silent and depressed ride home, Mark got on the phone with the Iowa transplant department. No way in hell was he going to let Holcome interfere in the next transplant evaluation.

"This is Mark Hampton. We were wondering if you had received records from Holcome so we can set up appointments for kidney transplant evaluation for Nick Hampton in the near future. We've been talking about this on and off through summer."

"Oh sure. My name is Tamara Brown, I'm the transplant coordinator. We finally received the records from Holcome and the prescription for the dialysis run. It took forever. I believe we can have everyone, nephrology, cardiology, social services, child life, everything available October 5th through 7th, with a consult on the morning of the 8th, is that okay? If we have time, we want to initiate blood and kidney tests for you and your wife as possible donors."

"Oh gosh, thank you so much. I mean the kid's been in kidney failure since last November and Holcome hasn't done a transplant evaluation yet. We've got to get out of there."

"Sure, I understand. Your kid needs it, let's do it. We'd be very happy to help you."

Mark liked that attitude. Then he added, "By the way, it came to our attention that the social worker from Holcome called Harbison before our eval there and passed on some detrimental information – lies, actually – about us to interfere with our chances of getting listed through them. I want to warn you that they may try to pull the same stuff there. Gwen Deeds would be making the call."

"Thanks for that information." Tamara gave a small laugh. "Don't worry, we're well aware of the little tricks Holcome plays and we don't play along."

"The worst part came with the comments by the Harbison transplant coordinator about the prospects for transplant," Mark added. "We were never told Holcome had done any transplant testing on Nick or about any test results. But the coordinator thought we knew and kept talking about the six markers for transplant, most people need to match only three but Nick has had so many interventions and blood transfusions, the transplant requires a match for all six markers and the expected wait is over five years, if it can be done at all." He sighed. "I thought I would drop dead from shock."

CHAPTER 45

At eight o'clock Wednesday morning, Patrice found the signed permission form on her desk, allowing the Miscellaneous Records file to be sent to the Hampton family. Who was here so early? She looked around, moving her long and flowing hair off her violet blouse. She went to show Mrs. Kirkpatrick.

"Don't just stand there, what do you want? I'm busy."

"This was at my station this morning. This is written permission for records access and it's signed by Dr. Loomis."

Kirkpatrick snatched them. "Can't be, that guy never rescinds anything." She looked at the papers. She held them up to the light, that was his signature all right. She turned the paper over. He used a felt-tipped pen, so there shouldn't be any pressure marks on the reverse side. And there weren't. It had to be legitimate. How odd.

"Are you going to call him to verify?"

"Are you crazy? No one second-guesses that guy. Put it through and make it snappy. I don't want him down here bitching at us for being a day late. It takes 30 days to process and he'll have it timed to the minute." But as she thought of it, perhaps it would be wise to send for verification that Dr. Loomis okayed this. She pulled up an internal fax form on her computer and the keys began to click.

Upstairs, early in the afternoon, more unsettled thoughts. Nick was ornery. They were trudging along the boring creamy ivory hallway toward the dialysis center, like a prison procession, behind the gray-uniformed plow horse of a guard. She had a sway back, so her massive behind shifted with every step. Nick was aping her every move, his orange and white shorts swaying in time. Callista was grateful for the warm weather, still shorts weather, she didn't want to consider buying more jeans for her growing boy. Heart patients usually looked peaked; kidney kids looked wasted. Nicky was neither, just lean and, today, mean.

"Ohh, Nicky, how *are* you today!"

Oh God, Lindsey again as the dialysis nurse, Callista thought, all perky in her navy blue scrubs with the Holcome International logo on her big right chest.

"How is my little boy today?" Lindsey ruffled his blond hair.

"I'm not your little boy," Nick muttered.

"What, sweetheart?" in her sickeningly sweet little girl voice.

"I'm not your little boy, I'm not your sweetheart," Nick replied distinctly, emphasizing every single word. "Please take your hand away and don't ever touch me except for dialysis stuff."

Lindsey stepped back. "What's the matter, aren't you feeling well today, honey?"

"Leave me alone, would ya?" He sat on the edge of the bed and slid up his shirt so she could access the catheters in his chest.

"Poor baby."

"Poor baby, you don't get it, do you? I'm hungry! Hungry! Because of my stupid kidneys, I can't eat what I want, I have to watch my potassium, gotta be careful of phosphorus between trips to dialysis. Oh, poor baby! I'd like to see you try it, honey." The sarcasm dripped like acid from his voice. "I can't have more than a single piece of pizza, no French fries! I want a Hershey bar, you hear me, I want a candy bar and I can't have it. I can't go to school, my friends don't even remember me! I'm ten years old, I want a life, but I'm stuck here three times a week having dialysis. I hate it!"

He didn't exactly look like he was about to cry, but he seemed angry enough to have tears running. He did that sometimes when he got really, really mad at something. Or he punched his brother.

"Well, perhaps I should call Child Life for a consult or a psychologist," Lindsey began. "You aren't dealing with this very well."

"You will not call anyone," Callista intervened. "You have no clue what his life is like because he's stuck on this hemodialysis. Just get on with your job, all right, so we can get out of here." She glanced at the guard to see if she was taking notes about bad behavior, but the woman was engrossed in her phone, as usual.

Lindsey was staring at her and Callista glared right back until Lindsey shrugged and in a minute, the red and blue connections were made and the machines began to whirr.

As Callista edged toward the chair in the corner she glanced up and saw Dr. Place. He looked puzzled. Dorian had never heard Nick say much of anything: no frustration, no pleasure, no emotion whatsoever, just Yes-No answers. This outburst was like a stab to the heart. Then Nick saw him and a look of terror crossed his face.

"I didn't mean it. Honest, I didn't mean it. I just hate her touching me. Don't take my mom away. Please don't take her away." Callista stared at him and then back at Dorian, who was saying, "Nick, stay calm, your blood pressure will go up." But by now Nick was sobbing, "Don't take her."

"Who take her?" Dorian asked. Lindsey sat up straight, all ears.

"You," Callista said. "Don't you read anything? It's right in the record, in the famous behavior plan Loomis and Holcome slapped me with in June. If I cause a scene – or Nick, do you think? – I will be removed and another caregiver would have to come with him, hospital-appointed, I presume. Haven't you noticed, the kid is shit-scared to make a move, to say anything to anybody for fear of retaliation.

"I had no idea,..." Dorian started to say, but she got back at him before he uttered another word.

"If I read every flipping word of everything you send to me, I expect you're supposed to do it too. And by the way," she glared at Lindsey's back. "Little Miss Lindsey there and Pauline keep jiggling his catheters, trying to 'straighten' them. Tell them to keep their hands off. It hurts Nick. He just grabs the blankets on the bed and holds on. He's too scared to tell them they are hurting him."

"Oh that's not true," Lindsey snapped, turning toward them. "I don't do that."

"You do, and it hurts him."

"Enough," Dorian said. "Lindsey, hands off, do you understand me? Who knows whether your actions can dislodge the lines and he'd be headed off to surgery again. Don't do it," he commanded. He heard a sharp intake of breath from Callista.

What had he said? Dislodge the lines and surgery again, Callista thought. Is that what happened last May? She sat on the bed and hugged Nick, wiped his tears. Was there no deliverance from this hell?

✳✳✳

"Out of sight, out of mind," Mark said as Callista and Nick finally got into the Ford Escape after dialysis. He'd stayed in Stanton, working from the vehicle and making several phone calls during dialysis. As they drove up to Tera's in Orion, he looked puzzled. "I don't remember this house at all, were we ever down here?" He saw burned rubbish piles and clumps of sawdust from the tree removal. "Looks like a lot of damage around here." He saw debris on the lakeshore and trees maybe a quarter mile away totally stripped of leaves and broken branches askew. For sure, no fall color in an otherwise picture-perfect location.

"Two big trees, I mean big, down by the house and lots of branches," Callista said, getting out of the vehicle. She brushed back her brown hair with her hand. Nick swung open the back door and took off for the house. He was pounding on the front door when it opened and he fell inside. "I don't know if we should do this, Mark. I have to keep track of Nick's food intake and what does Tera know about that stuff, or taking care of kids for that matter? She's dumber than a post sometimes. It's Friday, can we be away until Sunday?"

He grabbed her around the waist. "If we don't do this, we'll forget what it's like to be married to each other. Just us. She's not an idiot, you know." He waved as Tera came out of the house, Nick like a puppy behind her.

"It's all yours," she said, handing him a set of keys. "The code for the garage is 4321. I'm sorry if I didn't get all the dust."

Mark studied her, eight years younger than Callista, same height, same build for both of them. Hair – he still felt the dark, dark brown was a dye job. Looked like fresh blonde highlights. If it was Callista's length and color, they would be very similar, except for the eyes, light blue versus chocolate brown, and most likely both could blaze hot. Stunning women, I'm glad I captured mine.

"So how long have you had this place?" he asked, getting the suitcases out of the back of the Ford Escape.

"Been here three years." She offered nothing more, certainly no reason for not having any family over in all that time. "Okay, you have everything written out for me?"

"Yes, but I'm not sure...."

"That I can handle it? You'll find out, I'm sure your darling daughter will let you know if I get out of line." She sent Nick for a small duffle bag and hugged them both. "Don't worry."

Then she opened the door of the Mustang like a valet and waited for Nick to get in. He hugged his mom and dad and bounced in.

Mark threw his arm around Callista and drew her in for a kiss. "Better than a hotel, eh?" They headed toward the door. Beyond the entry was an opening to a huge kitchen and then the great room, a fire burning in the massive gray stone fireplace. On the small gray marble table was a tray with a blue glass carafe etched in gold and similar glasses surrounding it. A bottle of champagne was in a matching blue and gold ice bucket next to it.

"Bavarian art glass," Mark said in surprise. "Did she – they – buy all this stuff?" he asked, looking around. There was a large painting on the wall above the built-in bar, which held several sizes of crystal decanters. The visible bottles of liquor were all of expensive European brands.

"When she was a kid she never knew what day of the week it was. She liked her hair short and she would just shake it in the morning and not comb it. Trust me, Tera wouldn't know Bavarian from early Wal-Mart," Callista sniffed, but the set looked incredibly delicate and rich.

"She said everything came with the house, even that 911 in the garage. The guy wanted out and they wanted in." She faced him, taking his hand. "And I didn't come here to talk about my sister."

CHAPTER 46

They took the long way out of the neighborhood, if you could call two houses in a mile stretch any kind of neighborhood. Nick was in his glory, Tera was hitting the curves fast and hard, downshifting and then cruising, winding through the countryside until they found a county road that went back to highway 72. When they arrived in Trent an hour and a half later, it was close to 7:30, shoes were strewn in the entry way, the basement door open, and the house literally shaking.

"Max is banging the punching bag," Nick explained. He threw his bag in the middle of the floor and ran downstairs. Tera looked around, school bags on the steps going up, she could smell something from the microwave. There was a lot of yelping downstairs with the shuddering as the punching bag took a hit. On the kitchen counter were the written instructions Callista had left for the kids. Load dishwasher, a quick look showed that undone, a pile of dishes in the sink. Get laundry and fold. There were instructions for Tera to make a light supper and be sure to follow everything correctly and write it down in the logbook.

It was almost nine when the food was eaten. "Let's watch a movie," Sienna said. She headed for the living room when Tera caught her arm. "Just a minute, please, both of you."

"Yeah, what do you want?" Her hair was lime green, and some obscenity was blanked out on her black shirt. Max looked like he skipped his shower for the fifth day, his hair matted down on his forehead.

"Sit down. I went over your online class work, the grade book, stuff like that." Tera sighed. "Max, you win at last year's art competition at the county fair with a drawing and yet you're three assignments behind in art? And an F in social studies? It's only the third week of school! What are you using your brain for? And Sienna, grades sagging in math and English. You're both smarter than that, what's going on?"

"Who cares," Max said. He was picking up his laptop to go upstairs when Tera jerked it out of his hands. She opened it and saw the game he was playing while they were eating. "You aren't going anywhere in life playing stupid games. No more of this crap while we're eating."

Sienna was busy looking at her phone, laughing as she Face-timed with Trevor.

"That's enough." Tera reached over and hit the end button.

"What are you doing?" Sienna yelled.

"Tomorrow you're up by ten. You'll catch up on all outstanding work, and there's an English paper due, Sienna. And Max, you have art and make-up work to get your grade up in social studies."

"I did those, the teacher just doesn't have the grade book up to date."

"Really? Then show me proof. And for sure, you'll be down here working where I can see you. All you do upstairs is play games and stuff your face with candy. I found the wrappers under your pillow."

"Aren't you a snoop." That was Sienna.

"You'll be down here in a different room, so Mr. Boyfriend isn't the center of your attention. If he wants to come over here and work, that's fine, otherwise, off-limits."

"You're a fine one to be giving orders," Sienna said with an attitude. "Mom says you never did any school stuff and probably slept with every guy at your school instead."

Tera blinked. Image was everything but that was definitely the wrong image. What the hell was Callista saying that for? "Not even once. I didn't go to your school where you could get graded on that."

"Ouch," Max laughed. He reached again for the laptop, but Tera sidestepped him. "No, not tonight, you understand, Max? You've got to earn your free time back by finishing your work." How strange, he was tall enough that they were looking at each other eye-to-eye and he had a little dark mustache. Where had the time gone?

"Who are you to tell us what to do. You went to reform school." Sienna again.

"Excuse me? Well, in a way it was. Smart kids, who could go either way, gambling, drug dealing, hacking, anything to outwit the system. They all got their asses kicked out of regular schools and were sent to Aquinas to get their attitudes reworked." She gave a little laugh at the thought of her wild menagerie of classmates.

"Stupid."

"Not exactly, competition was used as motivation. You were nothing if you didn't *exceed* an A, if you didn't beat the guy sitting next to you. Maybe a quarter of the students were starting college classes during their high school years."

"All the schools do that, you do a class or two a year and get college credit. Big deal."

"No, this was fourteen-year-olds starting as college freshmen, through an arrangement at St. Mary's. Some people got a college degree along with their high school diploma."

"Holy shit," Sienna said. "What a bunch of geeks."

"No, misfits, every last one of them, but smart misfits. Even as freshmen, a group of guys smuggled in weed and sold it at neighboring schools until Sister Agnes busted them. They had to *volunteer* to strip and re-wax the pews in the local church. Another group snuck out really late and ran a gambling operation in the woods." She didn't add that she was the one who unlocked the doors when they came back.

"What did you do to get sent there?"

"Hacked into the French Lake district computers. They have all kinds of personal information in there, bragged about security. I wanted to prove they were wrong. They thought I was holding it for ransom so I got expelled."

"So instead of juvenile detention, you got sent to a Catholic jail school." Sienna was laughing raucously.

"The curriculum was more like brainwashing. It must have worked, the school has a long list of alumni who became lawyers, doctors, missionaries in India, a couple politicians, and teachers. Not your usual reform school." She didn't think it wise to mention one-fourth of her classmates were sitting in the state prison in Oak Park.

"You must be a real disappointment to them, you're such a loser. You're doing nothing but sitting in an office being a clerk for a stupid doctor."

Loser? Tera thought about the night the bandits attacked the WHO medical outpost in the Highlands of Guinea, shooting up everything and everyone in sight; her wild run to try and get the women to safety. The bullets, the screams, women being dragged off, others with their pregnant bellies slit, dead babies stomped into the ground. I'm the loser because I couldn't protect them. I'm still a loser, I've lost my husband and we're all going to lose Nick if I can't nail that bastard doctor. She looked at Sienna.

"I should smack you across your face for saying that." She grabbed the phone. "Get the hell out of here and remember, ten o'clock in the morning, sharp!"

"You bitch."

"That's *Aunt* Bitch."

Morning came too soon. The kids were sleepy, but they were working. No phones, just the scratch of pencils on paper. The blinds were open in the three rooms where the kids worked, all facing the huge garden with the woods beyond. To the left, maybe a football field away, tall grasses waved around a pond, swamp, wetland, whatever the current correct descriptive, to the right, tall trees in various stages of fall colors. Beautiful, peaceful. Unappreciated.

"Smooth lines," Tera said, looking over Max's shoulder. He was ensconced in the living room, his pencils spread out on the coffee table. The television was a dark rectangle on the wall and opposite his position on the floor, two mounted deer heads stared down on either side of the fireplace, their amber glass eyes like Big Brother watching his every move. And so were Tera's blue eyes, the prison guard.

The kid has talent, to be sure, but those games are a distraction, she thought. If he could just focus his mind on his work – the back end of the car done with *cray-pas* was amazing. It was the Mustang. She'd clandestinely taken a picture and sent it to Rusty.

Sienna was working on pre-calculus. She had the workbook and she had notes, Mark's notes.

"Your dad is doing a good job teaching you," Tera commented, recognizing Mark's writing. "Your teacher is just reciting whatever is in the book they gave her to teach from. It must be written word for word but she doesn't get it. A good teacher knows the material and can teach it two, three different ways to make sure everyone understands it."

"How would you know?"

Tera paused. Nonentity, that's me, or else they'd know I've been teaching applied math at Imperial College almost longer than they've been in school. "I had a math tutor when I was a freshman," she said, no need to go into details. It wasn't pre-calculus, it was a college honors class and she really hadn't needed tutoring at all. Sienna's classmates still couldn't spell or make correct change at their jobs, thanks to current fads in teaching.

On to Nick, who was sitting at a card table in the den and holding his head up with his hand.

"I don't get this stuff," he said. "My regular fifth grade class is learning about wetlands and water cycles in science but I can't go to regular school because of the stupid dialysis. I'm in this online academy, I have to figure out how fast a puck will travel across the ice in an indoor rink based on the outside temperature."

"I had that in ninth grade," Sienna yelled from the other room. "Same teacher. She's teaching fifth grade online because she's afraid of Covid but she's teaching her usual stuff. Mom's really mad about this."

"Are you planning for a career in the NHL?" Tera asked. That brought a laugh from Nick and she sat down next to him. "What else is there...you're having a problem with long division?"

"Well, I wasn't there after last October. And Mom kept begging them to send me homework and all they said not to worry about fourth grade and now I'm in fifth and don't know fourth!"

"You haven't heard half of it," Sienna called. "His dialysis days mess everything up. He's got a social studies class at 8:30 each morning, but the teacher won't archive it so he can watch it later, so he gets crappy notes and all kinds of work to do, but never gets to see what she teaches in class. Mom is trying to teach him without the benefit of knowing what they want him to learn. It sucks."

As if kidney failure isn't enough to deal with, Tera thought. There were options. The Office of Civil Rights could nail this one. He was medically disabled and you can't discriminate against the disabled. The threat of a civil rights action would easily fix the archived lesson problem.

"Okay, Nick, first, division," Tera said, picking up a pencil. "I don't care how they teach it now, this is how it works...."

Hours later, curled up in bed, Tera felt exhausted by the mental gymnastics. I don't think I'm cut out for this mom stuff, operating on all these different levels with kids and their moods and the school work, chores, keeping on them for all of that. And a husband? I don't know how Callie does it.

CHAPTER 47

Neil Hawthorne wasn't happy as he quickly tapped out a text of two words: *Heliport. 10*

Loomis rolled his eyes, why couldn't he just call me. It was the second Monday; the monthly team meeting was in the afternoon. He was supposed to be making rounds, but was still in bed at home, his wife was downstairs, probably hitting the bottle again, after all, it was eight in the morning, can't be off schedule. She always drank, heavily, the morning after. I can't stand her, I can't stand even touching her anymore, the lush. 20 years! I need to find a lawyer.

He rolled out of the extra king bed and looked over the closets and dressers, the highly polished walnut floors with the Persian rug sprawled beneath his feet. Wonder how much she'll take me for. The large plantation-style home in the doctors' gated compound looked enormously chic and costly, especially with the glorious rose gardens in the back. She's got the bottle problem, she should just be kicked out, he thought. The boys are over 18, no problem there. What's the likely settlement, half and half? Or is it something based on her earning ability versus mine? He threw his shorts on the floor and went into the shower. I will not make this mistake again.

Hawthorne was leaning over the railing, gazing at the October brilliance of sunlit multi-colored leaves when Loomis came through the glass door at the heliport. "What's the big problem?"

Hawthorne looked up at him, nicely tanned, new suit and tie, the epitome of an executive at the height of his game. And that was the operative word. Game. He straightened. "Aren't you decked out today, like you're ready to go to the annual gala. Too bad we aren't having it because of Covid. I'd love to see Jeanette again."

"What!"

"She's nice to look at, if you could keep her away from the bar. And funny, too. It was great last winter at the welcome for Rexalt when she announced you were the head of a department and you thought you were important." He laughed. He enjoyed putting this preening rooster in his place once in awhile.

"You *would* like that," Loomis snapped. "I'd be perfectly happy if I came home and she was dead from alcohol poisoning."

"That bad, huh? You in the market for something new? How about your admin, bet she'd look great on your arm, decked out in black silk with diamonds around her neck."

"You have the hots for her? Maybe *you* should trade up, or in this case, down. She's a drinker too. Caught her twice, pretty hung over in the office, barely functional." Not true, but what would Neil know about that.

"Maybe she broke up with her boyfriend and drank away her sorrows. Dave says they aren't a thing at the Hazel Nut anymore." He laughed a little. "Me, I don't dare stray too far, Candace would destroy me. She knows this job is long term and no administrator in this country has the brains or balls to run Holcome." His wife was a divorce lawyer much in demand by cast-off women. "But I can look, can't I?" He chuckled, knowing some wishes came true occasionally. "I'd forgive a couple of slips, if I were you. Try being nice to her and see what it gets you."

"So did you call me here to talk about my sex life?" Loomis was agitated, he didn't like being put on the spot, it made him feel less of a man to have an albatross of a drunken wife around his neck when he'd rather be on the free range. And Storm? He clenched his teeth.

Hawthorne leaned with his back on the rail. "No, I called you because I want you to do something about the Hamptons. Our little harassment is backfiring. The last thing I want is them going to the press and that Mark guy is smart enough to make it work."

"What the hell do you mean?"

"Cut off the portal, cut off appointments, you said. Cut off, cut off. Screw up the billing. The damned idiot keeps calling *me* to fix every little thing that goes wrong, like he did this morning. They won't take no for an answer, he zeroes in on me. Zora is useless. He doesn't call her, insists he was told in the care plan to deal with the team, her name wasn't mentioned, mine was. Do something, Chuck. Break them! I want them so bothered they can't think straight. Keep them so frazzled they can't move or react. Up the dialysis somehow."

Loomis leaned over the railing, hands clasped. "Uhhh, I'd have to think about that." His brain was racing for possible causatives. "That's going to be a problem, it's not usually done this early. Insurance may balk at it." He took an angry breath. "But insurance isn't likely to be the real problem, it'll be the Hamptons themselves. They're sharp, Neil. You tell the wife something and she calls the guy and he's back at her with every possible medical idea to oppose what we say. They will explore every option and fight like hell." He laughed. "Not that it will get them anywhere."

"Think about it. I want something in place in a week or so. Just don't do anything to kill the kid, he's worth big bucks." And Hawthorne walked off, laughing.

※※※

Downstairs in dialysis, Callista was pensive. The trip to Iowa had gone well. The mood of staff, particularly the transplant coordinator, was so upbeat it was contagious. They felt really good about the place and they were now listed for kidney transplant at both Harbison and the University of Iowa. It was strange how they worked the donor stuff, the country was divided into regions; if a kidney became available in an eastern region, the surgery for Nick would be at Harbison; if a kidney was in a western region, then surgery would be at the University of Iowa. The Mississippi River was the great divide.

She settled into the lounge chair. Nick had a good start on his homework in the truck, but what was done in the truck stayed in the truck. It was hard to concentrate in the dialysis bay with the nurse checking this line or that. Plus certain ones gushed over Nicky and wanted to see his homework and talk to him about it. Enough to make a person want to puke, she thought, they were so phony. The file of Miscellaneous Medical Records had finally arrived on a small flash drive; it would take forever to go through the thousands of pages of documentation. Their lives were stuck in a holding pattern.

The phone pinged. Text from Mom?

Ad in Stanton paper, lawyer looking for clients. Data breach of Holcome patients.

Callista froze. Data breach? There's all kinds of stuff in the records here, addresses, phone numbers, bank information, social security numbers, employment, medical stuff,... *pictures*. Her skin crawled at the thought.

C: *When?*
E: *May 21, 2020.*

That was the day of the fight in the dialysis bay, Callista thought. Were these two things connected? Who could do this, there are access keys and security codes. It had to be an inside job. She hurriedly texted Mark with the news, and Tera.

C: *Did u know a data breach at Holcome? May 21. Lawyer looking for clients, have to call, see if Nick or Sienna had their info stolen.*

Tera shoved the phone into her pocket. Loomis was leading the way as he, Dorian Place and Gwennie came in. And then Loomis was in front of her, his Adventus after shave lotion overpowering. He thought it made him more sexy. He was kind of restlessly moving, looking over his shoulder at the others.

"Yes, Doctor, do you want something?"

He handed her a Post It with a phone number. "Call this number. Leave a message."

"No particular name or person?"

"Don't ask questions, just do exactly what I tell you." And I'm supposed to be nice to this bitch who second-guesses me all the time?

"Just say 'Anytime'."

Tera's eyebrows went up. One word from the great one and kingdoms fell? He joined Gwen and they headed back to his office. She retrieved her phone. Roger would know about the breach, but she hesitated. Would he even pick up?

Data breach May 21? Lawyer advertising in News

While she waited for a response, she used the hospital landline to make the call for Loomis. It was an answering machine, some guy who sounded half asleep. "Leave a message."

"Anytime." She hung up but created a contact in her own phone, it might be useful. She texted herself the details. Roger pinged.

R: *Oh hell, it's out? Massive. 1500 FEMALE info. Inside job. CYA now, usual BS letter sent.*

Tera forwarded it to Callista, then she replied to Roger.

T: *Usual letter?*
R: *That files only looked at briefly, nothing downloaded. BS. You want to sell SS numbers, pictures, you download.*
T: *Employee?*
R: *Had access code. Likely. Happened more than once. No one will get records of anything starting from now on.*

Elsewhere, in Loomis' private office, "Gwen, did you manage to get through to Iowa?" he asked, taking a wine glass from his office cabinet and returning with her wine from the bar.

"No, I didn't. I talked to someone named Tamara and she told me they didn't want my information. I told her I was a social worker and I have the child's welfare as my priority, but she still said no. And then when I tried to call twice more, the call wasn't put through." Gwen was very insulted. Loomis did not look happy at all. He didn't mention that he had tried to call the kidney transplant team at Iowa and had also been ignored.

Damn them, the Hamptons got ahead of us on this, he thought as he poured the Grey Goose into his glass. He downed it quickly. What was it I said to Place when he asked about the breach, he thought, pouring another drink. They could see everyone who accessed records if they asked for the right information? I've been in and out of the Hampton records, even Mark Hampton's records when I blocked him. I've got to secure that. I'll have Patrice blank out my name. I hope they got that letter that they can't revoke me because I'm the head of Pediatric Services. He rolled the vodka around in his mouth and then swallowed. He waited as its warmth went through him. I've got too many things going on to keep track of, but somehow, a lot of them center on the Hamptons, damn them. Wish I'd never set eyes on them. How the hell do I figure out how to tie them up more than the three days for dialysis? He looked over at Gwen. Maybe she can come up with something, maybe a court order. This has to be airtight, he thought.

CHAPTER 48

There was a trick to unhooking the desk drawer from around the rollers. And it was heavy work, even with the fifty files taken out. But it had to be done, perhaps a paper, or papers had fallen over the back and into the cavern of the drawer frames. The flashlight picked up...a dirty tissue, some frayed crumbs of paper. Nothing. With a heave-ho, Tera had the drawer up and back on the rollers.

Looking down, she saw contact paper on the bottom. What neatnik did that? Tera ran her fingers over it, one sheet of paper wouldn't make a ridge, but a couple-three might. On the side, was something bunched up? She aimed the light at the side to the back. There was a triangular piece of paper peeking up but partly submerged under the contact paper. With a box cutter, Tera slowly went around the section and lifted it up. The triangular piece of paper was stuck for sure, but it was only a scrap; there were some other papers there folded up near it. Homework. She dropped them into her purse.

Sitting cross-legged on the floor next to the built-in file cabinets, Tera had been at it all morning, with Miranda's emailed account of what happened a year ago in her lap. The incident with the black woman who wanted to see her child's doctor and was taken away by security was a big red flag. Miranda had noted the smallest detail, even the silver lapel pin on the black woman's collar, R with wings of some sort. How on earth can I find her, Tera thought. It's not like you put an ad in the paper for a woman whose kid died at Holcome. Roger said there was a rumor about a child being killed by a doctor – was it Loomis?

To her right sat the files she'd gone through. How many people had been there since Miranda, three? All had quit, they couldn't stand working for Loomis. Three months and he ate them alive. But the single, unlabeled folder Miranda described was nowhere to be found.

Tera began to restack the load of folders when she detected a faint odor. Disinfectant! Were the desks disinfected after each use? And previous files removed, lest a piece of the virus would crawl out and kill someone?

This is impossible, she thought, discouraged. There is no way to locate anything that was taken away from here. All I have are some scraps of paper and a silver pin, with angel wings. I think there's one person who could help me on that end, I can see him tomorrow, but this could all be a dead end.

The door to the offices opened and she caught the aroma, Dior Sauvage. Oh God, Hawthorne. Tera hastily grabbed another pile of folders and began to put them into the drawer.

"Here, let me help you with that. Housecleaning day?"

She quickly grabbed another bundle. "That's fine, sir. No need, just another day in the life of a peon."

She was on her knees and gathered up the last batch, but they squirted out and he was down helping her pick them up. There was something off about this, Tera thought, being alone with the hospital administrator.

Brushing herself off, she looked up, "Thank you for your help. You *do* know that this is a late day, Dr. Loomis is in Wisconsin and due back" she made a show of looking at her watch, "in a half hour."

"I'll wait."

She settled back into her chair cautiously. Cat and mouse time.

"So, Ms. Storm, what do you do in your spare time?" He was lounging against the desk. Today he was garbed in a deep blue wool suit, with red pinstripes an exact match for his tie.

"A little personal, don't you think?" But he was waiting. "Go home, eat, read, sleep, same as everyone else."

"I can't believe this place is your whole life. A woman like you should be involved in a lot of things."

"Church knitting group? Bar hopping? No sir."

He started laughing at the images. "You'd be the perfect accessory to any executive. Black silk and diamonds, night life. How does that sound?"

"Out of my price range. Especially the diamonds." How well she knew that, her own collection – gifted by a generous husband – was safe at home. Life in London wasn't all books and students; once she'd broken Craig of his habit of spending all his time in the classroom, they'd enjoyed every minute of the city's cosmopolitan life.

"Not if they were a gift. Are you married?"

Gotta shut this guy down, she thought in panic. "Wouldn't you be more comfortable in Dr. Loomis' office? I understand he has a supply of liquid refreshment...."

"You know about that?" He was looking at her a bit differently; then, "Want to join me? He's got a good selection of wines and...."

"I'm working, sir."

"He says you're known to have indulged. So why not...."

"Gossip? You men gossip?"

Neil was enjoying this back and forth immensely. "So tell me, Storm, why is it there's nothing in your personnel records here?"

It was a split second hesitation, but he caught it. Got you.

"There's nothing down there? They must be lost, you're the administrator, you know a person doesn't get hired here without an arm's length of a resumé and certainly not put into Elite without extensive checks."

"Exactly. So where did your records go? Dave says you're the one who made a fool of Mrs. Harris in a monthly meeting. She let it be known you trained in Europe. Is that so? Where are the records? What is your work history?"

"You're talking about an international transfer. I have no idea how that works. They must have been here or *I* wouldn't be here."

"And why is there nothing about you online, Storm? Nothing."

Gotta stop this, she thought in a panic. "What is it you want to know? If I can transcribe? Use a computer? Read medical script? I went to Sorbonne." Lie. "Then to Italy for a master's." Lie. "I'm trained, I do what I am asked. Isn't that enough?" Too much edge in the voice, she thought. Take it down.

"Is my work unsatisfactory?" She forced herself to sound anxious. Did an eyebrow go up there? Then she heard the elevator.

"Mr. Hawthorne, here comes my boss, and your peon. Thank you for the visit."

They weren't gone a minute before she called Regina Harris only to find out Hawthorne had formally requested her personnel history and Harris was unable to stall any longer. There will be plenty of homework tonight, Tera thought, inventing an alternate Teresa

Storm, and covering eight years of fake work history, references, forged letters of recommendation, for sure nowhere near anywhere I've been with WHO or even London. I can throw together a list of hospitals, Heidelberg, Rotterdam, Paris, but if he checks with just one, I'm toast.

※※※

Staring at Hawthorne who was looking absently out the window, Loomis asked, "So what's your problem now? I've got work to do." He dumped a couple of files from his briefcase onto his desk, and shrugged out of his suit coat. "Neil!"

Hawthorne had poured himself some Barr Hill, but was lost in thought. Why would a drop-dead gorgeous woman be content with a silly job at a hospital, and have no life other than this and reading at home? Where was her home? A tiny apartment in town? Where had she worked? There was more to her than met the eye, she was far too polished, cultured. He could sense it, even in the way she talked, the European accent when she'd rattled off the schools. And why was she cleaning the drawers, unless she was looking for something. His eyebrows raised.

"Chuck," he took a swallow, thinking how to phrase this. "Chuck, remember when we were looking at the death certificate for that little incident a year ago and the paperwork you left on the desk, and your administrative assistant couldn't find it? Did you ever locate it?"

"What? That's old news. She probably threw it away and forgot about it. Anyway, she's gone, she won't talk, if that's what you're worried about." He went over to get his Grey Goose. "You came up here to talk about that?"

"No, what progress are you making on increasing that Hampton kid to dialysis four times?"

"Jesus, you think that's all I've got to do here is plot things out for you?" Loomis glared at him, hoping that would distract him.

"Get rid of her."

"Who? Storm? You want her in your office, I suppose."

"Call down to Elite and demand she gets canned." But he said no more, certainly not about the lack of personnel records or the uneasy feeling that was stirring in his mind.

Loomis again, "Yeah, sure. Later. So what's the latest on this breach stuff?" Hawthorne looked all wound up, even after a full glass of his gin. What the hell's wrong with him, Loomis wondered.

"Well, McDonough and Cranston from the Cities have taken it over, looks like a class action brewing. 1500 women's records viewed by some damned former employee here using a stolen access key is bad news. They probably will pick a dozen and make a show of going to trial with them. We're sending out a letter, saying nothing was downloaded. The usual response. The IT group looked to see if that was the only breach in the past year, but it seems that access key was used a few other times. Legal is not going to have fun with this one, damn it."

Loomis turned away and appeared to be enjoying his liquor. Lucky for him his *anytime* texts were just that, and not directly traceable to a breach date. There was just too much for him to keep track of.

CHAPTER 49

Fr. Tom Kressly shifted in the seat uncomfortably. He was in the confessional, a little box of a room, seven by nine feet, to the right was the kneeler with a screen, and before him was a chair for those who wished to confess face-to-face. Not many of those, the old folks didn't learn it that way and the younger ones didn't think they sinned. He felt wedged between the arms of the swivel chair. Either the guys from yesteryear were by nature diminutive or they fasted more than his twice a week. He couldn't help his large bone structure, good farm boy stock, except he'd never been on a farm in his life, he'd just come that way.

It was nearing 3:30, the end of Saturday's run when the confessional door opened. The person knelt at the screen.

"In the name of Christ our Savior, welcome and be reconciled to Him."

"Bless me, Father, for the grace of a good confession. It has been three months since I last confessed." There was a pause. "I am guilty of getting drunk, a whole weekend of it."

No news there, Tom thought, Covid made everyone want to get drunk, especially since liquor stores were open the whole time, being designated as an "essential service" by the governor. But this was a woman, they didn't exactly come across so bluntly.

"It was suicidal," she added. "I was depressed."

"Are you more at peace now or has this happened a lot lately?" he asked. "Is this a habit?"

"Just once, four-five months ago."

"Go on."

"I'm married, I was tempted to commit adultery. I...I wanted to, but in the end, it didn't happen."

"Was that temptation while you were intoxicated?"

"No, the drunk was after a put-down by the guy. I...I...."

"Okay, you don't need to spell it out, I get it. Go on."

Other items, deception, a problem with anger, oddly rather insightful. She seems to be wanting to right things, he thought. He spoke about fidelity in mind and body being important in married life; he spoke about the need for prayer.

"You pray, don't you?"

"Not enough."

"Then do it more. You are a child of God, keep in touch with Him. For your penance, please pray a Rosary, for Our Blessed Lady to help you get your act together. Pray it like you mean it. Now make an Act of Contrition."

They were finished. But the door didn't open, she didn't leave. Then suddenly, she was standing in front of him.

He shot back in the chair hard against the wall. "Teresa Blakely, Storm, whatever your name is now. What are you doing here?" He looked as if he'd seen a ghost.

Tera looked at him, strangely. "I went to confession. I'm tired of TV Mass and decided to...."

"I mean in here, now?"

How odd, she thought, he looks like he's in a panic.

And he was. Good God, he thought, I can't be seen in here with a nice-looking woman. She was actually wearing a white mantilla of Spanish lace and a very modest dress, oh hell, nothing could tame her looks, she'd always be a knock-out. Didn't she know about the sex scandals that tore apart the diocese? No, she probably wasn't even in the country when the rules were made, the little windows put in the doors so no hanky panky could occur in the confessional space. He looked frantically at the diamond-shaped window. I can't be seen in here with her. She was speaking, he turned forward.

"Tom, I need your help."

"Then come to see me in the office. Please leave."

"I don't want to run the gauntlet of your church busybodies."

"Teresa...Tera, please go. I can't be seen in here alone with you."

"No one is here, Tom. There was no one when I came in and now the church is locked, your cleaning staff won't be here for 20 minutes. I'll be gone then. But I need to talk with you."

"Sit over there," he gestured to the chair a sufficient way across from him. Then a thought occurred to him. "Did you really make a confession or use that as a way to...."

"I know the rules, Tom, you don't lie in confession. It was for real, I swear. What's wrong with you?"

He took a deep breath, remembering the comment he'd overheard from the church secretary that priesthood was a waste for a good-looking man like the new assistant. Another bet ten dollars he'd be out of vestments in a year. If anyone ever found out he and Tera met in a secret meeting, or worse, that in their past, they'd considered marriage....

"Tom!"

"Okay, okay, what is it?"

"I have to find someone. A woman. All I have to go on is this scrap of paper. My cousin Miranda used to work in the office I'm in and she told me about a black woman who came in demanding to see a doctor because her kid had died at his hands. She was taken away by security. Later in the week, Miranda found papers on her desk, one looked like a certificate. She threw them into her desk and forgot about it but her boss came at her later demanding the papers. She couldn't find them. She thinks there's a link between the two encounters. And there's a story at Holcome about a doctor causing some kid to die, no one says who it was. I tore the files apart and this was wedged on the inside of a drawer, it has a few letters of a name or maybe the letters of a street with a number. The format is like the death certificates I've had to fill out. I need to talk with her. That doctor is treating my nephew, Nick. I think Nick's in danger."

"What have I got to do with it?"

"I want to look at your church computer records, or have my IT guy do it. Or you can do it. I've got to find her." She tossed a little stick pin at him, which, flustered, he missed catching. "I think this is from your parish, the R with wings and a cross? St. Raphael the Archangel? I got this from your cabinets in the back of church. It matches something Miranda saw on the woman's collar."

"When did you go through our stuff?" He was angry now.

"You guys have no security at all. The cleaning people come in to sanitize, they don't lock the doors. Anyone could walk in. You think you got all the paper out of the place, anything that you could touch that could have the virus, well, no, you haven't."

Tom covered his face. The name Storm suited her, blasting away at everything. No rules left unbroken.

"Look, don't give me the name. People with pins are usually on some committee or another. Just send me the name of committee members if you find one that could be a match. She's a black woman, professional. I'll track the rest down. I'll have my mom call her. Everyone likes Ellie."

"I've got to think about this. Honest to God, you put people in the worst situations!" He remembered her in debate, opponents wasted; maybe she was on the edge with the ethics, but as sure as hell lethal in her arguments. "Please, just go. Now."

She bowed her head; it was a reflex movement, he blessed her, and she was gone. He got up and was making sure the room was in order when his phone buzzed. The anointing alert for the Covid Corps priests. He went toward the sacristy to pick up the anointing kit. Two more soon on their way to eternity.

Much later, the church was dark, only the sanctuary lamp lit, casting butterfly-like flashes across the golden tabernacle on the altar. Tom was on his knees in the first pew, he was frequently there at the midnight hour. So many needs came before him during the day, he felt he had to lift them to the Lord before taking his own rest. The Covid deaths were increasing amid reports about another surge of infection. He was at the hospital almost daily, anointing and blessing those taking their last breaths on this earth. And there were visits to those not yet heading for eternity – all of them needing the prayers of their priest.

And tonight, a prayer for guidance. What do I do, Lord? Yeah, always a problem when Tera enters the picture. I've been twisting this way and that on the whole thing and bottom line, I shouldn't do this, that information is a sacred trust. She's right, there is a danger, but I can't see a way to do this. You've got to show it to me. Watch over those entrusted to her care, I really believe there's evil here. Watch over her, especially, she's way out there in the storm. Amen.

CHAPTER 50

"Boys, settle down!" Callista called as Nick and his friend Brian raced through the hall next to the kitchen. They were laughing and shouting in a game of tag that she didn't want to end up in a heap at the foot of the stairs they were fast approaching.

"Give me back my sweatshirt, I've got to get home on time or my mom will go ballistic. C'mon, Nick!" Brian was laughing too hard to be taken seriously.

They skidded to a stop in the entryway and collapsed on the floor.

"Mom! Can Brian stay for supper? That will save him from the wrath of mom! That sounds like a movie, your mom can be the monster." And they laughed some more.

Callista sighed. Things were always crazy when the boys got together. Brian was a good friend, he'd stuck by Nick even when hopes of school dissipated for him. As long as Brian followed the house rules – don't visit if feeling ill, stay distant – he was more than welcome to come by and hang out. He didn't even mind having to mask up now and then. The boys had spent time building with Legos, riding bikes, and, over summer, just sitting under a canopy with their feet in a wading pool and talking endlessly. Their latest venture was remote-controlled cars. They were designing a track in an empty space in the yard to race their cars.

"Brian, we're just having fettuccini with meatballs. Are you interested in that?" Callista called to them. Brian's mom was into health food and Callista didn't want to get him into any trouble with her.

"Meatballs? Oh yeah," Brian called back. He ran a hand through his brown crew cut. "I'll run home and ask." And he was gone. He only lived a couple of houses away, Callista was surprised there wasn't a well-beaten path in the back yards between their houses.

Nick flopped down at the kitchen table, blue eyes alight and a crooked grin on his face. "Thanks, Mom. We're having so much fun, I don't want to quit just to eat supper. Did you know his mom won't let him go trick or treating on Halloween this year? She's afraid of Covid. I just want to go out, you know? I got cheated last year, no way was I gonna go door to door in that RV camp in California. Anyway, that was the night before surgery and I was so scared of another operation and I had meds to take. I can't wait to go out this year, even if it's only two houses. I hope I can walk that far, I still don't have all my energy back." He took a breath, he often ran things together when he had a chance to talk.

"It sucks I can't eat the candy I get, but I just want to touch it! Maybe I'll save it until after I get a kidney and stuff myself then. Nine days until Halloween! I tried on that hat, Indiana Jones here I come!" He laughed as he pretended to flick a whip. Callista played along, ducking behind the counter.

The front door slammed. "Hey, I'm back!" Brian yelled. Nick jumped up from the table. "Let's go!" And they disappeared up the stairs to Nick's room.

From his office, Mark watched them go. He and Callie were trying hard to make life as normal as possible for Nick, working around dialysis days and school assignments so he could just be a kid, not a medical disaster with cardiac and kidney problems.

"Hon, how about we all go out for Halloween? We can go on the four-wheeler and just buzz the area. We can dress up, too, what do you think?"

"Are you serious?" Callista hadn't thought of that, but it could be fun. It seemed so long since fun was in her vocabulary.

"How lame," Sienna said as she trudged into the kitchen with her laptop. "You trying to be kids again? Trevor thinks adults acting like kids are stupid."

"Too bad for him," Callista retorted. "I'm all for it. That way Nick can go farther than two houses, maybe all the way down the cul-de-sac if he doesn't have to walk. He's right, he was cheated last year. If you aren't coming, you can have door duty handing out the treats." She thought for a minute. "You know, I have a coverall, I can be a Ghostbuster. Mark?"

"I'll just put on my hunting gear, that's freaky enough. And Max is going as a pirate. He's bummed there aren't any parties this year, except at school they can dress up a couple of days. Yeah, let's do it."

Sienna made a face. "Seriously? What kind of freaks are you people?" But she felt a little jealous. Should have kept my mouth shut, she thought. Now I'm going to miss all the fun.

CHAPTER 51

The next day, Dr. Dorian Place strolled into #1 dialysis bay. He nodded at the security guard who was on her phone and didn't even see him. Shaking his head, he hooked his finger over the strap of the face mask and pulled it to the side, letting it dangle from his ear.

"Hi, there, Nick, how is it going? Your blood pressure is a little elevated, but otherwise your numbers look good for the run today."

Nick ignored him. Too much reading homework.

Callista looked up. "I need to talk to you," she said to the doctor. So far she and Mark had spent two days going through the Miscellaneous Records – it would take forever to get through 13,000 pages! It wasn't an organized search, just bits and pieces, but it was enough to raise questions and tempers.

"Oh? Now what?" he asked looking toward her.

"Now what?" She was trying to keep her voice low so the guard wouldn't notice, but it was hard, she was so very angry. She yanked out some papers from her carrying case. "We finally received a copy of our so-called Miscellaneous Records. You knew! You've known all along that Nick had End Stage Renal Disease! That biopsy in January showed it yet you let Loomis string us along and not list Nick for transplant. How could you do that?"

Dorian took a step back, a deer in the headlights look on his face. "I don't know what you're talking about."

"Don't you read anything? I'm talking about Nick's medical record. I thought you guys had to read the records to know your patients and how to treat their illnesses. Too long for you? You knew his kidneys were so damaged they couldn't recover but you said nothing about it. That makes you just as guilty of negligence as Loomis is. Negligence! And accusations in these records against us are *false*!

"I do keep up with the current stuff, but maybe some of the stuff far back...."

"Just current?" Callista waved the papers in his face. "Like we've got nothing else to do but look for the lies this place tells about us. Mark and I have been going over this for a couple of days and we know half the stuff in Nick's Holcome record didn't happen *here*! It's stuff dredged up from when we were at Ridley and it's all lies. We've been trying to get them to correct it. Why is any of it even in here?"

Dorian kept his mouth shut. There was no answer to this, except his own why.

"We're accused of intimidation! Have you seen us try to intimidate anyone?"

"I...I...didn't know, I haven't seen it." His head was spinning. He knew more than he wanted to admit. Loomis threatened him: either keep his mouth shut or be fired.

"And while we're at it, who's Linda O'Brien?" Callista was fuming. "Her name is listed on the Stanton Police report as a contact about the incident in May. She gave information to help Dominic Dorrance who was mysteriously gone the day of the police investigation. I never saw her, never met her, she wasn't even here, because she works at Croixpoint in Wisconsin! How could she say anything about it? Yet she says like a great authority that they were warned about us and these behaviors *before* the May 21 incident. Why was she warned if she doesn't work here? How did she get the information from Nick's confidential medical record?

"Do you remember calling Mark that day when Nick had the Interventional Radiology treatment? Why did you do that? It wasn't about the procedure at all like you said because you didn't open the report until *after* you called Mark. It says so in the records.

"Damn it, that whole disorderly conduct thing was a set-up! You made the call and then the cops came after him while he was on the phone with you. We were told all our meetings were cancelled because we were dangerous, but they were cancelled *before* the incident! It's all in the records we just received! Did you know that Loomis and Richardson spoke *before* the Transplant Committee met at Ridley and agreed there would be no transplant?"

"Look, the best I can do is ask about this stuff," Dorian said as he started backing toward the door.

"Go ahead, ask about this stuff. It might be pretty eye-opening.

If you plan to stay here on staff, maybe you should know what you're getting into." She shook her head. "You've been used, Dr. Place. Quit being a yes man, a doormat, and stand up for what's right. We need help here and all you can say is you'll ask about it. Good luck with that," she said, turning away. "You'll need it."

***

"They've got the Miscellaneous Records?" Loomis was aghast. "How did they get those? I blocked their access!" He was standing behind his desk, so angry he was shaking.

"Blocked it, you can't do that. They have a right...."

"You did it, didn't you," he accused. "You forged my signature! You've been pals with that female and she got you to sign off on it, didn't she. Just like the requests for Harbison and Iowa for records for transplant eval. Who do you think you are?"

"You weren't even available when those hospital requests came in, you were busy with Gwen," Dorian said evenly. "They have a right to go to another hospital for a second or even third opinion on transplant, especially since we haven't done anything about that. And why is that?"

"That's my business and the hell with their rights. That kid is my patient and I'll do what I want with his care. He'll get his fricking kidney when I say so! Get out of here."

The word "doormat" flashed into Dorian's brain. Is that what I am? Out of the corner of his eye he saw Loomis head toward the files with the built-in bar. Oh great, he thought, as he jerked open the door. And there, just outside the door, obviously eavesdropping, was Tera. He stared at her. What was going on around here?

"Sanitizer," she said quietly with a smile. "Have to see that everything is topped off."

"Without the refill jug?" he asked angrily. He took her upper arm and moved her toward his office.

"I've got stuff to do," she said, pulling back. No way was she going to get cornered in an office with him, but he was relentless. "Quiet or he'll hear you."

Quickly, he closed the door. "What's going on, Ms. Storm? Why were you parked out there like James Bond?"

"Whatever are you accusing me of, Doctor?" She pretended to

glance around his simple office, file cabinets, a cheap gray steel desk, printer, and bookshelves. Not even half the size of Loomis's empire. Such was the life of a lower level ant.

"You did this and you didn't give a damn who got ripped apart for it. You tricked me on those hospital permissions, but this. I know I didn't do it, which leaves you! I didn't even know he had a block on it."

"Don't be silly, how could I, a lowly administrative assistant, remove a block by the great and mighty Dr. Loomis on a patient's medical record?" The tone was a tad too insolent.

"Because I was here when a fax came from Medical Information for verification." He yanked open a desk drawer and pulled out the paper. "They sent it to the wrong computer. What's your game, Ms. Storm?"

Tera's eyebrows arched slightly. Another error on her part. But he covered it. He must have initialed and verified it. Should I tell him, she wondered. Should I tell him they're messing with my nephew's life and screwing over my sister's family? Should I tell him he'd better man up and get out or he'll get taken down with the others? Can I trust him?

"What's *your* game, Doctor? You've been around at some pretty prestigious hospitals. Tell me, have they been run like this? Have you *ever* worked for anyone like Loomis? Is this your goal in life to be that guy's doormat? Man up and do what you know is right. Now, if you'll excuse me," she went toward the door. "It's almost closing time."

❋❋❋

Loomis poured himself another Grey Goose. He'd downed the first so fast the liquid was still warm. How could they have gotten the records? He didn't believe Place for one minute. There simply was no one else who could have authorized the file release and sidestepped the verification.

His anger was still rising. And the Hamptons, of all people, to get their file. They needed a setback in their almighty plans to leave the state for treatment. A hefty swallow and he opened his middle drawer and then the upper drawer on the side. Everything was in order. No sign of tampering. He yanked open the bottom drawer and reached under the hanging file. Phones in place. He grabbed the blue one and although he usually used it for texting only, he called someone.

"This is Shane," answered a drowsy voice.

"Get out of the sack. I've got something for you to do."

"You want me to do more you've gotta pay more."

"I'm paying you plenty. Get over to the Emergency parking lot right away. A woman with long brown hair with a kid will be leaving about 4:45. She needs to be scared shitless. Follow her up 72. Drive at her, I don't care if you hit her." He gave the license number he'd copied from the police records. "It's a Ford Escape. Make that two women. Both driving alone. The second one drives a Mustang. Same thing. Ram her if you have to." He took another swallow. "And the other thing, anytime, got that?"

He hung up. As he put the phone down, he caught the faint odor of sage. Damn! Storm! What was she doing in the drawer? Had she seen the phones? He picked each one up. There it was, a bit stronger. Damn, damn, damn. It's been her all along. What does she know?

Tera was down the darkened hall making sure the lights were off. Gwen left stuff on all the time, once a candle was left burning. Sure enough, a flickering light on the back file cabinet. As she came back into the hall, a powerful hand grabbed her wrist tightly, jerked her around and pushed her so hard into the wall she bounced. His other hand pressed hard against the opposite shoulder. There was hardly any squirm room. He pushed again, over and over, bouncing her into the wall like this was part of a drug deal gone bad in a back alley. Her head hit the wall and she nearly blacked out.

"It was you, damn you! You had those records sent! No gun with you now."

Tera stared into the wild-looking black eyes. What the hell? Loomis reeked of liquor, absolutely soaked in it, his clothes disheveled, and breath horribly nauseating. He was taller than she was, heavier, and he was pinning her to the wall at an awkward angle, breathing heavily. How did he know about the gun incident? She could feel fear building inside. She tried to pull her wrist free from his grip, but he tightened his hold and pushed her hard into the wall again. The other hand, she thought, my only hope. He eased slightly for another push and she dropped her shoulder. He lost his balance a bit. It was enough. She reached over and pushed as hard as she could against him to get a tiny bit of leeway, then grabbed the wrist holding hers and raked her fingernails downward as hard as she could.

"Owww, you bitch." The grip relaxed ever so slightly and she jerked the hand off, then gave him a hard knee to the groin, pushing him into the other wall. As she quickly walked down the hallway, her back crawled with the sensation of his stare, and she wondered if he would come back at her. She heard shuffling footsteps coming from behind, mumbled words that sounded like "She'll ruin everything." Tera reached her desk, grabbed her purse and went to the main door almost at a run and turning off the lights behind her. It's dark enough, he's drunk enough to have trouble with the door, she thought, but there's no way in hell I'm waiting for the elevator. She yanked open the door to the steps and started down, her breathing coming in short, frightened gasps.

CHAPTER 52

"Look at that jerk," Nick said. Although long bored with the ride, his favorite pastime during the long journey up and down Highway 72 was car watching. He never knew what he'd see, sometimes a Model T going to a car show and once a white Maseratti. "He just pulled up behind us after passing three people at top speed. I didn't know a car that old could move that fast."

Callista looked in the rearview mirror. "V-8." A gray and white old Impala, as big as those boats from the '70s, was behind her. She'd noticed it behind her since they'd left downtown Stanton. Now it was very close, practically touching her bumper; she slowed down. The only way to get rid of him was to drive like an old lady until he got the message and moved on. Only he didn't. He stuck to her tail.

"Yeah, okay. So why doesn't he keep going and pass? What's wrong with him, nobody likes it when you go this slow."

Stalking, Callista wondered. Why else would he be stuck on her like glue? "Can you get his license Nicky? I'll call Dad and see if he can call the cops or something."

"No, I can't see it, it's smeared with mud. He's moving up now, Mom."

Yes, yes he was, now he was even with her and staring at her. Watch the road, she thought as he dropped back. She looked in her mirror and saw there were no other cars around for at least a mile. Was he going to pull something, run her off the road? Now he was coming up again, edging into her lane. She had to move toward the side or he'd hit her. Damn! Still being pushy. She was straddling the white line on the side. Who would do this? She was coming from the hospital...oh not that. Some goon put on her by security?

"He wouldn't do this if you were in your truck," Nick calmly observed. "Too bad it's in the shop or you'd knock the hell out of him.

This SUV is too wimpy for that."

Now the guy was pulling out what looked like a camera, she hoped, and not a gun. As he did, his car moved even closer and the front fenders almost kissed. He had a Twins baseball cap pulled down on his forehead and his features were indistinct. The road was still deserted, damn! She hit her brakes and he shot out in front, must have panicked and slammed on his brakes, swerving a bit. He was ahead of her now but still wavering. License somewhat muddy, but numbers kind of visible. The dashcam could capture it. Then she accelerated past him hoping the surprise would help her escape. "Catch me if you can, idiot."

He didn't try. He crossed to the southbound lane to go after his second mark. Soon, the Impala was next to Tera who was heading north on 72. Too preoccupied with her thoughts, Tera was oblivious to traffic around her until the Impala was edging over in her lane constantly, as if trying to push her onto the shoulder. A stupid move, a lousy driver, Tera thought. Top a dirty white, bottom a gray, part of a bumper missing, I'm surprised it can hold the road, she thought. What a shitty day, like she enjoyed crazy doctors and all the head games. She was still shaking inside from the incident with Loomis. What the hell made him go berserk?

Suddenly, the Impala sped up and swerved in front of her, then the idiot driver hit the brakes. Oh God, we're going to crash, she thought in cold fear. Strike first! She gunned the engine on the Mustang. The roar was usually enough to scare the hell out of people and again it worked its magic with maybe only a few seconds to spare. The guy suddenly swerved over to the left, cutting in front of another speeding vehicle. Horns blared and he wobbled, heading fast toward the other side and a ditch. Good riddance, Tera thought. Her exit came up at Orion and as she downshifted, she noticed her hands were shaking uncontrollably. No surprise, a day in hell would do that to you.

It was dusk already, October. She opted to go straight home, maybe a brandy would help, or not. Liquor still turned her stomach. No computer, her concentration was shot. Besides, she'd been over the accounts and files so many times she could recite them, the threads coming together on the billing, the collusion – creating picture that was increasingly nasty, and downright criminal.

Through the burnt shambles of the little town and off toward the south on the now-dirt road, numerous shadowy trees waving in the wind like a choir of spectres closing in beside her. The open spaces of the golf course were blobs of darkness – a fitting Halloween prelude. The forest green house was hardly visible among the trees. She drove beyond the extended portico and circle and straight into the garage. The Porsche was there, a sad reminder of another life.

Once inside the back door, warm air surrounded her. Odd, it should have been cooler as dictated by the program in the thermostat. As she reached out for the light, she smelled something...edible? Food? Who the hell was in the house? And now, a step behind her. No more, please God, no more today, she begged as fear began to mount and she began to shake. She turned slowly.

He was right there as if he'd never been gone. Jeans and sweatshirt, needing a haircut, his dark hair was down his neck and curling at the edges, just like during that reckless year at Aquinas. The wire-rimmed glasses were new but did not detract from his rugged and handsome face.

Her voice was a whisper. "Craig?" I don't remember him being so tall, she thought. I feel like I'm looking at a stranger, it's been so long....And then anger swept over her.

"Why did you leave me here alone, Craig Storm-Livesey?" she said evenly. "You get me into that hellhole of a hospital and then you take off to jolly old England and your cushy teaching job. You bastard!" She was taking short breaths, trying to get her trembling body under control before he noticed.

Craig's eyebrows rose. "I've missed you too." His words, with the slight British edge, were touched with humor. "Senior staff, you know. I have to be there one term a year," he went on. He studied her, something was off, she was edgy, distraught. But his feelings were about to erupt.

"You're different, the hair,..." He sensed a barrier, as though he'd walked in on a life in which he no longer had a part. Something... No. Not now, he thought, grabbing her arm and pulling her to himself. Hands running across her back, and then tightening, he whispered, "It's been a living hell without you."

There was no hesitation in her response, just before their lips met, "Hold me, just hold me." Don't leave me, she thought. I can't take it without you.

CHAPTER 53

Total absorption in each other would be the best way to describe those first few days, but then, things were back to two people hardly in contact with one another, even less than on a strictly professional level. The relaxing evenings before the massive fireplace never materialized. Craig's job as acting director of the Insurance Coalition turned into a hell of its own. He was soon drowning in a massive backlog of paperwork, endless meetings, policy problems, and run-of-the-mill office duties no one seemed to want to do.

Adding to the confusion were people who had been working from home now drifting back to the various departments and needing direction. Even Ellie got waspish as she did her best directing staff, but it was a losing battle. The workers, intent on renewing social interactions, seemed to have forgotten what their jobs were and more than once Craig was required to redo the work of underlings. His mood darkened more each day. Adding to the pressure was the approaching deadline to make a final decision on investigating the Hampton case, still a vague shadow of criminality; and the calls from Imperial in London never stopped coming. There just weren't enough hours in the day to do everything that had been dumped on him. Overwhelmed, Craig moved his things into a spare bedroom to avoid distractions. He was gone before daylight and home late, a ghost of an existence. And the headaches returned.

Pediatric Services was reasonably professional. Did Loomis remember what happened? Tera thought it doubtful he would connect the gouges on his wrist to the attack, to her – he'd been so drunk that night. Yet, she felt an uncomfortable undertone within the walls as the days passed, a bit like waiting for a delayed firecracker to go bang. It was Mark who lit the fuse with a message to Dr. Place, about the need for peritoneal dialysis at home and the desired transfer to Ridley for transplant. Of course Dr. Loomis roamed through private messages addressed to Dr. Place. Why not, how else could he control things in his domain? The Hampton message sent him into orbit. None of this, he thought, they're getting none of this! He was up and out of his desk chair in seconds and down the hall.

"Zane! Where are you? Zane!" He knew where she was, it was Monday and she was busy on the computer. Zora looked around quickly in her office, like a deer hearing the first gunshot of hunting season. She got up and went to the door.

"Yes, Dr. Loomis. Is there a problem?"

He berated her right in the doorway for not taking down the Hamptons. Then he turned and stared at Tera, who was seemingly engrossed in writing something on a legal pad on her desk.

"What the hell are you doing?"

"I'm creating an inventory of the files here, it seems no one has alphabetized them."

His eyes drilled her. A memory was stirring inside his brain. He remembered the phone call to Shane and then, the dark hallway, he shook his head, not quite clear. Damn her, she's staring at me with those piercing eyes, like she's reading my mind. What was it Neil said? Something not right? Get rid of her? He must think she knows something. Why list the files, why go through the desk? She knows something! She knows!

"Can I help you, Doctor Loomis?" Tera felt vaguely afraid. Something was roiling through his mind, something so bad she could feel it.

He turned abruptly and made his way back to the office where he immediately got on the phone to Regina Harris of the Elite Corps.

"Harris, I want Storm out of here!"

"Dr. Loomis, I can't do that," Mrs. Harris said coldly. "You do know Holcome laid off 10,000 staff. You do know people working at this hospital have died from Covid. I have 60 people and ten are out with illness, and 18 more in quarantine. You're lucky you have her full time and not sharing her with some other department."

"I'll gladly share her, I'll gladly do without her. I want her out."

"It's not happening. You don't run my department. I report directly to Dr. Rexalt. She stays."

The call ended abruptly. Regina Harris glanced back at the tall figure behind her.

"Good," Craig nodded. "She stays, no matter what."

"Are you sure?" She studied him, not even close to 40, dark hair and eyes, still very good-looking, a bit on the thinner side, the antique gold wedding band kept sliding down his finger. The black wire-rimmed glasses were a new addition, perhaps to make himself look older, although she'd read eyeglasses afforded some protection from the coronavirus. Craig still had the habit of working the notch on his upper lip with his teeth, but the rest of the scar from the early surgery was hardly visible. He was wearing a dark gray gabardine suit with matching tie, perfect white shirt and polished shoes. A charcoal gray mask with *Imperial* embossed on it in gold was hanging out of the upper pocket. Clearly he was presenting himself as every bit the executive as Hawthorne or even Rexalt himself. Except for the phone, he was staring at his phone constantly, then clicking away.

"Yes. The information points to major irregularities. This has gotten bigger than the insurance complaint, we may have to turn the case over to government investigators. I don't care how she does it, legal or not, she's got to pull it together." He hesitated, a very slight smile on his lips. When they'd met those years ago at Aquinas, that outlaw trait was what attracted him the most. He shook his head, no time to dwell on that now.

It was an odd comment, Regina thought. She'd taken a sabbatical from Holcome for six months and worked with a medical team attached to WHO. There she'd met them, they were newly married and intense about each other and about the work in West Africa trying to prevent an Ebola outbreak. He'd been competent, approachable, kind, and had been known to join in soccer games with a local team. And just over a year ago, when Teresa had been placed into Holcome for investigating, he'd been the same, gracious and friendly. Had his prolonged dealing with crisis after crisis in Britain over the past year changed him? Surely this had been the year from hell for everybody, but his attitude bordered on harsh, especially in reference to his wife.

"Doc," Regina started. He looked up, and she figured no one had dared call him that since those days in Africa. There he was just "Doc," not the brilliant, highly-thought-of medical expert recently returned to Britain to help with the Covid crisis. No one had dared to call him "Doc" there, she thought.

"You need to get her out of here pretty soon," she said. "The hospital administrator's been snooping around for her files. We just barely put something together for it; I hope he doesn't try to check anything. He may be on to her. If they suspect anything, they could destroy the computer files to cover what's going on. And I don't think this will be safe for very long."

"What's the problem?"

"I truly believe the doctor she works for could be dangerous, maybe even physically dangerous." Then she murmured, "*L'agent provocateur*, you know what I mean? I think she's riding him, hard."

He thought a minute. "Yes, probably, no surprise there, but he's our only link to the people running this scam. She stays, Regina, she's got to get this done." And he was gone.

Regina Harris shook her head at Craig Storm-Livesey's new attitude, wondering if he'd begun to believe his own press, and other people were merely at his disposal.

CHAPTER 54

As he made his way into the parish office after morning Mass, Fr. Tom Kressly was still wrestling with the Tera question. It had been two weeks of wrestling, always coming back to helping her would be crossing the line into illegal. Wouldn't have been a problem in his past life, but now? The white collar he wore made a difference. He stopped in the entryway, the literature rack for parish bulletins and Care Notes and schedules for ministry had been emptied months ago, according to CDC guidance that the virus could live on ordinary household items like paper. It's like the churches, he thought, cleaned out. There was a cabinet to the side and he opened the doors and bent to look in.

Damn! She was right. There was a mess of papers shoved in the back. He began pulling the trash out and could see a larger booklet with a colored photo on the cover way in the back – a church directory dated two years ago. He flipped through the pages. I've been here about ten months, why haven't I seen this? There were some black families among the parishioners, good Lord, he thought, is this the answer?

In the seclusion of his office, Tom Kressly tore off his mask and began cross-referencing the committees and families in the directory. He had the scrap of paper, the numbers and a couple of letters of a name or address, he wasn't sure which. He took note of the wings and R logo. A parishioner had designed the pins for the committee members, a perk, so to speak, the pat on the head so many needed to encourage their participation in volunteer work.

And there she was, Carolina Burntside, a comely woman with five children, two boys, three girls, member of the finance council, her husband an usher. The letter B and the numbers of the address, then the letters *Cou* – Coulter Street. So the funeral would have been maybe summer-fall of 2019? It would be in the computer program and there was a book provided by the publisher of the church bulletins he could search.

An hour later, Tom was at his computer, he had Tera's email address up on the screen. Send the committee members and I'll figure out the rest, she'd said. They were all listed. But if that bastard is as dangerous as she said, this needs to stop, he thought. She needs to know.

※※※

Gwen Deeds – Ms. Deeds. Her desk looked nice and neat on top, but all she could show for herself were two drawers filled with a mess of scattered papers and a box of masks from Amazon. Her file system was layered by month, with blank colored sheets between piles, with November at the very top. Papers and more papers with large colored vinyl paper clips holding somewhat related pages together about monthly reports, procedures to follow, reports on the few families she was working with. One batch with a purple clip had a Post It: Outgoing. Where? Tera put that one aside. Not likely that Gwennie would notice if it was out of place, or missing for that matter. A very large red clip held all things pertaining to Hamptons, including all notes to and from the overlord, Chuck Loomis.

As she flipped through them, Tera could see printouts of messages between him and Gwen, some with the words *Add here*. Add what? All had page numbers, so it was from something to this. Tera put them aside to scan and forward to her personal email and print out at home. Home. As sterile as a hospital. Craig was hardly there, even if physically present. The separation between them was so acute the extra large king-sized bed had become her work area with papers neatly arranged by date from one end to the other, her clipboard and notes dead center. There was still so much to go over and the pages from this drawer would add to the mess.

Tera flipped to the last papers and saw something that looked like an official report. The words jumped out at her: *child protection background information page 5.* Farther along: *Must file in June.* Another note toward the back, not from Charles Loomis, it was in a woman's elaborate script: *You have to phrase it a certain way. I'll write it for you. MC.* Who? Who was so lucky to command the attention of three people to make an ironclad case, last June...oh my God. It has to be about Nick, Tera thought. Were they collaborating on the CPS complaint? Another note: *I'll submit it for you. You're going to be gone in July. I'll handle questions. MC.*

Tera looked around, still safe. She reached for the wad of paper held together with the purple clip: Outgoing. *Patient Care Summary Report* with Nick's name on the first line. And there were scrawls all over, with little stars on each page, calling attention to certain passages. And at the bottom, she found a letter from Gwen to the Ridley social worker, telling her the parents were unstable and repeating the same lies about missing appointments with a new twist added – it was doubtful that post-transplant appointments could be kept. Gwen recommended Ridley limit contact with the Hampton family.

This hadn't been sent, there was a FedEx label attached, but why was it to go to Cynthia Langley in dialysis? She wasn't to whom the letter was addressed.

There wasn't time to think about it, Tera grabbed the paperwork and got busy scanning it through the network to her computer. She had to get this stuff taken care of before they came in, not much time left. Conspiracy? Collusion? She shook her head. Why?

Finally, the end. She threw everything back into the drawer and got to her desk when the elevator door opened. Look busy, look busy. She hastily opened her scan file and forwarded the information to her personal e-mail. Another look around. They were standing outside the door, talking. Tera did a quick e-mail check and saw something in her inbox. The address seemed sort of familiar. A very distant memory rose to the surface. Tom. She opened it.

Wings behind an R with a cross logo in the corner. It was a scan from the parish directory with a list of the Finance Committee members of St. Raphael! Names, no addresses. Tom had come through! And what? There was a little asterisk by one name, Carolina Burntside.

Under the scanned page, Tom had written

+Robert, age 12. Aug. 30, 2019

The cross in front of the name meant Robert had died. It was true, then, all of it was true, a doctor had caused a child's death. Was it Loomis?

And there, at the very bottom of the page, Tom had written in big, bold, black letters:

NO MORE! KEEP ME OUT OF THIS!

***

"Damn it!" Mark came from his office. "Callie! Look at this letter we just got! It says Nick does not meet Holcome's transplant selection criteria. Get this, the reason this time is: 'Behavior pattern by individual or caregiver which is likely to interfere with post-transplantation treatment.' Great beginning to November," he ended in disgust.

"Behavior pattern that interferes with treatment? Are these people crazy?" Callista sighed heavily. "My kid's *life* is at stake! Let's hope our transfer meeting with Ridley next week will end this once and for all and get us out of Holcome for good."

CHAPTER 55

The Ridley meeting was on Zoom, of course, with Mark and Callista, the new pediatric nephrology director, Dr. Jenny Arms, Dialysis Nurse Manager Cynthia Langley, and the Ridley social worker, Rhonda Bellacourt, in attendance. It was U-Ridley now, the rebranding included emblazoning the new maroon and gold logo on every scrap of paper and vehicle and wastebasket in all venues in the entire metropolitan area. It was a formal meeting, with a formal agenda, the same format as with any other transfer patient, scheduled for nine o'clock sharp that Monday morning, November 9th, so that Nick and Callista could be off to Stanton before noon.

Surprisingly, things were slow to start, the social worker kept flipping from one page of the report in front of her to another. She even turned the papers in her hand sideways as if there was a note in the margin. Finally, she looked up.

"I see you want to transfer all care here to U-Ridley Hospital. Is that so?"

"Yes," Callista replied, wondering why she needed to state the obvious. "We've already met with doctors during the two months we were here for dialysis, so Nick is an established patient. We want to move nephrology here and get on with the transplant evaluation and getting a kidney for Nick."

Rhonda flipped a few pages again. Mark kept an eye on her, she seemed to be stalling. Then, after running her hand through her black flowing hair, she asked, "Dr. Arms, what do you want to do with this case?"

Arms wore a boyish cut to her brown hair, emphasizing her very fine features which were drowned by her oversized glasses. She shrugged and began reciting the usual expectations. "First, we get the records," she nodded to the pile of paper before Bellacourt. "Then we need to establish a dialysis schedule. Ms. Langley has worked with you in the past and will be in charge of setting that up. After a month we should have a good feel for what is needed. Of course, a full physical, echocardiograph, and vaccination update will take place in between. All routine. Then we can start considering the transplant evaluation."

"But some of that has already been done," Mark pointed out. "If you look at the Holcome records, you will see the vaccination status and other information. You're doing everything twice."

"We'll study it," Cynthia Langley intervened nicely, "and get back to you." In the end, she would have the final say, and she already knew what her answer would be.

"How soon?" Callista pressed. "It's been almost a year, we've got to get moving on this."

"Soon," Dr. Arms said, looking at her watch. "Thank you for your time." And then it was over.

A few minutes after the meeting, Loomis heard one of his Tracfones buzz.

What the hell, he thought. Like I need a phone buzzing in my desk. He stared at the red phone in his hand and recognized it was a call from Langley. He quickly pressed the phone icon to connect the call.

"Now what," he demanded.

Cynthia was laughing, a delicate sound. "We just had our meeting with the Hamptons. They want to transfer to Ridley for transplant and a time schedule for when they can get it done." She laughed again. "Thought you needed an update, Doctor."

Loomis sat back in his chair, and stared at the ceiling. An idea was beginning to form in his head.

"So, Cynthia, how much power in this process do you actually have?" He switched the phone to his right hand so he could take notes. As the sleeve on his shirt edged backwards, he saw the scars on his left wrist. An impression of the dark hallway wafted through his brain but he shut it out, that question was unanswerable. He grabbed his silver pen and a pad of paper.

"What do you mean, Doctor? I'm the Dialysis Nurse Manager, you know that. I manage dialysis."

"And what else do you do, Cynthia?" There was a sly edge to his voice.

"I'm at a lot of the meetings, prepare the agenda, items for presentation...." She wondered what he was getting at.

"Any control over things?"

Ahh, that's what he wants. She thought of the FedEx package and its contents which she didn't share after all with Linda O'Brien.

"I can control what goes into a meeting and what goes out, if that's what you mean. If dialysis is involved in any way, I have a say in the conversation, and let's say the determination of who comes into the program. Like last May, when you and I agreed that it would be a no to the Hampton transplant."

Got them! Loomis chuckled. "So when a family comes into the program, you vet them. You personally?" He'd been doodling, but now was jotting down some ideas.

"I can. I have to go over their history with us and that of any other providers."

"Do you personally write up the plan of care?" Loomis was enjoying the whole idea he'd come up with.

"I have done so. Would you like a particular plan of care for the Hamptons, Doctor?" No use beating around the bush, she thought.

"Look at their records, I mean the copy sent to your social worker from ours. Work off of that. Do I have to tell you what to write?" He laughed. "The thing you want to concentrate on is they have a pattern of behavior, they disagree with treatment and they nag doctors to get what they want." All absolutely necessary tactics with that kid of theirs, he thought. No run-of-the-mill treatment for Nick Hampton, but damn it, enough to look like a pain in the ass accepting them at any other hospital if we play our cards right. The problem, though, is that these parents are usually right.

"And Cynthia," Loomis added, "Do you have access at all to any online measures, like scheduling and messages?"

"No need to spell it out, Doctor. I have a way to...to make things disagreeable for them."

"Do it. And Cynthia, I would be happy to meet you for a drink or two, the next time I'm up in the Cities. But until then, watch for my friends from FedEx."

As she ended the call, Cynthia looked around the office. No need to get the records, she already had them, which was why the social worker was fumbling through them during the meeting. Bellacourt hadn't laid eyes on them until the opening words. So, he wants a

Family Care Plan, does he, yes they wrote those, but never had to mention parental control. Most parents were scared to death their kid was going to die and never said a word about treatment, they probably couldn't understand a speck of it. Yes, these parents were far more competent. Extreme measures were needed for an extreme – and profitable – situation. She turned to the computer and wrote out instructions for scheduling:

All appointments in all departments for Nicholas Hampton, son of Mark and Callista Hampton, of Trent, are not to be accepted without my prior approval as a nurse manager.

I just don't need to approve anything, she thought.

❋❋❋

The office door opened and Tera caught the scent of Dior Sauvage. She quickly closed the file drawer. It wouldn't do for Hawthorne to see her dumpster diving into the files again. She grabbed a water bottle, dumped some of it onto the floor and came toward the desk with it half empty.

"Oh there you are, Storm." He was smiling. Light gray suit this time and green tie. His weekly clothing budget must be half my annual salary, Tera thought.

"Watering plants. May I help you with anything?" She took her seat behind her desk.

"You're a whiz at everything." He was smiling, too much. *En garde*, she thought.

"I finally got your personnel records, I can't imagine how they misspelled Storm."

"Inattention. It happens to the best of us."

"Loomis in?"

"Of course, Mr. Hawthorne. He's head of Pediatric Services, there's a lot of work to do being an overlord."

Neil couldn't help it, he started to laugh and almost forgot what he wanted to say.

"Storm, I called my friend at Gemelli University Hospital in Rome. It was on your resume."

"I'm sure you have friends everywhere, sir." Damn, damn, damn, I forgot that item. Tera shifted in her seat.

"You didn't work there, you were a patient there, five years ago."

"Not my fault they can't keep their records straight." Or names, she thought. In as Blakely and out with a wedding ring and name change. "It was a car accident. You know those Italians and their traffic circles. Splenectomy." Unfortunately, it was true, however not due to a traffic accident but bullets from the raid in Guinea. "Do you want to see the scar?" she asked boldly.

An odd look crossed his face, he wasn't expecting the totally inappropriate offer nor the plausible answer. He cleared his throat. "Pretty impressive resume, I guess you're worthy to be here with us. Masters, huh? In what again?"

"Public health, you know, health issues. It helps when working in hospitals." Thank goodness there was nothing in her made-up file about the real university in London at which she was still part of the mathematics faculty.

He nodded rather absently. "I'm sure it does." Everything adds up, he thought. Maybe I'm just getting jittery about all of this. "Thanks, Storm. See you later." But he didn't go down the hall to Loomis' office after all, he went right back out the main door.

Tera watched him go. Roger had returned the cloned blue and red phones that morning, they were in her purse, with a list of locations, but no names. I have to compare all the numbers, she thought. Wonder how many times Neil Hawthorne has been called by Loomis, and vice versa. About what?

Oh God, I hate this place, she thought, closing her eyes. I have to make myself act calmly and pretend Loomis didn't go after me two weeks ago. And now I have to keep one step ahead of Hawthorne. But if I don't do this, don't keep at it, Nick's not going to make it. I have to do this for Nick.

Several hours later, Tera sat hunched over the deluge of papers on the bed. There were so many interlocking threads, so many events that connected between emails and letters. The timeline Tera created, date by date, across all sources was huge, the ugly picture a paint-by-number canvas with Nick splattered in the middle. Yawning, she gathered the sections up, all carefully labeled with a summary on top and went down the hall to the office off the main entry. There she placed the pile on the table beside Craig's desk. It was almost two in the morning and he was in the shower. With a sigh, Tera gazed around the room, he was back to hiding behind his interior wall, alone with only work. Am I going to have to drag him into the real world again, she thought, seeing the schedules taped near the computer. Always a schedule. She wondered if he was washing his clothes on a schedule too. That rigid lifestyle had been put to rest years ago, revealing not a shadow, but a man, softer, kinder, eager to laugh and love with her at his side. Where had that man disappeared to? As if eaten by a returning cancer, his life had horribly regressed to a form of solitary confinement in which she was nonexistent.

"What are you doing in here?"

Tera turned slowly, "It's my office too," she retorted. She was so tired she felt as if she'd drop any minute. How could he keep up his abnormal pace? "Holcome. I wrote a summary connecting the evidence." She noted the jeans and a nice, professional-looking sweater. Why was he dressed up in the middle of the night?

"I'll look it over." He threw his towel over the doorknob and picked up his notebook. An occasional drip of water slid down from his dark hair and he brushed it away. "Your sister must begin filing official complaints against Holcome immediately. Do you think she and Mark are up to it? They need to file a complaint with the Office of Civil Rights, with details of statutes and infractions. That may take a bit of time. The immediate need is they file with respective licensing boards in this state against that Deeds woman and Loomis. There's a deadline for those complaints. It has to be done or there's no chance anything will ever happen. Call your sister and tell her to get on it right away, this weekend, in fact."

Craig tapped the keyboard of his computer and was waiting for the screen to come alive. "OCR is their best shot, though, one step, one person at a time." He didn't wait for an answer, just turned back to the computer and sat at his desk. "Close the door on your way out, I have a class in a few minutes."

"Class? In the middle of the night? You mean you're still teaching at the Medical School for Imperial from here? Your term is over."

"I'm still on staff, you know. A couple of professors have been ill and I'm the last man standing until the end of the term."

"And then what?" Tera felt anxiety rising. *I thought this part was over, the connection ending so we could quit being gypsies every six months flying to London and put some roots down here. He can teach* anywhere, he can play doctor anywhere. Oh God, he's going to leave again, I know it, she thought desperately. He knows I want to resign my position at Imperial when my sabbatical ends in January, he knows I want to stay here, but it doesn't sound like I'm a part of the picture at all.

"Close the door when you leave."

As she made her way out of the room, she didn't notice a photograph on the floor, wrinkled from months of abuse in a clenched hand. It was a picture of Tera and Craig together, from their time in France, newlyweds and well after she'd been released from the hospital, finally looking healthy and vibrant. It was the only thing that had kept him going those recent harrowing months in London. Even now, so many weeks later, the images came back to him if he let his guard down, the haunting sights of death, men and women like shadows on ventilators, alone, forsaken, the breathing machines keeping them alive; the families he had to tell of things they weren't prepared to hear; his medical colleagues who fell in battle, by illness or suicide. Denis Rank, who'd come to Rome to witness their marriage vows, hanged himself in despair at the sickness all around. Craig was convinced that only the anti-malarials he was still taking after Africa had saved him from disease. Disease, all around....

The ping when the computer connected across the miles brought him out of the despair. He shook his head to clear it as the medical students logged on. Why, he thought, why am I doing this to myself?

CHAPTER 56

U-Ridley's letter regarding transfer into their dialysis program arrived the Monday before Thanksgiving.

U-Ridley Health Care Systems

November 18, 2020

Dear Mr. and Mrs. Hampton,

The Pediatric Nephrology and Dialysis Group at U-Ridley Health Care Systems appreciate your involvement in the care of Nicholas Hampton and want to do our best as his care team to provide care to him that meets professional standards. We have developed the following Family Care Plan Agreement which must be signed by you before any treatment or consultations at U-Ridley may proceed. Please sign this document at your earliest convenience and return it to me.

Jennifer Arms, Director, Pediatric Nephrology
Cynthia Langley, Dialysis Nurse Manager

<u>Family Care Plan Agreement</u>

While recognizing that you were trying your utmost to care for Nick and to advocate for what you perceived as his health and medical needs during his care with our program, January through March, Nick's care team has concerns that his care could be compromised due to some of your behaviors. Behaviors of concern include: raised voice; inappropriate and/or disrespectful language and belittling comments; failure to cooperate with timing of visits or treatments; failure to notify the staff when you could not arrive on time for scheduled lab or hemodialysis treatments; insistence on certain IV medications and lab tests; refusing to work with an attending provider; refusing to work with social workers; failure to follow dietary recommendations; complaints about the normal behavior of other patients in the hemodialysis unit; difficulties with

following the prescribed plan of oral medications and supplements, then insisting on IV doses. These behaviors contributed to a breakdown in the therapeutic relationship and also disrupted the safe and therapeutic environment in our clinic and hemodialysis unit.
In order to establish a trusting and therapeutic relationship with our medical care team, we have these expectations:

- You have the right to respectful communication by the care team and to receive clear explanations about Nick's care.

- You have the right to ask for additional explanation when you feel you are not receiving adequate information.

- You have the right to visit and to be present in treatment planning, care conferences, clinic visits, lab draws, and to have regular communication with the medical team, nursing staff, and other members of Nick's care team. Communication that is perceived as disrespectful or intimidating will not be tolerated, it is disruptive to the team caring for your child.

- You are expected to follow through with recommended treatments, including dialysis and outpatient requirements such as labs, medications, clinic visits.

- If Nick is scheduled for hemodialysis in the Dialysis Center, it is disruptive of our schedule if Nick's appointment time is missed or he arrives late. You must be here on time.

- Your treatment team will include a primary nephrologist who will be your main point of contact for Nick's health and medical needs.

- You will be expected to engage with interdisciplinary team members, including social work, psychology, etc.

- When you have concerns about Nick's care, you should ask to speak with the Dialysis Nurse Manager or the nephrologist on duty.

Thank you in advance for your full cooperation in these important care plan parameters. Please sign below and return as soon as possible.

Jennifer Arms, Director, Pediatric Nephrology
Cynthia Langley, Dialysis Nurse Manager

CHAPTER 57

Callista stared in disbelief at the Family Care Plan, with all its insidious undertones. "Where is it written that *we* can have any input in his care? We're the ones who know if the strength of the blood pressure meds is wrong and he's dizzy, if there could be heart ramifications if dialysis pulls too much of one element or another. Are they taking over Nick and we're along for the ride?"

"Looks like it. The stuff we asked to be removed is still there and amplified, like we were ranting rioters taking over the dialysis center. You know as well as I do no diet recommendations were given to us and they told us to adjust meds by ourselves. I can't sign it," Mark said. "I'm not giving up having a say in my child's care when I have information they need for his safety."

He worked all night. The reply to Ridley had to be carefully written, logically stated and very clear that they wouldn't sign unless serious revisions were made. Specifically he pointed out their lack knowledge of Nick's complete history and the dangers of ignoring the background of cardiac complications for any treatment. They, the parents, should be expected to be a contributing part of the team because no medical records could possibly convey ten years of ramifications of medical treatment in a pediatric patient. Ridley didn't have a clue about the cyclic vomiting Nick experienced with high blood pressure or the migraines when he got too little rest. Those were bits of information they, as parents, and only they could provide. He carefully revised their Plan to include several suggestions.

Then he sent a note on the portal to Dr. Arms, asking if she concurred with the original Care Plan, since he wasn't sure she'd even seen it. He had a gut feeling the whole affair had been orchestrated not by a team, but a single person.

Ridley got back to them with the speed of a poison-tipped arrow, through the Message Portal a day later. There was no question who was calling the shots, her name was plastered across the top of the missive.

U-Ridley Health Care Systems
~ From Cynthia ~

Mr. and Mrs. Hampton:

Thank you for providing our care team the opportunity to review your recommended revisions to the care plan for Nick. Our team has had many thoughtful conversations about your recommended revisions and whether we can accept Nick back as a patient. Before we can agree to have Nick return to us as a patient, we will require the following….

There was no avoiding it, the Family Care Plan had to be signed before any transplant discussions could begin.

Mark sighed. "We've got nothing." He leaned back on his swivel chair, just enough to stay balanced. "What's plan B?"

"I'll call Iowa Transplant," Callista said. "We've got to get Nick on peritoneal dialysis at home and be done with all this crap." But the phone call garnered a negative result due to insurance regulations. The entire dialysis staff had to pass special licensing and training requirements to treat a patient from their state. They could treat patients from four other nearby states with their current training, just not anyone from where the Hamptons lived. Without meeting this strange insurance requirement, peritoneal dialysis could not be initiated, supplies could not be sent to them. Callista broke down on hearing the news.

There was only one choice left, and it was announced at supper. After serving up noodles with Alfredo sauce and meatballs, Callista looked around the table.

"We have to move to Iowa. Nick has to get off hemodialysis and put on something we can do at home and only Iowa will do it. The problem is we have to be Iowa residents."

Not a jaw moved to chew. Then with a clatter, Sienna shoved her chair back and screamed, "No! No! No! You can't do this to me! I want a life! Here! I have a boyfriend, I have kids at school I hang out with. You can't make me go to Iowa. I won't go!"

"Sit down and be quiet!" Mark ordered.

"I will not! You can't make me!"

Callista tried to reason with her. "Look, we can probably find a way to work around the rules but for the first six months, we need to be residents so Nick can get treatment."

"I don't care about Nick. What about me? Everything here is Nick, Nick, Nick. What about me? What about Max?"

"Leave me out of it," Max muttered. He figured an explosion like this would come sooner or later. He didn't want to pack up and leave either, but he'd be more passive-aggressive about it than screaming at the parents at mealtime.

"Sit down!" Mark yelled, this time getting out of his chair.

"You only have one kid, not three," Sienna screamed. "Max and I are orphans!"

No one paid attention to Nick, who had been twirling fettuccini around his fork until his sister erupted. The very volume of the argument was so loud, he started sinking in his chair to get away from it. Now everyone was yelling. Well, not Max, he was shoveling food into his mouth, probably going to make a quick get away. Nick didn't feel hungry anymore. He had no idea Sienna felt that way about him. She always used to kid with him and make him feel good, he had no idea she...hated him.

"Sienna, calm down," Callista was saying urgently.

"No! Leave me alone. I hate you both! You're ruining my life!"

The yelling continued and Nick sank further down. Finally, while they were in a tiny circle talking at each other, he ducked away and ran upstairs. Only in the safety of his room did the tears burst forth. "Mom, Dad," he sobbed, "I didn't mean to do this. You don't have any time, driving me around to doctor visits. You had to go to California for me. I bet you don't like me either. I am wrecking everything." He sat alone listening, just when he would calm down the tears would come again.

It would be better if I wasn't here, he thought. I want to die, and then it will be okay. The room was dark, he hadn't turned the light on, and he didn't want anyone to know he was there. They didn't miss him, no one had come upstairs yet. He looked around the room at his stuff. Nothing, absolutely nothing so important anymore, not even his musical aquarium that he listened to each night as he fell asleep.

It had eased his stress ever since his first heart surgery nine years ago, but not tonight.

It would be better if I wasn't here.

God, he sobbed, I know I shouldn't hurt myself, but they hate me. I can't make it better for anyone any other way. I have to die. He lay in the bed and yawned. Crying made him so tired. He felt under his shirt for his tunneled catheter lines. He'd heard the talk in the ER after that goof-off nurse did the dialysis wrong, the heparin and all that. No one could stop the bleeding when the stitches pulled loose. They all thought he was just a kid and didn't know anything, but he knew they were connected to the main blood vessel in his neck. All he had to do was pull.

Tears were flowing again. I shouldn't do this. In religion class they said you go to hell, but that guy with the nice smile that I saw after I coded wouldn't do that to me. He'll understand I'm just trying to help my family. This is the only thing I can do. He yawned again and wound his hand around the lines. "I'm sorry," he whispered.

CHAPTER 58

Callista rolled over in bed. Oddly, it was still dark. She looked at the clock. 10:30! Then she remembered no school for the older two on the day before Thanksgiving. Her head still hurt, she'd had a terrible migraine after all that yelling. She'd wanted to throw ice water on Sienna to shut up her uncontrollable screaming. How do you punish a girl who just turned 17, didn't drive, didn't go anywhere, and said so many ugly things last night?

Maxie and Nick totally disappeared during the fracas. When she'd looked in on Nick he was so still, he'd put himself to bed. Max was sprawled in his bunk, an arm over the side, candy wrappers strewn on the floor. No eating in the bedroom, and who listened or followed rules anymore.

What are we going to do, she wondered. Tear everything apart and take Nick to where he could get care? Or let him die because they couldn't move to the only other pediatric hospital in the state that could do hemodialysis and the relationship was tenuous – even dangerous – with Holcome, there was only so much harassment they could take. She sighed. Hell couldn't be much worse than their life.

She had to get Nick up and ready to leave in 45 minutes to get to Holcome on time. She trudged across the hallway to his room. Still dark with the drapes closed, she was careful not to step on the matchbox cars he set up on the floor in car show formation. He was still asleep, so still, hands....Oh my God. She bent over him, eyes on the fingers of his left hand which were tightly wound around the catheter lines. The lines were taut. Did he pull on them in his sleep? It was too dark to see if there was any blood. She stumbled across the hall to get a flashlight.

"Mark! Mark!" she grabbed his foot on the bed and pulled. "Nick. He's, he's still asleep, I think, I don't know." She was breathing heavily.

"I can't see if there's blood."

Mark was out of bed and across the hall with the flashlight in ten seconds. When she got there, he was slowly unwinding Nick's fingers from the lines. The kid wasn't stirring.

"Do we call 911?"

"He's breathing. But I don't know if he yanked on them in his sleep or pulled...." Mark didn't like the thought that crossed his mind. Nick was in the room when Sienna went wild. Would a ten-year-old try suicide? "Nick, Nick, come on buddy, time to get up."

They gave a sigh of relief when he moved his head. "Call Dr. Place," Callista said. "Ask him what we should do, look for. C'mon Nick, time to get going."

Still in his boxers, Mark took the stairs down two at a time to call from the office. He didn't want Nick to hear the questions.

Callista got Nick up to the bathroom, looking over him carefully for any bleeding. The fact Nick was so lethargic wasn't good. Even if the lines were okay, maybe his numbers were off. He seemed genuinely sad at resuming his morning routine.

Sienna heard the running footsteps. What now in this stupid house? She got up and peeked out of the door of her bedroom to see her mom sort of helping Nick toward the bathroom. Then her dad was coming upstairs at speed – what was he doing still in his boxers? Did something happen? She was afraid to ask, so she ducked across the hall to Max's room.

"Max, Max, get up. Something's going on. Go find out what."

"Do it yourself."

She dug her nails into his ankle.

"Yew! Leave me alone!" He was sitting up and nearly hit his head on the ceiling. "What'd you do that for, stupid? That hurt."

"Go see what's going on. I don't want to talk to mom and dad."

"Oh geez, am I your ears and mouth now?" But he obediently slid down from the bunk and strolled out of his room toward the bathroom. Callista was helping Nick to dress. The kid seemed really down, wasn't kidding around at all.

"Uh, yeah. Uh, hi."

Callista turned toward him. "We're leaving for Stanton in a half hour. You and Sienna see that the dishes are done and then see if you can make that cool whip dessert with the apple chunks. Thanksgiving is tomorrow and we're going to Grandma and Grandpa's."

"Grandma and Grandpa Hampton? They live in South Dakota."

"And we have dialysis Friday. No, Grandma Ellie and Grandpa Paul. Now listen, Max," she came forward and spoke into his ear. "Nick may have pulled his catheters out a bit. I don't know if he will need to be admitted. And I don't know if it was an accident."

"Oh shit!" Max said, suddenly very awake. "What...."

"You heard the argument last night. How do you think he felt?"

The ride was torture. For an hour and a half Callista was torn with guilt about Nick and the argument and wondering what he'd done or wanted to do. He was just mindlessly staring out the window of the truck. No game device, not saying a word. If he tried to take his life, would he try again, she wondered.

Same routine at the hospital, same stupid Covid questions, same wave to the guard, same death march up to second floor. Dr. Place was waiting for them. He was cheerful enough, said he had to check him over and take notes, his boss wanted additional information. Callista almost choked. Loomis wanted notes? She opened her mouth, but Dr. Place turned to her and winked. The guy had a heart after all. When he was done he nodded for her to follow him out into the hall.

"Everything is intact. What made you think he tried to commit suicide?"

Dumber than a post. Did he truly have no idea the hell they were going through? "Our only path out of here is moving to Iowa where Nick can get PD and survive until he gets a kidney. Our other kids, well, our daughter specifically, had a screaming fit over this last night and Nick heard all of the ugly things she had to say about him. That reason enough for you?"

"You want a social worker or psychiatric consult?"

She shook her head. What did she expect him to say or do? He was part of the problem.

❖❖❖

The phone buzzed with a text message. Tera pulled it out of her pocket and saw it was Callista. They were at dialysis today downstairs.

C: *Got a problem. Nick is really down. I think he tried to kill himself last night.*

Tera's heart was pounding as she read the words. How could a ten-year-old think of that? And for him it would be easy with those damned catheter lines into his jugular. One yank and he'd bleed to death. The message continued:

C. *We've been coming here day after day after day. And all our avenues are exhausted. Can't get to Ridley because of the Care Plan. Iowa can't do PD unless we're residents. I told the kids we had to move to Iowa and World War III erupted. That Sienna went off on us, she said so many bad things.*
T. *Did Nick hear?*
C. *Of course, have you ever heard her scream at people? Wake the dead.*

Tera sat back in her chair. Although everything was quiet, everyone was present in the office. She couldn't leave to go down and visit, maybe help Nick.

T. *How long are you downstairs?*
C. *4:30. Long day and dark drive home. I hate it.*

Loomis is behind this, Tera thought. She'd seen Ridley's Family Care Plan while cruising in his desk and it was a piece of crap. Finding it there was just one more piece of evidence both hospitals were conjoined in their plans for treating Nick. But that isn't important now, she thought. Nick needs help. She quickly pressed the buttons on her phone.

"St. Raphael's. How may I direct your call?"

"Fr. Kressly, please."

"Father is about to go into an important meeting. I can give you his voicemail."

"Father will want to take this call. Just tell him it's Teresa and it's an emergency."

"I'm sorry, I can't do that."

"This is an emergency, lady. Sacramental emergency! Should I call the pastor next? The Bishop maybe?"

The call went through.

"You're such a bully," Tom answered, his voice not at all teasing. "You scared that poor woman badly. I don't want to talk to you. I still haven't made peace with myself about that last stunt you pulled."

"I'm not sorry in the least about that. I needed that information. And now I need help. Well, not me, but my nephew, Nick. My sister thinks he tried to commit suicide last night."

"What? The one on dialysis?" His voice was low and urgent. "Details."

She told him what she knew. "I don't know what to say, how to help him. He feels life is caving in on him and it's all his fault."

"Not your job," Tom said. "Where are they?"

"Dialysis today, two floors down from my office in the Maxwell Building. Second floor, until 4:30."

"'K, I think I'll wander over."

"You can't get in the dialysis center, it's locked and I don't think the collar will work this time, not many people need Last Rites there."

"Waiting room?"

"A little tiny thing right outside the doors, but...."

"Okay, I'll go there, bring Communion. Want to meet us there?"

Tera thought it over. "No, I can't and I can't. Still at my desk, I can only leave if the building collapses. And I can't do it, I can't receive. My husband is back and things...things just aren't right. There's nothing." She hesitated, "I'm thinking of leaving him."

"Running away again?"

"That's not fair! I've been married to him for five years. There is nothing between us anymore! Nothing! We don't talk to each other anymore, we don't even sleep in the same room!" She sounded desperate.

Tom sighed, he'd heard stuff like this before. "Look, why do you want to help your nephew? Why are you fighting so hard for him? He's not your kid."

"Because, because he means a whole lot to me. I love him."

"And what about this guy you thought you loved so much you vowed your life to him? You're not going to fight to save your life together? Why do you always run, Tera, or try to drink yourself to death? You need more help than Nick does."

CHAPTER 59

Snow was just starting to fall when Mark and Callista and the kids pulled up at Ellie's. The long row of lilacs was nothing but sticks and brown dead leaves were twirling along the yard and driveway in the wind. They parked to the side of the blue Mustang.

"Aunt Tera's here!" The kids tore out of the car and raced to the front door. It opened but they seemed suddenly frozen in place.

There was a tall fellow by the door, dark hair, glasses, with a light brown long-sleeved dress shirt and dress slacks -- something a person would wear to church, if people still went to church, what with the Covid restrictions, Mark thought. Craig Livesey still looked more like a rakish playboy than medical man, except for the intensity he projected, an aura of command.

Mark took the lead. "Craig," he nodded in greeting, a bit slowly.

"Mark, Callista. How have you been?"

"What are you doing here?" Mark asked bluntly.

Unperturbed, Craig replied, "Family, you know." The British accent was slight, barely noticeable, definitely upper class.

The kids edged around him. Behind his back, Sienna was clandestinely pointing, eyes wide and mouthing, "What's he doing here?"

"Well, let's get out of the doorway," Callista said hurriedly. If she remembered correctly, Craig was very perceptive and would know exactly what the kids were thinking. As if reading her thoughts, he turned. "Paul is waiting for you to help with setting the table and Sienna, watch your manners."

Nick was not perceptive. "I don't remember you very well. Who are you?"

"He's Uncle Craig, Nicky, go take your jacket upstairs."

"Uncle? You're my uncle? How?" Came the dawn. "You're married to Aunt Tera? Where have you been all this time?"

Over in the kitchen, Ellie and Paul were preparing the last items for the Thanksgiving meal.

"Didn't think Craig would have the guts to show up," Paul muttered to Ellie. He slid sideways as she started the electric mixer to mash the potatoes, there was no telling what would get splattered when she used that thing.

"It's Thanksgiving, family stuff and all that. He's here, it wouldn't look good if Tera came alone. He's good at keeping up appearances, you ought to see him at the Coalition. Dressed to the nines, vest and all like a commander-in-chief, but nothing hides that look in his eyes. Utter disdain." She looked down. "Instant potatoes next year, this is such a mess. What I'm really worried about is this stuff after dinner, getting everyone together to go over the Holcome mess. Roger will be coming around seven." She began to scoop the fluffy potatoes into two serving bowls.

"The guy was certainly skittish when he was over here," Paul said, as he opened the oven door to get out the pan with sliced turkey. "If you hadn't forced that beer into his hand I think he would've had a stroke or something. Then when Tera came in, if I didn't know better...."

"She has that effect on all guys."

"Ellie dear," he said, turning toward her. "You're wrong. The first time in your life, maybe, but you're wrong about that. It was like a bolt of lightning between them. A guy knows these things, from a guy's point of view. It wasn't exactly anger, or it was anger and something else. Do you know what I'm talking about or do I have to spell it out?"

Her eyebrows rose. Not that it was impossible, maybe she just didn't want to think in that direction. Tera and Roger had been seeing each other too much for her liking. He and Craig would meet later in the evening. Just what I need, she thought, two studs facing off in my family room.

A few minutes later, in the serving area in the dining room, Tera began arranging the cut vegetables on a tray, carrots, plenty of black olives, pickles, table onions. Nick was stalking her, and snatched the olives when she turned her back.

"You little devil!" She grabbed his arm. He gave her a hug, he knew he could always disarm people with a hug.

"So that guy Craig, you're really married to him?"

"Where did that come from?" she asked, carrying the tray, with the olive section refilled, toward the festive table set up in the middle of the room. "See this?" She flashed her fingers at him, the wide golden wedding band, its diamonds brilliant in the evening glow of the fireplace. "Yes, I am married to him," I think. She deposited the tray on the table.

"He must be stupid or something, not being here," Nick said as they went back to the serving area.

Although she agreed, Tera patiently repeated the party line, "He was teaching at a university in London, then couldn't get home because the airlines shut down."

Spying more olives in the open, Nick snatched another one. "Don't tell mom, she'll get all uptight about potassium crap. You know what happened yesterday?"

"Dialysis?" Tera was putting cranberries into a large bowl.

"Yeah, well, after, there was this guy in the waiting room. He stood up when we came out of the locked doors, real tall. He reminded me of that face I saw when I was 'somewhere else' that I told you about. Then I saw he was a priest. He was so cool. He knew my name and Mom's name, seemed like they knew each other, and he asked how we were and if we needed a little prayer or if anything was bothering us." He hesitated. "There was something I had to tell him, it was like confession. He made it all right. And he gave me this." He pulled a white rosary from his pocket. "He said in the darkest time of the night to look at this and it would be glowing to remind me I'm not alone, Blessed Mary is with me."

Tera looked down at the bowl she'd filled, she didn't want him to see the tears in her eyes. She recognized the white of the beads, luminous color that would glow in the dark. Tom to the rescue, as always. Nick would be safe now, from temptation at least, and God willing, from the other devils around him.

"He talked to Mom, and then said some prayers and gave us Communion, right there in the waiting area. He said an angel sent him." Angel? Tera nearly lost it right there and the bowl of cranberries started to tip. Why would Tom say that? He, of all people, knew how tarnished she was.

"Tera, the food! Quit daydreaming!"

"Yes, Mom, I'm coming." Taking a deep breath to regain control, Tera hurried to the dining area.

The plethora of food was amazing as well as tasty. The youngsters looked like power shovels with their forks, not that the adults were far behind them. It was odd having no conversation directed toward him, so Craig was alone with his thoughts and the meeting to follow later in the evening. Paul asked him a question about the house and he'd replied, "You'll have to ask Teresa."

"Who's Teresa?" Nick asked.

Craig looked at him oddly. "Your aunt, Teresa."

"Oh, I get it, she shorted it. So how come you have a different last name from Aunt Tera?" Nick went on, looking at Craig who was carefully cutting a slice of turkey.

Craig looked at Tera. "It's the same last name for both of us, Storm-Livesey. She chose to delete part of the name, apparently." There was no mistaking the edge to his voice.

"Seriously, Nick, Teresa Meredith Storm-Livesey is too long to write," Tera said quickly. "Storm has a nice ring to it." She gave a twisted little laugh. Watching the interplay, a small smile played over Craig's lips. She hardly looked evil with the jade sweater and curly hair.

"Like watch out for trouble?" Max teased, his voice rumbling from his shoes. "Like when you babysat us and...."

Sienna quickly interrupted, let's not go there, she thought. "So what do you do, Mr. Livesey?"

"Sienna! He's your uncle, you can call him uncle," Mark said. "Sorry," he said to Craig. "You're a novelty."

I hardly know these people, Craig thought, uncomfortably. We've been elsewhere for years, I don't even know what to talk to them about. "Indeed. So ask what you will."

"I just did."

"I'm a medical doctor."

"What's your specialty," Nick asked. This was his department. "Cardiology, General Practice? Maybe you're a shrink? You look like you could be in charge of something."

"No specialty," Craig said. "Just a doctor. A lot of the time I teach at a medical school."

Nick wrinkled his nose. "You teach? What a waste, that's for old guys who don't want to see patients anymore."

"You don't see patients at all?" Callista asked. "So you just wear a suit and preach about how to be a doctor? Seriously?"

Craig shifted, obviously annoyed. "My employer seems satisfied, and for the record, I did see patients in my residency. And when called out into the field, there were people who needed care."

"What field? Sports?" Max asked quickly, showing the first spark of interest in a boring conversation.

Tera cut in. "He...we...worked as attachés with the World Health Organization." Craig was not being very talkative nor informative. "We went to foreign countries, like Africa, where there were outbreaks of disease," Tera explained. "He was supposed to determine if an epidemic was starting, and give advice in handling and preventing disease."

"What did you do? Are you a nurse?"

"No, I gathered data and analyzed it to determine the progression of the epidemic. But if we were at a site in the back country, I also supervised hygiene, quarantine, teaching people how to avoid getting sick when things got bad. It's very different from how we do things here for an epidemic. In some places, houses would be burned to the ground to get rid of contagion. It would have been far better to avoid the sickness with proper procedures." It sounded good. In reality, it was stupid to teach hygiene when there was no clean water, she thought. And it was so hard to get people to abandon age-old customs such as ritually washing the bodies of dead family members and re-clothing them, thus getting exposed to disease and restarting the vicious death cycle. "A doctor can't just stand by when a person is injured and bleeding, you know. There was some stuff like that." Craig was adept at hands-on care, including surgery. Not in his job description and nothing he ever talked about, but if it was needed, it was done.

"So why were you gone so long this last year?" Callista asked Craig.

"Passport difficulties and with the Covid shut-down, it took awhile to get it straightened out with British authorities."

"When did you get back, then? Did you have to quarantine on the East coast? I heard they were doing that to people."

"Yes, they did enforce quarantine." He said no more. It's my business what happened during quarantine, he thought, those interminable video meetings with WHO and the CDC for my take on the Covid epidemic. He turned away and saw Tera studying him. "Is there a question, Teresa?"

Teresa? He's acting as if we're mere acquaintances, not husband and wife, she thought. She shook her head in answer and then got up and walked away. What *was* he doing during that quarantine, why didn't he call?

When the meal was close to ending, Ellie and Paul brought out the pies and Cool Whip and started taking orders: pumpkin, apple, cherry. No seconds until everyone had their firsts.

Observing the table, Craig thought it a waste of time to be there when there was so much paperwork needing completion to launch a criminal investigation by federal authorities of Holcome. It wouldn't get done while partying, but Ellie had trapped him into being the star performer at the gathering she arranged. She told him in no uncertain terms he owed an explanation to those who had gathered the evidence whether he liked it or not.

"Wake up," Ellie said, handing Craig a slice of apple pie. "Not enough sleep lately?"

"I can't remember the last time I had four hours of sleep," he replied, looking up at his sometimes abrasive mother-in-law. "Thank you, Loretta. Everything was very nicely done," and he meant it. "Truly a feast."

"Loretta, who's that?" Max asked, looking around. The kids were puzzled.

"Loretta, your grandmother." Craig looked around at their confused faces; the adults seemed to be enjoying the confusion. "Don't you know your grandmother's given name?" he asked. The situation almost made him laugh.

"Did you think my name was Ellen, Eleanor or Elaine?" Ellie asked. "L.E., Loretta Enright Blakely."

"That's kinda weird," Sienna said.

"There's a lot that's weird in this life," Ellie retorted, thinking of the coming meeting. "Get used to it."

A short while later, Mark cornered Craig who was standing by the fireplace cleaning his wire-rimmed glasses. "What's this meeting about tonight?"

"You filed an insurance complaint. This is a chance to bring everyone up to date on what has taken place, what has been discovered. Besides family, others have been working on it. This seemed a good time to do this while I'm still here."

"While you're still here?"

Craig didn't bother to look up. He seemed overly interested in the invisible spot on the lens.

"Didn't you have contacts the last time you were here?" Mark asked slowly. Craig finally put on the glasses, they made him look older and even less friendly than he already was.

"I left them in London with my other things."

"Why would you do that if you're living here?"

There was silence.

"Jesus, you're not staying, are you, if you left your stuff there. What's going on?"

"None of your business, Mark, now leave me alone so I can prepare."

"You're going to go off and leave Tera again? Does she know this?"

Silence again. No getting through to the guy. "You're a real son of a bitch, aren't you?"

Craig looked him straight in the eyes. "I asked you to leave me alone. Please. Mind your own business."

CHAPTER 60

The dishes were stuffed into the dishwasher when the dramatic tones of Beethoven's Fifth Symphony spilled from the doorway.

"Meeting time," Ellie said. "That's Roger." Paul was gone in an instant. Mark and Callista were sitting around the oak table in the family room, the golden glow of the tea lights in the centerpiece flickering on the gleaming surface. The kids were upstairs playing an old Wii game. Tera was filling glasses with ice, ready for whiskey, vodka, Irish Crème, brandy, everything on deck with beer as well.

Roger, the computer whiz he'd heard so much about, Craig thought. He glanced toward the door, and his eyebrows arched slightly when he saw the good-looking black man.

As Roger entered, he saw a pleasant family gathering. He already knew the players, Miranda was a nice addition. She waved to him. And Tera, over by the liquor. She looked as attractive as ever in the jade sweater. Nice. Then there was the tall dark-haired guy with the wire-rimmed glasses by the fireplace. Not even a hair out of place. Pleasant enough looking, maybe overdressed.

Craig turned and was giving Roger an appraising look. He'd missed nothing, particularly the glance toward Tera. He cast a quick look to the side, she had her head down, but no longer busy. Good God, something has been going on here, he thought as he went forward uneasily.

"I'm Teresa's husband, Dr. Craig...." He extended his hand, a bit of an edge to his voice.

Roger wouldn't take the hand. "I have no respect for you, man, not for any guy who leaves his wife here all this time alone."

Usually unruffled, Craig was taken aback. "I had business in Europe to attend to and then this Covid stuff...." They stood there, same height, Roger still every bit the athlete in build, Craig by no means diminutive, but definitely with the air of a man more likely to command a business meeting than a football field.

"That's your story. Are you totally clueless, or didn't you know about stuff like your *wife* getting attacked in the parking ramp at the hospital?"

Silence fell over the room and Tera dropped the ice cube tray. "Uh, Roger, no need to...."

Roger wouldn't stand down. "Does he know you were stalked by those two jerks again and again? Did you tell him when they were in the ramp, you had to pull a gun on them?"

Roger glared at her and then at Craig. "This isn't for laughs. She doesn't know what those guys planned to do. I heard them, guys talk. That's why I was there in the background watching, every single day, so she'd be safe. Where were *you*?" Craig cast a sideways glance at Tera with a very obvious flash of anger.

"Help yourselves to refreshments," Ellie broke in cheerily, like some clueless old lady. Like hell, she thought. Things were about to get explosive. Her comment threw some cold water on the tempers that were flaring. Roger turned and took a seat next to Miranda. Ellie wondered what the real story was behind his abrasive words, Tera had cut herself off from them, saying nothing about this terrifying stuff.

"Cool it," Ellie whispered to Roger as Craig watched the drinks being served. He was as hard to read as ever, she thought. Working directly under him for the month since his return from London wasn't pleasant and he ran – ruled – the Insurance Coalition with an iron hand. The only thing saving her job, even if it was only temporarily taking Tera's management place, was the fact she could produce what he wanted, when he wanted it, and how he wanted it. The addition of the work on the Holcome investigation only added to the tension. And now the results of the foray were right before them all.

"To begin," Craig started, then waited until all eyes were on him. It was hard to tell if he was angry or merely intense, his British accent was clipped and precise. "Thank you for interrupting your holiday evening and coming to this meeting. To acquaint you all with the players, of course you know Loretta and Paul, who are hosting this discussion, Tera, Mark and Callista Hampton, Nick's parents, Miranda Coates," he paused slightly, "and Roger Allen. One other person, who provided invaluable information, declined to participate to protect his or her identity." He looked around. "Each of you has played an important part in getting this plot uncovered. It is a bit involved, but I will simplify as much as possible." The dark eyes roved the room.

"Is he calling us stupid?" Mark whispered. The guy would be a devil in the classroom, he thought, an absolute devil, eyes not missing a move. And Craig was staring at him.

"Mark? A question?

"Uh, you weren't even here, how do you know what was going on?"

An eyebrow went up. "It was my job to know, to have people gathering details. You know, the office job you disparaged earlier? I was kept informed. Now if I may continue...."

You goddamn prick, Mark thought. He looked toward Tera. Why the hell did she marry *him*?

"Over the past few years, complaints of fraud were filed with various members of the collaborative under the Insurance Coalition umbrella. Usually these complaints were ignored, miniscule in the global picture of things. The only standout was repeated claims in rehabilitation or transitional care, about people put into rehab when they didn't really need it or being kept in rehabilitation much longer than the industry norm. This did not occur in large numbers and people concerned with it did not produce requested evidence.

"When I took over as Director of Medical Review two years ago, Teresa was managing the office part-time, doing policy and other analytics and she compiled the data on these reports for me to review. A little over a year ago, a detailed complaint was received about Holcome International; that was something we *could* investigate.

"We'd had contact with Regina Harris during her sabbatical a few years ago, and she agreed to place Teresa in the Elite Corps and assigned her to transitional care where the suspicious activity originated."

Roger sat back. Mrs. Harris went to Guinea in West Africa to assist a WHO team during an Ebola outbreak. *They* were with the team? He'd seen the pictures, but couldn't remember who was in them, and some of the medical workers wore the space suits. He looked over at Tera. Man, I seriously underestimated her. But I was right, she wasn't at Holcome long enough to know which snake not to step on. He shook his head with regret at their past relationship which ended so abruptly. But then, if this was her husband, it was better it ended as it did, for her sake, because the control freak *doctor* didn't look like anyone to mess around with.

"Dialysis began to be another problematic area. There are no clear rules about its use and before End Stage Renal Disease is declared, things get easily blurred. Dialysis is costly, less oversight, patients aren't knowledgeable about their own treatment; they just do what the doctor says. The costs mounted, the payments to the hospitals and dialysis centers increased. No one paid attention. And then came a complaint against Holcome.

"Miranda was already working there, and was to be transferred to Nephrology, preferably to dialysis, but the orders got changed and she ended up in Pediatric Services. Nothing of interest there, until a child mysteriously died. Miranda, would you care to continue?"

Miranda hadn't expected to speak before the group. She quickly pushed her Irish Crème to the side and then nervously brushed back the brown hair cascading over her shoulders.

"A woman came into our specialty circle and asked to see a doctor, she wanted to know why her child died. The doctor I worked for, Charles Loomis, was watching her through the blinds and had me call security to get her away. Then a few days later when I came in early to work, I could hear three voices arguing in the back conference room. Dr. Loomis came out of the offices screaming at me for being early, ordering me not to say a word to anyone about anything I'd heard in that office. Later on, Loomis was after me again, demanding the papers he'd left on my desk. He had me rattled so badly I couldn't find them. The next thing I knew, I was demoted to part-time in a different department and within a month, my employment ended."

Craig's long fingers were drumming against the back of an empty chair, his gold wedding band like a warning beacon on his finger. Impatience? The story too long?

"The child died from medical negligence; he had kidney problems, his blood pressure was forced too high, and his body couldn't handle it. Staff on the floor did not treat the child as rapidly as they should have. Cerebral edema caused his death."

"That could have happened to us," Callista breathed. "Oh my God! Was it deliberate?"

"I don't know that, I wasn't there," Craig said rudely. "The case was buried, the family literally threatened with bad publicity if they revealed the cause of death. Thanks to our absent informant, we have the family name and the mother was willing to speak with me and agreed to meet with lawyers about the case."

"Lawyers took the case? We had a similar experience and no one will give us the time of day," Mark interjected.

"Your child is still walking this earth, thus no damage," Craig said harshly. "Hers is not. Of course they took it, an easy win for damages, their percentage puts plenty of money in their coffers."

Mark was shifting angrily in his seat. Callista put a hand out and stroked his arm. This was their case and getting into an argument with the lord of the realm wasn't going to help.

"The mess on Miranda's desk likely was Loomis' attempt to alter the original death certificate and have a new one entered into the records. But that is neither here nor there. The details were unknown in the general hospital population, the death only a rumor at the time, no department indicated.

"Moving on," Craig looked over the room. The Hamptons now looked as if they were struck dumb. Good, no more questions, he thought. "In all places with complaints, such as Houston, the plan appeared to be the same, keeping patients in high-priced situations. And it seemed to me the next likely area of incursion would be pediatric dialysis. For children, hemodialysis is used initially, the dialysis catheters are introduced into the arterial system, usually the jugular, and that type of dialysis can be performed only at a hospital. According to the plan we thought would be implemented, hemodialysis would be introduced, parents made to believe it necessary and required with more frequency, having the weekly times increased significantly so as to bring in tens of thousands of dollars a month to the hospital. When Nick Hampton came along, we had our way in to find out what, if anything, was going on at Holcome."

Callista sat bolt upright. "You used us, damn it! You used us!" She was standing now. "You knew what was going on and let it happen, let Nicky get abused by these...."

Mark grabbed her arm and pulled her down. "Shhhh. Let him talk."

"No!" she yelled. "He knew what was happening and...."

"Of course you were used," Craig asserted calmly. "We had to see how it played out. I believe everything that happened is part of a script, the treatment neglected at the hospital to lure you into an angry response, like the one you just had. The onerous behavior plan, all of it, even the lackadaisical care at Ridley was likely part of the plan. Our research found a similar case in rehabilitation a few years ago. Meetings with hospital officials in that case were nearly word for word as the ones you reported from last winter. I am positive the May altercation at the hospital was constructed specifically to provide an excuse for keeping you at Holcome, holding you there for alleged security reasons."

Tera was staring at the table. Why is he being such an ass about this? The sound of his harsh voice was actually making her feel ill. She looked up and caught Roger's eyes on her. She held his gaze until he glanced briefly toward Craig, there was no mistaking his disgust.

Mark couldn't stand it any longer. "*Why*! This makes no sense. It's insane. Someone *planned* it this way? They could've killed Nick! They still could!"

Craig hesitated, I need to tread lightly here, he thought. "This at Holcome may be a test for implementing the fraud scenario in pediatrics cases elsewhere. Nick was unique because of having cardiac difficulties as a complication, but they went ahead with it. It seems a likely scenario for duplication if it works, and it has been, hasn't it? You haven't been able to move an inch away from the mighty Holcome International, have you?" There is a lot going on outside of simply trapping them in expensive dialysis, he thought. Should I tell them or shouldn't I? The intimidation, interstate coercion, child endangerment and negligence that I am obliged to report to federal authorities – can they understand it isn't just about them anymore?

"How can you stand there so calmly and act like this is just a classroom recitation!" Callista hissed through clenched teeth. "Get us out of this!"

"I cannot get you out of this." Craig nailed her with his glare. But she wasn't intimidated, wouldn't back down.

"Then what good are you standing there like some god making pronouncements."

"I'm your best chance of getting *yourself* out of this!" Craig shot back angrily. "I told Teresa to get you to file the Office of Civil Rights complaint. You did, didn't you? *They*, not me, are your so-called best hope. Piece by piece, do you understand me? Person by person, you need to take them apart because this has happened to *you*, your child. You are the ones hurt by this, I can only give you information, advice, and hope to God you follow it. Start with licensing and don't stop." His voice was raised. He'd caught the look between Tera and Roger and he had to work hard to keep his anger in check.

Paul pushed his chair back. "Time out on the field!" he called. "Anyone need to use the restroom, it's down that hallway. Drinks? Ice water? Time to take a break and cool things down." There was a lot of noise as chairs were pushed back, but the silence was overwhelming.

CHAPTER 61

Callista turned to Ellie. "I can't believe this. He stands there like God himself telling us what to do! Who put him in charge?"

"You did, actually," she replied. "You filed the complaint. Once he got Tera's timeline, the bits and pieces suddenly fell into place. He could see it through all the random incidents. That's what he's good at. Then Roger here got drafted to do some computer work," she cleared her throat, "you know how they remote into computers to fix them?"

"Don't say any more," Mark said. "I work for people who track the Rogers of the world down and have them arrested." He looked over, Roger and Miranda were in a friendly conversation. He was definitely someone the girls would go for, Mark was glad Sienna was upstairs. He wasn't ready to deal with that kind of stuff.

"He was merely looking for clues, directions to go in," Ellie said. "Looks like we're resuming our chat." As people moved to their seats, she went up to Craig, who was staring a hole into Roger's back. "Need anything to drink?" She meant liquor, to calm him down, she'd seen that temper more than once.

"Coke, please."

"Just what you need, more caffeine," she replied, he'd already emptied four cans in two hours. But she got a cold can and handed it to him. He popped the tab and drank half of it. "God, I hate this people stuff." He was about to turn back to the group when Ellie said, "Geez, you're a doctor, how can you hate people?"

He turned on her, angry. "*This* stuff, Loretta. Dealing with people *this* way. It's just like telling people their loved ones are dying of that goddamn virus within an hour. I hated doing it and I hate this. I hate the office. I'd rather be back in Guinea practicing real medicine than here."

She choked down a startled cough and decided it was time to retreat. He'd done hospital work with Covid patients in London? A little PTSD, then? He was facing the group, his eyes frigid.

"None of this talk about fixing things is any good unless we get the man in charge, the fellow whose wicked mind came up with this plan. We're not even close to that," Craig said, thinking all of you, get off my back for not getting you through your crises. "Loomis is a loose cannon, devious and a psychopathic liar, perhaps the perfect front man." He looked at Mark and Callista. "His job is to keep you in control, spinning stories to you and about you. He told you Dr. Arthur released you to transfer to Ridley. She didn't even know there was a transfer attempt, nor did your other specialty physicians. And you didn't have a clue. You were told they all agreed to get rid of you."

"I can't believe this," Callista said. "How can he be pulling all these strings?"

"He has *power* over people," Craig said, frustrated. "He provides whatever they want, usually money." It was a shot in the dark, but the most likely scenario. "He might even be acquainted with the former resident who was apprehended for the breach, the fellow who was downloading indecent pictures of female patients, possibly for sale on the internet."

Callista gasped, "Holcome never told us about downloads. Nicky's file was breached!"

"Yes, and it seems while Mark was being assaulted in the dialysis center, *his* files were breached. Not likely by the same person or for the same reason, but someone *was* in his files because on that day all care for Mark Hampton was cut off forever. Someone had to be *in* his file to do that. Roger has been trying several ways to access it and all have been foiled, there is extra security on that particular item. It's unfortunate for the son of a bitch that he did it on the same day as the major breach by the former resident. Whoever the interloper is, he *will* be linked to the breach and take a hit for it." Likely Loomis, Craig thought, whether he likes it or not, he will be implicated up to his balls in the dirt. The feds will nail him and the press will eat it up.

"As I said, we haven't figured out the brains yet. And meanwhile, you are chained to Holcome, you need dialysis, you cannot have a transplant, and you cannot transfer. You may be sure Ridley will deny you. You're stuck and have to wait out everything they throw at you until some federal agency decides to investigate this intrigue." Craig looked over the room one last time and sighed. That was it, his part was finished, now just the last few minutes of obligatory small talk and they could leave.

Callista sat back, it was dizzying. And he was so matter-of-fact, so cold, she wanted to slap that look off his face. If she hated anyone, it was Craig Storm-Livesey at that moment. Doctor? Brother-in-law? Bullshit. Killing the messenger? So what, I want to kill *someone*.

What a mess, Paul thought. He reached over and rubbed Callie's hand. "It'll work out. They'll get it done." He didn't know who *they* were, but she was desperate for encouragement.

Mark was exhausted and wished they'd gone home before any of this meeting stuff started. The kids were downstairs, hanging out by the table and scarfing up stuff from the dessert tray. Nick wasn't into dessert, he was sneaking olives and crackers, until a hand came over his.

"No," Tera said. "You can't do this, your mother will kill you." If Holcome doesn't. She was short of breath, her heart seemed to be racing. The day was way too long, and she just didn't have much of an appetite. The anticipation, the stress of this meeting – Roger and Craig face to face, especially – tied her in knots, even now when it was over. Craig could sense things other people couldn't. It made her afraid that he knew she'd wavered in fidelity. She took a quick breath. She still felt nauseous, in fact, and a little dizzy. There was a tap on her shoulder. Craig nodded toward the stairs.

"We need to talk." She couldn't read his mood, past that professional face of stone.

She turned, saw the kids had suddenly disappeared, probably upstairs again while the adults talked away. She shrugged. "Okay," and started up toward her old bedroom.

Craig paused, noting that Roger was leaving. And then he was out the door, right behind him. Paul caught the action and went to the window, watching out the sheer curtains.

"Allen!"

Roger turned. What the hell? "What do you want? I need to get home."

"What do I want? I want to know what the hell went on at that place, those guys you mentioned. What did she do to make them go after her?"

"What did she *do*? She didn't do anything. They just came on to her," Roger looked at him, hair still perfectly in place, totally the executive, but perhaps not so much an office slave as he appeared. "You got a problem with that then you should've been here to mind the store." He turned.

Craig grabbed his arm and jerked him around. There was more power in the so-called doctor than met the eye. "You're not telling me everything."

"What's there to tell? Have you looked at her? There wasn't a guy in the place that didn't want a piece of her. All she ever did was walk by. You get it or are you blind? Even the hospital administrator was after her. His kid was the one facing the gun in the parking ramp and he was telling his pals his father would have better luck than he did." He stopped. Pure hatred was standing before him.

"And you? What did you want?"

"Go to hell." Roger turned and walked away.

Craig stared after him and then deliberately walked toward the house. By the time he got inside, he made for the stairs, taking them two at a time.

Paul looked around, where were the kids? Callista and Mark were about ready to leave. And Tera? Upstairs? This is not going to be good, he thought.

CHAPTER 62

Callista swung the Ford Escape down the driveway for the trip home. It was relatively quiet, the kids were full of ice cream and pie and sedate, even though they didn't like being crammed together in the back seat.

"God! What an ass! 'Of course you were used.' I could've choked him!" she said about Craig's comments. "If I never see him again it will be too soon."

"That guy is such a cold bastard, what did she ever see in him?" Mark complained. "Too bad we're related to him."

"We don't have much to do with them, we're safe," Callista yawned.

"Uhhhh, what about Christmas? We'll be over at your mom and dad's, them too."

"No! Go without me. I can't think of anything worse than being with people I hate. And right now I hate him."

"You're not the only one," Sienna said. They'd forgotten just because the kids were quiet didn't mean they were struck deaf and dumb. "They were having a loud...um...argument upstairs."

"What were you doing upstairs? I mean, I know you were downstairs awhile and then disappeared again, but where were you that you heard anything?"

"In Grandma's room."

"Yeah, you guys were still yapping, so we went back up to do a little, uh, exploring. Grandma shops early," Max explained. "We decided to kill time looking for our Christmas presents in her room. In the closet."

"You were in my mother's closet? Snooping?"

"Didn't you ever snoop?" Max asked. "Of course we were looking around. Found some interesting books, did you know she reads spy novels? And there was a mysterious bag with boxes." He was laughing with a little hiccup. "That's where we were when they started arguing."

"I'm surprised you didn't hear them," Sienna interrupted. "They were *yelling.*"

Mark laughed. "They did disappear for awhile. In fact, only Craig came to say good-bye, but I dodged him. Like I wanted to even say anything to him, he was icy hot, you know what I mean? Madder than hell. She didn't come down. Pity him, she's got a hell of a temper."

"You think?" Sienna said. "They both went at it so bad my ears were burning. Hate? He was telling her she wasn't going back to work at that bloody place, he had no idea who she was involved with and what she was doing."

Max interrupted. "And then it was, let's see if I can remember it right, she yelled, 'Who made you my lord and master'."

Mark winced. "Ouch," he said. "You girls are short on the wives shall be submissive stuff."

As Callista slammed him in the arm, the Ford Escape jerked to the side.

"Mom!" the kids yelled.

"Then she said, 'You want your damn proof, by God I'll get it or die trying'," Max continued. "Then he said, 'You're not....' You can guess the rest of the picture."

Sienna snorted. "You haven't heard anything yet. Then they got on the subject of Roger Allen."

"Oh, oh," Callista said quietly as she turned onto the freeway. Little red dots of taillights ahead were barely visible through the falling snow. She, too, suspected there was more than met the eye to the story.

Max picked up the story, "Oh yeah," he said. "They got into it bad about that. That's when we cut out. I kind of wish Roger would have punched that Craig guy out. Fight! Fight!"

"I'd put my money on Roger," Sienna said. "He's a hunk. I wish Tera would've married him instead of that Craig."

"Maybe you'll get your wish," Mark muttered. "I can't see Craig hanging around. In fact, he even said he left most of his stuff in London and got really pissed when I asked him point-blank whether he was leaving. What's he got to be mad about, you want to protect your property, you lock it up and guard the door. Serves him right."

"Property!" Callista swerved again. "You're on the sofa tonight, you jerk."

But both were thinking the same thing, was Tera cheating on him? Did he step out on her?

"Let's see what we don't know about the medical mystery man," Mark said as he opened the browser on his phone. "Medical doctor, served as an attaché to WHO in public health surveillance. What the hell is that? You just watch people get sick? British Army. Now acting director of the Insurance Coalition since Elgin died. This is too tame. He's going to be out of here ASAP. Professor at Imperial Medical School, he wasn't even old enough to be credible when he started teaching there. He's now on staff with their School of Public Health. That's what he went to Europe for in December, his classes. Oh my God."

"What is it? What is it?"

"When the pandemic started and the airlines shut down, he worked with Imperial's Global Infectious Disease Team on the projections for the virus, deaths and mitigation factors, those guys who did the modeling for Britain and the US and other countries." Mark was staring at the phone intently. There was a link to a story about grossly exaggerated modeling projections. Craig had challenged the team's work in the public forum? The guy laid waste to everything he touched, it seemed. But what if he was right? What if all those predictions really *were* exaggerated? There was more, but Callista's voice broke into his thoughts.

"He never said anything about that. I don't believe it. And how would someone so high on the food chain get in contact with my sister?"

Mark attacked the phone again. "When Tera graduated from high school, she got a degree in mathematics the same year? They never announced that. She's that smart? How the heck did she get into Imperial College in London? They take Americans? Maybe she and Craig met up there. Did you know she has a PhD in math?" He stared at the screen, Tera said she served as an attaché with WHO in public health, how did math fit into that, he wondered, but then saw her dissertation was titled, *Using Statistical Analysis to Predict Outcomes in Managing Public Health Crises*. Wasn't that what modeling was about?

"I was too busy raising kids to pay attention," Callista interrupted his thoughts. "Nick was busy having heart surgeries when she'd zoom in and then do a disappearing act. Am I supposed to believe she's some kind of genius? Don't make me laugh! She probably can't tie her shoes yet."

Nick was quiet in the back seat, tears beginning. It's happening again, he thought, everyone angry again. His fingers tightly gripped the white rosary inside his pocket.

***

The ride home to Orion was intensely quiet. The argument between Craig and Tera had been filled with accusations of infidelity and denials, harsh personal insults as cutting as a scalpel. Craig told her he would never be sure if a child she bore was his – an evil statement because they'd been told conception was impossible for her. She answered with a bitter laugh and challenged his manhood.

Tera pulled up under the portico and Craig was out of the car before the engine stopped. He was in his office before she even came through the main door. Flinging her purse aside, she saw a letter askew on the table by the entryway.

Picking it up, she glanced through it. London. It was a print-out of an employment agreement from Imperial, beginning early in January for all of 2021. She was before him in three steps.

"What the hell is this?" She held it out to him.

He turned slowly, deliberately, the dark eyes behind the wire-rimmed glasses boring into her. "You can read. They need me back. And I'm bloody well going."

"No."

"I am. They need...."

She wouldn't let him finish. "They can get another lackey to recite lesson plans."

"You have nothing to say about this. It's my life. I'm getting out of here as soon as I finish with the Coalition and get on a plane."

She tore the letter up into pieces and threw it at him. "The hell you are. No."

He stared at the torn paper. It was like his life, a torn puzzle of pieces. "I'm leaving. Do you understand me?"

"Oh, I understand. The great Dr. Craig Storm-Livesey at your service. I'm telling you now, if you go, don't come back, I'll be gone."

"Then you'll be free, won't you?" he said carelessly. "A handy little divorce and you can go off with your black lover. Don't think I can't figure out what's been going on, the way he was looking at you. You're already his and you want him. I was a fool to think you'd be faithful." He was just short of yelling in his anger. "What the hell have you been doing that these men are falling all over themselves for you? The hospital administrator! But this one...." His voice trailed off as he took a breath, shaking his head. The link with Roger had been almost palpable.

She was inches away from the square jaw. "Are you thinking all I did was whore around, that I slept with Roger? Nothing happened between us."

"I'm supposed to believe you? That you weren't burning inside for him?" He laughed bitterly. "You're a liar. You always have been. You're always saying image is everything but with you, it's really deception is everything. Deception, do you hear me? It's what you do best."

He was barely able to control his anger, at her and at himself for trusting her. I loved her so much, he thought, I thought she felt the same. It's over, or perhaps it never really existed.

"I took our vows at the altar seriously," Tera retorted. "Forever and faithful! I swear I've *kept* my part of it." Teeth nearly clenched, she laughed a little. "Maybe you didn't, though. The airlines opened up last summer, why didn't you come back? Or did you have some side action? Maybe with your little office girl, Naomi? She'd sell her soul to the devil to get at you." Tera was breathing hard, dizzy with anger.

"I'm a doctor, you idiot woman!" He stared at her. "I should leave a deadly medical situation and come back to hold your hand?" He turned away. How dare she say that, when the man she'd been involved with couldn't keep his eyes off her at that meeting!

"I hated you when you left last year," she yelled at his back. He just turns away like our marriage is nothing to him, she thought in rage. "And I hate you now!" She yanked the wedding ring off and threw it across the room.

"Don't raise your voice to me, you slut." He still didn't bother to turn around, trying to mitigate his anger, his life spinning out of control.

"Or what?" Her tone was a direct challenge. She was so angry her whole body was shaking, breaths coming very rapidly.

Rage consumed him. Everything that whole night, everything that happened the whole year, everything he feared, now in this moment, personified in her. He turned and violently grabbed her arm, and pulled hard at her, shaking her. He wanted to hit her, to shut her up; his other arm was rising.

"I hate the sight of you," he hissed.

Tera felt the intense pain of his hand on her arm and saw the other hand now on the downswing. She tried to pull away. "You're hurting me! Let go!" What's happening? I don't even know him, so angry. Heart pounding, gasping and suddenly very lightheaded, she started to lose focus, she couldn't think anymore.

It was then he noticed she was trembling, internally, as dramatic as insulin shock. What the hell? Her eyes. Empty....

And then he was jerked forward as she fell. He made a grab to support her but missed and she landed hard on the polished wooden floor. He bent down and then shook her none too gently. Nothing. He saw where his hand left deep marks on her arm, already starting to bruise. He'd wanted to strike her, to hurt her badly in his rage. And now this. She wasn't coming out of it. Not normal. He quickly reached for her pulse. Very rapid, skin too cold, very, very white, breathing difficulty. It's shock for certain, he thought, confused. How did I miss it? This was now a medical thing, a serious medical thing.

He gathered her up in his arms and reached for his phone.

CHAPTER 63

The weekend was a nightmare. Craig called an ambulance, and then got in a nasty argument with the attending physician in the emergency room at the little community hospital; the doctor wanted to call the police on him for assault, the bruises were obvious. Then the doctor started on her, demanding she file charges or he would, state law required it. There she was loaded up with an IV, EKG wires taped here and there, blood pressure cuff wound around her arm – the incident was caused by drastic dehydration and concomitant low blood pressure – and he kept demanding she have Craig arrested, which would have been a sure case for deportation with his paperwork not in order, not even a renewed driving license yet. The ER fellow finally shut up when she tore off the BP cuff and EKG lines and began to yank off the tape on the IV. It was time to get the hell out even if she couldn't navigate very well. He threw after-visit papers at her and told her she was in danger being with the man who attacked her. It was essential she take care of herself, he said, and told her to come back for an appointment – but by then they were gone.

She didn't remember the trip home, only that she woke up in bed sometime during the night. The sheer curtains were closed, but enough light was coming through so that she could see Craig asleep in a chair near the bed, keeping watch as she'd seen him do so many times for his patients. His internal alarm would wake him every hour to check on her. For all of his faults, Craig Storm-Livesey was a good doctor.

Why? Damn him, why! She stared straight up at the glittery textured ceiling. How can I ever trust him again? Her arm hurt badly as did her hip where she'd fallen, her other arm ached from the poorly placed IV, but nothing was as bad as the sense of emptiness. It's over, there's nothing left. She stirred. Maybe I deserved this. I *was* unfaithful, I was, in my heart and soul. Deception? I just wanted someone to be with me, to love me. She felt cold and tears spilled over until consciousness slid away again.

At first, he helped her when she was up, but even then his touch made her pull back. They didn't talk, not once, until Sunday night.

"You're finished at Holcome. I'm sending a message to Harris," Craig said, standing in the doorway. She was using her laptop in the master bedroom, away from their shared office and his entrance was silent. She turned and was surprised by his appearance, unshaven, and he'd obviously been wearing the same sweatshirt and jeans through the last few days. Work apparently was the only thing that mattered.

"You can't tell me what to do."

"You're not well enough. Your blood pressure is still low and you probably should have stayed at the hospital for more fluids. But as for Holcome, there's no point, no conclusive evidence, no way of getting it. You're done."

She got up to leave but he blocked her way.

"Teresa...." He reached out toward her as if to take her hand. But she could feel herself starting to shake at the very sight of him and she brushed the hand away.

"Don't. Just don't," she ordered, going around him and hoping he didn't see the unsteadiness in her walk or hear the shake in her voice.

"Teresa, please listen to me, I don't know what got into me. I'm sorry." She kept going. She knew his schedule. She'd be at her job and home without his even knowing it.

❋❋❋

It was the Monday after Thanksgiving, a late Monday but nonetheless, Dr. Dorian Place walked into the office before eight. There she was, armed with ear buds and fingers flying over the keyboard as she transcribed. Storm was in a class by herself. Out of uniform again, there would be an argument for sure, the navy and red blouse with the three-quarter length sleeves was very becoming. She'd done the curls again and he couldn't understand why she put up with the crap in that office, with Deeds and Zane joining Loomis in harassing her. She could get a job anywhere with her skills. And he felt what he saw didn't even scratch the surface of her real capabilities. Something in medical for sure.

"You know there's a transcription department at this hospital."

She whipped the buds out. "Loomis had some stuff he wanted done, he left me a message and by the time it would go through the queue downstairs, I can have it done." Actually, the guy left his recorder on his desk over the weekend and she was transcribing some interesting conversations. She heard the deep voice, couldn't identify it, and the transcription wouldn't be admissible, but the conversations filled in some missing facts nicely.

"You don't look well," Dorian said, looking closely at her. A shade too pale, a little stiff in movement. "Any Covid symptoms? You should get tested."

"Is that all you people think of is Covid?" she shot back. These doctors, badgering people all the time. The doctor in the ER on Thanksgiving night was another one. Come back, come back for an appointment. He was probably still talking to the revolving door.

"And you don't look so well yourself." She'd seen the antacids on his desk.

Dorian sighed. "There's an opening at Denver Children's in nephrology. I want to apply, even if I have to move the family again. It closes tomorrow and I have to get a recommendation from Loomis. I can just imagine what he's going to say."

"I'll write it. And do his signature."

"Charles Loomis?"

"C. Loomis. Man or woman."

He was tempted. "What if they call and ask about a surgical procedure in kidney treatment."

"I'll Google it while I'm talking." She knew she could handle it, she wasn't impressed with those medicos sitting in their nice comfortable offices in universities and hospitals, not after being in medical field operations in Guinea where her job involved a lot of improvisation both in teaching and even in surgery.

"Enticing offer, but I can't chance it," he said somewhat sadly, turning to head down the hall.

Not a risk taker, she thought. She double-checked the recorder, and hit rewind. Time to return it to the king.

Not a half hour later, Loomis made his way into the office. What was Place doing here so early? Storm was standing over the copier. He was on his way past her when he stopped. He was still angry about the morning's confrontation with Jeanette, the drunken thing who was his wife. He was moving her out in a couple of days. The end.

"You look sick," he said, glaring at Tera. "Hitting the bottle again? But that won't get you out of work, I'll see to that. I hate drunken women." And he shoved a load of case notes at her. "By noon, do you hear me?" Without so much as a blink, Tera appeared to miscalculate the distance to take the papers from his hand and they fell all over the floor.

"God damn it, you stupid woman! Pick those up and get to work!"

She worked very slowly, straightening the papers carefully, and then stood. "Yes, Doctor."

He watched her go toward her desk. Screw her, she's so infuriating, he thought. That was all deliberate, I hate her, I hate her.

"Uh, Dr. Loomis," Place was coming out of his office. "May I have a minute of your time?"

"Now what, Place. Can't you get through a day without me having to hold your hand?" He motioned for him to come along. "Make it short."

Dorian felt a sinking feeling in the pit of his stomach, but time was running out. "Dr. Loomis, I need a letter of recommendation. I want to transfer to Denver Children's."

The laugh could be heard in the outer office area. Tera shook her head, the lion and the mouse. No odds for who would win *that* contest.

Buzzzz. Her phone was in her thigh pocket. A quick look, Callista again. God, leave me alone, Tera thought. Then the office phone rang.

"Pediatric Services, may I help you?"

"Why?" It was Callista. "Why did you marry that fricking asshole! I hate him, I wouldn't even go to the funeral if he dropped dead and I wish he would."

Tera shook her head. "Leave me alone, I'm at work, I can't talk to you."

"No problem there, you're toxic if you're with him. I don't understand you, you leave home, then pop in whenever you want, like being in our family isn't even important to you, and now, when you've finally come back home, he's part of the package? He stands there like God almighty and yells at us? Tera, use your brain. He's a jerk and he sure as hell isn't good enough for you. Leave him."

Her turmoil of thoughts were running in the same direction.

"How did you get tangled up with him?"

"He spent a year at Aquinas as an exchange student when I was a freshman. He was the math tutor. When St. Mary's University placed me at Imperial in London for their upper maths program, I didn't know he was a doctor already and teaching in the medical school, he's only four years older than I am. My studies overlapped into his department. We started working together." She could feel tears welling.

"You'd have been better off if you'd married that priest guy, the one that met us at dialysis. I remember you were a couple for so long. You shouldn't have let him go."

CHAPTER 64

Wednesday morning brought another boring drive. It was December, a few snowflakes here and there. Callista was getting nervous, after all, the snow drifts wouldn't stay away forever, and the weather service was hinting about major snowfall in a couple of days. Maybe a lot. Saturday, please, not Friday.

Lindsey as the dialysis nurse again, Callista thought when they entered the bay. And she's supposed to be at that nephrology care conference they're springing on us Friday. If this isn't the week from hell, I don't know what is. She sank into the recliner next to Nick's bed. He, too, seemed down, in fact barely holding it together, his lower lip was trembling. Anger swept over her. I'm not going to look at that smirking idiot during the meeting, I'll bet she's reporting to Loomis every time I give her the eye. I'm going to block her. Armed with her laptop, Callista began writing. I made them change the social worker from Gwen Deeds and I'll make them ditch this freak too, she thought.

The ping came awhile later. Tera.

T: *Ever have a care conference?*
C: *No, but one coming. What is it?*
T: *Don't know. No one ever had one before. Could be bad.*
C: *Ya think?*
T: *Have you gotten into med record?*
C: *Mom tell you? Thousands of pages.*
T: *Flash forward to end October. Notes on Transplant Committee Meeting.*

Tera had overheard talk about the Care Conference meeting that morning. Loomis and Gwen were gabbing about it outside Gwen's office. They thought they were safe, the good little assistant had the ear buds in and the fingers flying on the keyboard transcribing some silly thing or another. But the ear buds weren't really in her ears, and Tera was busy transcribing their conversation. It wasn't good. They'd mentioned the care conference, Loomis was telling Gwen to come up with an agenda to discuss care – a little laugh there – and get her riled up enough to talk and record it all. No guess as to who they were talking about, it didn't take much to push Callista over the top these days. Loomis told Gwen whatever was said would fit nicely with the Transplant Committee report. That would be enough then to finish.... They moved into the office then, and Tera had sent the text.

None of this was good, she thought, and she didn't know how the pieces fit together, what the end game was. She'd seen a printed email in his desk, referencing the Transplant meeting. Across the top someone had written, "**How is this?**"

The Multidisciplinary Transplant Selection Committee met on October 30, 2020 to discuss your child's Kidney Transplant Evaluation. After careful review by the Selection Committee, it was determined that your child does not meet Holcome International Medical Center's Transplant Selection Criteria for the following reason(s):

Behavior pattern by individual or caregiver which is likely to interfere with post-transplantation treatment.

There was an **OK - Loomis** at the bottom and a date. Did Loomis have to approve what the Transplant Committee did? Or did he tell them what they were supposed to do? She hoped Callie could find the answers to that in the records.

Meanwhile, a few miles away, Cynthia Langley sat back in her chair in her dialysis office, and sighed contentedly. Her latest delight had just arrived via FedEx, twelve $100 bills. A bonus! Finally her skills were appreciated. I should thank the good doctor for his kindness, she thought, picking up her cell phone.

"Loomis."

"This is Cynthia Langley, Doctor. I just wanted to call and say thank you for your little package. It is *very* appreciated."

Loomis was playing with his pen at his desk, still angry at Dorian Place for daring to ask for a transfer. "Anything new on the Hamptons?" he asked.

She clicked her email. "I sent a little note to Markie about the team still *thinking* about Nick's case. He's dangling nicely."

This woman! Loomis thought. Nasty. "So now, Cynthia, what can you do to stick the knife in further? Delay him. Make it look official."

"Of course, anything you want."

"What I want is for them to be *here*. Stall as long as it takes. You up for that?"

"Absolutely." So what if she was stabbing Ridley in the back.

"Here are a couple of ideas," he said quickly, pulling over a note pad and starting to write as they discussed logistics.

"I can do all of that," she assured him. "Messaging, appointments. Easy. In fact, you know our doctors collaborate with the University and with Capitol City Children's Hospital. I can set it up that if the Hamptons go anywhere, there will be an automatic…um… *communication*, if you will, that explains they are such dangerous people."

He was laughing as he got up and went to his bar where he poured and quickly took a gulp of his Grey Goose.

"Dr. Loomis, are you there?"

"Yes, yes, I'm here. Do it, Cynthia, I like it." He settled back in his chair, semi-reclining and staring at the ceiling. He loved the effect the alcohol had on him.

※※※

Late that night, Callista sat at the computer. It seemed to take forever to course through the months and days of material, well, after all, Nick had been there for a year. It looked like every word, every thought was put down on paper. Who did this? Were the rooms bugged, she wondered. Why is this set of records so different from the ones we usually receive? Or is it the unsanitized version? She saw some notes from the incident in January when she yelled for help when Nick was throwing up blood.

October, October…there it is. She printed the entire month and then sat back to read. Mark had brought her a glass of Arbor Mist Raspberry Moscato. It was so nice of him. He was just so understanding, so tender at times.

She sat up suddenly, there it was, the Transplant Committee meeting, on October 30. She paged through, only a few sheets left in the month. No notes from the meeting? How unprofessional. You can't tell me there wasn't discussion, she thought. Then a copy of the agenda fell out of the stack; no name indicating whose paper it was. It had some writing in the upper right hand side:

Dr gave info for Hampton. Family unstable, behavior issues, possibly psychiatric issues. Will not be able to keep post-transplant appointments.

Callista froze. Post transplant appointments. Those were the words on the letter they received turning down transplant consideration. She snapped a picture of the page and sent it to Tera. Who was the doctor? How could he say this? She had a sick feeling in her stomach that she knew these answers already.

CHAPTER 65

"A hold on Nick's account? I thought the supervisor removed that two months ago," Mark said. He remembered that conversation well, one among many communications that day, but with a quick resolution, or so he thought.

"I'm sorry, Mr. Hampton. I don't know anything about that. There *is* a hold on your son's name. No appointments can be made without prior approval by the person who placed this block."

"And who might that be?"

"I'm not allowed to say."

Mark hung up, it was a waste of time. He paused, remembering Sunday night, his shock when he opened an email from Craig, of all people, suggesting that letting Ridley know ahead of time that their actions were going to investigated might allow the perpetrators a chance to clean up their act. It was worth a try, so he emailed Langley and asked for the name of her supervisor; the name of the person responsible for deciding to violate the provider agreement; and the justification for the violation. He reminded her Ridley's own ethics board had recommended that Nick be treated there and he told her point blank he believed she was responsible for the violations which would be reported to federal authorities.

Cynthia sat in her office laughing when she received the missive. Oh, poor Markie. Give him my supervisor's name. No way. He's running to the feds. Right. She picked up her phone and texted Loomis.

C: *Thought you would like to know Markie fit to be tied. Emails, threats about going to the feds.*
L: *We have him just where we want him. Keep it up.*
C: *I will forward you my next letter. It'll destroy him.*
L: *Make it good and you'll be well-rewarded.*

Loomis couldn't help himself, he went on a laughing jag. Best thing I ever did, he thought, getting that nurse manager involved. She's a genius, he thought.

U-Ridley Health Care Systems
~ From Cynthia ~

December 10

Mark Hampton:

The leadership team at U-Ridley Health Care is at present meeting to discuss how to handle your case. This decision can be made without any further information, however what they decide is binding regarding the procedure for your return to U-Ridley for health care. Cynthia Langley

---

As soon as the message appeared in the inbox, Mark was on the phone.

"Nursing service."

"May I speak with the Senior Nursing Director?"

"One moment."

Sandera Vann wasn't in the loop, thank God, and Mark explained to her pretty much what his last e-mail to Langley was about, that their access to hospital appointment scheduling was illegally being blocked and that constituted discrimination. He also mentioned the insurance investigation was likely to be followed by a federal investigation.

Her response was monotonous: "I don't know anything about that." "I don't know," and "I don't know." Finally, she said she would look into it, that the Leadership Team was meeting, would continue to meet, and she would pass the information on to them.

"And one other thing," Mark added. "Since we are confident that there *will* be an investigation, tell them whatever they choose to do, they'd better be able to defend their actions." That's what Craig told him to say and by God, he took great pleasure in saying it.

※※※

Craig stamped the snow from his feet as he came in and took a deep breath, there were too many things going on and he could feel a headache starting again. Though not exactly friendly, Mark was amenable to suggestions in the matter of U-Ridley, not that anything could help that situation. For sure Craig knew he'd be tied up for the coming week, maybe more, preparing the paperwork for the possible criminal investigation of Holcome by the federal authorities and the other institutions entwined in its tentacles. With luck, that and the mess at the Insurance Coalition would be wrapped up before Christmas. Maybe some down time. His phone buzzed. Text from Imperial. Good God, he thought, adding another class next term? When am I supposed to sleep? I'm sorry Dr. Rathengan died from Covid, but isn't there someone in London to take over his ten o'clock lectures? That's four o'clock in the morning here. He sighed, as though in pain, who am I kidding, this isn't going to be online, they're opening the doors and they expect me back in my office on January third, that's not even a month away.

Snow fell from the shoulders of his overcoat as he removed it. His glasses next, they were too fogged up. This is not Britain, that's for sure, he thought. Warmth! The heating system was engaged and he could see lights farther down the hallway as he made his way to the kitchen and hung his suit coat and tie over a chair. There must be clothiers at the Mall of America, nothing I have here now is up to this frigid air.

There, on the floor. Grocery bags? All in a nice row. My God, why did she do this? I could have gone for groceries. He paused. So why didn't I take care of this? What's wrong with me? I used to do it, we used to go together. He shook his head. We're operating in different worlds. He began inspecting the bags, they contained mostly dry goods, and folded up the empty ones as he went along. Opening the refrigerator he saw things well-stocked, they wouldn't suffer from a week-long blizzard. Last week's two days without power and nine inches of snow was a new experience.

He went through the great room, no sign of her, but she was here, he could feel her presence...oh, a light in the master bedroom. He continued down the hallway, surprised the door was open. She'd kept it locked the last two weeks and he wasn't about crash his way in. Pushing the door wider, he didn't see her, but wait! Definitely the sound of someone being ill in the bathroom.

What the hell is going on, he thought. I'm sure it isn't the first time for this. I don't even know if she's eating at all, she just sits at the computer, as if afraid to move. No eyes on him now, Craig went over to her dark computer, pressed a key and the black screen came alive. Google. Another press and her searches came up. Cancer. Pancreatitis. Nausea, vomiting, other symptoms. Self-diagnosis, why am I not surprised at this, he thought. At the sound of running water, he turned and was standing casually by the bed when the door opened.

Face wet, breathing a little heavy from the spasms, Tera blinked when she saw him waiting for her, glasses gone, tie off, shirt open – she wanted to melt into his arms. No! She shut her eyes. I can't even think in that direction.

"Teresa...." Alarmed at her distress, he put a hand out and took a step forward but then he stopped. "How long has this been going on?" he asked cautiously. There had been no communication between them in nearly two weeks, nothing face-to-face, the situation more frightening now that he saw her, the pallor, the unsteadiness, she seemed exhausted.

She backed away. She couldn't think. A week? Did too much today, the shopping alone was an ordeal, she thought wearily.

He looked as if he was going to come toward her. "I'm your husband, let me help you." He paused. "If there's something wrong, you're going to need tests. Please, please, let me help!" His thoughts flashed back to that night in London, not even a year after her arrival, a bad housing choice that ended up with her raped and thrown unconscious on the street. He'd seen her in a hospital ward during rounds with his residents; brought her to his flat to recover because there was nowhere else for her to go. Within hours, the trauma set in and it was only by the grace of God he managed to finally restrain her and save her from suicide. I'll do it again, he thought, even if I have to drag her out of here and up to the University hospital.

It was as if the same thought flew between them. "Don't come near me." She looked toward the door, but didn't move, his steady gaze holding her in place. One sign of weakness, she thought, he'll easily overpower me. No. Not now, I still have to find out who...I don't know what's wrong with me, but I can't let him near me or it's game over. "Get out," she said harshly. "I'm sure you have something more important to do."

I'm not leaving this room, Craig thought. "Teresa, please," he began, starting toward her again. "Tera, please listen to me. I'm sorry.

I never should have said what I did. I never should have laid a hand on you. I don't know why I did that, I swear I will never do it again. Can you forgive me?"

Tera felt the tears welling, but another wave of nausea was coming. "Go. Just go and leave me alone. Play doctor somewhere else."

Her tone of voice was like a slap across the face. He stepped back, a puzzled look on his face. He could see there was no choice and reluctantly he made his way to the great room and eased down on the sofa before the dark fireplace. He moved a fleece blanket with a tied fringe, then looked down at it. Lightning bolts and storm clouds and he could smell her fragrance. Storm. He fingered it gently. Oh my God, what have I done? She's the only woman I ever wanted all these years, since I first saw her at Aquinas. She's the only woman I have ever loved. I've ruined everything.

CHAPTER 66

Late Tuesday morning the phone began ringing, disturbing Nick while he was doing homework. Yes! he thought, a chance to sneak a break from math.

"Iowa!" Mark called.

Kidney? Callista ran to the kitchen.

The perky voice of Tammy Brown came alive on the speaker app. "I just wanted to let you know what's been going on down here for Nick. Several people have gone online to fill out the uiowa.donorscreening questionnaire."

"Really? Oh that's wonderful!"

"Some of them are having the blood sample taken, even got a guy from South Carolina."

"Rusty!" Callista and Mark said together. "My brother," she added. Rusty hated medical stuff. How generous that he wanted to help Nick.

"Oh, I get it," Tammy said. "He's hilarious. When I told him about the 24-hour urine collection, he said he'd have to keep a jug in his FedEx truck and what if he delivered it."

Nick was laughing so hard he fell on the floor. Mark shook his head. That was Rusty all right.

"Another one, a doctor, said he was an uncle, he made it through everything, but was incompatible."

"Must be Craig," Callista said. "He's incompatible with everything."

"Mom!"

She didn't realize Nick heard her.

"What was that? You remember all the six markers must be matched. He cleared four for sure but that's not good enough for Nick."

❖❖❖

"Storm! Now! My office, time for your employee review."

Tera looked up. What the hell? She got up slowly, hoping to keep the nausea at bay. Swilling Ginger Ale didn't help anymore. *I've got to get out of here, and if this jerk is going to go crazy on me again, I'm going to lie down and die. I feel like it anyway.*

"Be seated."

Tera sat across the glass and chrome desk from him, hands folded in her lap. The perfect employee. But that damned smirk of his was a tip-off.

"Okay, so we are obliged to discuss performance reviews with employees every six months," he began in a lordly manner. Obviously, he didn't know Elite members were not reviewed in the same way as everyone else, the meetings were with their director only.

"To be frank, I'm dissatisfied, Storm. Your work is poor and your office demeanor unpleasant, defiant, at times. And you're out of uniform a lot." Smirk. As if he didn't enjoy that part of the ticket, she thought. He was leaning toward her now, going for the kill. Strike first, she thought.

"My work is poor, Doctor? In what way?"

"Mistakes, Storm! All over the place. In the patient records, in your work in the office." A touch of anger.

"I don't make mistakes."

He sat back so hard the chair shifted. He wasn't expecting the back talk. "There are mistakes. You're incompetent, do you understand?" He pulled out sheets covered with scribbled text and literally threw them at her. "I want these corrections by noon tomorrow!" She realized that they were patient records, with numerous data changes for each. She looked up, *you damn bastard.*

"What did you say to me?" He'd heard her voice clearly. At least he thought he'd heard her.

"My lips weren't moving, *sir*." *Let's drive the knife in more*, she thought angrily. "I said nothing and those are not mistakes, those are added changes, after the fact. I didn't make them on first entry. *You* made them, afterwards, *sir*."

He was up and out of the chair. "And you've been in my computer. In my files. I can see changes in the entries!"

"If I was in your computer I'd have wiped it just to screw you," Tera shot back, all professional pretense gone. "Are you finished with this joke of a meeting? If I have all this shit to do, I'd better get going on it." She got up to leave and heard him coming behind her. Quickly. He was getting too close and her stomach contracted. She whipped around and saw his hand poised over her shoulder to grab her.

"You lay a hand on me again and so help me...." It had slipped out and he caught it. His eyebrows raised, and then he glanced at the scars on his wrist and at her hands. Fingernails, huh?

"Oh, you remember that?" he asked and then started laughing, a crazy sort of laugh.

She made it to the door and then to her desk. God help me, I can't take this anymore.

❋❋❋

The phone buzzed with a message as she was preparing to leave. Text from Callista.

C. *Had Care Conference yesterday. Gave social worker an earful, all about Gwen, and that they've damaged our entire family's mental health. When Place made his statement, he actually said Nick needs peritoneal dialysis for his health and Holcome won't do it. Or will but without Mark. Dangerous to not train the other adult in the house. Sounds negligent to me. New social worker now has an obligation to look into it because it was said at an open meeting with witnesses.*

Tera shook her head. They talked about all of this? Callie fell headfirst right into Loomis' plot. No wonder Place was so on edge the last couple of days, not even close to friendly.

T: *Who was the other SW? Saw some female buzzing around this morning.*
C: *Marissa Chamberlain. When we dumped Gwen, they brought this one in.*

Marissa Chamberlain, Marissa Chamberlain. Tera sat back in her chair, eyes closed. Name not familiar, but there had to be a connection somewhere. M. Chamberlain, M.C. Her eyes jolted open. The note in the file! The Child Protection report!

You have to present it a certain way...I'll write it for you. MC

Oh my God, Tera thought, are they going to try that again? She grabbed the Holcome staff directory. Marissa Chamberlain was in charge of child protection and court involvement for Holcome. Callie wanted to bring the new person up to speed on all the harassment against them, except the new person was already in on the scheme and likely helped to create it! Telling her about the destruction of the family's mental health just cemented the need for court intervention, Tera thought. This has got to end. We've got to find the brains behind this. She suddenly sat down as nausea and vertigo assailed her again. She was ready to grab the wastebasket under her desk. I can't take it anymore. I can't help you and I can't even help myself. She sighed, holding her head in her hands. Tomorrow, I can get into the files one more time, and that's got to be the end.

The drive home was uneventful, the air was cold, streetlights reflecting on the snow from the storms a week ago made thousands of glitters along the way. Cars with their headlights cutting into the night crossed the overpasses. Occasionally a red light, and then the red and blue flashes of police. Life going on minute by minute.

Empty. Everything empty as usual as she opened the door from the garage. And chilly. She threw her uniform into the laundry room where Craig wouldn't see it and grabbed a sweat suit. I guess I should make something for supper, she thought, maybe chicken wings, as she pulled Paul's recipe out of the box. Salt, baking powder. Can't wreck it too much. This took awhile to cook. Time to think.

She sat at her desk and took out the blue and red cloned phones and powered them up. Obviously two separate uses. Roger pinpointed some of the numbers from the blue phone. A few pinged to Wisconsin, perhaps a certain Linda O'Brien? And this other number, somewhat familiar, one-word texts, "anytime." But this last was a direct phone call...October 23. I can't place the date, it seems familiar but my mind just won't work. She put it down.

The red phone was special. Only four numbers on it, one used sporadically, the others more frequent, and she recognized two area codes from in the Cities. Richardson? That Langley babe? Hawthorne is one he calls every day like reporting in, she thought. But this other one, calls several months apart. Someone he didn't need? Someone out of town? Or someone he didn't dare bother? It was too hard to think. She took the phones to her bedside table and dropped them in. As she turned, she could hear the oven buzzer, time to turn the wings. Reset. A two-minute task and she was so exhausted she barely made it to the great room where she sank down on the sofa before the fireplace.

I'm so tired. The constant cat and mouse, the constant head games. I hate to admit it but Craig's right, I have to quit, Tera thought. I can't keep up the fight there anymore, and I can't fight *him* anymore, he's trying, trying hard to make amends, but I feel nothing inside toward him. Oh, God, I can't stand the way my life is going. With a sigh, she fell asleep.

The house was dark as night when he drove up. Where was she? Every day when he returned, he wondered if she'd left him. Still so distant, unresponsive, unwilling to engage even in the simplest conversation. He didn't know what to do. But then he saw the Mustang when he drove into the garage. And the house dark?

The oven buzzer greeted his ears, and there was light from the overhead range hood. The smell was not exactly familiar. Craig opened the oven and rescued the wings. They looked good, actually. He looked around. Where was she? He was earlier than usual, couldn't take the constant drivel as the board discussed over and over the candidates for Elgin's job. Tomorrow they would do final interviews of two, Dr. James Middleton from Connecticut, that would be online early in the morning and in the afternoon, Anton Gregory, currently managing a major entity in Houston, who was flying in tonight. That was an in-person meeting. It was between the two to become president of the Insurance Coalition. Most likely Gregory, with his experience in the market and his connections in the Cities, which was why he was flying in. His connections, whatever.

Craig went to start up the fireplace and saw her asleep on the sofa. He couldn't help himself, he bent toward her and gently brushed the hair from her eyes. And then he was staring in their blue depths, no confusion, no hostility. She seemed confused.

"I just sat down for a minute. Oh! The wings!" She started to get up.

"I took care of it. How are you feeling?"

"Always the doctor." She didn't object, though, when he sat next to her. She seemed worn down and depressed.

"Why are you so early today?" What was it Tom had said? The man I vowed my life to. I want to leave, I can't trust him, but I want to stay, stay, so badly. I don't know what to do. She was happy it was dark, he wouldn't see the tears on her face.

"There is only so much office I can stand. We have two candidates to interview tomorrow. I'm guessing the job will go to Anton Gregory, who's flying in from Houston. He's been in the Cities before, in fact worked at Holcome. He's been in town now and then, so it won't be much of a change."

"Houston?" Where some complaints were from? Worked at Holcome? "What did he do at Holcome?" Tera asked cautiously.

"Same as every place he's worked, Chief Financial Officer." Craig hesitated. "And I'm not always the doctor, you know that."

Surprisingly, she edged closer to him, and now his arm slid around her. She stiffened at first, but slowly relaxed into his side. He closed his eyes and his lips gently brushed her hair. It felt so good to hold her again.

CHAPTER 67

It seemed as if a phone was ringing in the distance and suddenly the bed lurched her awake as Craig jerked up and fumbled for his glasses. It was still dark in the room, no light coming through the drapes, plus a cloud-filled winter day again. He caught sight of the alarm clock. "Oh my God, it's eight o'clock. The meeting!" She watched him hesitate, as if getting his bearings in the master bedroom – they hadn't slept together in weeks. Then he was up, yanking a dress shirt from the closet and then rapidly going off down the hall in just his black and green sleep pants and bare feet. It was rather enjoyable to see not the great Dr. Craig Storm-Livesey but instead just an ordinary guy panicked at being late for work even if it was only a Zoom experience this morning. The big meeting was in the afternoon.

She sighed, her hand lingering over the warmth where he'd slept. He'd held her in his arms for most of the night, his warmth reaching every fiber of her body. It was comforting, but it wasn't enough, a shard of fear still existed deep inside – fear of what would happen if his anger ever erupted again. I don't know what to do, she thought. I don't know how to go forward, I'm so confused.

But now it was time to get moving. What did he say? Chief Financial Officer at Holcome. Could it be? And he was in town this very day. Tera rolled over and reached into her bedside table. She began scrolling through texts, it would have been over a year ago. And there it was, four or five around the first of September. Today. I've got to do this today. As she quickly swung out of the bed, the nausea sent her back down again, this was worse than last summer with all the liquor she'd downed. And it kept coming, every day now and more than once a day. Here lies the not-so-great Teresa Storm-Livesey hardly able to keep on her feet. What was this called in psycho-babble? An aversive response? Aversion to Holcome? For sure. What did that ER doctor say, come for an appointment? Maybe he wasn't so dumb after all.

It passed. She gathered some items from the closet and darted into the shower. She heard Craig in the office, logged into the Coalition meeting. She'd be out in a matter of minutes. He thought she was meeting her mom today. Ellie? Nine in the morning? Not.

❋❋❋

Everything was dark in the offices. Tera flicked on the overhead light in the king's office. The right bottom drawer was still a mess, but rearranged slightly, with more papers thrown in – the agenda for the Hampton care conference, with a note warning that Place needed to be kept in line. Beneath that some scribbles about what was going on at Ridley, about the Leadership Team evaluating the Hampton transfer. Copies made of all, Tera threw the stuff back in the drawer, but not before she sprayed her White Tea and Sage on the phones and entire contents, just to spite the son of a bitch.

Then the computer, they were up-to-date on that, thanks to Roger. She wanted that personal e-mail account. All open, unguarded by a password. There it was, all the back and forth on the same topics as the paperwork in the drawer, only in more detail, that slimy Cynthia Langley from Ridley begging for more help on handling the Hamptons, she was afraid they'd find out what she'd been doing: Mark was calling providers and asking what part they played in banning Nick from all appointments in every department of the hospital. Tera forwarded everything to her personal email, except for the one on Dr. Place, the one in which Loomis was discussing how he'd screwed the young nephrologist, not giving the recommendation to Denver, and then cancelling his contract at Holcome. That one she printed.

On to Gwennie's office. There, first item on the top of the pile, a written agenda with notes for the care conference, but wait, she wasn't supposed to have attended. Who wrote this, Marissa Cunningham? Another paper was attached with a list clearly noting that in November, Dr. Loomis presented the Hampton case to the Transplant Committee and told them to vote it down because of the possible psychiatric illness on the part of the parents which endangered the success and aftercare of the transplant. Then Callista's comment about the family's mental health being damaged by continuing hemodialysis was noted. Guardianship would be a *fait accompli* with that damning piece of information as evidence and it would occur quickly. Marissa Cunningham plainly wrote she would prepare the child neglect complaint immediately and that it would trigger an investigation and court action. Tera grabbed the papers, Gwennie wouldn't miss them, then sent a quick text to Roger.

T: *Meet courtyard, noon.*
R: *You crazy? It's cold!*
T: *Takedown*

The voice startled her. "What are you doing in here?" Dorian Place was standing in the doorway, looking at her as if she had a handful of diamonds from a jewelry store heist. Dark suit again, his thin face marred by dark circles under the eyes. He was wearing his glasses more, but they just made him look more downtrodden. The stylish upsweep of hair remained, but only half-heartedly tended today. And that's what a year in this office did to him, Tera thought.

"Checking the computer function."

"With a pile of papers from the desk drawer in your hand? I saw you take them. Loomis was right about you all along, wasn't he? I'm going to call security, you've breached our system, you've got stolen papers in your hand. Maybe you've been involved in the hacking too."

"Don't be an ass. Do I look like a hacker?"

"You're a hell of a lot smarter than some flunkie administrative assistant, that's for sure. You've been going through all of these offices and taking stuff, haven't you? Going into the computers and...."

He stopped abruptly as she got up and threw Loomis' printed email in his face. She wasn't feeling well again but meaner than hell at his stupidity. As he read, it was like watching a building implosion, the structure stood and then melted into dust. Finding out you're unemployed in two weeks would do that to a person.

He turned and went down to his office. She came in on his heels. "Look, Dorian, you've got a choice here. Keep your damned mouth shut about me or you're looking at jail. The Hamptons filed a complaint with insurance. Holcome has collected close to a million bucks from just them this year and with his chance of transplant at zero, Nick Hampton is a cash cow as long as he stays on hemodialysis instead of getting PD. There's more to this, HIPAA violations, collusion, conspiracy, and a patient died because of negligence. There's been an insurance investigation for fraud going on here, initiated by a major provider."

"You're with insurance? God, I can't believe this." Yes, he realized, he was used time and again, to keep the Hamptons in place and on a dialysis format originally designed to be temporary. "I swear I had nothing to do with making decisions. I just did what I was told. Loomis demanded the treatment and blocked everything else." He shook his head. "I can't believe this."

"It's over. Today. Do you know who else is in on this besides Loomis and Hawthorne?"

Place shook his head.

Tera sighed. It had to be Gregory, then.

"How did you get involved, is this your job?" Dorian asked.

One job among many, Tera thought. "Callista Hampton is my sister," she answered and then turned and left the room going back to Loomis' office. There she grabbed the red phone. Ever so carefully, she sent a joint message to the two principal numbers.

Emergency. Meet here today, 3pm.

Then she was out the door, stopping only long enough to grab her jacket.

Roger was standing by the gray bricks of the drained fountain. Snow was caked on the top over the ice created by the freezing of the water left behind. She came up behind him. What a contrast! He wore a heavy parka and a University stocking cap, heavy gloves. About six inches shorter, she wore a light jacket, no hat. She wanted to make sure she'd be recognized by any spies in the indoor hallways around the courtyard.

"You pick weird times for meetings. What's this about takedown?"

"Sit down," she ordered as she brushed snow from one of the benches. It was damned cold out here, better be as quick as possible. As he sat, she cuddled up to him.

"What the hell?" He looked down at her, now what was she up to? "Your old man know you're here?"

"Paul? What's he got to do with this?"

"Not your dad, the great and powerful Oz, your husband. I swear he hates me, he hates the ground I walk on and here you're cozying up with public enemy number one."

"Shut up and listen. We've got to blow this whole thing up. I found paperwork that says Holcome is going to file a child negligence complaint again with child protection services to try and take Nick away from Callista and Mark. Two complaints in a year? You know how fast they're going to act on that?"

"Shit. How're you gonna pull this off, you don't know the number three guy. Even I don't know who it is, I didn't recognize the voice on the tapes."

"Get closer, I'm getting cold."

He groaned as he wrapped his arms around her. "Better?"

"I sent them a text, meeting at three o'clock. I want you up there before then; you can watch from the office across the hall, at least until Hawthorne arrives. I think Number Three comes in the back way. Then come in. I want you to...." And she told him the plan.

"You're crazy. You can't get away with it. Don't do it." This was a different Teresa Storm. He'd finally figured out to Google her under her maiden name and realized she was no hothouse flower, her public health service record revealed time in some of the worst places on earth, and with the nasty Dr. Craig. "They'll catch you."

"They'll be looking for someone else. I'll be out of here, don't worry. Now say good-bye, we have an audience. Make it look good."

"You're killing me," he said as he held her close. She reached up and touched his cheek and then he held her hand in his. If only....

Then, with a smile, she was gone. It was time to get upstairs.

CHAPTER 68

Loomis crossed the office, his beady eyes surveying the reception area. There Storm was again, busy, busy, busy. He stopped at the desk and stared until Tera looked up.

"Yes, Doctor Loomis?"

"What's with you, Storm. There can't be so much work you're always pounding that keyboard. I heard Elite is short-staffed, some of you are doing double duty. Why don't you ask to be assigned somewhere else where you will be more...useful. Maybe two or three places, why don't you?" He ended on a mocking note.

"In fact, Doctor, that's what I'm planning. Right now I'm working on a technical guide to managing this particular office. I am especially stressing to be careful of working with you because you're a dictator."

"What did you call me? I am going to get you out of here once and for all."

"Go for it," Tera retorted. "You report me and I'll report you," she threatened, her voice even. "All you have to do is press 7 on my phone and it will connect to Mrs. Harris. Do it." She held the handset out to him. "I'll even do it for you."

He reached for her hand. The hallway. He jerked back as though burned. "I do not want to be disturbed the rest of the afternoon. Do you understand me? No interruptions." And then he turned. Tera had a flashback too. The call with the familiar text number made on October 23, it was the day he trapped her in the hallway and the day the car tried to run her off the road. He'd called "Anytime" – ordering him to go after her? What if she'd been killed? Tera suddenly felt very ill. Dorian was still watching Loomis walk down the hallway to his office when he heard the loud click of the main door. He saw Tera was retreating to the restroom by the elevators.

Just in time, it seemed, as she began to retch and vomit as soon as she made it to the stall. Aversion all right. Maybe I should have eaten this morning. Or not, who wanted to see puffed up circles of morning Cheerios floating in the toilet? The thought made her hurl again. She slid down the cold side of the stall and held her legs against her chest. Dizzy and so tired. All those times I wished I was dead, not now, please not now. Oh sweet Jesus, help me get through this. I don't want to cave in again and have those dirty pigs looking at me. Just give me two more hours, one more hour. For Nicky. I've got to get through this to help him. This is the only chance. The pounding heart receded slowly and the hot and cold feeling left. When she left the restroom, after using half a mouth spray canister, she could see Roger across the hall standing by the pediatric endocrinology office. Show time.

❖❖❖

"What do you mean he suddenly cancelled?" Craig interrupted the board meeting. The online interview with Middleton was finished and Anton Gregory just called to beg off from his 2pm in-person slot, saying he could participate at 4:30, something from his home office required a video conference from his hotel room. "That's not indicative of his interest in this job." He texted Smollett to call for a break from the phone conference.

After the others signed off, Smollett remained. "Craig, we said we'd interview the two prime candidates, we can't renege," Alex Smollett said tiredly. For hours the board went back and forth on Zoom, asking the same questions ten different ways. Picking a name from a hat and hiring the winner was more appealing.

"Alex, unless the man had a heart attack, what could possibly keep him from talking with us about running the nation's largest insurance carrier?"

❖❖❖

When Neil Hawthorne strolled in, Tera was leaning back in her chair, legs crossed and reading some papers, the smoky glasses and the tight leggings a pleasant visual.

"Hello there, Ms. Storm. The way you're sitting is bad for your back, you know."

She sat at attention. "Hello Mr. Hawthorne. How have you been? You haven't been around much lately." She smiled brightly. "Should I announce you or do you want to go in and surprise him?"

He laughed and winked and started down the internal hallway. It was 2:45.

When Hawthorne appeared in the doorway, Loomis was annoyed as hell. "Why are you here?"

"Emergency meeting. I got a text late this morning."

"I didn't get any text."

"That's because you're already here. That woman out there is breathtaking. Any luck with her?"

Loomis wrinkled his nose. "Not on your life." Damn that vodka. "I asked you, what are you doing here?"

Hawthorne looked at him oddly but before he could reply, the back door opened and Anton Gregory was there, cursing the hour drive down to Holcome, cursing the fact this little *tête a tête* likely may have cost him a job he could have manipulated to his purposes. He was impeccably dressed as usual, a dark blue wool suit with silver appointments. His tie clip alone must have cost two grand, with the diamond studs in it. The swarthy face, however, looked like the wrath of God.

"What do you mean dragging me out here for an 'emergency.' There are no emergencies in what we do. I am trying to get in a position to advance our little project and your emergency interrupted the proceedings. What the hell is going on?" His deep voice was wrapped in anger.

"What emergency?" Loomis looked around, and they stared back expectantly.

Roger strolled into the outer office phone in hand. The lights down the hall to Loomis' office were dimmed, and he could hear three voices. Damn but one of them was the deep voice from the tapes.

"He's here," he whispered to Tera.

She nodded and got up, carefully positioning her purse on the desk so she could grab it on the run. Then she went down the hall.

They were startled when the door burst open. Loomis was out of his chair instantly. "I told you no interruptions. Why the hell are you here?"

"I have two messages that are important, sir," Tera said quickly. Roger stood far enough back in the hallway to remain unseen. She looked around and entered the room so he had a clear shot. She took her time and looked carefully at each man to be sure she owned their attention.

"I thought you needed to know that 'Anytime' phone number you've contacted so many times has been disconnected. You called that number in October and told the guy to run me off the road but he crashed. When the police got there, they found his phone, laptop, and some meth. There was a flash drive in the laptop with pictures and pages of personal data. They think it's all from the breach here in October." It was a useful but untrue statement. "His number is in your phone, Dr. Loomis, and yours in his." Her voice hardened. "How soon do you think it will be before he rats you out and you're next on the list to be investigated?"

"Who are you, what do you mean coming in here like this!" Anton Gregory was at his full height and his face ugly with anger.

Hawthorne turned full on to Loomis. "What the hell have you...."

"And your pal, Cynthia Langley, from Ridley called," Tera added. "She asked what you want her to do." She heard two clicks behind her, they were perfectly framed because Gregory was right in front of her. "She said there's trouble, the Office of Civil Rights is preparing an investigation there for denying care for a pediatric patient, Nicholas Hampton." Another untruth, the OCR stuff against Ridley was still on Callista's desk. It didn't matter, though, it looked as if all hell was about to break loose. "I hope you all rot in jail." She was out the door, and grabbing Roger's hand, they made haste back to her desk. There, she stopped long enough to pull Roger close and give him a kiss. Then, snatching her purse, Tera was gone.

"Who's this Cynthia Langley?" Gregory turned on Loomis. "What have you got to do her, with Ridley?"

"Nothing, nothing, don't believe her. Storm!" Loomis yelled. This meeting, he never called it, but they came because they were texted. Jesus Christ, his phones. He sat down and yanked the bottom drawer open and the overpowering odor of White Tea and Sage assailed him. Then he was up and around the desk and running down the hallway.

She wasn't there. There was a black guy at her desk.

"Where is she?" Loomis yelled.

"Who?" Roger asked innocently. God, this guy is in a blind rage, he thought, and utterly dangerous. He felt a surge of fear.

"Teresa Storm, the admin...wait a minute, I know you. You're her lover."

"Lover! You've got the wrong guy, I don't do white."

"Liar! I saw you at noon all cozy in the courtyard. Where is she?"

"I swear, I didn't see any she." He held his phone against his leg. From the corner of his eye he could see Hawthorne and some other guy coming up behind Loomis. "I'm just here to fix the computers."

"Loomis, stop." That was Hawthorne, tall, imposing. He came forward and put his hand on his colleague's shoulder.

"You're lying to me," Loomis screamed at Roger. "Give me that phone. Press 7, she said." He jammed his finger on the button. Roger slowly turned toward the computer, pretending to do a keyboard test, but he was making 100 mistakes a minute.

"Harris! Where is Teresa Storm! This is Dr. Loomis. She just left here, she breached our files."

"She hasn't been here this week, Doctor. She left our employ last Friday."

"You're lying to me! She was here every day this week. She was here not ten minutes ago. I saw her. Stop her, damn you."

"I said Ms. Storm has not been here." She ended the call.

"Call security," Loomis yelled at Roger.

"Loomis!" The deep voice. Roger didn't know him. A lot of good this foray was, he thought, I can't identify the head guy. Then he saw the sign-in notebook. He took it in his hand and said, "I see you didn't sign in, sir, if you could come over and sign the notebook, we're required...."

Loomis jerked the notebook away. "You stupid n...." He stopped before uttering the racial slur. "Don't you know Anton Gregory, he used to be the CFO here, you dumbshit."

"Loomis! Now!" Hawthorne's voice boomed out.

"Security, this is Dr. Loomis. Teresa Storm just left here. She breached our computers. She's likely on the way to the parking ramp, about five foot-seven, drives a Mustang, wearing the blue uniform from the Elite Corps. Dark hair, blue eyes. Call the Stanton Police."

Hawthorne jerked Loomis away from the phone. "Chuck, get back in the office and shut your goddamn mouth."

As soon as they turned away, Roger pulled up his phone and began to send a text and the picture to Craig. She said to get it to him ASAP because Craig had to stop the vote on leadership at the Insurance

Coalition. Roger didn't think anything from him would be opened, but nevertheless, he hit send. "Open it, you jerk," he whispered.

In the Elite office, Tera had swiftly changed into street clothes, tight pants, subtle red, green and gold flowing top that came together in a knot at the hipline. She quickly slid her feet into spiked red heels. A little black sweater jacket rested over her shoulders. She felt a little shaky but forced herself to hold it together – she had to get out of there, fast.

"Take care, Teresa," Regina Harris said. "If I know the higher ups here, they'll have city cops in on this as well as hospital security."

Tera donned the dark glasses and looked over them. "They're not looking for this." She spread her arms out, looking more like a model than a humble administrative assistant. "Thanks for everything, Regina." Tera went forward and gave her a hug. "For everything." And then she was gone.

Tera walked boldly out the front door of the hospital and slowly past the gathering security people who were talking along the sidewalk and passing a paper around, a picture? A few guys gave her the once-over. They always did. She kept going toward the ramp. The Stanton police had already arrived, a massive guy was in charge and directing the uniformed men and women to go up and down the rows in the ramp. She just kept walking steadily.

"Miss! Would you please stop."

She stopped and slowly turned. The burly cop came up beside her, looking her over real well.

"Do you work here?" He looked at the picture, which was two years old. "May I see your ID?"

"Of course, officer." Tera pulled out her identification badge. He stared at it and at her. "You look like someone we're searching for, but it's really not the same picture." He handed it back. "Sorry for bothering you, Ms. Livesey." Tera turned. T. M. Livesey, Assistant Director of the Office of Hospital Oversight, once again made her escape.

And then she was at the car, leaning casually against the front, obscuring the Storm 2 license plate. She looked down the rows. Busy, busy, busy looking for the blue Mustang, but she had driven the black Porsche.

CHAPTER 69

The break was desperately needed. Craig was still wearing his sleep pants and had thrown the green shirt into the wastebasket. Still haven't shaved and hair unkempt, I look positively rustic, he thought, seeing his image in the bathroom mirror. They'd agreed to a two-hour break, it was a little after three now, he had to move faster if he was going to make it for the 4:30 meeting with Gregory up in the Cities.

The phone buzzed and he looked down. Roger Allen? What the hell does he want? Craig continued toward the bedroom to repair his wardrobe. The phone buzzed again. Craig was about to delete the message, but saw an image icon. Clicking it, he saw three men, the one in the center looking guilty as sin about something, and by God, Anton Gregory was standing next to him. He looked at the time signature, 3:08 pm. What was Gregory doing with these people? And they must have been at Holcome if Roger Allen had sent this.

C: *What is this? Some joke?*
R: *No, these are the three voices. The deep one is Anton Gregory.*
C: *What have you got to do with this?*
R: *T said you needed this right away.*

Roger grabbed the phone when it rang. "Yeah," he half-whispered.

Craig shook his head, why was he whispering? "Allen, what the hell is going on? What is this?" There was no mistaking his anger.

"Look, I'm only doing what I was told. Teresa set a trap to find out who that number three guy was and I was to take a picture when they all got together, then send it to you so you could stop some meeting."

"Teresa? She was at Holcome? She quit two weeks ago."

"Yeah, I asked her about that, she said you had no clue. She said you needed to nail these guys. I tried to talk her out of it, but...."

"Roger, where is my wife?" Craig interrupted warily.

"Honest to God, I don't know. She ran out of here like the devil was after her. He was. She baited that Loomis guy so bad he went right over the cliff and was out here screaming for blood not ten minutes ago."

Craig stared straight ahead. What's going on? Two weeks still at Holcome? How could I have missed this, he thought. Wasn't it just yesterday she was asleep on the sofa when I came home?

"Where was she going? Where would she go?" He put the phone on speaker and began to change his clothes rapidly. This is going to go badly, he thought, especially with her continuing illness. Whatever it is, it's more serious than a passing bout of dehydration. And now this added stress...."

"I don't know, maybe she'd go get sanctuary or whatever it is from the chaplain so they can't arrest her. Why don't you call him. Kressly."

That would be a last resort, Craig thought. Their last meeting two weeks ago didn't go well. Desperate and overwhelmed with guilt about the situation with Tera, he went to see a priest at the closest church – St. Raphael's – a week after the Thanksgiving incident. And in walked Father Tom, a formidable figure in any lifestyle, but doubly so in his black clerical garb.

"You're a *priest*?" Craig was stunned to see a former classmate before him.

Tom had made the connection immediately. Teresa Storm and here he was, Craig Storm-Livesey. It was just Livesey at school, what guy had a hyphenated name? But the papers recently featured a story on the Covid modeling team at Imperial, mentioning the member with global health experience. Who'd have thought this arrogant prick of a classmate would be out there helping mankind? Craig looked the same, a little more muscular, but now highly agitated, leaning forward, hands clasping and unclasping.

"Oh shit, she married *you*? She told me she wanted to bail on her marriage, had I known it was to you, I'd have told her to run like hell." He ignored the look of surprise on Craig's face. Tom sat down at his desk in the bright pleasant office with old wooden bookshelves, religious tomes lined up and stacked in every available space, including the floor. "What did you do now?"

They were rivals in mind and body at Aquinas, Tom, the brilliant freshman and Craig the foreign exchange student who was a whiz at everything, including soccer. Although four years younger, Tom was a powerful soccer midfielder and he and Craig, a premier striker in his few weeks at the school, were carded, thrown out of a game and suspended for fighting – each other.

"What is it you don't get about marriage?" Tom said angrily. "*It's not about you.* It's a *we* thing, I and thee. That's what the vow is all about, two now joined as one, you go forward *together*. After your relationship with God, this love between you is supposed to become the most important thing in your life; it's not I and me and *you* go off and do your own thing."

"Tell *her* that, she's out on her own, I have no idea what she's doing, damn it!" Craig snapped back. It was a wrong move.

"Then maybe you should have been here, helping her hold things together. But oh no, you just had to go back to Britain because you're *so* important. Did you ever talk to her about what's been going on? I mean really talk? The little kid, your nephew, wanted to commit suicide. Did you know that? Of course not.

"She needed you, she still needs you." Tom glared at him. "Listen, you idiot, this is how it works, you and your wife, it's *we* not me. This marriage thing is not one-sided, with you in command. You don't lay a hand on her because you're pissed off about something, you don't verbally destroy your woman. She had your back in every diseased backwards country you went to with WHO." Priest or not, he was yelling. "I read that stuff in the papers. What's wrong with you? Why don't you do the same for her?"

Tom paused to regain some semblance of self-control. "Did you at least apologize? Maybe *crawl* and beg forgiveness? Of course not."

The priest's anger brought back to Craig's mind that year at Aquinas, a year of arguments and even physical altercations with Tom, Pete, and some of the other guys. He sat back in the chair, stunned that the animosity still existed.

"Hellfire is better than you deserve," Tom was saying, "but maybe you're just stupid and believe your own press." He thought a minute. "First Corinthians, chapter 13. It's in the Bible, you know what a Bible is?"

Craig nodded dumbly, wondering how in hell Tom Kressly got ordained a priest.

"Read it until you own it. *Own* it in your mind and heart. Get your head out of your ass, Craig, fix this before you do any more damage." He shook his head. "And next time you come here, go to the confessional, maybe I won't be so tempted to smack you. And I'm a priest! God help me, even after all these years...." He said the prayers and was gone.

Craig shook his head at the bitter memory. It had not gone well at all, the words still stung. Calling Kressly was not an option.

"I've got to go," Roger was saying. "Back to my nice, safe IT job. They've been shouting like crazy in that back room. Do what you've got to do, and hurry up about it. She said to tell you to hurry."

"Wait!" Craig called out, then quickly gave Roger instructions to safeguard the computer hard drives. Hanging up, he glanced at his watch, 3:30. He punched in the numbers for Smollett.

"Cancel the meeting with Gregory," he ordered.

"What the hell?" Smollett had little patience in the first place and today had drained it all.

"Cancel it, tell him tomorrow, Thursday. Alex, there's an insurance investigation going on, I told you that, I told the board that. We've gotten complaints from locations around the country." A thought came to him. Some complaints were from Houston, and that's where Gregory was working now. He hastily scribbled a note to have someone compare Gregory's past hospital jobs with complaint locations. "There are three people spearheading the operation at Holcome and Anton Gregory has been identified as one of them." Craig was walking rapidly through the entry toward the garage. "I'll send you a picture, taken at a meeting of the three principals. This afternoon, in fact. Yes, he was at Holcome, not at his hotel room like he told us." Reaching the garage door, Craig pulled it open and saw the Porsche was gone. The Mustang was there, but the keys not on the rack.

"We can talk tomorrow morning," he said, starting to walk rapidly back toward the bedrooms. "I'll send you the picture. I swear it's valid. We have tapes of meetings about this scheme and I have someone who can identify the voices we have on tape." He sent the text on the run to the bedroom.

Her dresser was basically bare, a few items of make-up, a brush set, no jewelry scattered about, of course not, she didn't wear any, sadly, not even the wedding ring and he suspected it wasn't just missing because she threw it in a fit of anger, it likely was absent from her finger for several months. He saw her rosary, the one from her grandmother, brilliant white with gold filaments encircling each bead. He paused. Was she praying? Odd, neither of them were, had been, particularly religious, but then, why did he seek a priest for counsel? Looking for a divine intervention? He shook his head, so much had changed in the last year he couldn't sort it out. He turned back to his search, but there were no keys. One last glance around and he saw balled-up papers in the corner. He picked them up and started back to his office, smoothing them against his leg. His tension level was rising and already the scar on his upper lip was aching from his teeth clenched over it.

In the office, he glanced over the papers. Test results from the ER visit, he knew these tests and their ranges, no big deal. Visit summary. The last page listed more test results, stapled out of order. As his eyes raced down the page, he stopped in the middle. Oh my God, he thought, it can't be. He knew she didn't read any of this, from the way it was balled up and tossed aside. Every vile thing he said in their arguments shot back to his mind as he stared at the words in front of him. Neither of them expected this, but she should have known. How could a woman so brilliant in her work be so clueless? Or didn't she want to tell me? Dark suspicions began to rise within, but anxiety over Tera's whereabouts overtook him. Where the hell is she, it's been over an hour already. He went back to the great room and reached for his Glenfiddich 21.

He was still looking out over the lake, half-empty glass in hand, when the garage door rumbled open. Tera was through the door, the warmth of the house swallowing her. Safe. I'm safe, she thought. She suddenly felt like she was moving in slow motion.

Craig saw her come in, she was through the door, kicking off the red – red? wherever did those come from? – spiked heels. Certainly not wearing her blue uniform, but very attractive attire. He sighed in relief.

"Did you get that picture?" Her voice was hardly a whisper.

"Yes. I can't believe Gregory...." It was then she seemed to stumble and reach out toward the wall to support herself. He could see now that she was very pale, and her breathing was ragged. Oh dear God, not again! He scooped up the fleece blanket and went to her quickly.

"Tera, Tera,...easy...stay focused." He wrapped the blanket around her gently, pulling her close.

"Everything is going to be all right."

CHAPTER 70

There it was, among the greeting cards from friends that week before Christmas. This letter, however, was anything but friendly.

U-Ridley Health Care Systems

December 18, 2020

Dear Mr. and Mrs. Hampton,

This letter is to inform you that U-Ridley Health Care has decided that with the exception of emergency care, your son Nicholas will not be accepted to receive medical care and treatment at any of our hospitals or clinics. You will have 30 days from this date to transfer Nick's specialty care to another medical institution.

A Family Care Plan agreement was developed to provide clear guidance on how care would be provided and behavior expectations. This effort was undertaken to ensure a respectful and therapeutic relationship could be established amongst you and the care team.

Since the Family Care Plan agreement was presented to you, you have refused to sign it. Your response to the Family Care Plan demonstrates why we are unable to resume providing care to Nick. Your response has been to threaten legal action and business disruption against our organization. You have contacted outside organizations and asserted claims of discrimination and violations of the code of ethics against our individual providers. On Thursday, December 10, after making numerous and repeated phone calls across our system and to individual staff members, you spoke to Sandera Vann, RN, MSN, Senior Nursing Director. During that call you told Ms. Vann that you would be seeking legal, regulatory, and public action if U-Ridley Health Care did not resume nephrology treatment of Nick.

Our decision means the following to you regarding Nick's care:

• Nick will not be able to resume care at any U-Ridley clinic or hospital. However, should Nick need emergency medical care at any time, he may seek care at a U-Ridley Health Care emergency room.

• All scheduled or upcoming visits for Nick are hereby cancelled. Prescriptions will not be refilled.

        U-Ridley Health Care Leadership Team

 "You can't tell me this is for real!" Callista was shaking her head, her long brown hair swirling around her. "There's no name on it, there's no signature. It's just a stupid letter on Ridley stationary. She did this, that bitch, that dialysis nurse manager! What are we going to do?" she asked, seeing her husband was as aghast as she was.

 "I didn't threaten anyone," Mark said. "I was very low-key, I was just asking whether any of Nick's providers ever required a Family Care Plan, one that kept parents out of the decision process for care. Hardly anyone even talked to me! And Vann, all she kept saying was 'I don't know'." He shook his head. "I don't get it."

 "What if there's an emergency," Callista said, now jerking on her hair in anger. "All the stuff like blood work that the University Hospital in Iowa or the one in Harbison might need done! What if he gets sick, something way bad, like pneumonia or he's in a car accident. *We have nothing*! Ridley owns everything! They bought up all the clinics and community hospitals in the area. There is no place in this state we can go for care!"

 She burst into tears. "Why? My God, I can't stand this anymore, I wish I didn't have kids, I wish I didn't have Nick," she sobbed, "and I hate myself for even thinking that."

❊❊❊

 "Jesus Christ!" Ellie stared at her phone. The text from Callista about the U-Ridley decision seemed to burn in her hand. Paul looked up from the table, startled by her outburst. Not that Ellie avoided cussing, but even for her, this was over the top.

 "Those kids are snakebit," she told him angrily, after relating the message. "No matter what they do, where they turn, they keep running into roadblocks for Nick's care. How can these medical freaks get away with this?"

CHAPTER 71

"Save me!" Nick bolted out of the kitchen just ahead of his mother, a little plastic bag in his hand.

"Nicholas Michael, put that down!" Callista was at the door ready to pounce, her youngest was hesitating in the family room, his mom behind and Tera was moving quickly to block his route to the left of the large dining table.

"You're trapped, Nick!" Mark called out. "Surrender!"

It was good to be surrounded by all the activity and noise. Noise? It was always like this at Christmas or other events, the back and forth of chatter, food items, games, presents. And this year, a lot of over-the-top activity. After all, last year's Christmas was spent at Holcome, the hospital of the damned. This year's festivities were supposed to be even more low-key, thanks to the governor's coronavirus restrictions, only two or three families together and still a limit on the numbers in those groups and above all be sure to mask and social distance. How do you social distance at Christmas dinner, Mark wondered. The hell with it.

The fat Christmas tree was set up in a corner of the family room, ornaments reflecting the flickering glow of the fireplace, and little gold lights winked in the subdued light. There were all different sorts of gifts under the tree, and with the adjoining living room divided only by a small ledge on one side, the two rooms together were plenty spacious, all could easily visit with one another. Fake green garland wound with tiny lights adorned the walls and ran from one side to the other.

"Never!" Nick called back, rounding the table on the side away from Tera. He saw Craig at the end of the brown leather love seat near the fireplace and ran right at him, one step ahead of his mom.

"I'm safe! I'm safe!" He banged into Craig and then hurriedly sat down. "He's a doctor, he's got more smarts about what I can eat than you do." He slyly began to wiggle his hand between the cushions.

Craig was knocked a bit sideways in the encounter and turned to look at Nick, surprised at his boldness. "Leave me out of this, I would never do battle with a mother, and certainly not yours." He felt the cushion move as the hand slid down, hiding contraband.

"Begone!" Nick proclaimed, holding his hands up. "See, nothing! Hah!" Callista backed off and sank down on the nearby sofa next to Mark. She grabbed his bottle of Lonely Blonde and hurriedly drank some, muttering, "That kid will drive me nuts."

Mark was considering other matters. What a pair, he thought, gazing at his wife. Tera wore her signature tight black leggings and a glittery red flowing top and Callista was in black leggings – not so tight – and a glittery green flowing top. Both wore little jingle bell earrings. Did they coordinate this, he wondered, putting his arm around his wife. He glanced at Craig. "He's all yours." The emails the last two weeks between both men had eased some of the tension and Mark felt Callista's embargo no longer included him.

Craig now understood why Tera insisted on coming in spite of the nasty bouts of illness. She said she needed to be in this noisy and warm environment, and she was right, it was such that it fed the soul. This was their first Christmas with the family since the move to the States and nothing they'd experienced in all the years abroad could match the feeling of being part of a family. It was a totally new experience for him, his own family memories far darker than this. Tera was laughing as she chatted with Sienna. Then Paul joined their little group, teasing Sienna. Craig heard "*Grandpa!*" come out of her mouth. I don't care if I am the odd man in the group, wholly ignored, Craig thought, it was enough to see Tera finally have a spark of life in her actions.

While all eyes were diverted, Nick dug out his little bag of contraband from between the cushions and popped some candy into his mouth.

"Are you sure you can eat any of this?" Craig asked, careful to act as if nothing was happening. "I'm surprised your mother didn't prepare a baggie of edibles for you."

Nick looked up at him. "She did. Same old junk, and no chocolate. She even brought something for supper that she'll heat up. She has to measure and weigh *everything* twice. Do you know how hard this is?" Nick complained. "You doctor guys, all you do is sit at a desk and tell people what to do, but we gotta live with what you tell us to do. And it sucks!"

"A point well taken. I will remember that the next time I get to sit at a desk and tell people what to do. I don't recall having a desk in Africa or India though. I'll watch for one next time, if there is a next time."

"Don't count on it. Aunt Tera might lock you up and throw away the key." The boy studied his uncle intently. "You talk funny sometimes but you're sounding more American."

"Well, I did attend school here for a year, at Aquinas Academy and at the University, you know. I may have picked up a few mannerisms."

"Oh, so you've known Aunt Tera that long?" Nick sounded disgusted. "Why didn't you marry her sooner?"

"I guess I thought I was too busy," Craig admitted, thinking the delay one of the biggest mistakes of his life, the trip to London a year ago being at the top of the disaster list.

"What a waste. You could've moved here and had kids I could hang out with. I wonder if they'd talk like you do," he ended with a mocking British accent. He did it so well, Craig burst into laughter.

Mark elbowed Callista. "Look at those two, best buds."

"You've got to be kidding, Dr. No enjoying himself?" Laughing? Was that even possible? Callista watched them. Craig looked different, the perfect side part was gone and his hair was over the collar of the blue button-down shirt that peeked from beneath his wool sweater. And he'd ditched the wire rims. He almost looked pleasant.

"Cut it out," Mark's words broke into her thoughts. "Maybe they're comparing surgical notes."

Nick was relentless, as though on a mission to dissect his uncle. "Do you do any fun stuff, Uncle Craig? Sports?"

"I played football...soccer while I was here and in London."

"Oh really? Cool! I can't play, I might get hit by the ball here," he hit his chest and Craig winced. "And I can't run worth shit. Oops, sorry. But I love watching all the running." Nick dug into the sandwich bag and retrieved a couple of black olives. "I love these."

"You can have all you want if a kidney can be found."

"Yeah, I heard you offered to take the cut," Nick said, "but you were incompatible. Mom said she wasn't surprised, you're incompatible on everything. Then, on the way home from Thanksgiving, she said she wanted to choke you and would be happy if she never saw you again."

"Then you'd be an uncle short, now wouldn't you?" Craig said easily. "Maybe she'll change her mind and not choke me. Things can change, right? And, for instance, that kidney could be just a phone call away." Don't we all wish, he thought. Otherwise his prognosis truly lacks much of a future, only a few more years.

❈❈❈

It happened in the middle of the Christmas meal, as the platter of baked ham was being passed across the huge oak table.

"So, Dr. Know-it-all," Callista began, ignoring Mark as he covered his face, "what the hell is going on? We filed a complaint against the social worker's license with the State Board of Licensing. What can we expect them to do."

Craig paused, his tongue working over his top lip. "Nothing," he replied.

"What?" Callista was furious. "Nothing? No action? Then why did you have us write the damned report? Nineteen violations with a complete list of statute citations. Do you know how long it took me to do that? Nothing?"

"It's just a pissing contest," he said carelessly. Tera, next to him, dug her fingers into his thigh.

"Watch your mouth!" Ellie snapped, "The kids."

Craig glanced quickly toward the teens, but they were laughing, no virgin ears there. Max gave him a thumbs up. "Back and forth," he amended. "She said, you said. No one at Holcome would dare back you up and no notes exist. There's no way to prove your accusations, so what do you expect them to do? You'll get a letter telling you there was an investigation, they asked her side of the story and could find no need for action. Case closed."

"Then why did we do this?" Mark interjected. "If you knew it would go down this way, why did you insist on it? Why did we have to file against Dr. Yuki and Dr. Loomis to the Medical Licensing Board?"

Craig got a faraway look in his eyes. "Harassment," he answered quietly. "They've tormented you for over a year, it's time for a little payback. Not too much, not with Nick still entrapped there, but a little here, a little there, to let them know you aren't going to stand for this much longer." He sat back in his chair.

"None of this is going to be easy," he continued. "When you get to Loomis, you have notes and records from the hospital itself to use against him. Use it, use it all. Just keep at it. A big part of the problem with the medical board is that the members are political appointees in this state. No one will dare go against the current regime in office that believes Holcome does no wrong. Loomis will get a pass. Your best bet is filing with the Office of Civil Rights. You should be working on that, you are, right? It may take a year before anything happens. And it may take a year before the grand jury convenes to hear testimony on the Burntside case. You're in a waiting game."

Callista sat back, crushed. He was right, but she wanted him to be wrong, she wanted something to come through for them for a change. Now. She pushed her plate away.

"You're worthless," she said angrily. "I've got to go back there on Monday, kissing their asses while that Cunningham freak files her child negligence complaint. Loomis is there, Hawthorne is there and I'm stuck looking at their ugly faces." She glared at Tera. "Lucky you, you quit. You couldn't take it anymore, but I've got to sit and take every goddamned thing they can dream up. Alone!"

"Worthless," Craig snapped back, just as incensed as she was. "It wasn't you ferreting out the fraud, it wasn't you writing up the mountain of paperwork and chasing to Chicago this week to meet the feds with the documentation for the criminal case, the collusion and all that. And apparently, going after Holcome in this state is like kicking a sacred cow, I lost my damned job at the Coalition over this. It's not just you, and what you do, woman, we're all in this together for Nick!"

At that point, the faces began to zigzag before his eyes. Oh shit, not again, Craig thought. He knew he had his medication in his pocket, but damned if he was going to pop pills in front of the family. "If you'll excuse me," he said, abruptly leaving the table.

"On the run?" Callista said sarcastically. "Can't take it?"

"Knock it off," Mark ordered.

Tera looked around the table, then slowly stood, deliberately patting her flowing red top in place. The light blue eyes were frigid. "Craig gets migraines and they've gotten worse over the last year with all the hospital work and erratic hours. Yes, he *did* work with patients, Callie, so quit treating him like a do-nothing office slug. He ended up in the ER two days ago, if anyone cares." She didn't add the ER trip included herself for dehydration again. "Excuse me from this bitch session." And she was gone.

Craig had only gone as far as Paul's office, the first room away from the lights and noise. It would take awhile for the meds to kick in. In the dimming light from the window, he could see a couple of chairs around the room, the desk. The walls had makeshift shelves, many different-colored trays neatly labeled with client names, two computers, with a printer on a small table between them.

Tera found him staring out the window at the falling snow. "You okay? She's such an ass sometimes."

He turned. "She's right, you know. I've been an utter failure. Who knows what will come of all that data or how soon, with everyone working from home. It may take *more* than a year to get any action and she's going to be stuck there that long, facing the risk of retaliation." He sighed as he gazed at her, almost hopelessly. "I'm sorry for arguing, I should have stayed away. I don't belong here."

She stared back at him, horrible thoughts reeling through her head. "I've...I've thought about this." I don't want to say it, she thought, but he needs his life back. "If you want to go back to London, it's okay. Everything you do is back in Britain, the medical school, your writing. I have no right to hold you here. If you want to...to split up...."

"Split up? What are you talking about?" Craig felt a shaft of ice drive through him.

"If you want out, I won't stand in your way." They stared at each other as if figures in a tableaux.

He blinked. "You can't mean this...No!" He grabbed her shoulders. His hands were shaking. "No!" Voice raised. Anger? She started to back away, suddenly terrified at the outburst. But he pulled her forward. "I love you, do you understand me? I love you! I can't go forward without you." And he was kissing her with all the anger, then the passion he'd been tormented with.

When she finally pulled away, she was breathless and slightly dizzy, as she edged to a chair and sank down. She wasn't sure if she was going to pass out or not, the emotions so raw and powerful between them.

He knelt beside her, removing a jewelry box from his pocket. "Tera, I'm so sorry, sorry for everything." He took her hand, "Please, please accept this from me," he said, removing her gold wedding band, with its diamond interlocking hearts from the small box.

She closed her eyes. I'm carrying his child, but I was afraid of him not one minute ago. I can't do it, I can't. Not now.

"No," she said.

CHAPTER 72

Paul casually knocked on the office door before entering. He carefully kept an unconcerned face, though he'd heard a lot more than he let on. Their eyes were locked on each other, Craig staring in disbelief, Tera was looking up at him like a lost soul.

"Everything all right here? Craig, are you feeling better? Ter, mom wants you to help with dessert."

Craig's eyes followed her as she left, he seemed almost hypnotized, then shook his head as if to clear it. "Does it get easier, Paul, not doing the stupid things that can ruin a marriage? I don't know what I'm going to do," he added quietly. My God, my life just crashed, he thought.

Ruin a marriage? In 45 years, I can't think of a single thing that brought us to the brink of such a disaster, Paul thought. "I think it's something you grow into," he said carefully, "the more you're together." Five years ago, the shooting in Guinea, Tera's injuries, the airlift, Craig arriving days later from the WHO outpost – then and there they junked the plans to be married at Brompton Oratory in London and instead were wed at Gemelli Hospital's chapel. They were giddy in their happiness. Things must have blown up badly behind their closed doors, Paul thought, the bad feeling at Thanksgiving must have exploded to get to this point.

"Let's head back," he said quietly. Either the meds had taken effect or something ugly happened between them, Craig appeared to have wilted in minutes. "Are you okay on the job situation for awhile?"

"Oh, that. It's okay. Imperial will need to adjust their demands, I'm not planning to leave right now, and I'm done with WHO, things are getting too political with them and I refuse to go that route." He paused. "One thing strange has happened, though. On the way back from Chicago, I stopped at Holcome to meet with Rexalt, a courtesy call so to speak, to warn him of the coming hurricane."

"How did that go?"

"Bizarre. The first thing he said is 'You're younger than I thought you'd be'."

Paul burst out laughing. Craig didn't even look his 36 years.

"Then he tells me I have 15 minutes. So I told him to shut up and listen. After a few minutes he called his secretary and told her to cancel everything and asked if I wanted a drink, and I don't mean tea or soda. Then he started asking what I would do in this situation or that, my citizenship status...it was unreal. He even asked who he should fire first from this gambit. I told him no one, or else he'd tip his hand on the investigation. He wants to meet again next week, I have no idea why."

Job interview, Paul thought as they entered the dining room. Craig must be too stressed to figure it out.

"Tera, what are your plans, now that you're out of work at Holcome," Ellie was saying as the men returned the room. "Back to the Coalition or are you going to look for other employment?"

"She's not doing anything," Craig cut in as he took the seat next to his wife.

"I beg your pardon?" Ellie couldn't believe what she was hearing. Who was he to answer for her? All eyes were on him, his tone had been commanding. *Lord and master* flew into Mark and Callista's minds as they looked at each other. Here we go again.

Tera shrugged. "I'm...I'm not out much these days."

"Hyperemesis is nothing to fool around with," Craig said, exasperated. "I don't want to find you being sick in a snowbank by the side of the road." He looked directly at Tera. "I *am* a doctor, I'm good at something even if no one else thinks so. You're only two months along, you don't want to chance losing our child, do you?"

There was a collective gasp. He looked around at the stunned faces and then back at Tera. "You didn't *tell* them yet? Not even with all that woman talk this afternoon?"

"You're *pregnant*?" Callista burst out. "I thought you two were on the outs. You're not even wearing a wedding ring anymore. Whose kid is it?"

"We never expected this," Mark hurriedly put in. "The kids overheard you arguing upstairs on Thanksgiving." Wide-eyed and ashamed, the kids started edging down in their seats.

Ellie's eyes narrowed slightly as she appraised Tera. Guilty? Tera glared back.

"I didn't realize our marital status was in question," Craig interrupted quietly. He took the ring she'd rejected from his pocket. "I was going to give you this later in the evening. It was at the jeweler's for repairs," he added for the benefit of the stunned family members. As his lips grazed her cheek, he whispered, "For now," and he took her hand, slipping the band on her finger.

"How does the foot in your mouth taste," Mark asked Callista unkindly.

Paul found the tablecloth very interesting at that moment. Nice save, he thought.

"Craig is the father of this child," Tera cut in. "And he's going to be around whether you like it or not. Everyone argues. I'm sure Mark argues a lot, living with *you*, Callie. We had a disagreement! We're not saints, you know."

"Kressly would agree with that," Craig added mildly, they glanced at each other and began to laugh. Too true.

"Fr. Kressly?" Nick interrupted. "That nice priest who was at the dialysis center?"

Nice priest, like hell, he has a harsh tongue, and in school, too handy with his fists, Craig thought. I damn near got expelled because of him. Maybe nicer now…in atonement for his past sins. He *did* put us in contact with that poor woman who lost her child to Loomis. But he needn't have made such a big deal this morning when he saw us together at Christmas Mass.

"Yes," Tera said. "We all went to school together, gambling, drinking, carousing and sss…." She stopped, the sex part was not fit for family consumption; anyway, it was supposedly just a rumor, she'd had no part in anything like that.

"Good God," Paul turned to Ellie. "There was something in the news about a big gambling problem down there. Was that when she was there? And then the other stuff we found out about?"

Ellie nodded. "That was Pete Cordileone."

"The eye surgeon? The guy on the magazine cover as one of the best doctors in the state?" They both were a little shocked, though; apparently all was not good and holy at that school after all.

"I need something stronger than this dinner wine," Ellie whispered. Paul nodded and got up to get two glasses and the Jameson.

"It *was* a reform school," came Max's deep voice, interrupting the sudden quiet. "Cool."

CHAPTER 73

"Off to the belly of the beast," Ellie said as she heard the loud truck horn outside promptly at 11:15. Callista had begged her to come to dialysis that Monday morning.

"Keep your mouth shut," Paul warned. "Play nice in the sandbox." She punched his arm. "Smartass." He bent down to kiss her. "Good luck."

Ellie grabbed her overstuffed purse. An all-day trip meant snacks, a mini can of Coke, and the briefcase with the ancient laptop. "I'm off, see you later!" She lurched down the driveway under her load. "Do I need a ladder to get in this thing?" she asked staring upwards from the street. One big vehicle, but safe.

"There's a handle to pull yourself up and..."

"Oh shut up, I'm not decrepit." Ellie slid in the laptop case and her purse and made it easily to the seat. "Wow, this is a quite a view. Do you still drive like California?" They'd all picked up some bad driving habits from that short time out west for Nick's surgery a year ago. She looked over her shoulder. "Hi, Nick, comfortable back there?" He was tapping away at his DS game and nodded as the truck moved smoothly down the freeway toward 72 and Holcome. An 80-mile ride ahead, with more and more open spaces covered with sparkling snow.

"I'm sorry about Friday, Mom," Callista started. "I didn't mean to ruin Christmas. I just saw red when Craig said nothing would happen. He insisted we do all that work and for nothing!"

"For sure it would've been nothing had you *not* done it," Ellie reminded her. "You have to try everything you can and you have to be patient."

"Patient? How can I be patient when we're going to be facing child neglect accusations again? Twice in a year, you think that won't make someone sit up and take notice? Take action?" Her voice broke.

"Mom, I'm so scared of what's going to happen. If Nick didn't need dialysis, we'd run like hell away from here. I can't do this anymore."

"Callie, it's going to be all right. We'll help all we can, you know that." But she noticed Callista's shoulders were shaking and tears were running down her face as the miles went by.

"Is this where you had all your adventures?" Ellie asked as they passed through a flat and desolate stretch of terrain.

"Yeah, you'd think they'd put up some trees as a windbreak. We had that near-miss with the snow storm, there's no way we should've had to come down here with a winter storm brewing. But we had to," she was swinging off the freeway into downtown Stanton. "All because that damned behavior plan says show up or Nick won't get care at Holcome anymore." She thought back to the first time she'd seen that plan in June. I hate them all, she thought. "And then that tornado, right before Labor Day. I hate this road so bad." She gripped the steering wheel, knuckles on her hands white. "I hate it."

They'd just swung into a parking space when the phone rang through the truck Bluetooth. It sounded like a klaxon horn and Ellie jumped.

"Yeah," Callista answered. The truck was idling and it was hard to hear. "Let me put you on speaker," she said after a minute.

"I'm calling with an offer."

Offer for what, Ellie thought. Telemarketer?

"We have an offer for you. It's dependent on getting all the medical information verified and testing. We need to have an answer within an hour. If you say no, we will offer to someone else."

Callista's brain didn't seem to want to work. Offer?

"I don't understand," she said carefully. The woman talked some more.

"Wait a minute," Callista interrupted. "Are you saying you have a kidney?"

"Why yes, I thought you understood that was what I was saying."

By now Callista was dead white. "Please, hold on, I've got to put you on a conference call with my husband." Her hands were shaking so badly she had a hard time with the buttons as she held the phone and switched off the truck.

Nick was hanging over the seat, his breath smelling like the cherry candy he was twirling in his mouth. "What is it?" he said as he poked his mom. Ellie hushed him.

The conversation went on five minutes longer and when she hung up, Callista seemed dazed. She looked around at the towering brick buildings of Holcome International Medical Center and back at Ellie, whispering, "It's over. They have a match, an infant, the parents are donating his organs. Mark is coming to take Nick to Harbison in Wisconsin. You and I will go back home, I need to pack. Surgery is Wednesday."

Deliverance.

Later That Week

<u>Callista's Journal – December 31, 2020 – 1 day after transplant –</u>
Nick came through surgery fine. I know they were worried, a transplant just isn't done on a kid with cardiac issues, there is so much to watch out for. But he made it and those little kidneys kicked right in. I thank God for those parents who set aside their agony at losing their little baby and donated his organs so other kids could live. I am thankful to UW-Harbison Children's Hospital team for taking the transplant risk. Now we just have to get through this first year. It's scary that they have to suppress his immune system to prevent rejection, how is he going to fight off any disease? Covid is still around, the transplant coordinator said if Nick gets it he will die! I can't think about that. We have a year of blood tests, biopsies and doctor visits ahead of us, we'll make it work. This was Nick's only chance, we had to take it. Miracles do happen, thank God, and we are so grateful to have received this one.

❖❖❖

"You haven't heard from the police? Anyone?" Neil Hawthorne, tie loosened and white shirt open, was planted in the armchair in Loomis' office, a glass of the chilled Bar Hill in hand. It was New Year's Eve, everything so low key at the hospital there was no sense to hanging around in the office.

Loomis was hunched over his desk, face puffy, eyes a bit on the red side, must've been hitting the booze this week, Hawthorne thought, stroking his chin. He got what he wanted, no wife or kids around. Wonder if he's got some broad on the hook, awaiting his attentions.

"No, not a word. I tell you she was lying. She just did that to destroy me." Who the hell was this Teresa Storm, Loomis thought. She simply disappeared off the face of the earth when she left this room two weeks ago.

"Then why did she burst in here like an attack dog? Where did she get that information about the breach and the shit about you playing Langley like a puppet? Why did she bring up OCR?" Hawthorne snapped. He took a long drink of his gin.

"She was lying!" Loomis said between clenched teeth. "None of what she said was true, she made it up and disrupted everything." What better way to make me look like a fool, he thought, jumping into a private meeting and making accusations. He poured himself more of the Grey Goose. But he knew every word she said was true and he knew how she'd learned about his hidden actions: the scent she left behind would haunt him until his dying day. She must have accessed the phones, he thought, my desk, even my computer. By God, if I ever see that woman again, I swear I'll kill her.

❋❋❋

"When are you leaving?" Tera asked.

"Ten minutes." Craig was just slipping a sweater over his shirt, the outside temperature was much colder than he'd ever experienced in Britain. "The meeting with Rexalt is just after noon."

"I meant to London."

"London? I'm not going."

"But the contract said...."

"I'll make them change it." Craig faced her. "I'm not leaving you here alone. The damn airlines may shut down and who knows when I could get back." A thought came to him, with a sharp knife of sadness. "Unless that's what you want."

"Craig! No!" She came to him and wrapped her arms around him. "Please, I just need some time." She held him tightly, then pulled his face down and gave him a light kiss that began to linger; he felt that dizzy, ethereal feeling starting in again as he felt her respond. "Please," she whispered as he slowly stroked her hair. "Just a little time." She didn't pull away.

A short while later, Craig paused before the hallowed doors of Holcome International Medical Center. Why am I here, he thought. Does this meeting have anything to do with a new chapter of my life – or rather our life, for Tera and me, and perhaps Nick, the whole family?

A blast of warm air enveloped him as he opened the door. To the future, he thought, whatever it may bring for all of us in the months ahead.

AUTHOR'S NOTE

In every story there is a kernel of truth on which hangs the fiction. There is a child who needed a kidney and whose family was put through hell as they fought corporate collusion and medical incompetence to save his life. He was lucky. The Transplant Team at American Family Children's Hospital in Wisconsin gambled on a risky surgery and it paid off. The Transplant Team at Stead Family Children's Hospital at the University of Iowa was ready to do the same. Otherwise this story would be headed in a very different direction.

ACKNOWLEDGMENTS

First of all, a hearty thank you to the "Hampton" family for opening their emails, CaringBridge account, notes, and medical records to reveal the background needed to create this story. Thanks especially to my husband and daughter for allowing me to disappear for hours at a time while working on these pages. And a toast to Rhonda Klein, of Evergreen Press, designer *par excellence* and navigator into the Amazon expressway.

My nephew John Kinning, R.N., B.L.S., A.C.L.S., P.A.L.S. – how is that for an alphabet? – read an early version and liked it, especially the undercover ops, he said. He also provided some medical insights to make this story and the coming sequel real.

Many people offered encouragement. Jeffrey B. Burton of the Mace Reid series took the time to listen to the idea and told me to go for it. Dr. Tom Combs, ER physician and author of the Drake Cody series, helped tremendously by sending writer blogs to my inbox, the advice therein was greatly appreciated. Tom also allayed my fears of self-publishing and laughed at my qualms about naming names; he got away with it quite well in his medical thrillers that have a cliffhanger at the end of each chapter. A special thanks to Catherine Coulter, author of 27 outstanding books in her FBI thriller series. She's been aware of the story behind the story since day one, while "Nick" was at Stanford and her reaction to the inexplicable problems encountered in simple health care for a child made me feel I had a winner – after all, it takes a lot to puzzle a mystery writer. Michael Stagg, author of the bestselling Nate Shepherd books, was gracious enough to pass on several ideas about indie publishing and making a splash in the marketplace. I am forever grateful for their pushing me along. Writing is a solitary task, it's almost like being in a parallel universe and they all understand it so well.

ABOUT THE AUTHOR

It's not often a character jumps into real life from the novel you're reading but Ellie in *Deception* said she would write a book about what happened to Nick and this is it. Loretta Enright is the pen name of a journalist (BA, University of Minnesota) living in a large metropolitan area in the upper Midwest. Her years have been spent writing and editing countless news stories and managing a small foundation's magazine schedule. She and her patient husband have six grown children and nine grandchildren.

Catch some of Loretta's writing tidbits at Lorettawrites.com

CURIOUS?

Thanks for reading *Deception*. If you have questions or want to know more information about *More Deception*, please send me an email at LorettaEnright@hotmail.com. Meanwhile, I hope I've left you with some questions to ponder until the sequel answers them all:

• Will Nick Hampton make it through the first critical year after kidney transplant? As Nick soon will find out, there are life-threatening opportunistic pathogens lurking ahead to attack his immune-suppressed body. Will he be able to fight them off?

• Will the triumvirate of other pathogens – Dr. Charles Loomis, Neil Hawthorne, and Anton Gregory – ever see justice?

• Are there any more deceptions between Craig and Tera? It seems both of them are hiding a past.

As frequently happens, a chapter or two from a book gets tossed into the recycling bin to meet arbitrary page requirements. "The Snowstorm" is one of these from *Deception*. You can get a free copy of "The Snowstorm" by emailing a request to:

LorettaEnright@hotmail.com

-30-

Made in the USA
Monee, IL
30 April 2024

57568724R00203